Praise for the Capital Crimes Series

"Truman can write suspense with the best of them."
—Larry King

"Truman 'knows the forks' in the nation's capital
and how to pitchfork her readers into a web
of murder and detection."
—*The Christian Science Monitor*

"Political junkies of all stripes should find some-
thing to feed their appetites."
—*Publishers Weekly* on
Margaret Truman's Experiment in Murder

"Dead-on descriptions of Washington's most crack-
ridden streets and exclusionary shindigs."
—*USA Today* on *Murder at Ford's Theater*

"Ripe with suspense, Truman's mystery gets edgier
with each page. . . . A captivating,
fast-paced thriller."
—*RT Book Reviews* on
Murder at The Washington Tribune

"[A] satisfying tale . . . remarkably fresh in its
insights about politics, intrigue, money,
and sex in the city by the Potomac."
—*The News & Observer* (Raleigh, NC) on
Murder on K Street

| BY MARGARET TRUMAN |

MARGARET TRUMAN'S

UNDIPLOMATIC
MURDER

A CAPITAL CRIMES NOVEL

► DONALD BAIN ◄

FORGE®

A TOM-DOHERTY ASSOCIATES BOOK | NEW YORK

NOTE: If you purchased this book without a cover, you should be aware that this book is stolen property. It was reported as "unsold and destroyed" to the publisher, and neither the author nor the publisher has received any payment for this "stripped book."

This is a work of fiction. All of the characters, organizations, and events portrayed in this novel are either products of the author's imagination or are used fictitiously.

MARGARET TRUMAN'S UNDIPLOMATIC MURDER:
A CAPITAL CRIMES NOVEL

Copyright © 2014 by Estate of Margaret Truman

All rights reserved.

A Forge Book
Published by Tom Doherty Associates, LLC
175 Fifth Avenue
New York, NY 10010

www.tor-forge.com

Forge® is a registered trademark of Tom Doherty Associates, LLC.

ISBN 978-1-2508-7808-3

Forge books may be purchased for educational, business, or promotional use. For information on bulk purchases, please contact the Macmillan Corporate and Premium Sales Department at 1-800-221-7945, extension 5442, or write to specialmarkets@macmillan.com.

First Edition: July 2014
First Mass Market Edition: July 2015

For Robert Gleason,
whose friendship and savvy editorial instincts
I've benefited from and treasured for years

History is a series of random events organized in a seemingly sensible order.

—JAMES ATLAS, *THE NEW YORK TIMES*

PREQUEL

1

She was late, no surprise. Brixton's younger daughter, Janet, was habitually late, pathologically late. Brixton, on the other hand, was a stickler for being on time, which only exacerbated his annoyance.

He and Janet had been at odds for much of her teen and adult years about a variety of things, which Brixton sometimes found to be interesting in retrospect. Janet's sister, Jill, and she were polar opposites in personality and perception of life, which was usually the case with siblings. Jill had been the proverbial straight arrow for most of her life, her teenage years uneventful, and she'd breezed through college and emerged with a degree in accounting. Her ease with numbers amazed her father. Balancing a checkbook for him was akin to dental visits and watching TV reality shows. She had married a solid sort of guy—at least that's how Brixton perceived him; he shaved every day, enjoyed fruity alcoholic drinks with little umbrellas in them, and watched the History Channel—and they produced Brixton's first and only grandchild, at least for the moment, an adorable little baby boy whose smile melted Brixton the few times he'd been charmed by him in person.

Janet, on the other hand, defined for her father the term "flaky." She'd used drugs during her teen years, run with a controversial crowd, dropped out of college after one semester, and decorated herself with a pair of garish tattoos. She not only had pierced her ears, she wore a tiny gold nugget in her upper lip. Brixton couldn't even look at the lip when they were together, which hadn't been often of late. He hated the tattoos and the pierced lip. They detracted from her natural beauty, and the thought of having someone stick a needle through her lip caused him to cringe.

He wasn't sure how his daughter made a living; he just knew that whatever it was didn't always provide enough for her to pay her bills. He did know that she was involved in the city's club and music scene in some capacity, managing some rock-and-roll musicians, promoting concerts, working in recording studios—never anything steady. Her calls to him usually involved a need for money to repair her car or to keep the lights on and the telephone in operation, calls that he sometimes responded to despite resenting it. "Grow up," he told her on more than one occasion. "Get a real job and take the responsibility of supporting yourself." She always agreed with him, a smart technique when dealing with an irate father, but never resulting in a change in lifestyle. Meeting today in the outdoor café a few blocks from the State Department in Foggy Bottom resulted from one of those telephone conversations.

Hi, Daddy. It's Janet."
   "Hey, sweetheart. How are you?"
 "I—am—wonderful!"

He smiled at her happy tone. At the same time her calling him "Daddy" set up his defenses. She seldom referred to him that way unless she needed something.

"I've been going with this dynamite musician, Daddy, soooo talented, a real musical genius."

"Yeah? What's he play?"

"Guitar."

Brixton pictured this "genius" stalking the stage, leaping up and down, hair flying, amplifiers blaring, the air filled with colored lights and marijuana smoke. As far as Brixton was concerned, rock music shouldn't be called music. An inveterate jazz lover, he remembered what the great saxophonist James Moody had once said to an interviewer when asked what he thought of rock and roll: "You really can't play an instrument when you're jumping up and down," the gentle jazz giant responded. That summed it up for Brixton.

"Well, that's great, Janet," he said. What else was there to say?

"Daddy, Richard—that's his name—Richard has come up with an idea for a music app that will make him millions, and he wants me, *me,* to work on it with him—but he needs start-up money and asked me to help raise some and . . ." She paused for breath. "And so I thought that maybe you would want to get in on the ground floor and . . ."

"Whoa," Brixton said. "Slow down. You're talking to the wrong guy, sweetheart. I don't have money to invest in anything. I'm a working stiff. Remember?"

Her bubbly presentation instantly turned downbeat, as he'd expected it would.

"Won't you even hear me out?"

"I'm listening."

"No, I mean *really* listen to me. I can't do it justice over the phone. It's too—well, it's too complicated, and I have some stuff that he's come up with, a business plan and things like that. Can't we get together so I can show you everything and—?"

"Sure," he said. "When?"

"Tonight?"

"Okay. I have a meeting at State; should be free by five thirty. There's a bar and restaurant with an outdoor café a block from State, on Twenty-third. Buy you a drink, an early dinner?"

"That'd be great. I know the place. See you there."

What struck Brixton as ironic about their strained relationship was that in many ways she more closely mirrored him than did his more conventional daughter. Despite his dedication to order and routine in his life, he could be as impetuous as she was. His suspicion of authority butted heads with his having been a cop, first in Washington, D.C., and later with the Savannah Police Department in Georgia, where he rose to the rank of detective before taking a bullet in the knee and holding down a desk job for the months leading up to retirement. Like him, she marched to her own drummer and always had.

But what most closely linked them was their unwillingness to walk the straight and narrow and choose the safe route through life. Both their lives flirted with danger, his because of what he did for a living, hers because of a need to chase dreams and to spend her days with others for whom life was but a dream, chemically induced or not.

He finished off his mug of Prohibition Porter, a locally produced Belgian-style dark ale, checked his watch, grunted, and considered ordering a martini. He'd opted for beer rather than his usual drink to ensure that he had all his senses while conversing about Janet's "business proposition." He didn't feel deprived, because he'd had martinis at this place and rated them second-class.

Her arrival distracted him from having to decide. She looked terrific as she approached the café, tight jeans on her long legs, a snug, bright orange T-shirt that showed off her firm, ample bosom, and orange sneakers that matched the shirt. Her dirty blond hair was worn loose and caught the sun. She spotted him at a table next to the door leading inside the restaurant, smiled broadly, slipped past other tables, leaned over, and kissed his forehead before taking her seat.

"You look great," he said.

"So do you."

"For an old guy?"

"Oh, you're not old. How old are you?"

"Fifty-one."

"See? That's young."

"Drink?"

"A cosmo."

Because of its close proximity to the State Department, the café was a favorite hangout for diplomatic personnel, at least lower-level employees. With the weather clear and balmy, it had filled up since Brixton had arrived and commandeered the table.

"Nice spot," Janet commented as a waiter took her order for a cosmopolitan and a second beer for Brixton.

"You don't drink martinis anymore?" she asked.

"Yeah, sure I do. A beer appealed. Nice day for a beer. Besides, places with outdoor cafés usually make lousy martinis."

She laughed. "How can that be?" she asked. "Why would an outdoor café serve martinis that aren't as good as inside places?"

"Because martinis taste better indoors. I remember when I was in Paris. I really liked sitting in cafés and watching the parade go by, but they made lousy martinis."

"That's because they're French, not because you were outdoors. You should have had wine."

"I've had martinis in this place, too," he said. "They're not very good. Want another sage piece of advice? Never have a mixed drink in a Chinese restaurant. They haven't a clue how to make a decent one."

"If you say so."

Anxious to change the subject, Brixton quickly surveyed the menu and suggested calamari and an order of boneless ribs to go with their drinks.

They fell into an easy conversation about anything other than the reason she'd wanted to see him.

"A fat day," he commented, referring to the sunny, brilliant blue sky with a few puffy clouds to break the monotony, and a cooling breeze that caused their green market umbrella to flap.

"Did you go to Paris with that woman from Savannah that you were seeing?" she asked.

"Flo? Yeah. I met her in Savannah, but she was from New York."

"You still see her?"

"No. We split up."

"Did it make you sad?"

"Actually, I was kind of relieved."

Which was true immediately following the breakup. But he'd begun to miss her within a week and still did. Discussing his love life with his younger daughter made him uncomfortable, and he changed the players but not the subject.

"How's your mother?"

"She's okay."

"She happy with her new husband?"

"I guess so."

"You like him?"

"He's okay."

Brixton didn't like the guy who'd married his ex-wife, an attorney who looked like he spent all his time in a tanning salon and probably had a dental hygienist on a retainer to keep his teeth white.

"So, tell me about your business proposition," he said.

Brixton half listened as Janet explained what the music app was all about. It sounded silly to him, although he didn't do anything to transmit that reaction to her. She talked fast, her conversation filled with "like" and "you know" and "right?" He couldn't help but smile at her enthusiasm, her conviction that what she was excited about would change the world and everyone in it. Her eyes opened wide, then narrowed, speaking a language of their own. She paused occasionally in her soliloquy to see whether he'd understood, and took his nod to indicate that he had.

His attention drifted away from her words, captured by a couple who'd passed the café a few times. The woman appeared to be of Arabic origins. She wore a long, loose black dress and a scarf that covered her hair and neck. She looked young, a teenager, Brixton judged. Her companion wasn't of Middle Eastern origins. He was dressed casually—jeans, a blue-and-white-checked shirt, and a New York Yankee's baseball cap with longish blond curls sticking out beneath it. What attracted Brixton's attention were the furtive glances they cast on the crowd in the café, and he wondered why they hesitated coming in. There were a few empty tables, one directly across the doorway leading inside the restaurant from where Brixton and his daughter sat. It was on their third pass that they stopped and made their way to that table. A waiter asked for their order; the young man said, "Lemonade."

"Two?" the waiter asked.

"One," the young man said. "Just one."

Brixton tried to eavesdrop but wasn't able to hear because of the buzz of voices around him. He continued to glance at them. At one point the young man leaned across the table and spoke in low tones, his mouth almost touching the cloth that covered his friend's ear. She said nothing in return. She turned once in Brixton's direction, and he clearly saw her face—what he read on its unblemished youth was fear. Her companion also glanced at Brixton, who noticed the seawater green color of his eyes—eyes with no expression.

The waiter returned with the lemonade and placed it on the table. The young man pulled coins from his pants pocket, deposited them on the table, picked up the glass, and downed half of its contents. Then, after uttering something else to the girl, he stood and walked from the café, leaving her alone with the partially consumed drink.

"I'm sorry," Janet said. "I've been yakking away and the food is getting cold." She dipped a piece of calamari in the red sauce. "This is good," she said. "Yummy. Aren't you going to have some?"

Brixton took a piece.

"So, where was I? Oh, right. Richard's idea is sooo smart, Daddy. It's, like, it's right on with the music scene that's going on today, so *with it*. It's like, you know, like when Steve Jobs invented the Apple and—"

"Whoa," Brixton. "You're comparing this fellow Richard to Steve Jobs?"

"Well, maybe not like him exactly, but apps are big these days and . . ." She noticed that Brixton wasn't listening as closely as he had been. "Did you hear what I said?" she asked.

"What?"

She laughed. "What world are you in?" she asked.

"Let's get out of here" was his reply.

"Why?"

He slapped cash on the table and stood.

"Daddy! I haven't finished." She pulled sheets of paper that she'd wedged into the top of her jeans and placed them on the table. "Richard has it all figured out. See? Here are the numbers and—"

He grabbed her arm and tried to pull her to her feet. "Come on," he said.

She looked up at him questioningly. "Is something wrong?"

"We're leaving," he said. "Come on, we'll go somewhere else."

She stood. Assuming that she was following, Brixton moved to the sidewalk. He looked back for Janet, who stood tasting another curl of calamari.

"Hey, come on," he called.

As he again turned in the direction of the sidewalk, the young woman wearing the hijab suddenly stood and began screeching a chant in Arabic. Brixton spun around. Janet was looking at the woman as though she were a street performer entertaining passersby.

"Janet!" he barked, and started back into the café, his hands outstretched toward her. He'd gotten only a few feet when the explosion occurred, an ear-splitting blast whose force hit him in the chest, sending him sprawling on his back on the sidewalk, his head making sharp contact with the concrete. Parts of a splintered table came flying in his direction, and he threw his arms over his face to shield it from the wooden shards and other debris that rained down—plates, glasses, skin, limbs, eyeglasses, knives and forks, carafes of wine and mugs of beer, clothing, pieces of chairs, calamari, boneless ribs, pizza slices, and a toy gorilla that had been held by a child at a table two removed from where they had sat.

The lingering reverberation from the blast mingled

with screams, final sounds from the maimed, expressions of horror from witnesses to the carnage. Brixton's ears rang. He frantically discarded what had landed on him, twisted his torso, and used his hands to push himself up to a sitting position. He sat on the rubble-strewn sidewalk, blood dripping from the side of his face and back of his neck. He shook his head violently to try to clear the grayness from his mind, to make the incessant ringing stop, to make sense of what had just happened, of the legs and shoes of people rushing to the scene, of painful moans and wails of disbelief.

Brixton stumbled to his feet to see what moments earlier had been a bustling café filled with happy people. That a slaughter had taken place was vibrantly and visually displayed. Bodies were everywhere, some piled on top of others, blood covering everything and everyone.

He touched the side of his face and pulled bloody fingers away from the wound. He looked back into the café in search of his daughter but saw only a tangle of limbs and clothing where they had been sitting. "Oh, my God," he whispered, then yelled, "Janet!" As he took a step in that direction, a second blast occurred, sending a ball of flame from somewhere inside the restaurant through the entrance to the outdoor area, its heat searing his face and eyelashes and causing him to stagger.

Twenty-third Street had been busy with pedestrians at the time of the blast, and they were joined by people pouring out of office buildings and other restaurants. Despite attempts to get closer to the ruins, Brixton was caught up by the throng as they fled in panic. "My daughter! My daughter!" he kept crying out as the wave of people pushed him farther away.

He turned from the carnage and looked across the street to the crowd that had gathered there. He shook his head again and blinked rapidly to bring things into better focus. The ringing in his ears grew louder, and he cupped his hands over them in an attempt to silence it. He thought for a moment that he might pass out. But something caught his attention, and he focused on it. At first he didn't believe what he saw. Watching the chaos was the young man wearing the Yankees cap, who'd been with the woman who'd just blown herself up and slaughtered God knows how many people. Did he have a smirk on his face? Brixton thought that he did, and an anguished cry came from him.

A wave of nausea rose and he forced it back. That was the son—of—a bitch responsible for Janet's death. Cold now but focused, Brixton skirted the crowd, ignoring the uniformed policemen who'd arrived on foot, and the sirens of the squads of blue-and-white-marked patrol cars converging on the scene. He chose not to cross the street and confront the bomber's friend. Instead, he used the crowd to shield him from the young man's view. When he was certain that he wouldn't be noticed, he made his way across the street, bringing him to within fifty feet of the side of his target. Brixton moved behind the crowd until he was behind the young man. He had a decision to make—try to subdue him or look for a cop and point him out? A quick glance around made the decision for him. All the police were on the other side of the street trying to help the survivors.

Brixton squirmed past people until he was within striking distance. A few people saw the bleeding wound on his face, grimaced, and moved away. He poised to wrap his arm around the young conspirator's neck, but the man turned and a flash of recognition crossed his face. Brixton acted instinctively. His right fist landed squarely on the man's nose, flattening it and sending him crashing into others.

"Grab him!" Brixton hollered.

No one did.

The young man righted himself, turned, and pushed through the crowd, sending a woman holding a baby to the ground. Brixton stepped around them and took off after him. Someone yelled, "Stop that man!" and Brixton assumed that he was referring to the young man. Brixton's arm was grabbed. He shook it off and continued running.

The conspirator broke clear of the crowd and raced into an alley separating two office buildings. Brixton followed him and paused. His lungs ached, his right knee throbbed, and back spasms caused him to double over. Breathing came hard. He peered into the narrow passageway and saw the man scramble behind a large Dumpster. Brixton drew a deep breath, pulled his Swiss-made SIG SAUER P226 pistol from its holster nestled in his armpit, and slowly approached.

"Hey," he yelled, "I know where you are. Don't be stupid. You screw with me and you're dead."

The screeching, chaotic sounds from the restaurant where the bomb had gone off, and the incessant wail of sirens, pulsated down the alley like a computer-generated sound track run amok. The acrid smell of the bomb's explosive elements had by now wafted over the area and stung Brixton's eyes as he neared the Dumpster, his weapon held in both hands and aimed directly at it. "Come on, come on," he said, closing the gap. "Don't mess with me. I'm armed."

Brixton moved within a few feet of the Dumpster. He heard sounds from behind it, scraping sounds, something metal being turned over. Was the guy armed? Brixton had to assume that he was. Dizziness came and went as the pain on the side of his face intensified. He leaned against the wall of the building and twisted his neck against stiffness. "Come on, damn it, come out of there."

The bomber's accomplice emerged from behind the Dumpster. Blood was smeared on his mouth and chin from where Brixton had broken his nose. Brixton trained his weapon and ordered, "Get your hands up!"

His quarry appeared ready to do as he was told. But as he brought up his right hand, light glinted off something metal that seemed pointed at Brixton. Brixton didn't hesitate. He squeezed off one shot that found its mark in the man's forehead, sending him tumbling back against the Dumpster. Simultaneously, Brixton heard multiple hard footsteps behind him. He looked back. Four uniformed policemen ran into the alley, guns drawn and shouting orders. Brixton turned to face them. As he did, he realized that the weapon he held would be viewed as a threat and probably get him killed. He lowered the SIG to his side and raised his other arm.

"Drop the gun," one of the officers said.

"It's okay," Brixton said. "I'm a U.S. agent." He went to return his weapon to its holster, but a burly cop attacked, twisting his arm and causing the SIG to fall to the cement. A second cop pushed him against the wall and held him there, his gun inches from Brixton's temple.

"Take it easy," Brixton said. "You've got the wrong guy. Look across the alley."

The cops wrestled Brixton to the ground; one sat on him and pressed the heel of his hand against his head. People who'd seen the police run into the alley followed, pressing into the narrow passageway.

Brixton was allowed to sit up. The police attack on

him, coupled with the earlier impact of the explosion caused every inch to ache. He was pulled up to his feet and slammed against the wall.

"There, damn it!" he managed, using his thumb to point at the body.

"What?" a cop said.

"There," Brixton said, this time using his whole arm to point. "The guy on the ground was with the suicide bomber."

Two officers went to where the lifeless body of the young man was sprawled, his Yankees hat cockeyed on his head. One of them placed a call on his radio.

"Hey, look," Brixton said, "I don't feel good. I need to sit down." He'd no sooner said it when a wave of light-headedness swamped him and he keeled over into the arms of one of the officers, who let him drop to the ground.

"Name?" the officer said, kneeling next to him.

"Brixton," he managed. "Robert Brixton. State Department." He tried to reach back to retrieve his ID from his pants pocket, but it was too painful. "My wallet," he said. "My ID's in it."

The cop pushed him on his side, pulled out the wallet, flipped it open, and read the card indicating that Brixton was an agent for SITQUAL, an outsourced division of State's Diplomatic Security Service (DSS) apparatus. He waved over the officer in charge and showed him the card. The officer nodded. "Give it back to him," he said. The cop shoved the wallet into a side pocket of Brixton's suit jacket.

A siren separated itself from the general cacophony as an ambulance entered the mouth of the alley. It arrived almost simultaneously with a second vehicle that carried members of the Metropolitan Police Department's crime-scene investigation unit. By now the authorities had pushed many of the bystanders back into the street, but their numbers were replaced by officials examining the scene.

Brixton's eyes fluttered open and he tried to get up on one elbow.

Two emergency technicians stood over him.

"I was there," Brixton said, his voice raspy.

"Where?"

"The café."

"What are you doing in this alley?"

"Him." He pointed to the young man's body that was now surrounded by officers.

Two ambulances inched forward, their progress hindered by the crush of people clogging the alley. Sharp orders to disperse were issued as the EMTs helped Brixton onto the gurney despite his protests that he was all right and didn't want to go to a hospital.

"The Dumpster," he said to no one in particular.

"What about it?" the EMT asked.

"The kid, the young punk who was sitting with the gal who blew herself up. Look. He's there. I shot him."

"You *what*?"

"I shot him. He pulled a gun on me and . . ."

His voice trailed off as he was deposited in the back of the ambulance. The police officers decided that one of them should accompany him on the short ride to George Washington University Hospital on Twenty-third Street. His final thought before he passed out was of his, young, sweet, enthusiastic daughter who'd died at the hands of another young woman whose aspirations were decidedly and tragically different.

2

B rixton slipped in and out of consciousness as he was wheeled into an emergency room that was frantically gearing up to handle the influx of wounded victims of the suicide bombing. An EMT had applied first aid to the gashes on his temple and neck. The pain from the multiple bruises he'd suffered from the blast and having been roughhoused by the cops had lessened, but the devastating reality of his daughter's fate now gripped his mind and gut as though a huge boa constrictor had engulfed him.

"He's delusional," the EMT who'd ridden with him to the hospital told a nurse as she directed the gurney to a treatment area separated from others by a white curtain. "Keeps talking about his daughter and the guy he shot."

"He shot someone?"

"Yeah. He claims he's a government agent."

"What? FBI?"

"Beats me. Something to do with the State Department. All I know is he keeps rambling on about a daughter. He says the guy he shot is the one who blew up the café."

The ER was chaotic as its staff scrambled to find space for the incoming victims, some groaning, some screaming hysterically.

"I don't need to be here," Brixton protested in a moment of clarity to the nurse and an emergency room physician, who'd begun questioning him about his injuries. They ignored his protestation as they prepared to tend to his wounds. The police officer who'd accompanied Brixton in the ambulance took a call on his cell and entered the curtained space in which Brixton was being examined and treated. "Get him out of here," he ordered.

"What?"

"You have a private exam room?" the cop asked.

"Two, but—"

"Take him there."

The doctor and nurse looked at each other before grabbing the rails on either side of the gurney and wheeling Brixton out of the main ER and to a room down the hall. The cries of the injured mingled with terse medical orders trailing behind: "Bag 'em," meaning put a patient who'd recently arrived on a respirator. "She's circling, circling," the desperate words of an ER physician, shorthand for the patient circling the drain, with death close by. And "Jesus, there's more incoming scud," as broken, bloodied bodies continued to be wheeled into the area.

Brixton mumbled, "Janet. I want to see Janet."

"Take it easy," a doctor said.

Brixton tried to get off the gurney.

"Restrain him," the doctor ordered.

"Is she here in the hospital?" Brixton asked as they pulled straps across his legs and chest.

"No," the nurse said.

"My daughter was in the café when they blew it up. Is she—?"

"He needs a CAT scan and X-rays," said a doctor.

"Take these damn things off me!" Brixton growled as he strained against the straps.

As the doctor went to arrange for the tests, Brixton looked past the nurse and uniformed officer to see Donna Salvos, his partner at SITQUAL, standing in the doorway.

The cop still in the room challenged her. She showed him her ID, which satisfied him. She came to the side of the gurney, placed a hand on Brixton, and said, "Hey, pal, you doing okay?"

"What are you doing here?"

"Checking up on you. Mike got a call from the PD. They said you'd been hurt and brought here."

"I'm fine. My daughter, she . . ." He fought back tears.

"What about your daughter, Robert?"

"She was with me in the café when it went up." He struggled again to sit up. "Is she here, in the hospital?"

"I don't know, Robert. I didn't realize that—"

"Go find out, huh? See if she's here being treated."

"I'll try, Robert, but there's so much confusion and—"

"Her name is Janet, Janet Brixton."

As Donna left to seek information about his daughter, two men arrived. Both wore suits and had a bureaucratic air about them. Brixton read it immediately. They were followed by two other men, one of whom wore a D.C. PD uniform with a wall of ribbons on the chest. His colleague was in civilian clothing.

"How are you feeling, Agent Brixton?" one of the suited bureaucrats asked.

"How do you think I feel?" Brixton said. "I just stopped in here to take a nap. How are *you* feeling? Somebody please check on my daughter."

"Your daughter?" the man asked.

"Who are you?" said Brixton.

He introduced himself and his partner as FBI. He turned and indicated that the two other men were from the MPD, as though Brixton hadn't already figured that out.

"Can somebody get these damn straps off me?"

His plea was ignored by the FBI special agent. "You were in the café when the incident occurred?" he said.

"Yeah, that's right. I was there with my daughter." His voice erupted. "Will somebody find out if she was brought in?"

"You saw the bomber, Agent Brixton?"

"That's right, both of them."

"*Both* of them?"

"Jesus," Brixton said. "Stuff your goddamn questions." To the nurse who'd returned: "Please, get these straps off me. I won't try to get up."

She looked at the doctor, who nodded, and the straps were unbuckled. Brixton pushed himself into a sitting position and looked for Donna, then saw her standing in the doorway. "Is she here? Is she alive?" he asked her.

"There's no record of her, Robert, but there's chaos. None of the casualties have been identified and—"

"Casualty? She's a casualty?" He asked it despite the reality having set in that, based upon his recollection of the explosion in the café and the second fiery blast from inside the restaurant, there was no way that Janet could have survived. He never would have left the scene if there was a chance that she was alive. He had to battle against allowing tears to flow.

"How many dead?" he asked.

"Unknown at this point. You say that there were *two* people involved?" the FBI agent asked.

"That's right. The young girl who blew herself up and the guy she was with."

"The young man you shot in the alley?"

"Yeah. He came in with her to the café, bought a lemonade, drank some, and left just before the bomb went off. I saw him across the street and went after him. The bastard was smiling. I saw him and wanted to kill him, standing there gloating."

"And you did."

"What?"

"You killed him."

"Because he tried to kill *me*."

"Did he say anything to you before you—?"

"He said nothing. He tried to hide behind the Dumpster and came out carrying."

The agent cast a knowing glance at his partner before continuing. "You say that you were in the café with your daughter when the blast occurred?"

Brixton didn't respond. Thoughts of when he had tried to get her to leave, assumed she had followed him, and saw that she hadn't, were too painful for words to get through.

"We were leaving," he managed to say.

"Why didn't she leave with you?"

"Because—because she hung back for a few seconds to collect some things, I don't know, something she'd brought with her. I yelled at her to get her out. God knows I tried. I had a feeling. I had a feeling."

"Did you get a good look at the young woman with the bomb?"

"No. She was wearing one of those Arab getups. I saw her face once. Just a kid. She looked scared."

"What about the young man you allege was with her?"

"*Allege?*"

"You say he came in with her but left after—what?—drinking some lemonade?"

One of the ER doctors interrupted. "The patient has to go for X-rays and a CT."

"Stay with them," the agent told his partner.

Brixton was happy to get away from the questioning that had nettled what was already a frazzled psyche. As he was wheeled from the room, he passed beneath a TV set in the hallway that was tuned to CNN.

"Wait a minute," Brixton told the nurse as he heard his name come from the set.

"The number of victims in the suicide bombing on Twenty-third Street has yet to be determined," the anchor announced. "But CNN has learned that a State Department security agent, Robert Brixton, who was in the café at the time of the bombing and who escaped with his life, claimed that a second person was involved, a young man whom Brixton allegedly followed into a nearby alley and shot to death. According to our sources, Brixton has been taken to the hospital, where he's undergoing treatment for his injuries. More on this as details emerge. We now go to Roberta Dougherty who is standing by at George Washington University Hospital, where most of the injured have been taken for treatment."

Brixton wanted to linger by the TV to hear more, but the nurse pushed the gurney down the hall and into a room where a technician took charge of the testing that had been ordered.

While the insides of Brixton's body and brain were being viewed and evaluated, his ex-wife, Marylee, gasped as she heard the same CNN report in her Rockville, Maryland, home. "Oh, my God," she said as she frantically dialed her younger daughter's cell phone number, only to hear it ring unanswered. She hung up; Janet Brixton had a habit of letting her cell phone run out of juice or forgetting to pay her bill. Marylee next dialed her older daughter at home.

"It's Mom," she said. "I just heard on TV that—"

"I know, I know," Jill said. "I heard it, too."

"Do you know where Janet is? I tried her cell but it's not working."

"I talked to her this afternoon. She said she was going to meet Daddy for dinner and—"

"Oh, no," Marylee wailed. "Do you think she was with him when the bomb went off?"

"I don't know. From what I've heard, he wasn't inside the café when it happened. So she must not have been with him."

"Please, God, let that be true. I'll try some other numbers. Maybe somebody will know. If you hear from her, call me right away."

The CNN broadcast was also watched by Mackensie and Annabel Smith at their Watergate apartment. They'd befriended Brixton a year earlier when he'd come to Washington while working a case as a private investigator from Savannah, Georgia.

Mac Smith had been a top criminal attorney in D.C. until a drunken motorist ran into the car driven by his wife and only child and killed them both. When the drunk driver was given what Smith considered a slap on the wrist by the trial judge, Mac soured on representing criminals, closed his practice, and accepted a post as law professor at George Washington University.

Annabel had been a Washington attorney specializing in matrimonial law. After years of dealing with irrational, squabbling spouses for whom the children's interests took a backseat, she took down her shingle and pursued what had been a lifelong passion, pre-Columbian art, opening a Georgetown gallery, which prospered under her ownership. Following their marriage at the National Cathedral, they'd settled into the apartment in the Watergate complex with splendid views of the Potomac and beyond, and reveled in having found each other. Their names were on many A-lists in a city where such lists are currency, but they pledged to be judicious in which invitations they accepted. They might have fallen in love with each other but did not share the same affection for "official" Washington.

"There were two people involved," Mac said to Annabel, "at least according to this report."

"And Robert shot the second person," Annabel said. "They said that he escaped serious injuries."

"Fortunately. I'm going to call his apartment and leave a message on his answering machine."

"Is there someone at GW Hospital you can call?" she asked.

"Yeah, there is. I'll see what I can find out."

Also watching CNN with great interest was Willis Sayers, Washington bureau chief of the *Savannah Morning News*. He and Brixton had met while both lived and worked in Savannah during the period when Brixton was a detective and Sayers worked local news, especially the crime beat. The bombing in the café would, of course, be front-page news in every newspaper in the country, but Brixton's apparent involvement gave Sayers a local Savannah angle. He corralled a freelance photographer who did work for the paper, and they headed for the hospital, hoping to get an exclusive interview.

In New York, Flo Combes, Brixton's significant other while they lived in Savannah, breathed a sigh of relief when she heard the announcer indicate that Brixton had survived the suicide bombing. *Leave it to Robert to be where a bomb goes off,* she told herself as she called his Washington phone number and left a message.

While others in Brixton's circle reacted to the steady stream of news about the bombing, he was wheeled back to the private examination room, where the FBI special agents and local MPD authorities awaited his return. Donna Salvos, Brixton's partner at SITQUAL, dreaded seeing him again. There was no record of Brixton's daughter having been admitted to GW or to the other hospitals that were tending to the victims, which could only mean that she hadn't survived the bombing. Those in the room had been joined by Mike Kogan, Brixton's and Salvos's boss at SITQUAL. Kogan had worked with Brixton during the latter's four years as a Washington cop, and while Brixton's tendency to do things his own stubborn way had perplexed, even angered Kogan on occasion, he recognized in his maverick employee a top-notch investigator—and a guy you'd want at your back in the parking lot when members of a motorcycle gang decided to crack your skull.

Brixton was no sooner delivered to the room when yet another suit arrived; he introduced himself to the others as Clint Halpern, special assistant for public affairs to the secretary of state. No introduction was needed for Brixton. He'd met Halpern on a few occasions and hadn't liked him. Halpern was immediately followed by two representatives from the Department of Homeland Security. The cluster of blue suits in the small room was suffocating. "Why the hell are there so many people here?" Brixton growled.

"Take it easy, Robert," Kogan said.

"I'll take it easy when I'm out of here," Brixton said. "She's dead, isn't she?"

When no one replied, he said, "Janet. My daughter Janet."

"We don't have any news yet," Salvos said.

Kogan, his head shaved and his body built like an NFL linebacker, leaned closer to Brixton. "I've talked to the doctors, Robert. They're going to take you to a private room, where you'll stay the night."

Brixton sat up. "No, I want out of here."

Kogan's hand on Brixton's shoulder was firm. "Don't argue," he said. "They want to observe you overnight; you suffered a concussion."

"Concussion? I'm fine."

Their conversation was interrupted by another doctor and two nurses, who asked that everyone leave while they prepared to take Brixton to his private room. He continued his verbal protest, even as he realized that it was a waste of time and words. Followed by the entourage that had assembled, he was wheeled out of the chaotic ER area, taken to an elevator, and a few minutes later arrived in the room that would be his for the night. It was on the top floor of the hospital, and judging from its trappings, it was reserved for VIP patients. It was large, had a sitting area with four black leather chairs, and a private bathroom. As the room filled up with investigators, Brixton was shifted from the gurney into the bed. He looked around at the faces staring down at him. The only difference was that there was more room here for the crowd than the ER treatment room had offered.

Everyone was asked to leave while a doctor performed an examination, including the wounds on the back of Brixton's head and neck.

"It's not as bad as it looked when you first arrived," a doctor said. "Should heal up fine."

"Then why am I here?"

"An explosion like the one you've experienced could cause a concussion" was the doc's reply.

"I don't have a concussion."

"We'll know better after you've had a chance to rest overnight."

The examination completed, the doctor and nurse left, and the others who'd been asked to vacate filed back in.

"Feel up to a few questions, Agent Brixton?" the man from Homeland Security asked through a disingenuous smile.

Brixton didn't answer. He muttered to himself, "Just like that. One minute you're drinking a beer and eating calamari, the next minute you're blown up by some warped kid who thinks she's doing something wonderful."

"I understand that you left the café just before the explosion," Homeland Security said.

Brixton snapped back to the moment. "Yeah, that's right, I was almost out of there."

"You were leaving anyway? You'd finished eating and drinking?"

"No. I left because I smelled something was wrong."

"Wrong? In what way?"

"What does it matter?" Brixton said. "I don't know why—a look in the girl's eyes."

"That she was obviously of Middle Eastern background added to your suspicions?"

"No. Well, maybe. I mean, I don't go around suspecting every Arab of planning to blow up a café."

"No, of course not." His smile was still there.

"When the guy left, I had the feeling that something bad was coming down."

"But you didn't do anything," Homeland Security said.

Brixton flared. "Do anything? What was I supposed

to do, shoot the girl there in the café? Jump up and shout 'There's a suicide bomber'? All I thought of at the moment was to get my daughter out of there and . . ." His voice trailed off and he looked away.

The representatives from the various government agencies were in and out of the room over the next hour. Brixton could see them huddled in the hallway, where two uniformed members of the Washington MPD had taken up positions in chairs on either side of the doorway. At one point only Donna Salvos and Mike Kogan were with Brixton.

"What's going on?" Brixton asked.

"They're trying to handle inquiries from a dozen sources," Kogan answered. "The press is camped outside the hospital trying to get a handle on the number of dead and injured. That friend of yours, Sayers, sent in a note asking to see you."

"Will? I don't want to see anybody," Brixton said.

"And you don't have to," Kogan said. He managed a small laugh. "Not that you'd be allowed to talk to anyone, including the press—especially the press—until you're cleared."

"Cleared? By who?"

"Homeland Security, DSS, the MPD, FBI—you name it, Robert. The way it's falling, you're the only eyewitness to the bombing who's alive to offer something tangible about it. And there's the guy you shot."

"What about him? Who is he? Who put him up to it? Who brainwashed him and the girl to do what they did?"

"That's being investigated," said Kogan. He checked Donna's reaction before continuing. She said nothing, simply turned away and looked out the window at the city's lights. "In the meantime," Kogan continued, "they want you secluded in the hospital until the doctors clear you to leave. You might as well use the time here to rest up. There'll be a million questions for you once you're discharged."

"And what if I don't want to answer them? All I care about is that beautiful daughter of mine who died at the hands of those bastards." He looked at Salvos, hoping that she'd contradict him. When she didn't he struggled to keep from breaking down.

"Why don't you try and get some sleep," Kogan suggested, and nodded to Donna that they should leave. "I'll be back first thing in the morning."

Brixton watched them go. The profound sadness he'd felt about Janet was now accompanied by an intense rage at those who'd killed her and so many other innocents. He thought of the young man he'd shot in the alley and desperately wished he were alive so that he could confront him, question him, beat him up if necessary to try to make sense out of why he and his girlfriend would have done what they did.

As Kogan and Donna Salvos waited for the elevator, they were approached by the lead MPD detective who'd been dispatched to provide security for Brixton and to keep him from being approached by anyone other than authorities.

"Just thought you'd want to know that we've got the ID on the guy your agent shot," the detective said.

Kogan and Donna waited for him to elaborate.

The detective consulted a slip of paper. "Name's Paul Skaggs, age twenty-two."

"Any relation to Congressman Skaggs?" Kogan asked.

"Yeah, I'd say so. He's the congressman's son. By the way, he wasn't armed. The only thing he had was a cell phone in a silver case."

3

SUICIDE BOMBING STUNS D.C.
17 DEAD, SCORES INJURED
CONGRESSMAN SKAGGS'S SON SHOT: POSSIBLE
SECOND BOMBER?

That was *The Washington Post* front-page headline that confronted Brixton the next morning as he prepared to leave the hospital.

"Skaggs's son?" Brixton said aloud. "That's who I shot?"

He quickly scanned the long article. While most of it focused on the café bombing and its victims—those who survived were in critical condition at local hospitals—he got to the section about the shooting.

Details are sketchy, but sources have told this writer that a security agent for the State Department, who was in the café at the time of the blast, accosted a young man the agent alleges was with the suicide bomber just minutes before she detonated the explosives. We have been able to confirm that the victim of the shooting was Paul Skaggs, the son of Congressman Walter Skaggs. Witnesses say that the agent, Robert Brixton, followed the younger Skaggs into a nearby alley and shot him dead. Attempts to contact Brixton have been unsuccessful. He is reported to have been taken to George Washington University Hospital to be treated for injuries he incurred in the bombing. It has been further reported that Brixton might have been with a family member in the café at the time of the incident.

The doctor assigned to his case entered the room just as Brixton finished reading *The Post*'s coverage.

"How are you feeling?" Brixton was asked.

"I just want out of here."

The young doctor examined Brixton, including running him through a cursory series of questions to determine whether he was suffering any latent effects of the explosion. He evidently passed, because the doctor, who appeared to Brixton to be too young to have an MD after his name, gave him a prescription for pain meds, urged him to rest for a week, and said, "Lots of luck, Mr. Brixton."

Donna Salvos arrived as the doctor was writing up Brixton's discharge papers. She was followed by Kogan, Brixton's boss at SITQUAL; the State Department's Clint Halpern; two FBI agents; a Homeland Security Department representative; and a new face, a stern, young, prematurely balding man from the CIA who didn't bother giving his name. Salvos noticed the morning paper with its telling headline.

"You've read it?" she asked.

Brixton grunted. "Yeah, I've read it, full of the usual 'allege's. The Skaggs kid was there in the café, Donna. I'm not *alleging* that he was there. He *was* there."

One of the FBI agents took the newspaper from where it had been tossed on the bed and put it in his briefcase. "Time to go," he said.

Brixton and his entourage were taken downstairs in a service elevator, walked through a series of underground tunnels, and emerged through a back door leading to a loading dock, where a black limousine with tinted windows waited, its engine running. A marked MPD patrol car blocked access to the area for other vehicles.

Brixton said nothing during the short drive to his Capitol Hill apartment. The dread and sadness over Janet's death had firmly set in during his sleepless night in the hospital room. No matter how hard he tried, he could not replace the vision of her laughing face with something less painful. Sometimes the picture was of her as a small child getting into mischief, pulling the cat's tail or dumping salt into the sugar canister. At other times it was her sitting next to him in the café trying to sell him on the cockamamy idea of her latest boyfriend. Once, his mental projection screen showed a close-up of her pierced lip, and he had to bite his own lip to not weep.

But Janet wasn't the only visual that had kept him awake. There was the young girl of Arabic origins looking fearful as her companion sipped lemonade and prepared to leave her to commit mass murder of seventeen innocent people, including two children, according to news reports. And there was her coconspirator, a smirk on his face as he watched from afar the pain he and the girl had inflicted on so many. When those images flashed in Brixton's mind, he swore under his breath, fists clenched, eyes squeezed shut against the rage that consumed him.

Several times he had considered getting up and sneaking out of the room and the hospital. But he knew that he'd never get past the two uniformed officers flanking his doorway. He felt helpless—helpless to save his daughter and helpless to find out more about the people who'd slaughtered her.

There were people on the street when the limo pulled up in front of Brixton's building. Some were from the neighborhood, who'd learned about their now-infamous neighbor and were waiting for his home-coming. They were joined by reporters and a TV camera crew who were also there for the homecoming but with a job to do. The neighbors said nothing as the vehicle's occupants piled out and walked quickly toward the entrance. The reporters shouted questions, which Brixton ignored. He kept his eyes straight ahead as they took the elevator to his floor, where he unlocked the door and stepped inside. A telephone answering machine's red light blinked, accompanied by a series of beeps. Brixton went directly to it but was stopped by one of the FBI special agents.

"I can't listen to my calls?" Brixton growled. "My dead daughter's mother might have called. So might a lot of other people I want to talk to."

"No, go ahead," the agent said, pulling up a chair beside the small desk that held the machine and taking out a pad of paper and a pen. Brixton glared at him, to no effect. He pulled his own chair close and punched the button to listen to the nine messages.

Calls from Mac Smith and Will Sayers were duly noted. Sayers called a second time urging Brixton to call back: "Your involvement will be big news back in your favorite city," he said, snidely referring to the fact that Brixton was never a fan of Savannah, Georgia, where he'd spent twenty years as a cop. "Don't forget me, pal."

Flo Combes's call from New York touched Brixton. Their breakup had been contentious; some bad feelings lingered. She asked how he was doing, and hoped he wasn't too badly hurt. "If there's anything I can do, Robert—"

It was the two frantic calls from Brixton's ex-wife, Marylee, that meant the most to him. The first call was made before she knew that Janet had been killed in the blast. The second was pure hysteria. She'd received official word that Janet was among the victims of the bomber, and Marylee could barely talk, sobbing, pleading for word from him, screaming at times, invoking God at others.

"Satisfied?" Brixton asked the FBI agent, after he'd gone through the calls, which included messages from other reporters besides Will Sayers.

The agent didn't respond.

"Robert," Mike Kogan said, "everyone here has questions for you. Maybe it's best that we sit down and get it over with before—"

"Before *what*?"

"Before people without an official capacity get to you."

"I have to return some of these calls," Brixton said.

"You can do that after we've had a chance to talk," said the CIA agent.

"No," Brixton said, "I have to call my ex-wife. It's her daughter, too, who was killed."

Looks between the others resulted in the Homeland Security official saying, "I think that Agent Brixton should make that call." He looked at Brixton. "Of course, you won't mind that we listen along with you."

"Yeah, I sure as hell do mind."

Kogan said firmly, "He's entitled to speak privately with his ex-wife about the death of their daughter." To Brixton: "Go in the bedroom, Robert, and make the call."

Kogan wasn't challenged, and Brixton went to his bedroom, closed the door, and dialed Marylee's number in Rockville, Maryland. His older daughter, Jill, answered.

"Hi. It's Dad."

"Where are you?"

"Home. I'm home. How is Mom?"

"Oh, my God," she said and began to cry. "Janet's dead."

"I know, I know. I was with her when—"

His former wife, Marylee, was now on the line. "Robert? Janet is gone. You were with her."

"Yeah, I was. We were having a drink when it happened."

"'When it happened'? *Why* did it happen?"

"I can't tell you why the girl did what she did, Marylee. It's insane, nuts. She must have been brainwashed to blow herself up. There was this guy with her who—"

"The one you shot."

"Right."

"Why didn't you do something?" She was yelling now.

"Do what, Marylee? I tried to get her out of the café and almost did, except she lingered for a few seconds, just enough time to get caught in the blast."

"You could have done something, for Christ's sake, you and your guns and your badge and, oh, God—whatever. *Something!*"

Brixton tried to come up with what to say next, words that would get through to her, lessen her pain, make her less angry at him. He'd been wrestling all night with his own questions of what he might have done to save his daughter, barraged with what-ifs—listening to his instincts about the young Arab girl a few minutes sooner and leaving quicker; choosing a different restaurant at which to meet; having spent more time with her following his divorce; being a better father—a kaleidoscope of self-recriminations and second-guesses.

"She's gone, Robert," Marylee moaned, her voice soft and filled with final recognition of reality.

"Look, Marylee," he said, "we'll have to get together soon and make final plans about—well, you know. It'll be a while before the authorities will release bodies and—"

"I hate you," she screamed, before slamming down the phone.

Brixton sat looking at the receiver in his hands for what seemed to him an eternity. He hated being hated by her, but he knew what was fueling her rage. It wasn't him that she hated, it was the world and the warped people in it for whom other lives were irrelevant. He slowly replaced the phone in its cradle and rejoined the others in his living room.

"You okay, Robert?" Kogan asked.

"Yeah," he replied. He took in the others. "All right, you have questions; let me hear them. Then get the hell out of my house."

The CIA agent took the lead and asked Brixton to recount his every move, from when and why he went to the café, his observations of the suicide bomber, and the blast itself. Brixton corrected him: "I observed two suicide bombers," he said, "the young woman who actually detonated the bomb, and the guy she was with who I now know is Congressman Skaggs's son."

"We'll get to that aspect in a minute," said the agent. "You say that you left the café moments before the explosion because you—what?—had a feeling, a premonition of some sort?"

"That's right."

Mike Kogan chimed in. "Robert Brixton has the best instincts about people that I've ever experienced," he said. "His instincts in this case were obviously right."

The special agent ignored Kogan's testimonial and pressed Brixton to describe the suicide bomber.

"There's not much to say about her. Young, looked to be of Middle Eastern origins, scared expression. The guy she was with, Skaggs's kid, was talking to her, whispering in her ear, like he was telling her secrets. She never said anything. Maybe he was boosting her confidence, keeping her from calling it off. I don't know. The guy ordered a lemonade, drank half, and scrammed. That's when I told my daughter we were leaving."

"She didn't want to go?"

"No. I mean, she was confused why I was in a hurry to leave. I got to the edge of the café, turned around, and told her to hurry up. I was starting back into the café when the bomb went off."

Brixton's patience, already strained, became more so as he was asked repeatedly to recount every second of his experience in the café. Eventually the CIA agent turned things over to one of the FBI special agents, who said, "Let's get down to what happened, Agent Brixton."

"Sure."

Brixton was asked for a second-by-second recounting of his confrontation with the young man, the son of one of the House of Representatives' most powerful lawmakers. He meticulously recalled his first visual encounter, when the young man and the girl passed by the café a few times before entering and taking a table close to where he and Janet sat. He repeated how the young man leaned across the table to talk to her, downed half the lemonade, and abruptly left. Brixton went on to detail how he spotted the man across the street, pursued him into the alley, and fired when it appeared that he was armed.

"End of story," Brixton said. "Look, I'm sorry the kid is dead, but I'm not losing sleep over it. He's responsible for killing my younger daughter, who was with me in the café. Sixteen others died because of him, including little kids."

An awkward silence filled the room. Brixton looked from face to face in search of a response and was met with stony silence. Kogan broke the ice.

"The problem, Robert," he said, "is that you're the only person who can place Skaggs's son in the café with the bomber."

"I'm the only one? Can't be. What about others who were there?"

One of the FBI agents shook his head. "We've interviewed the people who survived the blast, including those taken to the hospital. No one recalls a young man as you describe him being with the girl. Anyone close to the table she sat at was killed in the explosion. The secondary explosion—a gas line inside the restaurant blew—wiped out the serving staff who waited on outdoor tables."

Brixton sat back and processed what was being said. It was patently obvious that the others in his living room were skeptical of his story about Congressman Skaggs's son being in the café, and he felt his frustration level rise. Finally he said, "Look, I'm telling you the truth. Why shouldn't I? Why would I make up something like this? What do you think, that I just decided to go shoot a young guy who was standing around because I didn't like the way he looked? I'm telling you that he came into the café with the girl carrying the bomb, and he split a few minutes before she set it off. Blue-and-white-checked shirt, jeans, Yankees cap. I don't give a damn whether anybody else saw him or not, and I resent the inference that I shot and killed somebody for no good reason."

Kogan, who knew Brixton better than anyone in the room, said, "I think every question that can be raised at this point has been asked. Agent Brixton has been through a traumatic ordeal. He's lost a daughter in the bombing and was injured himself. I suggest we let him settle down here and get the rest the doctors told him he needs."

With some murmurs of dissension, the others took Kogan's advice and prepared to leave. The Homeland Security representative said as he gathered his papers, "I'm sure you appreciate, Agent Brixton, that the government is pulling out every stop, utilizing every asset, to find out who was behind the bombing. The president will be addressing it at noon today, and Congressman Skaggs is calling for a congressional investigation of the killing of his son. It should go without saying that anything *you* might say to others outside the chain of command could jeopardize the investigation. In other words, Agent Brixton, you're not to speak to anyone unless specifically authorized. Understood?"

Brixton neither confirmed nor denied his understanding. He locked eyes with Homeland Security and with State's Clint Halpern, who'd said nothing during the questioning but whose consistent expression of disdain for Brixton never left his face.

"I'll catch up with you in a minute," Kogan told the others. When they were gone, he said to Brixton, "Look, Robert, the fallout from this has only just begun. The café bombing is one thing; you shooting the congressman's son is another. I'm putting you on paid leave until things settle down. Avoid the press. They'll be all over it—and you. The stakes are big, as you can imagine. Congressman Skaggs has already issued a statement about his son, and although he didn't cite you by name, he did talk about a 'rogue State Department security agent' gunning down an innocent civilian."

"Maybe he ought to launch an investigation into why his son aided a suicide bomber. Skaggs is a blowhard, and you know it."

"And a damn powerful blowhard, Robert. Cut him a little slack. He's lost a son."

"And I've lost a daughter."

"So you know how it feels. I'm sorry. Go take a nap. Read a book. Get some sleep. I'll be back in touch."

Brixton walked his boss to the elevator and got in with him. "I'm going to find out why that kid did what he did," he said grimly. "I'm going to find out who turned him into a mass killer. Count on it, Mike. I *will* find those answers."

"Just don't make things difficult for me," said Kogan as the elevator reached the lobby. "I've got your back and I'm with you all the way. But remember, you still work for me and SITQUAL. Don't do anything to make my job tougher."

When the elevator doors opened, they were faced with half a dozen media hounds, shouting questions at Brixton, who immediately backed into the elevator and pushed the button for his floor. Kogan pushed his way through the reporters and got in the car in which State's Halpern waited.

"I don't like him," Halpern told Kogan. "He's a loose cannon. We don't need a loose cannon."

Kogan closed his eyes. Halpern was right; Brixton could be a loose cannon at times. But he was also a top-flight investigator, and Kogan had meant it when he said he had Brixton's back. But he silently prayed to a god he didn't believe in that Brixton wouldn't go off the deep end—the way he did in New York City shortly after Kogan had hired him to work for SITQUAL.

BEFORE THE
BOMBING

4

Robert Brixton's involvement with SITQUAL had begun months before the bombing that had taken the life of his daughter.

He'd stood in the kitchen of his studio apartment in Brooklyn's Red Hook neighborhood, adding ingredients to his blender—apple juice, a banana, uncooked oatmeal, maple syrup, and multiple tablespoons of a granular substance that was said to contain every vitamin known to man, and some that weren't. His face was set in a scowl. The thought of starting the morning with the concoction was anathema to him, but it had become a daily habit, thanks to Flo Combes, a habit he intended to break now that she was no longer in his life.

He'd met Flo in Savannah through a mutual friend. He liked the fact that she wasn't of southern stock—originally from Staten Island, and Jewish to boot—which appealed to his Brooklyn sensibilities. Flo hadn't always been a fitness nut or "health nazi," the politically incorrect label of the type. When they'd first met, she pretty much ate anything put before her, which matched Brixton's view of how to live your life. He was a firm believer in fate; a large bell would peal when it was your time to pack it in, no matter what you ate. He had no idea who would ring that bell; he didn't believe in God or any other higher being. Maybe it wouldn't be a bell. Maybe it would be a referee's whistle—"You're ejected from life!"—or a factory horn signaling the end of your shift. Or maybe it was silence. Probably just silence.

Brixton had ended up a cop in Savannah after moving there from Washington, D.C., where he'd put in four years on that city's police department. He'd met his wife, Marylee Greene, in D.C., and both their daughters were born in the nation's capital. The marriage didn't set a record for longevity. Once their hormones had settled down, the excitement of being married to a young, handsome uniformed cop waned, helped by Marylee's mother's open dislike of the man her only daughter had chosen to marry. Marylee was a gushy blond southern belle who'd been a cheerleader at the U. of Maryland. She came from money. Her mother, a widow, was the most pretentious, self-righteous woman—person—Brixton had ever known. The old lady supervised the packing when Marylee and the girls moved out of the small apartment in the District and settled in the family home in Maryland, which was okay with Brixton. He'd had it with Washington and its weak-kneed politicians whose only goal was to get reelected, the nation be damned. And so after four years, he resigned from the MPD, headed for Savannah, where its police department was hiring, put in his twenty years, the last ten as a detective, took the retirement package, and opened "Robert Brixton, Private Investigator."

That misguided fling at entrepreneurship didn't even last as long as his abbreviated marriage. He'd taken on an old Savannah case that involved a dead former hooker and drug addict who'd done time for the stabbing of a druggie in the parking lot of a local bar where drugs were freely dispensed. The girl had been shot dead on the street after being released from prison—end of story. Except that her God-fearing mother was convinced that her daughter had taken the rap for the stabbing in order to shield the one who'd actually committed the crime, the daughter of one of Savannah's leading and most powerful citizens. When Brixton took the case—his office rent was overdue, as were a pile of other bills—he never dreamed that following the leads in the case would take him back to D.C., resulting in almost bringing down the then occupant of the White House and his first lady, as well as her best friend, Washington's leading social hostess. That made a lot of people unhappy, and powerful forces in Savannah and Washington turned loose a hired psychopath to ring his bell or blow the whistle signifying his demise. He narrowly escaped with his life.

He packed up, left Savannah and its cloying southern charm, and hightailed it back to his native Brooklyn, New York. Flo followed, and they moved in together until his growing cynicism about anything and everything drove her away, leaving behind her parting comment—"You have become an insufferable, depressing bore!"—and her recipe for healthy breakfast smoothies.

Not long after she'd left and flipped him the bird on her way out the door, Brixton got a call at his Red Hook apartment from Michael Kogan, a former boss at the Washington MPD.

"Hope I'm not disturbing anything," Kogan said.

"Actually, you are, Michael. I was about to put in a

call to my broker to sell my twenty thousand shares of Apple stock."

"I'm impressed."

"You should be. How are things in my favorite city?"

"Our nation's capital? Business as usual: lots of self-serving speeches and no action. Aside from your vast stock holdings, things good with you?"

"I got up this morning, drew a breath, it worked, so what could be bad? Why are you calling?"

"Aside from wanting to hear your sunny voice, I have a job opportunity that you might be interested in."

"In D.C.? I hate D.C."

"In New York."

"I'm listening."

"On top of running this agency in D.C., the brain trust has decided to open an office in New York."

"Tell me again about that agency you head up. You told me the last time we talked, but I've had other things on my mind."

"It's called SITQUAL."

"What's that stand for?"

"It doesn't matter. I report to DSS at the State Department. That's their security and intelligence division. State has a hiring freeze and outsourced some of its security functions. You've heard of outsourcing. It's all the rage these days in government. We're a private agency with a federal agenda. We help keep foreign dignitaries and embassies safe here in D.C. Now they want us to do the same in New York City. The NYPD has the primary responsibility, but they're overloaded and asked State for help in making sure that UN types and consulate staffs live long, happy lives."

"I thought those people had diplomatic immunity."

"They do. That's part of the reason the PD wants to back off. They're tired of ticketing official cars and arresting embassy types who claim immunity and walk away. DSS is used to dealing with them. Interested? I'm hiring. It pays well, Robert."

"I'll think about it," Brixton said.

Kogan laughed. He'd been one of the few superiors Brixton had worked for who wasn't turned off by his downbeat view of life. "Hey, Robert, last I heard you weren't exactly living the high life in Brooklyn."

Which was true. Since returning, he'd picked up a few security jobs that paid the rent on the apartment in Red Hook but not much else. Since Flo's abrupt departure, he'd been living pretty much on frozen dinners, an occasional lunch or dinner out with what friends he had left, and breakfast drinks that deposited grit between his teeth. And there was always a martini to cap off lonely evenings.

"What's the job entail?" Brixton asked.

"Mostly investigations when a consulate or UN official complains about something—an employee getting mugged or a pretty young thing being accosted on the street. Nothing heavy-duty. Think of it this way: You'll be getting a decent paycheck and contributing to world peace at the same time."

"Sounds like another government bureaucracy to me," Brixton said.

"You have a hearing problem, Robert? I told you you'd be working for a private agency funded by the government. Besides, you'll be working for me. Like old home week."

"I'm fifty-one years old, Michael. Sounds to me like you should be looking for Young Turks. Plenty of them crawling the streets of D.C. and New York."

"I need investigative experience, Robert. Young Turks, as you call them, are a dime a dozen. You've been around the block. Besides, Young Turks don't possess your infectious charm."

"Glad somebody recognizes it."

"Take a couple of days and come down to D.C. Your daughters still live in the area?"

"Yeah. I'm a grandfather."

"A loving, doting one, I'm sure. Look, I don't want to make a big deal out of this. I just thought that—"

"Day after tomorrow?"

"Perfect. Call me when you get in, and we'll grab dinner. Looking forward to seeing you again. By the way, you still get pissed off when people call you Bobby?"

"I *shoot* people who call me Bobby."

"I'll keep that in mind—Bobby."

Laughter accompanied his quick hang-up.

B rixton drove to Washington, where he spent a day with Kogan and visited his ex-wife and his daughter Jill, mother of his only grandchild. Kogan was convincing. The list that Brixton made of the pros and cons of taking the job was decidedly lopsided: a couple of minor cons and a lengthy list of pros, headed by a good-sized, steady paycheck and a chance to be back in some capacity of law enforcement. He signed on and endured a one-month condensed training period at FLETC, the Federal Law Enforcement Training Center, in Glynco, Georgia, which included the handling of the weapon he'd been issued—a SIG P226 9mm pistol, the same weapon used by Navy SEALs.

He began his new career as one of six plainclothes investigators for SITQUAL's New York office, located in a tall building on Manhattan's west side, which afforded a splendid view of the traffic-clogged West Side Highway and New Jersey beyond the Hudson River. The first three months on the job were relatively peaceful, and he enjoyed the paycheck and the official status his State Department ID gave him. He befriended a couple of NYPD detectives and had fun kidding them about not having hired him twenty-five years ago: "Savannah's gain, New York's loss," he was fond of saying.

It was toward the end of his third month that an event occurred that turned his life upside down.

There had been reports that some members of the Russian delegation to the Russian consulate on East Ninety-first Street had been using their sacrosanct diplomatic pouches to bring drugs into the city. Brixton had been effective while on the Savannah force in developing informants, and he applied his skill to fostering a relationship with a Russian member of that country's New York consulate team.

He'd met him while frequenting the bar at the W Hotel on Broadway, fifteen minutes from the Russian consulate and a favorite hangout of consulate workers. They got together early one evening for drinks at the W. His informant had begun to balk: "I have to be paid more," he said in a low, convincing voice over his half-consumed double vodka.

"More?" Brixton said, exaggerating his shock at the request. "I've already upped the ante, Gregory. I can't get you more."

The Russian sat back and slapped his hand on the small table. "I get more money or I tell you nothing. Nothing!"

"Hey, pipe down," Brixton said, aware that there might be others from the consulate in the room. He leaned closer to the Russian and said in a low but convincing voice, "What you've given me so far isn't worth a plugged nickel." Brixton laughed. "Or a plugged ruble. You give me some hard info, Gregory, and I'll see whether I can get you more money. Unless you do that . . ."

A rowdy trio of vodka-fueled Russians at the other end of the room got into an argument with two African-American customers. The fracas intensified, the voices got louder, and the scrum eventually spilled out onto Broadway.

"Get lost," Brixton told Gregory, standing and pressing his elbow against the SIG 9mm in his shoulder holster. "We'll talk tomorrow."

"Money, Brixton," Gregory said as Brixton took steps away from the table.

"Yeah, money, Gregory. Tomorrow."

When Brixton emerged from the hotel onto Broadway, a Russian had pinned one of the black men involved in the argument against the wall. He pulled a knife and held it to the American's throat. Brixton glanced up and down the street looking for uniformed cops, but saw none.

"Hey, put down the knife," he yelled.

The Russian sneered at him and returned his attention and knife to the American's throat, muttering racist slang as he did.

Brixton wanted to draw his handgun, but a crowd had gathered and pressed in close; too great a chance of an innocent bystander getting shot. Instead, he repeated his call for the Russian to drop the knife, and moved in closer until he was within a few feet. The Russian, taller and beefier than Brixton, turned from the American against the wall and thrust the knife at Brixton, who avoided the blade by stepping aside. The Russian thrust again. As he did, Brixton grabbed his arm, twisted it, and the knife fell to the sidewalk. The Russian cried out in pain as Brixton increased pressure on his arm until he heard a bone snap. He forced the Russian to his knees and brought his left knee up into his face, smashing his broad nose and sending him tumbling backward.

Wires in Brixton's brain crackled with conflicting thoughts. He considered for a moment stepping back and walking away. Instead he pounced on the Russian, digging his knee into his stomach and driving his fist into his already battered face. He would have continued pummeling him were it not for the arrival of a NYPD patrol car. Two uniformed officers jumped out and dragged Brixton from atop the bloodied Russian. A few bystanders applauded.

Brixton identified himself and told the officers what had happened. They asked him to come to headquarters to give a statement, which he did. The Russian was taken by ambulance to the nearest hospital, where he was treated for his injuries and released. As far as Brixton was concerned, that was the end of it. He filed the requisite report with Mike Kogan at SITQUAL in Washington and forgot about the incident until a few days later, when the Russian embassy filed its own report with the U.S. State Department claiming that its employee had been savagely attacked and beaten by someone representing the United States government. It demanded that the attacker be punished.

The Russian's protest and demands reached DSS in Washington, which instructed Kogan to interview Brixton and take appropriate action. Kogan summoned Brixton to Washington to get his side of the story.

"The guy threatened a U.S. citizen with a knife," Brixton told Kogan as they sat in Kogan's Washington office above a Thai restaurant in Arlington, Virginia, "and he tried to slash me with it. What was I supposed to do, take him back in the hotel and buy him a drink?"

"I know, I know," Kogan said, holding up his hands in defense, "but things are tense with the Russians these days."

"When weren't they?"

"My bosses at DSS want you removed from the New York office."

"Fired?"

"They didn't say that specifically, but you can read it that way. Look, Robert, I don't have any choice."

"So I get canned because I save a guy and myself from this drunken Ruskie. Great system we have."

"I didn't say I was going to fire you, but I have to follow orders and get you out of New York. I have an opening here in D.C."

"I hate D.C.," Brixton said.

"As much as you hate losing a good job? You're not getting younger, Robert. Jobs for a guy your age aren't that plentiful. I'm sticking my neck out for you. DSS would just as soon see you gone. Look, I know what you did was warranted. It's up to you. I tell my boss at DSS that you're gone from New York, like they wanted. You come to D.C., get settled, keep a low profile—and keep your job. I don't want to lose you, Robert, but if you don't get down off your high horse, I won't have a choice."

Brixton took the job, moved what little he possessed to D.C., and found a place to live on Capitol Hill through his old friend from Savannah, Willis Sayers, now Washington bureau chief for the *Savannah Morning News*. Robert "Don't Call Me Bobby" Brixton was back in Washington, in a one-bedroom apartment with a nice little balcony, reintroducing himself to the city that he loathed.

5

B rixton settled into his new job in Washington with SITQUAL. While he wasn't thrilled about being back in the nation's capital, he reminded himself that Kogan had stuck his neck out for him, and Brixton pledged to do nothing to violate the faith that Kogan had placed in him.

He and Donna Salvos worked as a team, which pleased Brixton. She was a sharp gal who had the ability to separate her disdain for the bureaucratic nonsense from the job she was paid to do, which suited Brixton perfectly. Thirty years old and compactly attractive with short blond hair, she'd been hired by SITQUAL after serving four years as an armed member of the 1,800-strong Capitol Police. What made her especially attractive to SITQUAL, a private agency reporting to the State Department's DSS security division, were her linguistic skills. She spoke half a dozen languages, which proved helpful when dealing with staffers from the more than 175 foreign embassies in Washington, D.C.

Most of the cases they caught—more like incidents—
were minor-league stuff. But one day they were called
in to help investigate the murder of Peter Müller, an
employee of the German embassy.

The story of Peter Müller's murder started in Marigold's, a gay bar in Dupont Circle. According to his
friends, Müller had intended to leave an hour earlier
but kept being drawn back into the conversation. That
meant more Blue Velvet martinis, a drink made of vodka,
and blueberry schnapps, introduced at The Abbey in
West Hollywood in 1994 in honor of the movie *National Velvet,* starring Elizabeth Taylor, one of the gay
community's favorite leading ladies.

Tall, blond, blue-eyed, and unmistakably Teutonic,
Müller had moved to Washington, D.C., from his native Düsseldorf, Germany, four years earlier to take a
job on the Defense Attaché staff at the German embassy.
Armed with a degree in ambient intelligence from the
Technical University of Kaiserslautern, he'd been recruited to join the team responsible for coordinating
German defense initiatives with the U.S. Department
of Defense. The position sounded more impressive than
what his duties actually comprised, poring over reports
and analytic papers and summarizing their content for
his superiors. "I'm a glorified clerk," he often told his
friends at Marigold's and other gay watering holes.

Müller had been a closeted homosexual during high
school. In college a number of female students had their
eye on the handsome young man, and he'd dated a few,
but not because he was attracted to them. He did it to
counter rumors about his sexuality, the coeds his
"beards," as gays sometimes refer to such women.

He'd continued to keep his homosexuality under
wraps when he applied for the embassy job. Although

sexual orientation was not a line on the application, nor
was he asked about it during interviews, he was aware
of a tacit understanding that homosexuality was frowned
upon when it came to government employment. Too
easy to be compromised, blackmailed, manipulated.
And so he kept it to himself until reaching Washington
and securely settling into his job. That's when he began exploring the city's thriving gay community in and
around Washington's Dupont and Logan Circles.

Being with other gays was liberating for Peter Müller.
He made friends, and a few months earlier had initiated
a romantic relationship with Eduardo "Lalo" Reyes, a
young Spanish man who worked in the Spanish embassy's Public Information Office. On this particular night
Müller and Reyes were supposed to meet for dinner, but
Reyes had to work late, so Müller caught up with a
group of friends for dinner and went barhopping with
them, their forays into D.C.'s vibrant gay-bar scene extending well into the steamy summer D.C. night and
ending at Marigold's.

"No, I have to go now," he said more than once in
defense of having announced that he was leaving. He
had an eight o'clock meeting the next morning; to be
even a few minutes late and groggy would not sit well
with his boss.

It was 1:00 A.M. The bar was hopping. Shirtless bartenders made drinks, flirted with customers, and sold
vials of "poppers"—amyl nitrate—over the bar to
couples about to consummate their evening. Two
supple young men in loincloths danced to ear-splitting
music on a tiny stage at the rear of the long room.

"Come on, Peter," a friend said, his words slurred,
"one more Blue Velvet before you go."

"No, no, I can't."

"Then come back to my place, Peter. Let's not let this
night go to waste."

"No, I—"

"Afraid that Lalo will know? My lips are sealed unless—"

"What?"

"Unless they are attached to yours," he said, giggling.

"*Das Luder,*" Müller said playfully as he threw money on the bar and waved to other friends.

"Huh?"

"German for 'slut.'"

"I love it when you talk dirty. Best to Lalo."

They hugged, and Müller walked unsteadily from the bar into the oppressive night air. A dome of heat and humidity had descended on the city two days earlier, and forecasters said it would remain in place for at least another day. Was there anyplace more hot and humid than Washington, D.C., in the midst of summer? He doubted it.

He looked up and down the street for a taxi. His apartment wasn't that far, but he wasn't about to stumble to it. Did other people on the street notice that he was drunk? It would not be good if they did. It invited trouble.

He fought not to stagger as he walked to the intersection. Still not a cab in sight. *Probably having their turbans cleaned,* he thought angrily as he turned the corner. So many taxi drivers in this city seemed to wear them.

He was now on a poorly lighted and less-populated street. Ahead was another major intersection, and he headed for it in the hope of finding a cab there. He concentrated on walking steadily and not tripping, unaware that someone who'd been loitering outside the club had fallen in behind him.

He paused halfway down the block and placed a hand on a lamppost. He was tempted to sit on the sidewalk but drew deep breaths against the urge and continued.

"Hey," he heard someone say.

Müller stopped, turned, and was face-to-face with a short, stocky man wearing a tan safari jacket.

Müller squinted against the dim light to better see the man's face.

Not another word was spoken. The man, who held a handgun at his side, raised it and fired two shots. One struck Müller in the face, the other in his chest. His assailant quickly walked away as Müller twisted and fell, his extended hands no help in keeping his face from crashing into the hard sidewalk. The contact wasn't painful. Peter Müller was dead before he ever reached the ground.

6

A young couple discovered the body minutes after the shooting. The husband called 911 on his cell phone. A man who'd left the club turned the corner, saw what was happening, and ran back inside to spread the news, which prompted dozens of club-goers to flock to the grisly scene. A marked MPD cruiser came to a screeching stop where the husband and wife had remained, followed by an unmarked police vehicle with two plainclothes detectives. The uniformed officers kept the onlookers at bay while the detectives bent down to get a better look at the body.

"It's Peter," a patron from the club exclaimed.

"You know him?" asked one of the detectives.

"Yes, of course," he answered. "Peter Müller. I was just with him at the club."

"What club?"

"Marigold's."

"The gay bar?"

"The nightclub" was the testy reply.

More police vehicles and personnel arrived. The street was closed off. A crime scene technician went to work photographing the body and outlining it on the sidewalk with yellow chalk. Uniformed officers took names while the detectives went to Marigold's. The dancers had stopped; the bartenders had donned shirts.

"Turn off the damn music," one of the detectives yelled at the owner.

The abrupt silence after the deafening music was jarring. Some patrons headed for the door but were stopped by the detectives.

"We have a homicide victim around the corner," the owner was told.

"Someone from here?"

"Right." The detective consulted what he'd noted on a pad. "Peter Müller."

"I don't know him," the owner said.

"I do," a customer said. "Is it true? Peter was killed?"

The detectives asked who else knew him. A number of young men affirmed that they did.

"He have a problem with anybody here tonight?"

The stunned patrons looked at each other and shook their heads. One said to the man next to him, "You were talking to him just before he left, Jimmy."

A detective took Jimmy's name and asked, "You have some sort of a beef with him?"

"No. We were friends. We kidded around a lot."

One of the detectives returned to the crime scene and dispatched two uniformed cops to the club to take down more names and contact information. "Nobody leaves there," he ordered. He turned to the crowd. "Who was at the club tonight when the victim was there?"

One man spoke up. "Somebody has to tell Lalo."

"Who's Lalo?"

"Peter's partner. The victim's partner."

"You mean his lover?"

"Yes. They were close."

"This Lalo, he wasn't with the victim tonight?"

"No. Peter was stag. Lalo—his real name is Eduardo, Eduardo Reyes—had to work late at the embassy."

"Where the victim worked," a detective who'd examined the contents of Müller's pockets commented to his partner.

"No," he was corrected by the man in the crowd. "Peter worked for the German embassy. Lalo works at the Spanish embassy."

The medical examiner had arrived and completed his on-scene examination. Ambulance workers carefully placed Müller's shrouded body on a gurney and slid him into the vehicle. Satisfied that everyone's names, addresses, and phone numbers had been recorded, the detectives got in their car and drove back to headquarters at Judiciary Square on Indiana Avenue NW.

"Wasn't robbery," one said as they pulled into their parking space. "He had his wallet, watch, cell phone, ID, cash in his pocket."

"Another gay maybe, jealous of this guy Lalo?"

"Maybe this Lalo *was* the jealous one. What's that saying about a woman scorned?"

"Lalo's a man."

"Same idea. The victim worked for the German embassy. State will get involved."

"I suppose so. They'll make a big deal out of it. Just looks to me like somebody who doesn't like gays got rid of one."

"Probably right. Let's check in and get out before we catch another. The natives are restless tonight."

Because the victim worked for a foreign embassy, regulations dictated that the Washington MPD notify the State Department's DSS, headquartered in Arlington, Virginia. The call to that agency was made an hour after the detectives had returned to their second-floor squad room and filed their preliminary report with their superior.

"You got statements from everybody?" the duty captain asked.

"We got what we could. The club was busy, lots of people. We've got everyone's contact info."

"Good. What's your instinct on this?"

"Wasn't robbery. No one at the club said they saw an altercation between the victim and other customers. Somebody said he was drunk when he left. Maybe the shooter saw him stagger out of the place, went to mug him, something spooked him, so he shot and ran."

The captain shrugged and sighed. "Looks more to me like a bias crime. The victim is gay, gets drunk at Marigold's, leaves, and some guy with a weapon decides to play out his homophobia."

"Problems with Marigold's before?"

"A few citizens complaining about the noise, cigarette butts, a couple of public indecency reports."

"We want to talk to this guy at the Spanish embassy, Eduardo Reyes, nicknamed Lalo. He and the victim were intimately involved."

"Might be better for DSS to question him first. You know how it is to get anyone at embassies to talk to *us*."

"Makes sense."

"We'll bring it up at the meeting tomorrow. Anything else?"

"State is notifying the German embassy?"

"As we speak."

A call came in about a stabbing in Adams Morgan.

"I'll ring in Public Affairs about the Müller shooting. They'll handle any press interest that comes out of it. You guys get out of here. Busy night. This heat makes everybody crazy."

7

Brixton and Donna Salvos were assigned to interview Eduardo "Lalo" Reyes.

"Why a public place?" Brixton asked her as they drove to where Reyes had arranged to meet Salvos.

"He's gun-shy about doing it at the embassy, you know, being gay and all."

"What about where he lives?"

"He balked at that too. What difference does it make, Robert?"

"I don't care. Just curious."

They pulled up in front of the Spanish bar on H Street, where Reyes was already sitting at an outdoor table.

Brixton pegged Reyes at no older than twenty-five. He looked nervous; a desire to flee was written all over his soft, malleable face. Large, limpid eyes and black curls dangling over his forehead testified to his youth. He decided that "pretty" was the best way to describe him. Sal Mineo could have played him in a movie. *Whatever happened to Sal Mineo?* Brixton thought as they introduced themselves and joined him at the table.

The first words out of Reyes's mouth were, "I hate this." He was obviously having trouble keeping his voice from breaking.

"I know this is difficult," Salvos said, "but we have to ask you some questions because of what happened to Peter Müller."

"I understand," he said, his words displaying only a trace of his Spanish heritage. Salvos's vaunted language skills—she spoke half a dozen languages—would be wasted on this interview. Brixton had always wanted to speak a second language but had never made the effort to learn one, like most Americans. Everybody else in the world seemed to be bilingual.

They all looked up at a waiter who'd appeared. "Would you like coffee?" he asked.

"Love it," Brixton said.

Salvos and Reyes declined.

Brixton's knee ached. He'd taken a bullet in it during his last year on the Savannah PD when he and a partner went to pick up an armed parole violator. His partner killed the fugitive, but Brixton endured six months of rehab and was assigned desk duty until his retirement. He never knew when it would act up.

"The Washington police have already spoken with you," Salvos said.

"Yes. They said things that made me angry."

"What things?"

"They make it sound like I was the one who shot Peter. That is a lie. I loved Peter."

"They're just doing their job," Brixton said, remembering how many people he'd interrogated during his career as a cop and how being accusatory effectively rattled them, sometimes resulting in unintended admissions.

The coffee delivered, Brixton took a sip and listened as Salvos said to Reyes, "It's our understanding that you and Mr. Müller were close."

Reyes nodded, his eyes focused on the table.

"You weren't with him the night he was killed."

"No. I had to work late. We had a press release to get out."

"When had you last seen him?"

"The night before. We had dinner and then we—"

"Mr. Reyes, we know that you and Mr. Müller were lovers," Salvos said. "That's nothing to be embarrassed about. We just have to know what you can tell us that will help bring his killer to justice."

"Yes, I understand," Reyes said. "It's just that my relationship with Peter was not something that I talk about at the embassy. Some people are—well, some do not like it."

I bet, Brixton thought, *the macho Spanish male culture coming to the fore.*

"Did you and Mr. Müller have any problems lately, you know, an argument or a disagreement?" Salvos asked.

He sat up straight and became animated, as though he wanted very much to dispel that notion. "No, no, we got along just fine. No arguments ever."

"That's unusual," Brixton said, thinking of the arguments he and Flo had had over the course of their relationship. "Most lovers have a spat now and then."

"Sometimes," Reyes conceded. "Just silly little things."

"They usually are," Brixton said.

"How long had you been involved with each other?" Salvos asked.

"A few months. We met—"

"At Marigold's?" Brixton said. "The bar where Müller had been the night he was killed?"

"Yes."

"So you know who his friends at that bar were?"

"Of course. He was popular, well liked." A dreamy quality came over him, accompanied by a small smile.

"Peter was . . . he was very handsome and intelligent. Others at the bar wanted to be with him."

"As lovers?"

"Yes. I was pleased that he chose me."

"Did he talk to you about people he worked with at the German embassy?" Brixton asked.

"Sometimes."

"He get along there, no problems with anybody because he was gay?"

Reyes's nostalgic expression turned serious as he pondered his answer. "There were a few people who made comments, nasty comments." Lightness replaced concern on his face. "Peter taught me the German word for 'fag.' *Schwuchtel*. He said that there were some he worked with who called him that."

"Must have upset him," Brixton offered.

"He said that he was used to it."

Salvos said, "You mentioned that there were other gay men at Marigold's who were interested in Peter as a lover. Do you think any of them could have been so jealous that they would shoot him?"

"No. That cannot be."

"You own a gun, Mr. Reyes?"

"Me? No. I have a rifle at home in Barcelona but no gun here. The police asked me that, too. I don't think they believe me."

"They probably do," Brixton said. "I do."

He smiled. "I am pleased to hear that."

"You say that you're from Barcelona," Brixton said.

"That is correct," Reyes said, "but I have lived many places—Portugal, Chile, Hawaii, England."

"You worked for embassies in those places?"

"Yes. Not in all of them. I like to travel and learn new things about new places."

"So do I," Salvos said.

It became obvious that there was nothing further to

be gained by continuing the questioning. As Salvos and Brixton prepared to leave, Reyes asked about plans for Müller's funeral.

"That'll be up to the Washington police," Brixton replied. "It's a murder case, so they'll want to keep the body until forensics is completed, the autopsy—things like that. They'll have to work it out with the German embassy."

"Have his parents been notified in Germany?"

"The embassy is handling that," Salvos said.

"I would like them to know how much I loved him."

"I'm afraid we can't help with that," Salvos said. "Thank you for taking the time to speak with us. I'm sorry for your loss."

Brixton and Salvos walked to where she'd parked her car.

"He's not involved," Brixton said flatly.

"I agree," Salvos said.

"You talking to people at the German embassy, like whoever taunted him about being gay?"

"Others are, from DSS. Glad you were available this morning. I always like it when two do the questioning."

"Had nothing better to do," Brixton replied. "What's next on our agenda?" he asked as they drove to Arlington.

"We tell Mike what came out of our chat with Mr. Lalo Reyes and see where he wants us next."

They met with Michael Kogan in his office above the Thai restaurant.

"Anything come of talking to Mr. Reyes?" Kogan asked.

"No. He didn't kill anybody." Brixton made a face. "You ought to tell those guys downstairs in the restaurant to put in some fans or something. Your office smells like their kitchen."

"I kind of like it," Kogan said. "You ever eat downstairs?"

"I'm not into Thai food."

"I am," Salvos said. "Good Thai food."

"Does the joint downstairs serve good Thai food?" Brixton asked.

"Very good," she said.

Kogan slid a file folder across the desk to them.

"What's this?"

"Another murder, a woman who worked for the Polish embassy."

"What is this, open season on embassy employees?"

Kogan shrugged.

"When did it happen?"

"Body was discovered in her apartment this morning. Why don't you two get over there and see what MPD's got. The info I have is in the folder. Name's Dabrowski, Adelina Dabrowski. I have a call in to the embassy to get more on her."

The apartment in which the murder took place was in a narrow row house not far from Brixton's apartment. The street was clogged with MPD cars and an ambulance. Brixton and Donna approached a uniformed officer and showed him their IDs.

"SITQUAL?" the officer read.

"State Department. Who's the lead detective?"

"Morrison. He's inside."

They entered the building and asked for Detective Morrison, who stood in the foyer. After introducing themselves, Donna asked what was known about the victim.

"White female, worked for the Polish embassy, the visa and passport office in the consular section on Wyoming. Her roommate discovered the body."

"How'd she get it?" Brixton asked.

"Looks like strangulation. At least that's the preliminary from the medical examiner. He's there now."

Brixton and Salvos went into the first-floor apartment—the three-story building contained three apartments, they were told—and surveyed the scene. The victim was naked when she was discovered and was now covered with a sheet. Another woman, who Brixton assumed was her roommate, sat on a love seat staring out the window. Crime scene techs were in the midst of photographing the setting and collecting evidence. The ME had concluded his on-site evaluation and was preparing to leave. Brixton stopped him. "Brixton, State Department," he said. "She was strangled?"

"Appears so."

"Any sign of sexual assault?"

"I'll know more about that later. Excuse me."

Detective Morrison entered the room as the ME departed.

"What about the roommate?" Brixton asked him.

"Came in this morning and found her."

"The roommate works for the embassy, too?"

"Yeah. I've questioned her. Be my guest."

Brixton gave Donna a questioning look.

"No, you go ahead," she said.

Brixton approached and waited until the roommate looked up and realized that he was waiting to speak with her. He told her who he was. "Mind if I sit down?" he asked.

She shook her head and blew her nose.

"I'm connected with the State Department," he said. "Whenever anyone who works at a foreign embassy is killed, we get involved. You work with her?"

"No. I mean yes, but not in her section. She was at the consular section. I work in the ambassador's residence." She spoke English without an accent.

"You're not Polish," Brixton said.

"No. I'm Canadian, from Toronto."

"And work at the Polish embassy?"

"I'm on the ambassador's catering staff."

"A cook."

"Wines and beverages."

"How long did you know the victim?"

The question restarted her tears. Brixton waited. She pulled herself together and said, "A year, maybe a little more. We were going to be married." ·

"Oh. You're—"

"We were in love. As soon as we got the paperwork straightened out, we were going to be married here in Washington."

"That's right," Brixton said. "Same-sex marriages are legal in D.C."

The ensuing silence was awkward. Brixton broke it by saying, "You discovered her. Where had *you* been this morning?"

"Working. We have an important luncheon for a visiting dignitary. I should be there, but I ran home to pick something up and—"

She sobbed, and Brixton put his hand on her shoulder.

"I'm sorry," she said.

"It's okay. You know anybody who had it in for your . . . your . . . ?"

"My fiancée? No. She got along with everyone."

"No idea who might have come here this morning and killed her?"

"I've been over this with the detective," she said. "Please."

"Sure. Thanks for your time. My condolences."

Brixton took a final look around the apartment; it

didn't appear that an intense struggle had taken place. He cast a quick glance at the covered body and went outside, where Morrison was talking with neighbors. He sidled up to hear the conversation.

"What did the man look like?" Morrison asked an elderly woman wearing a flowered housecoat and holding the world's smallest dog in her arms.

"I really didn't get a good look at his face. He was sort of . . . well, I suppose you could say he was medium."

"Medium in height, weight?"

"Yes, that's it. He wore a uniform."

Morrison noted her comments in a notebook. He saw that Brixton was standing next to him and said, "This lady saw a man enter the building this morning."

"You said a uniform," Brixton said.

"That's right. A green uniform like . . . like coveralls."

"Was the victim expecting anyone?" Brixton asked Morrison. "A repairman?"

Morrison answered, "They were having problems with their air-conditioning, and the victim made a call, according to her roommate. They said they'd send someone today but wouldn't specify a time. Typical."

"So maybe she thought the guy who killed her was here to fix the AC," Brixton said. As he spoke, a panel van with a sign on its side indicating it was from an air-conditioning repair shop tried to navigate the other vehicles in the street to get closer to the house.

"He's a little late," Brixton muttered. "The victim and the roommate were lesbians. They were planning to get married."

"Yeah, the roommate told me."

"You think they allow same-sex marriages in Poland?" Brixton asked.

"How the hell would I know?" was Morrison's response.

"Just curious," Brixton said. "Thanks for the info."

Donna emerged from the house a few minutes later, and they drove back to SITQUAL's offices in Arlington.

"Like you said, it look like open season on embassy employees," she quipped while checking herself in a visor mirror.

"Maybe, he said, "but maybe it's open season on gays and lesbians."

"Who just happen to work at foreign embassies," she said.

"Yeah, that too," he said.

8

What do you make of the two embassy murders?" Kogan asked Brixton and Salvos.

Donna shook her head. "Coincidence," she said. "Totally different scenarios. One is shot on the street in the middle of the night; the other is a daytime assault in her own home, probably sexual."

"You were at the scene, Robert. It look like a sexual assault to you?"

"She was naked, if that counts for anything. Funny the way the room looked, though."

"How so?"

"The clothes she'd evidently been wearing when she was attacked were neatly piled near her body, as though whoever did it might have stripped her *after* he strangled her, or made a neat pile after raping her. A neat rapist. Interesting MO."

"Why would he do that?" Donna asked. "Strip her after strangling her?"

"I don't know," Brixton answered, "unless he wanted

to make it *look* like it was a sexual assault. The ME will come up with whether she'd been raped."

"You're assuming she was strangled by a man," Donna said.

"Fair assumption," Brixton muttered.

"They were both homosexuals," Kogan said. "Reads 'bias crimes' to me."

"She was a lesbian," Donna said. "Homophobes don't usually go around killing lesbians. They get off on lesbian porn. It's gay *men* they hate."

"What about both victims working for embassies?" Kogan asked. "That's why we're involved in the first place."

"Coincidence," Donna repeated.

"She's probably right," Brixton said.

"Provided another embassy employee doesn't get killed," Kogan said. "Two's a coincidence. Three?"

"Or another gay guy or lesbian," Donna mused.

Donna and Brixton started to leave, but Kogan stopped them.

"What's up?" Brixton asked.

"I said before that the murders wouldn't be just a coincidence if another one pops up. Well, there has been another. I got the report from DSS this afternoon. The German embassy is considering Peter Müller's murder part of a possible terrorist plot."

"That's a stretch."

"Maybe not. This other murder of a German embassy employee took place last week, in New York. The victim worked here for a while but was transferred to the consulate in New York a couple of months ago."

"Male, female?"

"Male." Kogan opened a file folder and consulted its contents. "The victim had an important job, according to the embassy, not enough to warrant any notice by the press, but he wasn't a clerk."

"How was he killed?"

"Gunshot, late at night, on the street."

"Like Müller," Donna said. "I don't suppose he happened to be gay."

"They haven't said."

"Let's say that he *was* gay. That would mean there's a German homophobe knocking off gay German embassy employees." Brixton laughed. "How's that for a comic scenario? Sounds like a far-out movie that Mel Brooks would write."

"Ms. Dabrowski wasn't German, Robert," Kogan said. "The point is that German intelligence is looking at the murders as possibly being part of a terrorist operation, maybe tied to an al-Qaeda cell inside Germany. They've been having plenty of trouble lately with jihadists."

"Who isn't having trouble with them these days? But what's this have to do with us? That murder happened in New York. The one we have to deal with is Müller, here in D.C."

"That's right, but DSS has to take the Germans seriously. I want you to make an appointment tomorrow with someone at the embassy. His name's Axel Herrmann. He was Müller's boss in the Defense Attaché Office. See what he has to say about Müller."

"Does it matter what he says? A couple of employees get killed, and the Germans go to Code Red. That's the *real* threat the terrorists pose. They chatter on the Internet, and we scramble, spend another ten million bucks to secure a parade or football game. These employees get killed, most likely because somebody was after their wallets or don't like who they sleep with, and the government goes into full anti-Muslim mode."

Kogan leaned back in his chair, formed a tent beneath his chin with his hands, and smiled.

"I know, I know," Brixton said, "I'm being a pain in the ass."

"Glad you recognize it. Go have a drink and a good dinner." He handed Brixton a slip of paper on which he'd written contact information for Axel Herrmann. "These two murders might not seem important to you, but our German friends are taking them seriously, *very* seriously."

9

Brixton called Mike Kogan at his SITQUAL office first thing the next morning before setting a time to meet with Axel Herrmann at the German embassy. "Thought I should check in with you before I call Herrmann," Brixton said.

"Glad you did, Robert. I was about to call you. There's no need to call Herrmann. The meeting is set for four this afternoon. It won't be with Herrmann alone. Two members of the German intelligence service in Berlin flew into D.C. last night. They'll want to know everything that you and Donna know about Peter Müller's murder, including the interview you had with Müller's lover. Let Donna take the lead. Just make sure that the Germans know that SITQUAL is involved."

"I'll hang a sign around my neck."

"I can think of other things I'd like to hang around your neck sometimes, Robert—tight."

"What about the murder in New York?" Brixton asked, ignoring the comment.

"Donna has been briefed on that. I know you don't

think there's anything to this, no terrorist plot, and you're probably right. But the Germans have been having their problems lately with their growing Muslim population and are skittish. Can't blame them. Just take in what they have to say, tell them what you know about Müller, and call it a day."

They ended the call, and Brixton slowly finished his coffee. Kogan was right. Brixton had dismissed the murder of Peter Müller as a bias crime. That two German intelligence authorities would hop on a plane in Berlin and fly to Washington seemed silly, unless they were looking for an excuse to visit the United States on their government's dime. Maybe one of them had family to visit or were tired of German food. The reason didn't matter. They were here looking for information about the murder of one of their embassy staffers, and the State Department had an obligation to provide what help it could.

But his cynicism wasn't total. It was a dangerous world with crazed people looking to inflict damage on anyone who didn't see things their way. Maybe the Germans were right. Maybe Müller's murder was part of some conspiracy. Who would have believed that nineteen young Muslim men would hijack three commercial airliners and kill so many innocent people? Who would have believed that a guy would get on a plane with explosives in his sneaker and try to bring down the plane, or wedge a bomb in his underwear with the same intention? Who would have believed lots of things in what had become a turbulent, upside-down world?

During his phone conversation with Mike Kogan, Brixton had been told to attend an internal DSS briefing at the State Department from eleven until one that afternoon. He sat with Donna Salvos as a succession of DSS officials droned on about the most recent threats to American embassies around the globe and the potential for terrorist activity in the homeland. It was a little after one when Brixton and Salvos left State.

"Lunch?" Brixton asked.

"I'm meeting someone."

"See you at four with the Germans," he said.

His growling stomach alerted him that he was hungry, and he decided to indulge in seafood at a restaurant on "Eye" Street, next to the George Washington University campus in Foggy Bottom. But as he walked to it, he stopped in front of a red town house in which a known student hangout, Lindy's Red Lion, was located. Brixton had heard that the hamburgers there were good, and that the prices were right. He debated going in; being with a group of college students wasn't something he aspired to, but it was past lunchtime. Besides, it was summer when most of them—hopefully—were back home mooching off their parents.

He stepped inside, looked around, and opted to go up to the second-floor bar. He was glad he did. Sitting at a table were Annabel and Mac Smith.

"Don't want to disturb your lunch," Brixton said.

"We just finished," Annabel said. "Sit down."

He kissed her on the cheek and shook Mac's hand.

"You'll have to excuse me," Mac said. "I have to get to a faculty meeting."

"I thought professors had the summer off," Brixton said.

"Mac thought that, too, when he took the job," Annabel said. "He was wrong. What brings you here?"

"I'm killing time until a four o'clock meeting at the German embassy. I just came from a briefing at State."

"Anything interesting?" Mac asked.

"Nothing new, if that's what you mean."

"I read about the murder of that young German embassy employee," Annabel said. "Have they found the murderer?"

"That's the MPD's job," Brixton said. "The Germans want to make sure it didn't involve terrorists. I don't think it did, but it's not my call. They're looking for information, that's all. A couple of their intelligence people arrived from Berlin last night. That's who Donna and I are meeting with at four."

"Donna?" Mac asked.

"Donna Salvos. She's with DSS, State's security and intelligence office. Nice gal. She speaks a lot of languages. I pretty much go along for the ride. You had burgers?"

"We shared one. They're very good," Annabel said.

"So I've heard."

As Mac prepared to leave, Brixton perused the menu and settled on a Redskins burger, with salsa and nacho cheese, and a draft beer. "Sounds good," he said. "I like the name of the burger. The only thing I ever appreciated about Washington was the Redskins football team. They used a lot of older guys."

"They didn't do very well," Annabel offered.

"That's okay. At least they valued age and wisdom."

Annabel decided to leave with her husband. "Leave some room on your social calendar, Robert," she said. "We'd like to have you come for dinner one night soon."

Brixton laughed. "My social calendar is one big blank, Annabel. "You name the date and I'll be there."

Brixton's burger and beer were delivered, and he ate and drank slowly, reflecting on what he considered two wasted hours spent at State. As he ate, the room started filling up with young people, obviously students. He decided to run by his apartment to pay a few bills before the meeting at the German embassy, so he covered his tab and left. An hour later, after dropping his paid bills at the post office, he was in his car and on his way to the meeting with Axel Herrmann and the two representatives of Germany's Bundesnachrichtendienst (BND), its Federal Intelligence Service.

Brixton parked a block away from the German embassy and walked to the main entrance where Donna Salvos waited. A uniformed security guard checked their State Department IDs, and they were directed through a metal detector that worked; their handguns triggered a response, and they were instructed to leave them at the security post. Brixton gave the guard his best smile as he handed his weapon over and received a chit.

A phone call confirmed that they were expected, and they were directed to the Defense Attaché section, where a woman also checked their IDs before asking them to take a seat in a waiting area as stark as the building itself.

Fifteen minutes later a young man appeared and led them to an elevator that took them to an upper-floor conference room, where they were greeted by Axel Herrmann, a balding, middle-aged man wearing a three-piece black suit and small, round rimless eyeglasses; a woman of the same age with a perpetually stern expression on her chiseled face; and another man, tall, gray, and gaunt, whose name was Luka Becker. After some small talk about the recent good weather, complaints over the cramped seats on the plane that had brought them to D.C., and Becker's prediction of how the German national football team—"soccer to you Americans," he pleasantly added—would fare in the next World Cup, they got down to the reason for getting together.

"I must admit that your State Department's security forces are quick to react when we report problems."

"We try to be," Brixton said, despite not really feeling an integral part of the wider State Department security and intelligence apparatus.

"As you know," Herrmann said, "and I'm certain you

can understand, the recent killing of two of our embassy employees has led us to question whether their deaths are random and coincidental, or point to something more systematic."

"Terrorism," Donna said.

"Yes," the woman, Hanna Krause, said. "One of the victims was here in Washington, a second in New York City. While we have not established a link between those two deaths, it would be irresponsible of us to not investigate to the point that we can unequivocally rule it out."

"Do you have any evidence that terrorists are behind those murders?" Brixton asked.

"Not at the moment. However, we currently have at least a dozen leftist groups in Germany that support terrorism. Our intelligence convinces us that one or more of these groups are actively planning an attack not only in Germany but in cities where we have a diplomatic presence. We recently intercepted a young man who'd trained in Pakistan and traveled overland to Germany from Poland. He had in his possession, hidden in his underwear, a DVD of a pornographic movie that was confiscated by our agents."

When she didn't elaborate, Brixton said, "I don't get the connection between a porn movie and terrorism."

Becker elaborated. "Embedded in that DVD were more than a hundred al-Qaeda documents outlining plans for future terrorist attacks, including seizing cruise ships. It was their plan to dress the passengers in orange jumpsuits, like those worn at your Guantánamo Base where suspected terrorists are held, and execute them one-by-one, their murders videotaped and played for the world to see, until those prisoners at Guantánamo are released."

"They'd fail," Brixton said. "Our government wouldn't give in to blackmail."

"Yes, I'm certain that you are right," said Becker, "but I offer it as an example of how active al-Qaeda is in Germany. Hezbollah too has become more aggressive in recent months. Much of the material taken from that DVD points to a terrorist assault being planned here, patterned after the Mumbai attack."

Ms. Krause added, "There is also talk of launching smaller attacks on German citizens, targeting individuals."

"That's what I have trouble with," said Brixton. "Terrorists, at least based upon past activity, aren't content with killing individuals. They want to make a bigger splash, kill as many in one swoop as possible, grab the headlines. Granted, having two of your embassy employees killed within a short span of time raises doubts about whether their deaths were a coincidence. I'm not questioning why you'd want to see whether there's a pattern that might link to a terrorist organization. But there's another factor to consider: Peter Müller was a gay man. An employee of the Polish embassy in Washington was killed the day after Müller was. She was a lesbian. And I understand that your victim in New York might also have been homosexual. Isn't it possible that—?"

"That is not the sort of personal information that should be made public." Krause was angry.

"Hey," Brixton said, "I'm not going to the newspapers with it. But it has to be factored into any investigation. It could be that the 'terrorists' are only some nuts who hate gays and lesbians."

"Preposterous," said Krause.

Brixton shrugged. His initial reaction upon shaking Krause's hand was that he probably wasn't going to like her. He'd been right.

"What can you tell us of Peter Müller's murder, aside from what we already know?" Mr. Herrmann asked.

"There isn't much to tell," Donna said. "He was gunned down on the street early one morning. We're here because we were instructed to provide you with any information that might be helpful to your investigation of your embassy employees' murders. It's obvious that we can offer little beyond what you already know."

"Not true," said Herrmann. "We have a strong mutual interest in anything that is of concern to you and our presence in Washington. Chances are these two deaths are purely coincidental, but all information is helpful."

Becker smiled as he said, "Please don't think that our trip has been wasted. If you can think of anything, even the smallest detail concerning Müller's demise that might provide additional insight, we'd be most appreciative."

Brixton shifted in his chair against a stabbing pain that emanated from his back and shot down his leg. "If we think of anything else, Mr. Becker," he said, "we'll sure pass it along. But as far as I know, we came here today to learn from *you* about Peter Müller. And what can you tell us about the murder of your embassy staffer in New York? He was shot to death, right?"

"Yes. On the street late at night."

"Like Müller."

"Yes, I suppose the deaths are similar." Becker turned to Hanna Krause. "Maybe there *is* a connection with them both being homosexual."

"Highly unlikely," Krause responded.

"The news of Peter Müller's murder was tragic," said Herrmann, shifting attention away from Hanna Krause. "He was well liked by everyone in this section."

"No enemies? Resentments?"

"Peter? No, of course not."

"I ask because he was a homosexual. He was killed as he left a gay nightclub."

Herrmann formulated a response. "Some of us were aware of Peter's sexual preferences, but no one held it against him. You know, terrorism is not unknown to us. We haven't had a nine/eleven as you have, thank goodness, but such terrorist organizations as Hezbollah, al-Qaeda, and the Salafists have become increasingly active across the Continent, with Germany as their unofficial headquarters."

"I know about Hezbollah and al-Qaeda," Brixton said, "but who are the Salafists?"

"A Sunni terrorist organization," Herrmann replied. "Al-Qaeda is Shiite. The Shiites and Sunnis don't get along, as I'm sure you know. The lingering chaos in Iraq testifies to that."

"I have trouble keeping them straight," Brixton admitted.

"The point is that because of the increased activity in Germany, any unnatural deaths of people associated with our government must be carefully evaluated."

"I get your point," said Brixton, "but Müller didn't have a high-profile government job."

"High profile? No. But he was privy to a great deal of sensitive material."

"What about this other embassy staffer who's been killed? What was his job and background?"

Becker pointed to a file folder on his desk. "We received his personnel file before leaving Berlin. He worked here in Washington before being transferred to our chancery in New York. He held a midlevel job while here, primarily administrative. His duties at the chancery were roughly the same."

"Nothing high profile."

"No."

"Tell me, was he married?" Brixton asked.

Herrmann answered, "He was not married." A smile

crossed the German's face. "I know what you're getting at," he said.

"Homosexual?"

"The victim in New York was thought to be homosexual, although he evidently was discreet about it."

"Stayed in the closet."

Herrmann nodded.

"That's two out of two," Brixton said, referring to Müller and the New York victim.

Donna Salvos again brought up the murder of the Polish embassy staffer, Adelina Dabrowski.

"Yes, we've heard about that," Herrmann said. "How terrible."

"She was a lesbian. She and her partner were planning to be married," Salvos said.

"And so you believe that her murder and our two employees' were because of their sexual orientation."

"Not a bad bet," Brixton said.

"This may sound callous, but I prefer that scenario to one in which their deaths were for some warped political reason, terrorist assassinations," Becker said.

Either way they're dead, Brixton thought but didn't say.

Herrmann, who'd already spoken to detectives from the Washington MPD, asked whether Brixton and Salvos had anything additional to offer.

"Mr. Müller had a lover who works at the Spanish embassy," Salvos said.

"I wasn't aware of that. Is she—is *he* a suspect?"

"Not as far as I'm concerned, but the police will have to decide that. As far as I know, Müller's murder is the only serious problem your embassy has had recently."

"True, except for the recent death in New York."

"Let me ask you a question," Brixton said. "How does what looks like a bias crime on the street here in

D.C. and another murder on the streets of Manhattan add up to terrorism? People get shot every day in big cities."

"Of course," was Becker's reply, "but you also must realize that we are engaged in a war with those who would destroy our democratic way of life. There may be nothing politically sinister about these two deaths. If so, we can move on to other concerns. But until we can definitively rule out a terrorist connection, the matter must be pursued."

"Of course," Salvos said.

"All I can say is that we are extremely grateful to have the help of your State Department," Herrmann said.

"That's our job," Brixton said. It seemed the only thing to say. Better than "No problem."

Two days later the murder of another embassy staffer in Washington occurred. The victim was Antonio Conti, a middle-aged man who worked in the Italian embassy's Agenzia Informazioni e Sicurezza Esterna (AISE) office, Italy's military secret service. It occurred on Sunday evening as Conti left a restaurant after dining alone.

He'd taken a long walk to work off a large meal and ended up in Meridian Hill Park, also known as Malcolm X Park, a twelve-acre green space between Florida Avenue and Euclid Street. Once considered a possible setting for a presidential residence, the area had fallen into disrepair and had become notorious for drug dealing. Still, the magnificent formal gardens within the park and its Italianate sculptures drew its share of admirers. Conti was particularly fond of the statuary, especially Joan of Arc, Dante, and the two statues that flanked the James Buchanan statue, named "Law" and "Diplomacy."

It had grown dark, and he was about to return to his apartment near the embassy on Whitehaven Street, just off Embassy Row, when he was shot twice in the back, one of the bullets piercing his heart. A few visitors who'd lingered in the park heard the shots and ran to where Conti lay dead at the base of the Dante sculpture.

Brixton and Salvos spent time at the Italian embassy the day after the murder gathering information about the victim. They were told that he'd been at the embassy for seven years and was a highly regarded analyst. One person described him as a gentle man who loved history and Italian art. Another colleague portrayed Conti as someone with a small ego and large intellect. Everyone agreed that his senseless killing was a tragedy of the first order.

Brixton called Mike Kogan following their interviews at the embassy and was told that he and Salvos should come to headquarters at four to file a report based upon the interviews. With two hours to kill before the meeting, Brixton split from Salvos, ran a few personal errands, including buying two shirts and a pair of shoes, and returned to his apartment to drop off his purchases. He was about to leave for SITQUAL's offices in Arlington, when his phone rang.

"Hi, Daddy. It's Janet."

"Hey, sweetheart. How are you?"

"I—am—wonderful!"

"I've been going with this dynamite musician, Daddy, soooo talented, a real musical genius."

"Yeah? What's he play?"

"Guitar."

"Well, that's great, Janet."

"Daddy, Richard—that's his name—Richard has come up with an idea for a music app that will make him millions, and he wants me, me, to work on it with him—but he needs start-up money and asked me to help raise some and . . ." She paused for breath. "And so I thought that maybe you would want to get in on the ground floor and . . ."

"Whoa, slow down. You're talking to the wrong guy, sweetheart. I don't have money to invest in anything. I'm a working stiff. Remember?"

"Won't you even hear me out?"

"I'm listening."

"No, I mean really listen to me. I can't do it justice over the phone. It's too—well, it's too complicated, and I have some stuff that he's come up with, a business plan and things like that. Can't we get together so I can show you everything and—?"

"Sure. When?"

"Tonight?"

"Okay. I have a meeting at State; should be free by five thirty. There's a bar and restaurant with an outdoor café a block from State, on Twenty-third. Buy you a drink, an early dinner?"

"That'd be great. I know the place. See you there."

AFTER THE BOMBING

10

With Kogan and the others gone from the apartment on the day after Brixton had returned from the hospital, everything was suddenly and eerily quiet. He opened the French doors leading to his small balcony and leaned out. Sounds of media on the street below drifted up to him. Parked across the street was a TV remote truck, its antenna extended. He closed the doors and went to the kitchen, where he looked in the refrigerator and freezer for something to eat, took out a frozen slice of pepperoni pizza wrapped in foil, and put it in the toaster oven. He took a half-consumed bottle of Wild Turkey bourbon from a cabinet, poured three fingers in a glass, and sipped as he leaned against the counter. He felt numb, drawn, exhausted, devoid of feelings and without the energy to think. His head and neck ached, and bile burned his throat.

When the pizza bubbled, he put it on a plate and carried it and the drink to the balcony, sat in a webbed chair, and watched the circus below, which now included residents of apartment buildings who'd come out to see why the media had gathered. The first bite of pizza tasted metallic. He placed it on a table and finished the bourbon. He might have dozed off had he not seen the TV cameraman climb up on top of the truck and aim his camera at the balcony. Brixton successfully stifled the urge to extend his middle finger and returned inside, where he kicked off his shoes and collapsed on the bed.

He slept fitfully, the ringing of the phone and the tinny incoming and outgoing messages on the machine keeping him from going completely out. There were two calls from Marylee, two from his journalist friend Will Sayers, another from Mackensie Smith, and a succession of messages left by the press. Donna Salvos called to ask how he was doing and offered to bring him dinner. He liked her a lot and enjoyed being paired with her on assignments. She was a no-nonsense woman whose simple hairdos, minimal makeup, and distinctly non-designer clothing accurately mirrored her approach to life. He might have considered trying to turn their professional relationship into a personal one, except that she was more cerebral than he was. Besides, she was seriously dating an orthopedic surgeon. Better to keep it professional.

He finally fell off the edge and slept until four.

Returning the calls was a chore that seemed beyond him when he awoke, but he poured another drink, sat at his desk, and called Donna Salvos to thank her for offering to bring him dinner.

"You holding up, Robert?" she asked.

"Yeah, I'm fine, considering I've had my legs shot out from under me. Jesus, Donna, this is like something out of *The Twilight Zone*. You're too young to remember that but—"

"No, I'm not. I watch all the reruns."

"Did you see the statement that Congressman Skaggs put out?"

"Of course."

"I'm sorry his son is dead, but damn it, Donna, he *was* with the girl with the bomb, whispered in her ear, then split. He came out from behind the Dumpster carrying what looked to me like a weapon. What was I supposed to do, hug him?"

"I don't blame you for being upset, Robert, but—"

"*You* believe me, don't you, that the kid was there in the café?"

"Sure I do, Robert."

"What about Mike?"

"He— I suppose he does. He hasn't spoken about it."

Brixton was disappointed in her response. He knew that his boss would speak about it; how could he not?

"Thanks for the dinner offer," Brixton said, wanting to end the conversation and not challenge her. "We'll keep in touch, huh?"

He knew that he should call Marylee back, but couldn't summon the will. Instead, he returned Mac Smith's call. Annabel answered. "Robert, how are you? We've been worried about you."

"I'm okay," he said. "Sore but nothing terminal."

"We heard about your daughter. We're so sorry, Robert."

"Thanks. Sometimes I believe it, but most of the time I'm in denial."

Mac came on the second phone. "Holding up?" he asked.

"Yeah, sure. The alternative is worse. I got your messages and wanted to get back to you."

"What can we do to help?"

"I can't think of anything," Brixton said. "The docs

told me to rest up. I don't have a choice. I've been put on paid leave."

"Want to come here to recuperate?" Annabel asked.

"I may take you up on that," Brixton said, "but not now. The media vultures are at my door, so I think I'll just hang out here."

"Do you have food? We can bring you something."

"Thanks, but not needed. There's a slew of takeout places that deliver. I haven't turned on the TV or radio. The president was supposed to give a speech about the bombing. Did you see it?"

"Yes, we did," Mac said. "I'm sure it will be repeated all evening."

"What about Congressman Skaggs? He was supposed to release a statement."

Mac and Annabel's hesitation said to Brixton that what the congressman said wouldn't be something that he wanted to hear. It was Mac who said, "Aside from offering his condolences to the victims and their families, he talked about his son's death and—"

"Mentioned me?"

"Yes. He's threatening to hold a congressional hearing, but that's another matter. Congressman Skaggs is, as I'm sure you know, bombastic. Look, the offer holds for you to come here while you rest up. We have the spare bedroom and—"

"I'll let you know," Brixton said. "Thanks."

With that call ended he turned on the TV news, where an anchor was leading into a replay of the president's speech. Brixton gritted his teeth as he waited for President Jack Shearson to come on the screen. Brixton liked Shearson. He seemed to have been more forthcoming than his opponent—or most other politicians in Washington, for that matter.

"Here's what President Shearson had to say about the horrific suicide bombing yesterday," the anchor said.

"My fellow Americans," Shearson said from the Rose Garden, where he was surrounded by members of his cabinet, including top officials from Homeland Security, the CIA, the FBI, and the Pentagon, all appropriately grim-faced. "The first lady and I extend our sincerest condolences and offer our prayers to the families of the victims of the senseless tragedy that occurred yesterday._ It was the work of a warped young woman, whose motive at this juncture is unclear. But I assure you that *why* she committed this cowardly act that killed innocent American citizens will be unearthed, and that those behind her action will be identified and subjected to swift and sure justice. Every resource of my administration will be brought to bear to root out those who have so little regard for innocent life. They will be identified, and *they will pay the price*. I also extend our prayers and thoughts to Congressman Walter Skaggs and his family for the loss of their son, Paul Skaggs, in the aftermath of the bombing."

The TV anchor followed by reading the statement issued by Walter Skaggs, the Mississippi representative, the words scrawled on the screen over a photograph of the congressman. Skaggs had wielded immense power in the House of Representatives for more than thirty years. Red-faced, overweight, and with a southern preacher's style of oratory laced with southern phrases intended to mitigate the venom in his attacks on others in Congress—and lately in particular on President Shearson—his statement read:

"To the families of those whose lives were snuffed out by yet another Islamic zealot for whom life isn't worth more than loose pocket change, I pray that you find comfort and solace in your faith and in your fellow citizens, who will be there for you in your darkest hour of need. I truly share your grief. My own son, Paul, also lost his precious life in this savage attack on all we hold to be decent and true. But his death, at the age of twenty-two, was at the hands of one of our own, a federal agent licensed to carry a weapon and who has said that my son was an accomplice in the bombing. Not only was he unarmed and gunned down in cold blood, he's been slandered and libeled by this same agent, who is employed by a private security agency known as SITQUAL, funded by our State Department. I will not rest until my son's name is cleansed of this outrageous assault on his character, and until this trigger-happy agent is no longer able to abuse the powers granted him."

Brixton swore under his breath and snapped off the set. Up until reading and hearing the congressman's statement, he'd felt defeated, the air gone from him, in a meltdown. But anger and resolve replaced those defeatist feelings.

He called Marylee, whose anger at him had abated. She tearfully spoke about the need to make funeral plans for their daughter and asked him to come to her house the next day to discuss it. He told her that he'd be there first thing in the morning, hung up, and called Willis Sayers at the Washington office of the *Savannah Morning News*.

"You're alive," Sayers said.

"I'm not sure," Brixton said. "Sorry I didn't get back to you sooner."

"Hey, buddy, I understand. Look, I feel terrible about your daughter. I've got two of my own back in Savannah and—"

"Just as soon not talk about it, Will."

"Sure. I want to get together with you. Where are you?"

"My apartment. The media ghouls are out in the street training cameras on my balcony."

" 'Media ghouls'? Present company excepted, I presume."

"Most of the time. I'd suggest we meet up tonight, but I need some time here alone. How about lunch tomorrow?"

"I'll cancel a date I already have. Noon, twelve thirty?"

"I'll be with my ex-wife in the morning. Make it one."

Brixton hadn't been hungry since returning home from the hospital. But as evening approached, he developed a sudden craving for Chinese spareribs and shrimp fried rice. He called the Chinese restaurant in the neighborhood and placed an order to be delivered. In anticipation of its arrival, he made himself a martini (with gin, of course, straight up and shaken) and awaited the arrival of his dinner. A half hour later his intercom sounded. "Delivery," the voice said into the box next to the building's front door.

Brixton buzzed him in and waited for the knock. When he opened it he was face-to-face with a young Asian man carrying the greasy brown bag of food—and a small tape recorder.

"Mr. Brixton, Jerry Chi from WTOP radio."

"Why are *you* here?"

"Just a few questions, Mr. Brixton. Did you have any idea that the man you shot and killed was Congressman's Skaggs's son?"

Brixton tried to grab the bag from him and shut the door, but the reporter hung on to it and wedged his foot inside. "Just a few minutes of your time, sir," he said.

"Gimme that bag," Brixton growled.

"Then answer my questions," the reporter demanded.

"Like hell." Brixton opened the door slightly, then slammed it against the reporter's foot. Simultaneously he ripped the bag from his hand.

"I paid the delivery guy for that," the reporter said, "and tipped him, too. Come on, just a few questions."

Brixton opened the door and held the bag up in the reporter's face. "You've heard that there's no such thing as a free lunch?" he said, a grin on his face. "Don't believe it."

With that, he slammed the door again against the foot of the reporter, who pulled it back, allowing the door to fully close.

The reporter banged on the door. "You at least owe me for the food," he shouted.

"What I owe you is a flattened nose and black eye. Get lost before I call the cops. You're trespassing on private property."

The rapping on the door eventually stopped, and Brixton settled at his kitchen table to eat. The confrontation had energized him. At the same time he knew that he would continue to be badgered by the press. After putting the empty food cartons in the garbage, he called Mac Smith's number.

"Mac, it's Robert Brixton. Your offer still good for me to spend a few days with you and Annabel?"

"Of course."

"Starting tonight?"

"We're not going anywhere."

"I'll be there in an hour."

11

Escaping the media pack was easier than Brixton had anticipated. He went down a back stairway to the parking garage beneath the building, got in his car, and roared away before anyone could react and set chase. After making sure he hadn't been followed, he parked in the Watergate complex's underground garage, and the doorman on duty in the lobby of the iconic apartment complex called the Smiths. Small suitcase in hand and with a Smith & Wesson 638 Airweight revolver that he'd brought with him from New York, which he was licensed to carry, nestled in his Fobus ankle holster (his SITQUAL-issued SIG SAUER P226 had been confiscated after the incident in the alley), Brixton arrived at their door and was warmly greeted.

"Glad you decided to come," Mac said. "I can only imagine what you've been going through."

"It's all a blur at this point, Mac. I caught the president's statement, and Skaggs's too. He said that I'm slandering and libeling his son. That's not true. It's just not true, damn it! He was there in the café."

"I don't doubt that for a second, Robert. It's unfortunate that there isn't someone to corroborate it."

"There's got to be somebody."

"Let's hope that somebody surfaces."

Annabel came from the kitchen. "Good to see you," she said.

"I really appreciate this," Brixton said.

"You're welcome to stay as long as you like. I put on fresh sheets after you called."

"Don't make a fuss about me," Brixton said. "I would love a drink, though."

"Coming right up," said Mac.

Drinks poured, they sat on the terrace, which afforded a sweeping view of the Potomac River and the spires of Georgetown University beyond. Brixton had declined their offer of something to eat and told them of his encounter with the young Asian reporter from WTOP. "I was tempted to tell him to eat it since he'd paid for it, but I was hungry. I give him credit for ingenuity."

"He's lucky he didn't end up with a sparerib up his nose," Mac said, chuckling. "By the way, Will Sayers has been trying to get hold of you," Mac said.

"I talked to him before I left the apartment. We're having lunch tomorrow."

Sayers had become friends with Mac and Annabel after moving to D.C. to reopen his newspaper's Washington bureau and had introduced Brixton to them when Brixton came to D.C. from Savannah. They'd hit it off immediately, and Brixton treasured the couple's honesty, a trait he'd not found in abundance in the nation's capital.

"I'll be going to Maryland in the morning to meet with my ex-wife about our daughter's funeral arrangements."

Annabel winced. "I can't imagine anything worse," she said. "Mac and I don't have any children but—"

"I had a son who died in a crash," Mac said.

"I know," Brixton said. "It's devastating. You just never think that any of your kids will die before you do. I keep asking myself whether I could have done something different, acted a minute sooner, saved her in some way. I knew—I just knew that something bad was going to happen and told her we were leaving the café. But she hung back, picking up some papers she'd been showing me, and then . . ."

"The young man you shot, Congressman Skaggs's son," Mac said. "Have you learned anything about why he was there with the girl?"

Brixton slowly shook his head and sipped his drink.

"It's fairly common knowledge that the congressman is estranged from his children," Annabel said.

"More than one?" Brixton said.

"Yes," said Annabel. "Someone in the building who knows the Skaggs family told me that it's a dysfunctional family with a lot of bitterness within it. There's an adult daughter."

"Do you know what the son had been doing the past few years?" Brixton asked.

"I have no idea," Annabel said.

"I'm determined to find out what I can about him," Brixton said. "Why he would have accompanied a suicide bomber is the big question. I've got to know. If I can get an answer to that, maybe I can prove that he was there in the café."

Mac and Annabel respected the silent reverie Brixton slipped into as he looked out over the river and slowly sipped his drink. He broke the mood by saying, "You know, in all my years on the force, here and in Savannah, I never killed a man."

"I suppose it's something every law enforcement officer dreads," Annabel said.

"I've been close to cops who killed somebody in the line of duty. Even though the person they shot was the scum of the earth, taking a life hit them hard." He paused. "My father killed a man once."

Mac and Annabel drew a breath and waited for the rest of the story.

"My old man was a bartender in Brooklyn. Not a weekend bartender or anything like that. He was a pro, worked bars his whole life—and don't let anybody tell you that it's fun, you know, like show business, entertaining customers, putting on a show. It's damn hard work."

Mac agreed. "I know people who've gone into the restaurant business because they think it *is* show business, you know, standing at the front in a suit meeting and greeting customers. They soon find out what a tough business it is."

"Yeah, my dad worked hard, and the joints he worked in weren't what you'd call 'high end'—they were neighborhood bars, shot-and-a-beer joints, every once in a while a nicer place. He owned a few, too. Anyway, one night he's dealing with an obnoxious drunk who gets combative because my dad refuses to serve him more drinks. He threatens my dad—and you should know that he was a tough dude, a take-no-prisoners sort of guy. Anyway, the guy leans over the bar and grabs his neck. What does my father do? He grabs a baseball bat he kept behind the bar for protection and gives him a whack on the head. The guy goes down, and my father figures he's knocked out, will wake up with a hell of a headache and sorry that he acted like a jerk. But he doesn't wake up. The bat must have caught him in just the right place. My dad calls nine-one-one, and the guy dies on the way to the hospital."

"You couldn't blame your father for doing what he did," Annabel offered.

"Yeah, that's right, except that, like cops who shoot a murderer or rapist or drug dealer, my old man didn't feel that way. Sure, he was justified in hitting the guy, just like a cop is justified in shooting a bad guy. The police—my dad knew a slew of them who used to hang out in his bars when off duty—told him he was justified, and he was never charged with anything. But it changed him. Man, did it change him. He was never the same, became moody and introspective, lost his sense of humor, lost his edge."

Mac and Annabel said nothing.

"And now *I've* killed somebody."

"Because he helped blow up a restaurant and killed your daughter and others," Mac said.

"Tell that to the rest of the world," Brixton growled. "I'm the only one who can place him in the café with the bomber. His father is a powerful congressman. The media doesn't buy my story that he was in the café. Nobody does. My boss, Mike Kogan, puts me on leave until the dust settles. Mike's a good guy. I'm being paid while I cool my heels. But I hate it. I hate being called a liar. I hate having to defend what I did, because what I did was right. I thought he was armed. Turns out he had a cell phone with a silver case in his hand, no gun."

"But why did he run from you?" Annabel asked.

Brixton managed a snort that would do for a laugh. "They asked me that at the hospital, some of the suits who arrived from the FBI, the CIA—everybody with questions. One of them said that if he were a young guy who saw me, somebody with blood running down his face and neck and waving a gun, he'd run, too. Of course I didn't pull my gun until I cornered him in the alley."

Recounting his father's experience seemed to have

drained from Brixton whatever energy he had brought with him to the apartment.

"You look exhausted," Annabel said. "The guest room is made up, fresh towels in your bathroom, a TV. If there's anything else you need, just yell."

"You won't mind if I head for bed? It's early and—"

"Of course not."

"I hate to end the conversation, but it's better than passing out in front of you."

Mac laughed. "Try to get a good sleep," he said. "By the way, we're having your buddy Sayers for dinner tomorrow night."

"How about that," Brixton said. "Lunch *and* dinner with the whale."

"We have another guest coming," Mac said. "I hope you don't mind. Her name is Asal Banai. She and Annabel became friends through a book club they belong to."

"Asal Banai?" Brixton said. "Unusual name."

"She's Iraqi American," Annabel said. "She works for a nonprofit organization that promotes better relations between our country and Iraq."

Brixton's brow furrowed.

"I mention it, Robert, because I'm not sure you're up to having dinner with someone of Middle Eastern origins after what's happened to your daughter."

Mac and Annabel had discussed it prior to Brixton's arrival and thought it only fair to give him an out.

"No," Brixton said, "I don't have a problem with it. Every Arab isn't a suicide bomber."

"Glad you feel that way," Mac said. "Go on, get to bed. We'll have breakfast in the morning and send you on your way."

Brixton lay awake in the Smith's nicely furnished, serene guest room and fought to put his thoughts in order. So much had happened, so many issues to resolve, so much anger to get under control. He tried to apply what friends who were in AA had told him: Change what you can, accept what you can't, and be wise enough to know the difference, or something like that. Janet was dead! He couldn't change that. Others were dead, too, unsuspecting people who'd been enjoying themselves in the café. Too late to do anything about them either.

He dreaded meeting with Marylee in the morning and was hopeful that he could maintain his composure, be a brick upon whom she could rely. There would have to be a funeral; nothing could change that reality. Marylee, a devout Roman Catholic, would want the works, every bell and whistle the church had to offer. He wouldn't argue. Robert Brixton believed in individual faith. Some people required a higher power to turn to when things got rough and they needed comfort. But he turned skeptic when the faithful got together. Religion had probably inspired the bomber who'd slaughtered his daughter. Religious differences had fueled so many wars resulting in millions being killed. For him the only way to leave this world was in a simple pine casket and hopefully earning a few tears from friends while you were lowered into the ground. The lyrics for "St. James Infirmary," the Louis Armstrong recording that jazz-lover Brixton played over and over, summed up his view of dying:

> When I die, I want you to dress me in straight laced
>   shoes
> A box-back coat and a Stetson hat;
> Put a twenty-dollar gold piece on my watch chain
> So the boys know I died standin' pat.

But he knew that he couldn't impose his beliefs, or lack of them, on Marylee at her time of personal pain and sorrow.

His jumbled thoughts didn't keep him from falling into a deep sleep, and he awoke early the next morning surprised that he'd slept as soundly as he had. After showering and changing clothes—and applying to his head and neck wounds the fresh dressings provided to him when he left the hospital—he joined Mac and Annabel for eggs, bacon, toast, and two cups of strong coffee.

"We'll see you tonight?" Mac asked as he walked Brixton to the elevator.

"Sure. You run a first-class hotel, Mac."

"When Annabel and I decorated the place, we wanted it to be as luxurious as the best hotels we've ever stayed in."

"Well, you succeeded. See you at—?"

"Will Sayers and Asal are coming at six."

The sky was overcast as Brixton drove from the underground garage and headed out of the District to Rockville, Maryland, where Marylee lived with her new husband, Miles Lashka. He'd met Lashka when he'd visited his daughters at the stately white colonial home, and was surprised when Marylee announced that she and Lashka were getting married. Brixton hadn't liked the smarmy, tanned, and glib attorney from the first handshake. The attorney seemed to live in tennis whites and considered everything he said to be gospel. Worse, Marylee always agreed with him—"Miles says" or "Miles thinks" or "Miles knows a lot about that." Brixton couldn't fathom what Marylee saw in him. He knew, of course, that such speculation was a useless exercise. What attracted women to certain men, and men to certain women, had always intrigued and amused him. Maybe what made it especially interesting was that Lashka was his polar opposite. Go figure.

This would be the first time he'd visited the home without Marylee's mother being there. The old lady had died of lymphoma while Brixton was back in New York, and he'd suffered a brief moment of sadness after receiving the news. He was sad when anyone died, whether he liked them or not. Dying was the price you paid for living, someone had once said, and Brixton related to that bit of philosophy. But he decided that to attend her funeral would represent hypocrisy and he begged off, much to Marylee's chagrin, although he suspected that she was secretly relieved.

The elderly Mrs. Greene had never tried to mask her disdain for him, and he blamed her for contributing to the breakup of the marriage.

"Rest in peace, Mrs. Greene," he'd said after learning of her death. It would have to do.

Marylee's house with its white cedar shakes, moss green shutters, three-car garage, and blacktop driveway was in a grassy neighborhood with tall, stately trees and with plenty of basketball hoops. If you didn't know the address, you'd have trouble finding it; it was identical to every other house in the community. Parked in the driveway were matching silver Mercedes sedans. One's vanity license plate read PLEABARG.

Brixton's older daughter, Jill, answered the door. "Oh, Daddy, you look terrible," she said, giving him a quick hug.

"Hi, sweetheart," Brixton said, and kissed her on the cheek. Beyond her in the large living room decorated in white and gold were Marylee, Miles Lashka, and a Catholic priest.

"Is Joey here with you?" Brixton asked, referring to Jill's son, his only grandchild.

"No. He's with a sitter. Come on in."

Jill's husband, Frank, intercepted Brixton on his way to the living room. Frank was a tall, ruggedly handsome ex-marine who carried his military bearing into civilian life. He'd gone back to college after his discharge and earned a master's degree in hospital administration, which he put to good use at Walter Reed. He was a man of few words, which Brixton appreciated. He liked his son-in-law, probably because Frank made it obvious that he liked him.

"You okay?" Frank asked.

"Yeah, I'm okay. You? How is Jill holding up?"

"Doing fine, Robert. Glad you're here. Wish I saw more of you."

Brixton was next greeted by Lashka, who shook his hand and uttered his condolences.

The youngish priest introduced himself as Father Monroe. "A difficult time, I know," he said.

"Yeah, tough," Brixton agreed.

He went to where Marylee sat on a couch and extended his hand. "Not much to say is there?" he said.

"No, not much to say."

Lashka quickly slid in next to Marylee and put his arm around her.

"I've arranged for the funeral," she told Brixton. "The funeral director said that it will have to be—" Sobs choked off her final words.

"Closed casket," Lashka filled in. "Understandable." He handed his wife a white handkerchief.

Brixton took a chair next to the priest, who sat talking to Jill. "I just want you to know, Father, that anything Marylee wants is okay with me."

"I try to personalize the service to whatever extent possible," the priest said. "Will you wish to speak about your departed daughter?"

"No, I'm not much of a public speaker," Brixton said.

Father Monroe looked to where Lashka sat with Marylee. "Her stepdad will be saying a few things," he said.

"Good," said Brixton. "I'm sure he'll make a very nice speech." His tone said that it would be best to not pursue the topic.

Marylee, red-eyed but composed, came to them. "I tried to reach you on your cell phone," she said.

"I haven't turned it on since—since the bombing. What did you want?"

"I wanted you to bring any pictures you have of Janet for a photo wall at the funeral parlor."

"You kept most of the photos, but I have a few. I'll get them to you."

"The young man she's been seeing—his name is Richard—I've asked him to bring his band and play at the funeral. She said he's very talented."

All Brixton could think of that moment was that it was this Richard's cockamamy idea for a music app that had lured Janet and him to the café. It also struck him as inappropriate to have a rock band at such a solemn occasion—maybe solo jazz piano, Shearing, Peterson, Garner—but he knew that it really didn't matter what music was played. Regardless of what words were said or how elaborate the ritual would be, nothing would change. His daughter was dead, and the rest of it was for those left behind.

"That sounds wonderful, Marylee."

Brixton didn't know the protocol for such a gathering. His knee and back had started to ache, and he would have preferred to leave. He had every right to be there, yet he felt as though he didn't belong. He passed the next half hour talking with visitors and nibbling on cookies and cakes brought by neighbors, offerings that Marylee had arranged on the dining room table. When he felt that he'd put in the requisite time, he told Marylee that he was leaving.

"There's another thing before you go, Robert. I don't want to see Janet's funeral turned into a media circus. That would be totally inappropriate."

She sounded like her departed mother, imperious and self-righteous.

"Why tell *me*, Marylee? I've got nothing to say about it."

"It's because of you that the media might show up, your shooting the congressman's son and all. I've had calls from reporters asking about you."

"That congressman's son just happened to be in cahoots with the suicide bomber who took our daughter's life." He was unsuccessful in keeping the anger from his voice.

"Yes, I've read about that," the priest said.

"Are you okay, Daddy?" Jill asked.

"Me? I'm fine. Look, if there's nothing more to discuss, I'd better get going. Like I said, Father, whatever Mrs. Brixton wants is fine with me."

"Mrs. Lashka," Marylee corrected.

Brixton kissed Jill good-bye and walked from the house, followed by Marylee's husband.

"Can I do anything for you, Robert?" Lashka asked.

"Can't think of a thing," Brixton said.

"It sounds to me as though you could run into legal trouble over the shooting of Congressman Skaggs's son. If you need legal advice, you know where to turn." He handed Brixton his business card and adopted what passed for a serious, concerned expression.

"That's nice of you, Miles," Brixton said. "I'm really touched. See you at the funeral."

Brixton got in his car and silently cursed. There was a moment when he might have taken a swing at the ambulance chaser, but he'd managed to restrain the impulse. He waited until his anger had passed before starting the engine and pulling out of the driveway. He stopped a block away and turned on his cell phone, which was filled with messages, including those from Marylee. Most were from media requesting—some almost begging—for an interview, which he ignored. He made a note of a few calls worth returning. One was from his former paramour, Flo Combes, calling from New York. "I'm worried about you, Robert," she said. "If there's anything I can do, come to D.C., just name it. We may not be lovers anymore, but we can still be friends. Please call me."

The other call that he cared about was from Donna Salvos at SITQUAL. He reached her on her cell phone.

"What's up?" he said.

"Where are you? I've called the apartment a number of times and just get that damned machine."

"Making funeral arrangements for Janet."

"Oh. I'm sorry. Can I help?"

"Everybody asks what they can do for me, and I appreciate it. I really do. But what I want and need is to find out why Skaggs's kid was with the bomber, who he was, what his game was. I'm being portrayed as some trigger-happy whack job who goes around shooting young men who just happen to be passing by."

"I know, Robert, I know. Look, Mike Kogan wants to meet with you."

"About what, reinstating me?"

"I don't know why. I'm just passing along the word. He's been calling your apartment, too."

"Tell him I'll give him a call."

"I will. And keep in touch with me."

He drove back into the District and made a pass by his apartment building. The media crowd had thinned out, but the TV remote truck was still there, along with a smattering of reporters. It struck him that being a reporter was like being a cop—endless hours spent hanging around and waiting for someone or something to happen. He'd spent plenty of time on stakeouts when he was a cop in D.C. and Savannah and had hated every minute of it.

He parked on E Street and passed the time walking through the National Law Enforcement Officers Memorial, in which federal, state, and local cops who'd died in the line of duty were honored. It wasn't his first time there. He stopped to read some of the nineteen thousand names engraved on the memorial's long, curved, blue-gray marble walls and felt as though he'd personally known them. Savannah had its own memorial to fallen cops, located just outside police headquarters, and Brixton had often lingered there too, gaining solace from the experience. No one at Marylee's house had talked about a headstone for Janet. It had to be a nice one, not too elaborate, but dignified. He'd bring it up the next time they talked.

Eventually he returned to the car and drove to the restaurant where he was to meet Will Sayers for lunch. Sayers, whose mother was Czechoslovakian, was a self-proclaimed foodie. He'd complained about the absence of a good Czech restaurant in Washington and had latched on to this place the day it opened. He'd been a regular ever since. Sayers had already arrived and taken a table inside in a corner. The weather was nice, sunny and with a gentle breeze, the way it had been when the bomb went off. The restaurant had a pleasant outdoor dining patio, and Brixton would have opted to eat there but wondered if he'd ever feel comfortable again in an outdoor café. Besides, he was self-conscious wearing his white bandage and was glad that Sayers had chosen a less-public table.

The large, imposing bureau chief was dressed in what was almost a uniform: wrinkled khaki pants, a button-down shirt, a putrid green tie, blue suspenders, a tan corduroy sport jacket rendered shiny from wear, and brown Space Shoes that were broken down from carrying his weight, which clocked in at just south of three hundred. Completing the outfit was a signature red railroad handkerchief hanging from his rear pants pocket. Willis Sayers would never win anyone's best-dressed award.

"Hey, pal, good to see you," he said as Brixton sat across from him.

"Good to see you too, Will."

Brixton hoped that the subject of Janet wouldn't come up right away, and he picked up the menu as a distraction. "What's good here?" he asked.

"Everything," Sayers said. He motioned for the waitress: "Two Pilsners and a plate of the chicken schnitzel to start, with the panko crust, nice and crisp, huh? And some potato salad." He looked at Brixton. "Okay with you?"

"Whatever you say. Not especially hungry. So, what's new in the swinging, swirling world of big-time journalism?"

"A lot less than what's new with you, Robert. You okay?"

"I've been better."

"That hurt?" Sayers asked, referring to the white dressing on Brixton's wounds.

"Only when I laugh, which isn't often these days. I'm staying with Mac and Annabel Smith."

"So Mac says. You'll be at dinner tonight."

"Right." Brixton leaned across the table. "Will, I've got to find out why Skaggs's kid was with the bomber in the café."

"Why did I think I'd be hearing that today?" Sayers said as he pulled folded sheets of paper from his inside jacket pocket. "I did a little research on the kid."

Brixton managed a smile, his first of the day. Leave it to Sayers to anticipate what he'd be asking.

"I don't know if what I've come up with means anything, but it's a start. You do know, of course, that the Skaggs family is not all sweetness and light."

"Annabel mentioned that, nothing specific. I don't keep up with politicians from foreign countries."

"Mississippi's not a foreign country."

"Says who? Go on, I'm listening."

"The congressman's son, Paul, age twenty-two, lasted one semester at UCLA, dropped out, played beach bum for a while, surfed, strutted on the boardwalk—who knows? He evidently got tired of sunny California, because he left there and lived in Hawaii for a while.

"Damn, this schnitzel is good," Sayers proclaimed after it had arrived. "Just the way I like it." He saw that Brixton was annoyed. "Okay, sorry, you know me. I get excited over good food. More about Paul Skaggs. A few years back, when he was in high school in Mississippi, he attacked his father with a gun, threatened to kill him."

"Lovely. Why?"

"Aside from being nuts, he hated his father's stance on Iraq and Afghanistan. The old man is the loudest hawk in Congress. His son's a self-proclaimed peacenik."

"There are lots of peaceniks who don't threaten to shoot their father, or stand by while others are blown up."

"Right, but what the kid did was in keeping with other actions. None of this was ever reported: The family kept it hush-hush, aside from the predictable leaks, and the local media played along with the family. The kid was a foul ball all through high school—suspended a few times, got in fights. My source down there also says that junior knocked up a classmate, but his old man, the esteemed congressman, bought off the girl and her family. The kid ended up in some quasi-military school where screwed up kids are supposed to learn discipline and find God. I don't know how he did there. The next thing I know, he goes to UCLA in California—he's allegedly damn bright despite being a nut job—and lasts a semester."

"But he obviously came back to D.C. When?"

Sayers shrugged his large shoulders and finished the schnitzel. "How about an order of beef goulash with bread dumplings, and bratwurst? Their sauer-kraut is terrific. By the way, what do you hear from that lovely lady you used to live with in Savannah?"

"Flo? She's still in New York. Our split wasn't what you'd call amicable, but we're still friends. She's been calling. She's a good gal, only—"

"Only she got tired of Robert Brixton's jaded view of the world and everybody in it."

"Something like that. Order whatever you want. So, Paul Skaggs comes back to Washington, hooks up with a teenage girl whose sense of fashion and religion is to strap TNT to herself. He accompanies her into a busy café around the corner from State, where she blows everybody up including my daughter. *Why?*"

"I don't have an answer for that. Did you read the list of victims?"

"No."

"The number of dead is now at nineteen, two not making it in the hospital. Seven worked at the State Department."

"No surprise. It's a block away."

"Just wondering whether that café was chosen be-cause of who hangs out there. One of the other victims was Marjorie Krim. Name ring a bell?"

"No." Brixton summoned the waitress and ordered a martini, straight up. Sayers stuck with beer.

"Who is she?"

"An activist for LGBT rights here in D.C."

"A lesbian?"

"Yeah. She worked for the State Department."

"So?"

"There's something brewing in the D.C. gay community, Robert."

"Such as?"

"You know Congressman Ken Wisher from Georgia?"

"I've heard of him. A real right-winger."

"Right, a real right-winger, champion of family values, leads the fight against gay marriage . . ."

"And?"

"And maybe a closet gay."

It was Brixton's turn to sigh. "I gotta tell you, Will, I couldn't care less about a congressman's sex life."

"Even if he was compromised because of his sexual orientation?"

"Who compromised him?"

"Don't know. That's what I'm trying to find out. I've got a lead on someone who allegedly was Wisher's lover on occasion, a guy from the Spanish embassy. He calls himself Lalo."

"Lalo Reyes?"

"You know him?"

"I interviewed him about the murder of that German embassy employee, Peter Müller. Reyes and Müller were lovers."

"He gets around. Did Congressman Wisher's name come up during the interview?" Sayers asked.

"No."

Brixton grunted.

"What?"

"Reyes told us—I was with my partner, Donna Salvos—he said that he'd lived in a lot of places."

"And?"

"One of them was Hawaii. I wonder . . ."

Sayers jotted something in the reporter's notebook he seemed always to have at the ready.

Brixton brought the conversation back to Paul Skaggs. "What else have you learned about him?" he asked Sayers.

"Not a hell of a lot. He had a sister, Morgana."

"I heard about a sister. What's her story?"

"She's ten years older than her brother. Best I can put together, she split from the family years ago and hasn't been a guest at their Thanksgiving dinners since. The son either."

"They both split, huh? Sounds like the Skaggs kids weren't anxious to hang around with Mommy and Daddy."

"Be an interesting dinner if they showed up."

"Where's the daughter?" Brixton asked.

"Hawaii. At least that's what I'm told."

"You said that Paul Skaggs was there, too."

"The blow to your head didn't affect your hearing, Robert. Yeah, he was in Hawaii, too. The island of Maui. Ever been?"

"No."

"Beautiful place."

"I'll put it on my bucket list."

Conversation came to a halt when their lunch was delivered. Brixton was anxious to hear more from his journalist friend but decided to wait until the platters were clean, which didn't take long.

"That was good," Brixton said.

"Always is here. Ready for some more tantalizing tidbits?"

"I was counting on it."

"The Skaggs daughter, Morgana, is still in Hawaii."

"What's she do there?"

"Works for Samuel Prisler."

"Prisler. Prisler. The arms dealer?"

"Not according to him."

"There was a feature on him a while back in a national magazine."

"Here," Sayers said, handing Brixton a copy of the article he'd dug up on the Internet. In it, the author alleged that Prisler was a middleman between foreign arms manufacturers and certain Middle Eastern countries.

As Brixton scanned the article, Sayers said, "From everything I've learned, he's got connections with Iran, Iraq, Afghanistan, Mali in Africa, and especially strong ties with Pakistan. It's alleged that young Paul Skaggs lived in Prisler's compound for a time."

"He has a compound?"

"It's a cult. Causes lots of controversy on Maui. Prisler manages to skirt the issue because he's got clout on the island. He runs local businesses—aside from selling arms around the world to less-than-savory people."

"So what?"

"So, wise guy, maybe there's a connection between Paul Skaggs getting involved with a Middle Eastern suicide bomber and falling under Prisler's spell. *Allegedly,* of course."

Brixton shook his head. "That's too much of a stretch. It sounds like an Oliver Stone screenplay."

"Just playing the what-if game."

"You say the daughter is in Hawaii? Maui?"

"According to my impeccable sources."

"And she's part of this cult Prisler runs?"

"My sources say that if you hook up with him, you're in for life. He doesn't take kindly to members of his community abandoning him."

"So Morgana Skaggs is a member of his so-called cult. What's the connection with Prisler and the bombing?"

"I don't have one. All I know is that after Paul Skaggs

left California, he joined his sister on Maui and lived there for a spell. You'll have to connect the dots, Robert, if that's possible. That's all I have, but I'll keep digging. Oh, by the way, Morgana Skaggs changed her name when she got to Hawaii." He consulted one of his sheets of paper. "Kamea Wakatake. That's the Hawaiian name she goes by now."

Brixton added to the notes he'd been making on the papers Sayers had given him.

"There's a guy who knows more about Samuel Prisler than Prisler knows about himself, Charles McQuaid, retired from the Justice Department. While he was at Justice he headed up a task force that tried to build a case against Prisler. They never did, but Prisler has been an obsession with McQuaid. He's a friend of mine. If you want, I'll call and get you two together."

"Thanks," Brixton said. "I appreciate it."

"See you tonight at Mac and Annabel's," Sayers said as they parted outside the restaurant.

"Yeah. Do you know anything about Annabel's friend who'll be there?"

"No, never met her. Take care," Sayers said, slapping Brixton on the arm. "I know you're going through hell, pal. I'm here for you."

"What can I do for *you*?" Brixton asked.

"An exclusive interview about the bombing—but only when you're up to it."

Brixton watched Sayers waddle away and struggle to get into his car. Since the bombing and death of his daughter, Brixton had begun to wonder whether he had any friends in this world.

Sayers had answered the question.

12

Brixton made another pass at his apartment building after leaving lunch and was pleased that the media had departed in search of other stories. He parked in the underground garage, went to his apartment, and called Mike Kogan at SITQUAL headquarters—if the offices above the Thai restaurant could be called a headquarters.

"I've been trying to get hold of you," Kogan said.

"I've been running around, had to make funeral arrangements for my daughter."

"I'm sorry."

"Thanks."

"You didn't turn on your cell."

"I wasn't interested in hearing from the rest of the world. Donna says you want to talk to me."

"That's right, I do. You free now?"

Brixton checked his watch. "No. How about in the morning?"

"Okay. You staying out of trouble?"

"If you mean have I not talked to the media? Yes, I've stayed out of trouble."

"Play it smart, Robert. Don't complicate things for yourself."

"Or for you."

"Right. For me too. Be here at eight. I have a nine o'clock with DSS at State."

Brixton was curious about why Kogan wanted to see him. He'd already been suspended; the next move could be dismissal. On the one hand, he didn't care. If Kogan fired him—and if he did, Brixton knew that he would do it with regret—he'd simply pack up and head back to Brooklyn, where people talked straight, even the mobsters he knew there. On the other hand, he liked working for Mike Kogan and knew that Kogan had been right when he'd said that finding good jobs wasn't easy for a fifty-one-year-old guy.

He also second-guessed agreeing to join Mac and Annabel Smith for dinner. Attending a dinner party wasn't something that he, or anyone else who'd lost a daughter, should be doing.

But what was the alternative?

Sit alone in the apartment, get stinking drunk, and cry? Find some down-and-dirty bar where he could do the same thing and have the bartender call for a cab to take the sot home?

Besides, he was still staying at the Smith's apartment. What was he going to do, sulk in the Smith's spare bedroom and listen to the dinner-table chatter through the closed door?

And he was anxious to spend more time with Will Sayers. Who knew what the rotund editor would have come up with about Paul Skaggs between lunch and dinner?

Before leaving he dialed the number for Flo Combes in New York.

"I was hoping you'd call," she said.

"I've been busy and—"

"You don't have to explain, Robert. It's just that I'm worried about you."

"No need, sweetie. I'll be fine. I'm staying at the Smith's apartment. Remember them? You picked me up there after my tussle with that psychopath who tried to kill me."

"How could I forget? They're such nice people."

"Things okay with you?" he asked.

"Things are fine. Negotiations with the bank for a loan to open the dress shop are stalled, so I'm cooling my heels while they straighten it out. In other words I'm free and can come down to help while you go through the mess you're in."

"Come to D.C.?"

"Yes. I know, I know; tough guy Robert Brixton doesn't need anybody to help him. He'll do it himself. But sometimes we need someone, Robert, at least somebody who cares. I'd really love to help."

"Look, Flo, I appreciate the offer but—"

"Just thought I'd ask."

He heard the tears in her voice.

"Hey, what's wrong?"

"I miss you, damn it! I wish that we were together again. I'm sorry for all the hateful things I said. I'm sorry that I called you a loser and a hopeless cynic and—I'm just sorry about everything."

"Maybe when things blow over we can take a stab at it, Flo. Right now my head is swimming with Janet's funeral, being suspended from the agency, the media chasing me, and trying to prove that the congressman's son was with the suicide bomber in that café. I just can't handle another complication."

"I understand," she said.

"I hope you do. Look, I'm sorry to cut this short but I have to run. I'm having dinner with the Smiths."

"Okay. I just want you to know that I'm here for you, at least in spirit, and that . . . and that I love you."

"I love you, too, babe," he mouthed silently into the dead phone.

Brixton's visceral reaction to Asal Banai when Mac Smith introduced her was that she was strikingly beautiful. Large brown eyes were set in a perfectly formed oval face the color of coffee with cream. Her pitch-black shoulder-length hair, carefully tended to frame her face, shone in the overhead lights. She was about five feet five inches tall. He surreptitiously took in her figure, the sort of body that stayed in shape without hours in a gym, rounded and firm, classic. Still, he detected a subtle sadness that came deep from within, source unknown.

Brixton figured that maybe before he arrived, Mac and Annabel had suggested to Sayers that the topic of the café bombing be avoided unless he raised it. They studiously ignored that subject, and Brixton was grateful for the opportunity to talk about other things. Asal may have been given the same suggestion, because she didn't mention it during the initial conversations when, drinks in hand, they had settled on the terrace. The mood was kept lighthearted, with Sayers telling tales of when he'd been a reporter in Savannah and the characters there he'd run across.

It was Asal who shifted conversational gears after dinner, when she asked Brixton about homeland security and whether he thought the nation was adequately protected in light of the café bombing. Mac and Annabel's expressions indicated that they weren't sure what voicing that question would spur in Brixton. To their surprise—and relief—he enthusiastically opined about the terrorist threat to the nation and how he evaluated the government's lame response.

"So you don't think all these agencies and people make us safer?" Asal asked.

"Hell, no," Brixton replied. "SITQUAL—the agency I work for, or *did* work for—is one of two thousand private companies charged with homeland security. Two thousand! Add them to the thousand of other government intelligence agencies in the business of protecting us from terrorists, and it becomes a joke. Everybody reports to the director of National Intelligence, and he reports to the president. You think *he* knows what the hell is going on? With more than three thousand separate agencies all doing the same thing and not talking to each other and turning out fifty thousand reports a year? He doesn't have a clue. How could he?"

Mac Smith laughed. He and Annabel had become comfortable with Brixton's cynical view of the government and how it worked, finding it amusing at times and almost always thought-provoking.

"What does SITQUAL stand for?" Asal asked.

"Ready for this?" Brixton said. "Strategic Intelligence Tasking. Don't ask me what QUAL means. I think they decided they couldn't just call it SIT because it sounds too much like a command you give a dog, so they tacked on the QUAL."

"For 'quality'?" Sayers asked lightly.

"If you say so."

"It is part of the State Department?" Asal asked.

"We report to them," Brixton said. "We're supposed to gather info on people working at foreign embassies here in D.C. A couple of congressmen decided that staffers at the embassies might be infiltrating our security system and promoting terrorism, so they told State to add more investigators. Naturally, Congress wouldn't give them more money to do it, so they outsourced it. State hired my buddy, Mike Kogan, to put together a group to keep tabs on these people." He guffawed. "He hired all former cops. Mike's a good guy, got us top-secret security clearances. You know how many people working on homeland security have top-secret clearances? Eight hundred and fifty thousand. That's more than the whole population of Washington, D.C. Don't think I'm telling tales out of school. *The Post* did the exposé, named names, laid it out for those who think we're safer after nine/eleven because of the overkill."

"The government always operates on the theory that if something's worth doing, it's worth overdoing," Sayers chimed in.

"Tell Asal why you left New York and came here to D.C. to work," Mac suggested.

Brixton laughed. "It's a long, sordid story, something to do with my roughing up the wrong person who worked for the Russian embassy in New York. He got drunk and pulled a knife on someone and then turned on me. They said I used excessive force. He's lucky I didn't break his neck. They even suggested I take anger-management courses. Can you believe that? Hell, I'm the original flower child. It was me that Joan Baez and Bob Dylan were singing about."

Sayers laughed, shaking the table. "Robert Brixton," he said, "the original flower child. Believe that and you'll believe I'm a bathing suit model. Time for me to drag my bones home."

Asal also took the opportunity to call it a night.

"You can't leave because you're living here," Annabel told Brixton.

"You're welcome to stay as long as you like, Robert," Mac added.

"I know that, and I really appreciate it, but I made a

pass by my apartment before coming, and the media types have departed. I think I'll head back. Things to do."

"Whatever you say," Mac said.

Before he left, Sayers took Brixton aside. "I called Charlie McQuaid, the guy I told you about. He said he'd be happy to meet with you about Samuel Prisler. Here's his number."

Brixton packed his belongings, and he and Asal Banai left together ten minutes after Sayers. On the ride down in the elevator, he asked, "Up for a drink?" He wasn't concerned about offending her Muslim background, because he'd noticed that she'd enjoyed wine during dinner.

"Oh, I don't know, I . . ."

"Come on, just a quick one. I'll drive you home after that."

Her smile was welcoming. "All right," she said.

They walked across the vast Watergate property and settled in a secluded corner of the infamous complex's hotel bar.

"I've never been here before," she said.

"I've stopped in a couple of times. Makes me feel like a D.C. mover and shaker."

"Are you?"

"A mover and shaker? Afraid not."

"I hope you don't mind my saying that I know about your daughter and that I am very sorry for your loss."

"No, it's okay. I have to get used to it. Reality. That's what it is, reality."

"But so painful."

"This helps," he said as he lifted his martini to her. "Here's to meeting you."

She clicked the rim of her glass against his.

"I like your friend Mr. Sayers," she said. "He's funny."

"Yeah, he's always got a story to tell. He's a *good* friend."

"He's helping you with . . . ?"

"With the situation I'm in? You've read about it."

"Yes. They say that the man you shot, the congressman's son, wasn't there when the explosion happened."

" 'They'?"

"The newspaper and the television."

"Newspapers and television are wrong. The congressman is wrong."

"I believe you."

"Glad to hear it. That makes two believers—you and Will Sayers."

"The Smiths?"

"Oh, them, of course. The number is up to four. Mind a question?"

"A question about what?"

"The young woman who blew herself up. As hard as I try, I can't even begin to imagine what could make her do that."

Asal cupped her hands around her wineglass, and her expression became thoughtful. She said, "Are you asking me that because I am an Arab woman and should have some deep understanding of why another Arab woman would do such a thing?"

Brixton nodded. "I suppose I am," he said.

"I could take offense at that question."

"I don't mean to offend you. I'm just trying to understand why my daughter is dead."

"I don't know why anyone does terrible things," she said. "It is not only Middle Eastern terrorists who kill innocent people. There are hundreds of hate groups here in America that kill other innocent people. Your Ku Klux Klan is an example. The man who blew up the building in Oklahoma City is another. So many."

"I know," he said, "you're right. Where were you born?"

"In Iraq."

"You're a Muslim?"

"I was raised in the Muslim faith but don't practice any religion these days. I sometimes go to a Unitarian church near where I live. I like the minister there and what he preaches."

"What *does* he preach?"

"To love and respect all living things."

"Shame that suicide bomber didn't hear a few of his sermons."

"There is nothing in Islam that says you must kill innocent people. I respect my heritage and the religion I was brought up in, but I now live in America. People shouldn't stereotype all Muslims because of the actions of a few."

"Do you think I'm doing that?"

"I hope you are not."

"I'll try not to."

As the conversation shifted to less-contentious topics, Brixton took the occasion to appreciate her physical beauty. Her occasional laugh was playful yet sensual, her voice pleasing with a touch of an accent. Funny that he never thought of Middle Eastern women as being particularly beautiful. He'd obviously missed something. *There I go stereotyping.*

She ordered a second glass of wine. It was a refill for Brixton.

"I didn't think Arabs drank alcohol," Brixton said. "Is that stereotyping?"

She laughed. "The very pious ones don't drink alcohol, but liquor stores—alcohol shops, they're called in Iraq—are very popular. Iraq is one of the most secular countries in the region. There was a time when Saddam Hussein was in power that most were shut down, but since he is gone, many have opened again. I have friends in Saudi Arabia, where to drink alcohol is punished severely. But when my friends travel, as soon as the plane takes off, they are asking the stewardesses for bourbon or Scotch. Or flight attendants, as they are called now."

"I still call them stewardesses," Brixton said. "That's hypocritical if the Saudis punish people for drinking and then go ahead and drink themselves."

"You don't like hypocrisy, do you?"

"Who does? That's why I got out of Washington years ago—couldn't hack the hypocrisy."

She changed the subject, either because she didn't want to pursue it or because she had other things on her mind.

"Tell me more about what you do for the State Department. You work for . . . ?"

"SITQUAL."

"What do you *do* there?"

"Keep everyone at the embassies safe. Want to see my cape?"

"Your cape?"

· "My Superman cape. Robert Brixton, savior of mankind, protector of the innocent and—"

Her laugh was more spirited this time.

"Funny?"

"You remind me of that man Rooney, who was on television every week."

"Andy Rooney? I loved him. He told it like it is, pointed out all the stupid things we do, like texting while you're driving. Can you believe that we have to have a law prohibiting people from texting while they drive, a law so that dunderheads behind the wheel know they shouldn't do it? Pathetic!" He realized that he had gone off on a tangent and said, "Here I am mouthing off about things you couldn't care less about. Tell me about you, Asal. What's this organization you work for?"

"It is called the Islamic Partnership, a nonprofit agency. We have offices here in Washington and Baghdad. Since the American troops left Iraq, there has been a great deal of trouble. The Shiite majority oppresses the Sunni minority. We try to bring pressure on the Shiite government to be more inclusive."

"You're a Sunni."

"Yes."

Her eyes became moist for no apparent reason.

"Is something wrong?" Brixton asked.

"I am sorry. It is just that there are times when I think of my brother and—please excuse me." She pulled a tissue from her purse and dabbed at her eyes.

"What about your brother?" he asked, not certain whether he should pursue what was obviously a painful subject.

"He is a prisoner in Iraq."

"A prisoner? What'd he do?"

"He was born a Sunni."

"And he's a prisoner because of being born?"

"He's a prisoner because he has stood up to the new Shiite government. When Hussein was in power, the Sunnis prospered. Now it is different. My brother led a protest group against the oppression of Sunnis. *That* is why he has been taken a prisoner and remains in an Iraqi jail—no lawyers, no contact with anyone, including me."

"There's nothing you can do?" Brixton asked.

"I am doing what I can. A friend is helping me, but I do not know how successful he will be."

"We never should have gone into Iraq. It was all based on a lie."

"It is a shame that your President Bush didn't agree with you."

Brixton decided to get off politics and asked, "So what do you do with this partnership group of yours— raise money, that sort of thing?"

"We are always raising money. One of our major projects is bringing deserving young Arab women to the United States for education at your universities."

They traded life stories, Brixton abbreviating his and hoping that he didn't come off as a lunatic. There had been a lot of violence in his life, now that he thought about it. He realized how much he enjoyed spending time with this quiet, gentle woman whose soft voice was soothing.

His cell phone rang, and Brixton cursed under his breath. "I should have turned it off," he said. "Excuse me."

He went outside to take the call. Brixton railed against people who talked on their cell phones in restaurants.

"Robert, it's Marylee. I don't want you to forget the pictures for the funeral home."

"I'll be back home in an hour. I'll gather up what I have and get them to you tomorrow."

"And I don't want the media there."

"Look, Marylee, I'm doing everything I can to avoid the media. If they show up, there's not a damn thing I can do about it."

"Then maybe you shouldn't come."

"I'll forget you said that. Even if I didn't come, there's no guarantee the press won't be there looking for me." He heard a sigh. "I don't want to get into an argument. You'll have the pictures in the morning."

"Important call?" Asal asked when he rejoined her.

"Nothing that couldn't have waited until I got home."

He looked at the cell phone that he still held in his hand. "I hate these things. You ever notice how everybody walks around with one glued to their ear, like they're all really important, expecting a call from the president or some other big shot, or they sit staring at it hoping they'll get a message that they won the lottery?" He placed his credit card on top of the check.

"That's what Andy Rooney would have said," she quipped.

"Yes."

"Come on, I'll drive you home."

There was an awkward moment as they sat in Brixton's car in front of her apartment building. He had the feeling that she wanted a good-night kiss, but he didn't want to make the move, nor did she.

"Thank you," she said, "for the wine."

"Hey, what's a guy for? I'm sorry about your brother."

"And I am sorry about your daughter. So much sorrow in so many peoples' lives. Good night, Robert."

"I'll call you, maybe have dinner?"

"I will be disappointed if you don't."

With that she was gone, and he wished that she was still there.

13

After showering and dressing early the next morning, Brixton poured the ingredients of his morning shake into the blender he'd brought with him from New York. *Old habits die hard,* he thought. His fingers hovered over the switch while he weighed whether or not he could stomach another healthy smoothie. He decided he could not.

After checking that the media hadn't returned, he jogged to a local deli, picked up two egg-cheese-and-bacon sandwiches, orange juice, and a large coffee, and brought them back to the apartment, where he sat on the balcony with his breakfast and read that day's *Washington Post.*

A long front-page article that was continued inside the paper was a report on the café bombing, researched and written by three *Post* reporters. Brixton scanned the piece in search of anything that would bolster his claim that Paul Skaggs had accompanied the bomber, but there was nothing. The section devoted to Brixton's shooting of Skaggs focused on a new statement by

Congressman Skaggs, in which he chastised the Justice Department for not moving fast enough in its investigation of Brixton and why he'd killed his unarmed son. It was noted that reporters were unable to reach Brixton for his comment.

There was, however, new information on the bomber herself. The article identified her as Shahinaz Chamkanni. She was eighteen years old. Her family belonged to one of the many Pashtun tribes in Pakistan that provide warriors to the Taliban and whose government is based upon Islamic sharia law. A serious face looked out from her picture in the paper. Although details of her arrival in the United States were sketchy, sources indicated that she had come to Washington on a student visa. However, when contacted by the paper, officials at myriad local colleges and universities had no record or knowledge of her, leading officials at Homeland Security to conclude that her visa and accompanying papers had been falsified. Her whereabouts since arriving were unknown. The local address she'd listed on her visa application proved to be an abandoned storefront in southeast Washington.

"What the hell is wrong with our immigration people?" Brixton growled to himself. "How does she come up with phony papers and disappear until she's called upon to blow up a café?" He was also impressed that they'd been able to identify her so quickly, considering that she'd entered the country using false papers and had undoubtedly been blown into little pieces.

He read the article a few more times until satisfied that there was nothing of value to him regarding Paul Skaggs. As he finished his breakfast and sipped what was left of his cold coffee, his thoughts shifted from the story to the previous evening.

He was glad that he'd had dinner at the Smiths'. He needed to get outside of himself and not wallow in his misery. The physical wounds he'd suffered in the bombing had healed sufficiently for him to abandon the dressings, but he knew that his psychic wounds also had to be administered to.

He was pleased with himself that he'd invited Asal Banai for a drink. The time spent with her had been easy and pleasant. She was one of those people who practiced the cardinal rule of a good conversationalist: She listened. Her large dark eyes had focused on him as he recounted more about his life than he'd intended, his failed marriage, his two daughters, the years spent with the Savannah PD, and the retreat to his Brooklyn roots. It occurred to him that he was on his first date since Flo ended their relationship. That made him smile. He was too old to be on a "date." English seemed to lack an appropriate term for a mature unmarried relationship. When people used to ask how his girlfriend was, he often responded that Flo wasn't his "girlfriend." That was for teenyboppers and lovesick college kids. But no matter what you called sitting with a lovely Iraqi woman in a cool, dark bar, he knew that he'd enjoyed it, so much so that he intended to repeat the experience.

After slipping four photographs of Janet into a manila envelope, he went to his car and headed for Arlington and his eight o'clock meeting with Mike Kogan.

Kogan was on the phone when Brixton entered his office. Two other SITQUAL agents sat on a small couch near a window.

"Hey, Robert," one said, getting up and shaking Brixton's hand. The other agent also greeted Brixton but stayed seated and waved.

"How are you feeling?" the more enthusiastic agent asked.

"I'm okay."

"Your daughter. Man, I am sorry."

"Thanks."

"Have the arrangements been made? I mean for the funeral."

"I'll know more later today."

"I'll be there. You can count on that."

"I appreciate it."

Kogan motioned for the men to stop talking so he could better hear his phone conversation. The agent returned to the couch, and Brixton took a chair across the desk from his boss. A minute later Kogan ended the call, looked at Brixton, and said, "Thanks for coming by. Give us a minute." He pointed at the agents on the couch. "Give me an update on the cases you're working on," he said.

They had little to offer. One had worked undercover near the Canadian embassy on Pennsylvania Avenue. There had been two purse snatchings of female embassy employees in the vicinity, and Canadian security officials had asked State to investigate. SITQUAL had sent in a plainclothes agent dressed in casual clothing to blend in, but as far as Brixton was concerned, he had "cop" written all over him. MPD help had also been requested, resulting in a marked patrol car making a pass each day. Lots of luck.

"I hung around the embassy," the agent said, "but there was nobody who fit the description of the perp. I talked to one character who looked like he didn't belong there—white, scruffy, middle-aged, a street guy. The snatcher was young and black, according to the women."

"And grabs purses in daylight," Kogan said. "Go back this afternoon. His MO is late afternoon. Put in some time around then. Give me a report that I can show DSS, so *they* can show the Canadians that we're on it."

The second agent had been assigned to investigate

anti-Semitic graffiti that had been spray-painted on cars belonging to members of the Israeli embassy who'd been attending an art exhibit by Israeli-born sculptor Dalya Luttwak at the Kreeger Museum.

"Whoever did it is no artist," the agent reported, "just painted 'Jew bastards' on two cars. He doesn't spell so good either." He laid photos he'd taken of the cars on the desk. Bastards was spelled BASTADS. "MPD says they're looking into it."

"Stay on top of it with MPD," Kogan said, "and give me a written report end of the day."

"You take care, Robert," one of the agents said as he and his colleague left the office.

"So," Brixton said, "business as usual."

"If I had my way, I'd tell the embassies to investigate their own purse snatchings," Kogan said, "but I don't have it my way. Look, I asked you to come in because I can use you."

"To do what, help stake out the Canadian embassy and nab the purse snatcher?"

"I want to pick your brain about the bombing."

"It's already been picked clean, Mike. Read the papers; watch TV."

"I know you've told everybody what you experienced, but maybe you can help fill in a missing piece for me."

"How come SITQUAL's involved?" Brixton asked.

"Because of where that café was located, and because a number of embassy staffers were victims."

"You think they might have been targets?"

"Nobody knows. The FBI, CIA, and Homeland Security have raised the possibility with State, and I have to follow through on it. Can you think of anything that you saw or overheard that would give that theory credence?"

"No."

"Skaggs's son. You said that he spoke with the bomber before he left. Did you hear anything he said?"

"No. He whispered in her ear. I didn't hear a word."

"Was there anything in the café that indicated that State Department employees were there?"

"Like what, a neon sign?"

"Like maybe some customers still wore their State ID tags around their neck. You said the bomber and Skaggs's son passed the café three or four times before deciding to come in. Possible that they were scoping it out looking for embassy types?"

Brixton shrugged. "Sure, it's possible, Mike, but I can't tell you anything that would back it up. Sorry."

"I just thought—is there anything I can do for *you*, Robert?"

"Like provide an eyewitness that Skaggs's son was in the café?"

"I wish that were the case. You do know that I tried to avoid suspending you."

"Sure."

"That blowhard Skaggs wants your head, and mine too. If it weren't for him I—"

"No explanations needed, Mike. Actually, it's better that I'm on my own trying to prove that Skaggs's son was with the bomber. Keeps the heat off you."

"Any success?"

"No, but my friend Will Sayers has put me in touch with a retired guy from Justice, Charles McQuaid."

"What's he got to offer?"

Brixton explained that McQuaid had devoted much of his tenure at the Justice Department trying to build a case against Samuel Prisler.

"Prisler. Sure, the cult leader."

"International arms dealer."

"Same guy. He lives in Hawaii, doesn't he?"

"So I'm told. On Maui. Paul Skaggs's sister lives there, too, and works for Prisler."

"'Works for him'? You don't work for Prisler, as I understand it. You sell your soul to him."

"Will Sayers also told me that Paul Skaggs lived there for a period of time."

"Interesting, Robert, but he just could have been visiting his sister. State has a thick file on Prisler. He's clever, has a bunch of corporations. One gets investigated, he shifts everything into another. He's tight with some of the Middle Eastern countries, Pakistan in particular."

It took Brixton a moment to respond. "You read in today's *Post* that the bomber came from Pakistan?"

"Yeah."

"Paul Skaggs lived on Maui before coming back to D.C."

Kogan leaned back and rubbed his eyes. "That'd be a tough connection to make," he said through a yawn.

"Sure it is. Maybe this guy McQuaid can help make it. As it stands, I don't have anything to link the Skaggs kid to the bombing other than what I saw. What I have to find out first is how long Paul Skaggs was here in D.C. before the bombing, where he was staying, what he was doing. You've got a good line into MPD. Will you make a few inquiries for me?"

"Happy to."

"I appreciate it."

Kogan walked Brixton to the stairwell.

"Why don't you tell those guys downstairs in the restaurant to get an exhaust fan?" Brixton said. "Your office smells like a Thai kitchen."

"I kind of like the smell," Kogan said.

"To each his own. Thanks for the time, Mike. I'll stay in touch."

Kogan returned to his office, sat in his chair, closed

his eyes, and thought about the predicament Brixton was in. He was out on a limb that was quickly snapping off. He'd shot and killed the son of one of the House of Representatives' most powerful voices, Congressman Walter Skaggs, a my-way-or-the-highway politician from Mississippi, chairman of the House's most influential committees, and an unabashed champion of the invasion of Iraq: "I don't give a damn whether those weapons of mass destruction were there or not. Saddam Hussein was evil and had to go. Well, he's gone, and the Iraqi people can live in freedom and peace. We get rid of a few more like him, and maybe this world will be a better place."

Brixton had no one to corroborate his claim that Paul Skaggs had been in the café with the suicide bomber. It was only his word; anyone who could have backed up his story was dead. On top of that, Skaggs's son had been unarmed, carrying only a cell phone in a shiny silver case.

And Brixton had lost a daughter in the bombing.

Unless the ghost of someone who'd died in the bombing came to life and testified that Skaggs had been there, Robert "Don't Call me Bobby" Brixton was dead meat.

And Mike Kogan couldn't do a thing about it.

14

MAUI, HAWAII

Samuel Prisler walked into the dining room of the main house on his twelve-acre estate outside of Kapalua. His acreage jutted out into Honolua Bay and delivered not only spectacular sunsets over the bay and Pacific Ocean, but he could also see the island of Molokai in the distance. The massive table had been set for one; it could accommodate thirty. A fresh vase of red hibiscus had been placed on the table moments before his arrival, along with that day's newspaper, a shortwave radio, and a pink legal pad and Flair pen. His multicolored aloha shirt—reds, yellows, and greens, especially made for him out of imported fabric—was worn loosely over white muslin slacks secured with a drawstring, and he wore sandals. He was an imposing man, well over two hundred pounds and standing six feet three inches tall. A hair transplant, which took on an odd shade of pale orange in certain light, provided cover for his bald pate and hung down over the collar of his shirt and his ears. His face reflected his mixed parentage—European and Hawaiian—strong, angular features and a natural tan.

A member of the staff delivered his breakfast—fresh pineapple, pastries baked that morning in the kitchen, and strong Kona coffee.

"Anything else, sir?" Prisler was asked.

"No, thank you. I'll call when I'm finished."

He tuned the radio to the BBC and listened while nibbling at his food and scanning the local paper. Prisler was addicted to his shortwave radio, taking pleasure at all hours of the day and night hearing reports from around the world. He devoted his total attention to the radio when the announcer reported about the bombing of the café in Washington, D.C. The report ended with: "The father of the young man killed following the bombing, American congressman Walter Skaggs, is pressing for an inquiry into his son's death and into the U.S. State Department agent, Robert Brixton, who shot Paul Skaggs and who alleges that the young man was involved in the bombing. This is BBC World News."

Prisler summoned the young woman who'd served his breakfast to remove the plates. He left the dining room, walked through the expansive living room, and emerged into the front gardens, where a team of landscapers busily tended to a vibrant array of plants and flowers. He walked past them in the direction of a series of three two-story white structures housing thirty small apartments. They bordered a one-story building in which the occupants of the apartments took their meals, attended meetings and seminars hosted by Prisler, and from where his sizable business empire was administered.

He was greeted with great courtesy bordering on reverence by those he passed, some who worked in the complex, others who were on their way to their offices at various Prisler businesses on Hawaii's second largest island. He entered the one-story building and went directly to an area where an attractive young woman sat at a desk just outside a conference room.

"Is Kamea here yet?" Prisler asked.

"No, sir."

Prisler checked his watch. "Call her," he said. "She's late. I'll wait for her inside."

The conference room's walls and floor were covered in bamboo. The oval table that accommodated twenty people was polished to a burnished glow, its armchairs covered in rich tan leather. Two vases of freshly cut red and yellow hibiscus were the only items on the surface.

Prisler took a chair at the head of the table and drummed his fingers on it. He didn't take kindly to people who were late. After five minutes he was about to go back to the receptionist when Kamea Wakatake knocked, then entered the room. "Sorry I'm late," she said. "I was on the phone to the mainland and—"

"Speaking with whom?" Prisler asked.

She hesitated before saying in a low voice, "My mother."

"She called you?"

"Yes."

"About Paul?"

"Yes."

"What did she say?"

"She said—well, she wants me to come home to attend Paul's funeral."

Prisler said nothing, but his stern expression implied a great deal.

Kamea, whose given name was Morgana Skaggs, which she changed her first year living on Maui, avoided Prisler's hard stare as she said, "I told her I didn't think I could."

His face softened, and a small smile crossed his lips.

"Did she accept that?" he asked.

"She was angry."

"Which is to be expected. But she'll get over it. You haven't been home in what, five years?"

Kamea nodded.

"You do remember, of course, why you left home in the first place."

A shadow crossed her round, plain face framed by lank brunette hair. She didn't respond.

"I remember vividly the day you came to see me. You were extremely upset with your family, and your view of yourself was negative, almost suicidal. Do you remember that?"

She nodded.

"My heart went out to you that day, Kamea, but I knew that what the center offered would provide you with the chance to shed the shackles your family had put on you and allow you to grow into the splendid young woman you are today."

"I know," she said, "and I am so appreciative of what you've done for me."

"It's important that you recognize that. The minute you forget it, you are in jeopardy of falling back into your old self-destructive pattern. We wouldn't want that to happen, would we?"

"No, we wouldn't want that to happen."

He sat back, laced his fingers, and rested his chin on his hands. "I must say that I was disappointed in your brother. He did not follow the instructions he was given."

"He was— My mother is very upset."

"And your father?"

Mentioning her father, Congressman Walter Skaggs, caused her thin lips to tremble.

"Your father was at the root of your problems, Kamea. I hope you haven't forgotten that."

"No, I—"

"You've come a long way since deciding to get out

from under his thumb. As you know, it hasn't been easy for you to achieve your freedom from his tyrannical grip. Had your brother followed the instructions he was given, he would have returned to the center. Unfortunately, he paid the price of disobedience."

She started to say something but stopped.

"What is it, Kamea? You're free to speak. We don't keep secrets from each other at the center."

"I . . . I want to go home for the funeral."

His disapproving expression returned. "I'm sorry to hear you say that."

"It's just that—"

"You know that going home will set you back, Kamea. The progress you've made is because you've discarded all the negative baggage your family burdened you with. You've achieved the freedom you so desperately sought when you came to me in California. But if you return home, even for a short visit, you'll quickly slip back into your life the way it was before—misery, anger, questioning whether you even deserved to live. I can't let that happen. I *won't* let that happen."

"Please don't misunderstand," she said in a small voice tinged with pleading. "I know that what you say is true and has always been. I am so grateful for what you and the center have done for me, and for Paul too. But my mother was so upset—I haven't spoken with her for years—and because Paul is dead and I'm their only child and— Oh, I don't know what to do."

Prisler reached and patted her hand. "I know that Paul's unfortunate death has upset you and has upset your mother too. But such things are always out there, poised to undo all the good work that we've accomplished. I want you to go back to your apartment and read The Book. You have always found solace and wisdom in The Book, haven't you?"

"Yes."

"The outside world is a dangerous place, Kamea, especially our own country. It is controlled by evil men—like your father and his ilk—who impose their greed and hatred on all the downtrodden, the millions of decent people in other lands who want desperately to be freed of the slavery our country imposes upon them, including our own people. But we have found a better way here at the center. It is imperative that you not begin to question what is in the Book. Immerse yourself in it, my child, and you will soon feel differently about going home for the funeral. Thomas will hold a ceremony here in Paul's honor within a few days. I'm sure that you will find it a warm and comforting way to remember your dear brother. I'll be away on business, but Thomas will make sure that everything runs smoothly. "

She stared at him with glassy eyes, her body rigid. He stood and beckoned her into his arms. His embrace of her was prolonged.

"Thank you," she said when they disengaged.

"I love you, Kamea. We are your friends here, your *only* friends. Always remember that."

S amuel Prisler claimed both a Ph.D. in behavioral science and a master of divinity, although no graduation certificates adorned his office wall. What he *did* possess was a charismatic personality that convinced others, at least those lacking healthy egos, that his view of mankind and human relations was blessed by some unseen, irrefutable being.

He was born in Hawaii to a German father who'd settled there, married a native wahine, and made a fortune in real estate and sugar processing. They had little contact with their son once he'd become an adult and left the islands to strike out on his own. With a certificate in social work from a California community college, he worked a variety of low-paying jobs, most funded by local government welfare agencies and community churches. But he'd long harbored a dream of establishing a center over which he could reign.

The thousands of disgruntled young people flocking to California in search of an alternative lifestyle, who were also missing a father figure from their lives, provided the human capital that allowed Prisler to turn his dream into reality. The death of his first wife only a year after their marriage—the car she was driving veered off a fog-shrouded California road and plunged into a ravine—and the large insurance payout from a policy he'd taken out on her months earlier, provided him the financial capital to buy the land on the California coast and to officially begin the Prisler Center for Healing. Crash investigators initially questioned whether some of his wife's injuries would have been caused by the accident, but their speculations were dismissed.

The twenty lost souls who comprised his first batch of followers were recruited from the churches and welfare programs with which he'd worked. Prisler rented trailers to house them as they set out to build permanent structures. Those who found jobs in the area contributed their salaries and wages to the center and recruited new members. Their number grew to more than thirty. The center's buildings took shape. At the same time, California authorities began to investigate the center's claim that it was a legitimate religious sect and exempt from taxation. Too, a disillusioned member bolted from the center and told a local newspaper reporter that Prisler sexually abused some of the younger male members of the cult.

Sparked by the resulting article, the authorities brought increasing pressure on Prisler and his center.

As he struggled to ward off their attempts to tax him and the organization, and their probes into charges of sexual abuse, fate and human frailty intervened. His father died in Maui, and while his will directed that most of his wealth go to relatives in Germany—Prisler's mother had died two years earlier—he left his twelve-acre estate on Maui to his only child, Samuel T. Prisler.

Prisler didn't hesitate to pack up the California complex. With his loyal acolytes in tow, he moved the Prisler Center for Healing to the island of Maui and the spectacular tract with its ocean views, stunning sunsets, moderate climate, ample sunshine, and, he hoped, a less contentious legal situation. As the membership rolls swelled, he invested in various businesses—real estate, restaurants, a fishing charter service, and gift shops. It was during this period of impressive growth that Morgana Skaggs, daughter of U.S. congressman Walter Skaggs, fell under his spell.

Prisler returned to his office in the main house after Kamea left the conference room, and he pondered the conversation they'd had. He'd sensed a growing anxiety in her over the past six months and had increased the number of her group therapy sessions—long, brutally confrontational sessions in which the center's philosophies as contained in The Book were hammered home, souls laid bare, tears flowed, and wails of anguish reverberated within the four soundproofed walls of the facility. At the end of these sessions, the participants were left exhausted, bodies drenched in sweat, minds dulled. But there was also the requisite hugging of "friends," as cult members were called, and negative thoughts that anyone had brought to the session were left on the floor, wrung from their spent bodies and minds, and all was well again.

Prisler checked his watch. He had to get ready for the trip he would take in the morning to Washington, where he would meet with his own private lobby, two men who oversaw his interests there and whose allegiance to Prisler was unassailable, not because they came under his charismatic spell, but because they were highly paid to keep tabs on the nation's capital and how its machinations might affect his operation.

Before leaving the office, he called his second-in-command, Hawaiian-born Thomas Akina. Akina had signed on with Prisler from his earliest days on Maui and had earned his trust—to the extent that Prisler trusted anyone.

"Thomas, it's Sam. I've just met with Kamea. She's naturally upset over her brother's death, but I'm afraid that her faith in the center and its mission is wavering. I want you to keep an especially keen eye on her while I'm gone. Pay particular attention to the tap on her phone, and don't allow any mail to reach her without reading it first."

"I'll see to it, Sam," Akina assured.

15

When Brixton swung by Marylee's house to drop off the photos of Janet, he was relieved that her new husband, Miles Lashka, wasn't there. Jill answered the door, and he followed her in to where Marylee and two neighbors sat in the kitchen. Marylee introduced Brixton to the other women, who took his presence as an excuse to go.

"I can't thank you enough," Marylee said to them as they left. "You define what good neighbors are all about."

Brixton handed her the envelope with the photos. She took them out, carefully studied them, then began to cry.

"Yeah, it's tough looking at them," he said, squeezing the bridge of his nose. He waited until her tears had subsided before asking, "How are plans for the funeral coming along?"

She answered by handing him a printed sheet from a local funeral parlor on which the schedule was detailed: The closed casket would be on display for two days beginning tomorrow at two in the afternoon. The church service would follow the final day of viewing—if you could call it that—and burial in the Greene family plot.

"It sounds fine," he said.

"I dread it," she said.

"I know."

"How are you, Robert?"

"Me? I'm taking it day by day."

"You're in trouble, aren't you?"

"Trouble? What trouble?"

"The congressman's son that you shot. They say that—"

"I'm tired of hearing what *they* say, Marylee. I *know* that the kid was involved in the bombing. I just have to prove it."

She went to a small desk in the corner of the kitchen and returned holding a copy of the local newspaper.

He assumed that she wanted him to read an obituary of Janet. But a cartoon in the lower right-hand corner told a different story. It was of a man who looked somewhat like him. The cartoon character wore a large six-gallon Stetson. He held two pistols. Smoke came from both. One hung at his side. The other was held to his mouth as he blew away the smoke. The character had a satisfied grin on his face. A badge on his shirtfront read STATE DEPARTMENT AGENT.

Brixton dropped the paper on the table in disgust.

"I'm so embarrassed," she said.

"Embarrassed?" he said in a voice more angry than he'd intended. "You believe what *they* say?"

"He wasn't even armed, Robert. All he had was a cell phone."

"That's right. He had a cell phone—and blood on his hands, our daughter's blood."

"Will there be media at the service?"

"I have no idea and I don't care. Look, Marylee, I didn't come here to have you sit in judgment about something you don't know squat about. I came here to deliver the pictures and—"

His raised voice brought Jill into the kitchen. "Why are you yelling at Mom?" she demanded of him.

"I wasn't yelling, I was— Oh, what the hell, thanks for the information about the funeral. I'll see you both there."

Once he got into the car, his anger was more directed at himself than at his ex-wife. She had the innate ability to bring out the worst in him, although he also acknowledged that the worst of him was there to begin with.

He looked back at the house before he drove away, and realized that apart from their two daughters, his marriage to Marylee meant little. It was as if their four years together in D.C., when he was a uniformed cop, had never happened. This big white house, the manicured lawn, the fancy cars in the driveway defined Marylee and her family. It meant nothing to him. He was neither nostalgic nor envious, but detached from what had been a momentary blip in his life.

He thought of Flo Combes and hoped that she would follow through on her offer and come to Washington. She was present tense. She was reality.

As he drove toward the District and his scheduled meeting with the retired Justice Department lawyer Charles McQuaid, he was struck with a renewed sense of purpose. When with Marylee and his daughters, he tended to shrink into a defensive shell. He'd done the same thing since the shooting of Paul Skaggs, talking a good game but unsure of whether he could play that game and pull out a victory. He didn't feel that way now. He knew that he was right. He also knew that there were people who could give him the answers he sought, and he was committed to seeking them out and exonerating himself.

He owed it to Janet.

When he'd called Charles McQuaid about meeting, McQuaid seemed pleased to hear from him.

"So you're a pal of Will Sayers," the retired Justice Department official had said.

"Afraid so," Brixton had said, laughing to lighten the comment.

"He's a character, that's for sure," said McQuaid. "Of course, I knew about you before he called. I read the papers."

"I try not to read them," Brixton had said. "I really appreciate the chance to get together. Have any time available today?"

"I always have time. That's an advantage of retirement, Mr. Brixton. Or maybe a curse. Too much time. Sure, come on by. You get seasick easily?"

"No. And please call me Robert. But not Bobby. I have a thing about that."

"Fair enough, Robert. But you can call me Charlie."

"Sounds like a deal."

"Good. We'll take a spin in my boat, have some lunch and a few drinks, and talk about Mr. Samuel Prisler."

McQuaid lived in a modest ranch house in the southwest quadrant of Washington, the city's waterfront area and the location of myriad fish restaurants and markets. As Brixton drove up he saw why McQuaid lived there. Across the street was a boatyard at which a few dozen craft were docked, some approaching the size of a luxury yacht, most of them smaller boats that Brixton associated with middle-class families who enjoyed a Saturday on the water after a week working mundane jobs. Brixton knew that the area attracted many government workers because of the moderately priced homes, and he assumed that McQuaid had been drawn to the area for that reason, as well as a convenient place to park his boat.

The man who answered the door was small in stature. Even his face seemed smaller than average, although Brixton had no idea what an average-sized face was. McQuaid wore glasses tethered by a red cord around his neck, pale blue jeans that were too big for his frame, a yellow T-shirt with I'D RATHER BE FISHING written on his chest, and shoes commonly known as Top-Siders. For a small man, his handshake was firm. He enthusiastically greeted Brixton and led him to the kitchen that overlooked the boatyard.

"Trouble finding it?" McQuaid asked.

"No, no trouble at all. I take it that you enjoy fishing."

"I love anything involving the water, although I don't fish anymore. I used to bring home some beauties, gut 'em, fillet 'em, and cook 'em for dinner. But since my wife died, I don't enjoy cleaning fish. Take-out from the restaurants around here does just fine. Beer? Whiskey? Coke?"

"A beer would be fine."

They settled at the kitchen table with their beers. McQuaid raised his can to Brixton's. "Here's to life," he said, "or what's left of it."

Brixton wasn't sure what to say in response but clicked his can against McQuaid's.

"Let's get the unpleasantness out of the way," McQuaid said. "I am very sorry about what happened to your daughter."

"Thanks. I appreciate that."

"I have three grown children, all living in different parts of the country, two grandchildren too, and another on the way."

"I have one, a grandson. I don't see much of him.

My wife and I were divorced a long time ago. My daughters—daughter—lives in Maryland with her son. My wife remarried."

"When I read about what happened to you, I became angry, damned angry. I felt as though I knew you. And when Will Sayers called and asked if I'd agree to meet with you, I didn't hesitate to say yes. I don't know if I can be any help, but I certainly want to try."

"Can't ask for more than that," Brixton said, realizing how much he liked this man after only a few minutes.

McQuaid took a healthy swig of his beer and said, "I made up some sandwiches—hope you like tuna fish; it's on fresh rye bread—and potato salad made by my neighbor. Best potato salad I've ever tasted, plenty of beer too in the cooler, and chips." He stood. "Let's go. They say there's a front coming through later today. No sense getting ourselves wet."

McQuaid's boat was smaller than Brixton had anticipated, eighteen feet long, according to its owner, and had been meticulously maintained. The hull was painted a vivid red; the wooden canopy above the controls was a glistening white.

"It's more like a small fishing dragger," McQuaid said as he went through his machinations to prepare the craft to leave the dock. "Not fancy or sleek like most boats this size, but I prefer it, like its classic lines. It's all wood, no plastic; takes more work to keep her shipshape but worth it."

Brixton had to smile at McQuaid's immense pride in his little boat. Brixton didn't care about boats and had no interest in owning one. Marylee had wanted them to buy one when they were married, but he'd balked— "Nothing but work," he'd said—which sent her into a two-day pout. But he did enjoy going out on other peoples' boats, and he found himself relaxing as

McQuaid guided the small craft along the Washington Channel and into the Potomac River, the breeze playing on his face, the rumble of the engine pleasing to his ear, like a low, sensual voice of a sexy woman. The boat was named *Alicia* after McQuaid's deceased wife. "I couldn't name her after my girlfriend, now could I?" he'd quipped as he stood proudly at the wheel, every bit the captain in command.

A half hour after leaving the boatyard McQuaid pulled into a shallow inlet and dropped anchor. "Hungry?" he said.

"Yeah," Brixton replied, "hungry for information about Samuel Prisler."

"I'll feed you plenty of that," McQuaid said. "Let's sit down and eat—and talk. First of all, tell me what *you* know about Prisler."

"Not much. I'm told he runs some sort of cult on Maui in Hawaii. He's also been accused of being an arms dealer. That's it."

"Not a bad start, Mr. Brixton. You're right on both accounts. Sam Prisler is an evil guy, a twisted son of a bitch, the Antichrist, if you're into that sort of thing."

Brixton was taken by McQuaid's bluntness. "I'm not into higher beings," Brixton said, "but go ahead. I'm listening."

While McQuaid methodically set up their lunch on a small folding table, each item placed just so, napkins neatly folded, plastic utensils lined up with the napkins' edges—Charles McQuaid was obviously a well-organized man—he spoke about Samuel Prisler and the years he'd spent at the Justice Department trying to build a case against him.

"I suppose you could say that Prisler became an obsession of mine," McQuaid said. "I used to get kidded a lot about it when I was at Justice. I deserved it, I guess. I even took trips to Maui to try and dig up information about him from the locals there, used my vacation time for my wife and me to make those trips, and on my dime, I might add."

"What was it about Prisler that caused you to—well, to become so obsessed about him?"

McQuaid laughed. "You mean to cause me to go off the deep end?"

Brixton added his own laugh. "I didn't put it that way."

"Wouldn't bother me if you did," McQuaid said. "It's hard to explain, Robert. I spent most of my later years at Justice in a division whose responsibilities included building cases against arms dealers. We worked with the CIA and other intelligence groups, although it's never easy to get disparate government agencies to cooperate with each other. The arms smuggling world is a fascinating one. These smugglers share a few things in common, like a total disregard for who their weapons end up slaughtering, and a penchant for being able to rationalize the morality of what they do. It doesn't matter to them who ends up with the weapons, what their goals are, or who pays the tab. As far as gunrunners are concerned, they're helping to right wrongs, giving honorable people the wherewithal to accomplish what *they* consider to be lofty aims. Sometimes it works out that way. The overthrow of a brutal dictatorship is an example. The common people, the downtrodden and disenfranchised, take up arms and bring down a despot. That's a pretty lofty aim, isn't it, helping oppressed people achieve freedom through democracy?"

"You're talking to the wrong guy about lofty aims and bringing down tyrants. That's the way politicians talk. I avoid politics."

"That in itself is a lofty aim, Robert," McQuaid said, laughing and emptying more potato chips from the bag onto a paper plate. "But there's really no way to escape politics, especially here in Washington, D.C. The point is that there are times when arming people, even when done illegally, can be justified. But then there are times when those being armed are anything but noble. Those are the people who use arms and munitions to kill the innocent, to terrorize—people such as the young woman who blew up that café and killed your daughter, and those who provided her with the weapon. Those people are Samuel Prisler's clients, Robert. He sells weapons and munitions to terrorists."

Brixton ate a few chips and finished his beer while McQuaid carefully gathered up the remnants of lunch and placed them in a plastic bag.

"Let me ask you something," Brixton said. "You talk as though you've got the goods on Prisler. You and the people you worked with at the Justice Department spent how many years building a case—five, ten?"

"More like five."

"Okay, so you spent five years trying to nail the guy. Why didn't you?"

McQuaid smiled. "You're asking why we failed?"

"I suppose you could say that."

"A number of factors, Robert. First, it wasn't as though we had a large department whose only job was to make a case against arms dealers. Far from it. There were just a few of us, and every time we thought we might be getting close, we were pulled off to deal with another case. We were always shorthanded; other priorities kept coming up."

Brixton interrupted him. "What could be a more important priority than making a case against a guy who arms terrorists, the same people who are out to kill us all? I lost a daughter to one of them. Maybe the bomb that young Islamic woman used was provided by Samuel Prisler."

Another McQuaid smile, more rueful this time.

"That's always a possibility, although Prisler isn't the only man providing weapons to terrorists." He paused and seemed to Brixton to be weighing what he would say next. Content that he had the right words, he said, "You say that you have no interest in politics. I envy that. Working for the Justice Department—for any government department, for that matter—is all politics, or so it sometimes seems. Not only is Sam Prisler a very clever man—of all the arms dealers I've tracked, he's the absolute best at covering his tracks—he also knows how to curry favor with those who call the shots."

"Politicians?"

"Certain ones. He has a number of them in his pocket, including . . ."

Brixton cocked his head.

". . . including Congressman Walter Skaggs."

Brixton sat back and bit his lip. He said, "Skaggs is in Prisler's pocket?"

"According to what I've learned. Of course, Skaggs wrapped himself in the flag when derailing any progress we were making in building a case against Prisler. It was always something about national security—isn't that the usual convenient reason? Skaggs's staff claimed that Prisler was in sensitive negotiations with freedom-loving groups in the Middle East and that we were to do nothing to jeopardize those negotiations. Skaggs has always been a law-and-order man, a hawk when it came to the so-called war on terror, a real saber rattler. Of course, he never personally interfered with me or my colleagues, but the higher-ups got the message. They knew which side of the bread was buttered for them. Skaggs's committee holds the purse strings for Justice. You don't bite the hand that feeds you." McQuaid laughed. "My dear departed wife always said that I was too fond of clichés."

"They're okay if they get the point across."

"Exactly my thinking. You do know that Skaggs has a daughter who lives inside the Prisler cult and works for him?"

"Yeah. Will Sayers filled me in on that. I also know that the guy I shot, Paul Skaggs, the congressman's son, spent some time on Maui with his sister, which means he also spent time with Prisler." Brixton processed what he'd just been told. "What I don't get is that if Skaggs is in Prisler's pocket, as you claim, and Prisler had something to with Skaggs's son accompanying the young girl into the café just before she blew the place up, why wouldn't Skaggs be out for Prisler's scalp?"

"Maybe between us we can get answers to that question and others. I may be retired, Robert, but that doesn't mean I've stopped looking into Prisler's dealings. In a sense, having gotten out from under the yoke of working for the Justice Department has freed me up to keep digging without anyone looking over my shoulder. I've put together quite a set of files since retiring. I'm happy to share what's in those files with you."

"Mind if I ask why you'd do that for me?" Brixton asked.

"As I said when you first arrived, I became angry when I read about what had happened to you, the loss of your daughter, and the incident with Congressman Skaggs's son."

"You believe me when I say that Paul Skaggs was with the suicide bomber, and that I shot him because I thought he was holding a weapon?"

"Why wouldn't I believe you, Robert? I know that Paul Skaggs spent considerable time with Sam Prisler in Hawaii. His sister has been with Prisler for years. Prisler runs a cult in addition to dealing arms and munitions to terrorists. Those facts don't necessarily add up, of course, to linking Prisler to the café bombing. But I'd say that there is that possibility. Wouldn't you?"

"A possibility? Yes. But nothing more than that."

"Unless you can nail down the link."

When Brixton didn't respond, McQuaid continued. "I told you that I was well aware of you and the dilemma you're in before Will Sayers called and asked that we get together. I should have also mentioned that I had your FBI file pulled. You've had an interesting life: four years with the Washington PD, twenty years with the police in Savannah, your marital history, the woman you've most recently been involved with, a Ms. Combes, I believe."

Brixton stared at McQuaid.

"There was also, of course, your fracas with a member of the Russian consulate in New York City, and we can never overlook the case you worked on here in D.C. that struck fear in the heart of the city's leading social hostess and in the hearts of the occupants of the White House itself."

"Why did you go to the bother?" Brixton asked, feeling both offended and impressed.

"Let me put it this way, Robert. I'm afraid that unless I can finish what I've started where Samuel Prisler is concerned, I'll never enjoy a peaceful death. From everything I've read about you, one of your trademarks is tenaciousness. I admire that. I also assume that you have sufficient motive to want to get to the bottom of your daughter's tragic death. If that involved Prisler, I'm sure that you'd like to see justice done."

McQuaid turned from Brixton and peered into the western sky. "That front's coming in faster than was forecast. We'd better be getting back."

The two men didn't speak during the return trip to the dock, where McQuaid secured his boat and deposited garbage in a bin. He'd been right; the rain started coming down the minute they walked into McQuaid's house.

"I apologize if I've confused you, Robert," McQuaid said. "It's obvious that I'm obsessive about Samuel Prisler."

"Apologize for what, wanting to rid the world of somebody like him?"

"For being presumptuous about you," McQuaid replied.

The retired Justice Department lawyer walked from the kitchen and motioned for Brixton to follow him. They went into a small room off the kitchen that served as McQuaid's home office. Like the rest of the house and the boat, the room was neat. File folders on the desk were lined up square with each other. A computer occupied the center of the desk, along with two cordless phones in their bases.

"Sorry for the mess," McQuaid said, indicating a chair on which other file folders rested.

Brixton laughed. "You call this a mess?" he said.

"I don't usually leave things on chairs," McQuaid replied as he removed the files and indicated that Brixton should sit there, "but when I knew that you were coming I pulled out folders whose contents I thought you'd be interested in seeing."

Brixton opened the first folder and started reading.

"Coffee?" McQuaid asked. "Another beer?"

"Nothing, thanks," Brixton said.

McQuaid left Brixton alone in the office for twenty minutes. When he returned, Brixton said, "I'm having trouble keeping track of Prisler's corporations."

"Many of them are shells," McQuaid said. "As I told you, he's a clever man, always a few steps ahead of those looking into his business dealings."

"Maybe if I had more time to make sense of it," Brixton said.

"I'd suggest we stay and give you all the time you need, but I'm afraid I have to leave. My younger sister lives in Maryland, and I try to visit with her as often as possible. She's very ill—terminal cancer."

"I'm sorry to hear that," Brixton said.

"But how about you coming back tomorrow, say, for dinner? Those files you've been looking at are only the tip of the iceberg. I've put together a lot of information about Prisler's cult that you should see."

"Sure I won't be intruding?" Brixton asked.

"Not at all. It will be my pleasure. I see from the FBI file on you that you're a martini drinker."

"They even know that about me?"

"Afraid so, Robert. You should pay cash for your drinks. You have a preference in vodka?"

"Vodka? I'm a purist when it comes to martinis. Nothing but gin."

"Then gin it shall be. See you at five tomorrow?"

"I'll be here. Thanks for being so open with me, Charles."

"My pleasure, Robert. Maybe between us we can take Mr. Samuel Prisler down. And call me Charlie."

16

Brixton drove from McQuaid's house to Arlington, where he decided to drop in on Mike Kogan. He was in luck; Kogan was alone in his office.

"How are you doing, Robert?" his boss asked.

"Okay, I suppose. I've got Janet's funeral coming up. If anyone suggested that I'd be attending my daughter's funeral, I'd have called them nuts. But it's true. It'll be a closed casket because . . ." He fought against the catch in his voice.

Kogan said, "I made some inquiries at MPD about Paul Skaggs and his movements after returning to D.C. from Hawaii."

"I appreciate that, Mike. What did you come up with?"

"Not a lot. I did learn that he stopped off in New York City before coming here."

"Why?"

Kogan shrugged. "Airline records show that he flew from Hawaii to JFK three weeks before the bombing."

"How long did he stay in New York?"

"I don't know. I had my guy at MPD check plane, train, and rental-car records for the time between his arrival in New York and the bombing. Nothing."

"What did he do, walk here?"

"Or got a ride with someone."

"Why didn't I think of that? Who do you figure drove him?"

"Maybe he hitched a ride."

"I just came from a meeting with Charles McQuaid. I told you about him."

"Was he helpful?"

"Yeah, he was. I'm going back tomorrow for dinner and to go through material he's developed on Samuel Prisler. Did your PD contact have any info on where Paul Skaggs went and what he did once he was back in D.C.?"

"Just one thing, Robert. He got a traffic ticket a week before the bombing."

"He had a car?"

"Not his. Skaggs couldn't produce the registration, said it belonged to someone else—Zafar Alvi."

"Sounds Middle Eastern."

"Yeah, it is. You know about him, Robert?"

"No."

"He's a big shot in the Arab-American community here in D.C., an Iraqi, although he's wired into the Pakistan and Afghanistan embassies."

"And he loans his car to the Skaggs kid?"

"Evidently, unless Skaggs stole it." Kogan laughed. "I kind of doubt that. Aside from knowing that Skaggs was driving a borrowed car during the weeks before the bombing, MPD says there's no record of him, no credit-card use, nothing to indicate where he stayed—zippo, like he didn't exist."

"Maybe this guy Alvi rented him a room," Brixton said. "You have an address for him?"

"It's on this slip." He handed it to Brixton, who saw that the car Skaggs had been driving was registered to Zafar Alvi on Thirty-first Street NW, on the fringes of Georgetown.

"Thanks, Mike. I appreciate this."

"Just don't stick your neck out too far, Robert. By the way, you heard about another murder of an embassy employee?"

"No."

"A guy from the French embassy on Reservoir Road. He was found this morning in Rock Creek Park, shot twice."

"Anything else about him?"

"DSS is having a briefing. I'll know more then." He checked his watch. "I'd better get over to State. I wish your situation would resolve itself, Robert. With embassy people dropping like flies, I could really use you."

Brixton left the building with Kogan and watched him get into his car and head for the State Department. The rain had let up; it was more of a mist-cum-fog that hung over the area. He paused to look at faded color photographs of featured dishes in the window of the Thai restaurant, which didn't tempt him. Among many rules Robert Brixton had adopted over the years was to never eat in a restaurant that had color pictures of its food in the window.

Since signing on with SITQUAL, he'd explored Arlington watering holes. There were plenty of them near where he lived on Capitol Hill, but he was turned off by too much political talk, too many cocksure young men in suits and self-assured young women, all basking in the glow of the politicians they worked for. Working for a member of Congress never seemed to Brixton to be cause for celebration or ego gratification. Besides, the crowd that gathered at those watering holes tended to be twenty-somethings, a demographic with which he wasn't comfortable. Not that he considered himself old. At fifty-one and with a full head of coarse gray hair that he wore in a modified crew cut, he was confident that he could take any of them one-on-one. Not that any of them were issuing any challenges. Still, not a workout freak, he exercised regularly and had managed to keep his midsection fairly flat.

He'd liked Eventide's rooftop bar, and its next-door neighbor Spider Kelly's. But he finally settled on the downstairs bar at the Liberty Tavern on Arlington's Wilson Boulevard strip, preferring its dark atmosphere (which often matched his mood) and the quiet professionalism of its adult bartenders. He also appreciated its clientele, who tended to keep to themselves and didn't consider conversation a requisite for enjoying a drink.

"How are you, Robert?" the bartender asked as Brixton slid onto a barstool.

"I'm okay. My knee's acting up, but otherwise okay."

"The usual?"

"Sounds good to me."

The bartender delivered Brixton's cold, dry martini, shaken and served with a lemon twist, and said, "I've been reading about you and that bombing. I was really sorry to hear about your daughter."

"Thanks," Brixton said. He tasted the drink and said, "Perfection!"

"What I'd like to know is why Congressman Skaggs's kid was there with that suicide bomber."

"You and me both," Brixton said.

The bartender sensed that Brixton wasn't in the mood to discuss it and moved away to the other end of the bar, leaving his customer to enjoy his drink—and to ponder the jumbled bits of information he'd received and how they fit together—if they even did.

Before his suspension, he'd come to the conclusion

that SITQUAL's primary mission was to make it look as though the State Department was serious about protecting the foreign diplomatic corps that calls Washington, D.C., its home away from home. Not that adding a dozen agents was impressive. DSS already had more than two thousand agents dispersed throughout the world, protecting the secretary of state and America's diplomatic contingent in every nation in which State had a presence. The uniformed division of the Secret Service also played a role in providing security for visiting dignitaries, as did the Washington MPD and the Capitol Hill Police. SITQUAL had been lauded to D.C.'s foreign embassies as an elite organization whose only purpose was to enhance protection for the embassies and their people. But from what Brixton had experienced, SITQUAL was more like a small-town police department, rescuing stranded cats from trees and breaking up late-night parties that got too noisy for the neighbors. Or for investigating purse snatchings and biased graffiti.

But the stakes had obviously grown bigger.

Until now he'd felt that the Germans were wrong in trying to link the two deaths of its embassy people. A couple of their people get murdered, one in New York, the other in Washington, and they're about to declare war. He'd been convinced that Peter Müller had been the victim of a shooter who was out to kill a homosexual, and maybe Adelina Dabrowski's murder was for the same twisted reason. Then again, her death could have been nothing more than a sexual assault gone bad, the work of a whack job who got into her apartment by pretending to be there to repair her air-conditioning. Her sexual orientation might not have meant anything to a rapist who saw a pretty girl and decided to attack her.

What it had come down to for Brixton was that those

two disparate acts of violence didn't justify the German government trying to link them to some sort of terrorist plot.

But now that had changed.

Apart from Peter Müller, Adelina Dabrowski, and the dead German in New York City, there was now the Italian embassy staffer named Conti, and this most recent murder of someone from the French embassy. Was the Frenchman a homosexual? The newspaper report of Conti's murder had said that he'd eaten alone in a restaurant before venturing into the park, and had been a lover of art. Did that mean anything? Were these murders because of the victims' sexual orientation?

Brixton no longer thought so.

They were all employed by foreign embassies in Washington, D.C. That had to mean something.

Like parts of a large jigsaw puzzle, other bits of information occupied his thoughts as he sipped his martini and turned each item around in his mind, trying to make it fit into the picture.

Will Sayers had mentioned a pending homosexual scandal involving Congressman Ken Wisher and that a possible sexual partner of the congressman was Eduardo "Lalo" Reyes, Peter Müller's lover. When Brixton and Donna Salvos interviewed Reyes, he'd mentioned that among the places he'd lived was Hawaii. Not that that meant anything in and of itself. Lots of people lived in Hawaii. But Reyes, an embassy staffer himself, was involved with one of the embassy staffers who'd been killed, and Brixton made a mental note to take a stab at talking to the young Spaniard again.

Having stopped in to see Mike Kogan paid off in some new information about Paul Skaggs and his movements prior to the bombing. Brixton now knew that Skaggs had returned to Washington via New York City and had most likely traveled between New York and D.C.

in someone's car. Had this man, Zafar Alvi, provided the transportation? The congressman's son was obviously Alvi's friend; he'd been given Alvi's car to tool around Washington in. Zafar Alvi was Middle Eastern. Who was he? Was he involved in some way in planning and carrying out the bombing in the café? There was nothing tangible to say that he was, but it was a question that Brixton had to answer.

Having been put in touch with a retired Justice Department attorney was a bit of good fortune. Charlie McQuaid obviously knew as much as there was to know about Samuel Prisler, his cult, and his arms dealings with terrorists. There was nothing to tie Prisler to the bombing, though, and Brixton knew it. But as he finished his drink, he became more convinced than ever that there had to be a connection. Paul Skaggs had lived on Prisler's compound prior to returning to Washington and aiding in the bombing. His sister had lived and worked with Prisler for years. Prisler was suspected of being an arms dealer who sold to terrorists.

There had to be a connection.

He was tempted to order a second drink but conquered the impulse. Ever since Mothers Against Drunk Driving (MADD) launched its public-awareness campaign, he'd starting walking away from bars before ordering another. He thought of Mac Smith having lost his wife and son to a drunk driver and shared his anger at the lenient sentence the driver had received. Besides, he didn't need a DWI. Bad for the image of a dedicated representative of the United States government.

When he and Asal Banai had parted company after their drink together, she'd given him her phone number. He pulled out his cell phone and dialed it.

"Robert Brixton here. Hope I'm not disturbing anything important."

"Oh, hello, Robert. No, nothing important. I'm reading an excellent book about how the battle of Fallujah in Iraq was fought. It was such a peaceful city until the fighting began. Most of the city was destroyed."

"'War is hell.' Somebody said that."

"One of your Civil War generals, I believe. General Sherman?"

"Yeah, it was probably him. Doesn't matter who said it, it's true. I was wondering if you were free for dinner tonight. I know this is last minute but . . ."

Her laugh was warm and inviting. "You've saved me from having to eat leftovers. I would love to have dinner with you."

"Great. Any suggestions?"

"Since I'm in Foggy Bottom, not far from your State Department, I recommend the Founding Farmers restaurant on Pennsylvania. It's very good. I go there often for salads."

"A half hour?"

"That will be fine. It's between Nineteenth and Twentieth Streets."

"I'll find it, Ms. Banai."

"But I'll only come if you call me Asal."

"It's a deal."

Just don't call me Bobby, he thought as he ended the call, paid his tab, got in his car, and drove across the Arlington Memorial Bridge into the District.

CHAPTER

17

Brixton was on edge when he drove to the restaurant. He was still getting calls from the media, each fueling his irritation. It wasn't that he resented reporters doing their job. He'd come to the conclusion during his tenure in Washington, D.C., that the media was probably the only true check-and-balance on government. Its frequent excesses were dismaying, of course, but at least someone was looking into what the government was doing without their reelection chances dictating their views and decisions. But the constant bird-dogging by the press—and the reporters asking the same questions over and over even though he'd just answered them—tried the little patience he had left.

The relaxing evening he looked forward to with Asal Banai kept getting pushed to the back of his mind by recent events. He dreaded Janet's funeral—what father wouldn't?—but it was complicated by the horrible way that she'd died. He'd have to look down at the closed casket and envision her smiling face, lip ring and all, her verve for life, her determination to find her own way (with occasional help from Daddy). Too, there was the strained relationship with Marylee. What would her new husband, Miles Lashka, have to say at the funeral? Maybe he, her natural father, should have planned to speak. Too late now. Besides, public speaking ranked right up there along with weddings with loud, obnoxious DJs as situations to avoid. He also felt a modicum of guilt for not having insisted on being part of making the funeral arrangements. But he also knew that it was best to stay out of Marylee's way. Her anger at what had happened was also directed at him; his jaded approach to life, death, and religious rites wouldn't have been appreciated.

He was juggling the new information he'd recently learned from Mike Kogan, Willis Sayers, and Charles McQuaid as he found a parking spot a block away and walked into the restaurant. For a moment he had regretted having made the date with Asal. But seeing her seated at the table, the lighting casting her in a flattering light, a wide smile on her face, mitigated any previous unpleasant thoughts.

"I'm not late, am I?" he asked as he took the chair opposite her.

She looked at her watch. "Right on time," she said. "Did you have trouble parking?"

"No. I never do. I was born with a gene that always seems to find a parking space."

"I wish I had that gene."

"No you don't. It also assures that somebody will dent my car or knock the side-view mirror cockeyed."

She laughed softly.

"You look exhausted," she said.

"Do I? Yeah, I guess I am."

It wasn't a sleepy tired. He didn't need a nap to

recharge his batteries, wasn't sleep deprived. What he did need was to rewind the clock to the time just before he'd made the date with his daughter. If he'd been a motion-picture director, he would have left all the film shot from that moment to the present on the cutting-room floor. Failing that, he would at least feel whole again if he could confront the suicide bomber and Congressman Skaggs's son, ask them questions, maybe gain some understanding of why they did what they did. Of course, he also knew that unlike some people who lose a loved one to a shooter, deranged or not, he wouldn't be content to just ask questions. He'd have to strike out at them. He admired those who could display compassion for murderer and victim alike, but he wasn't there yet, probably never would be. Finding answers from Paul Skaggs and the woman he'd abetted was impossible, of course. What was done was done. Robert Brixton might feel exhausted for the rest of his life.

"What you're going through must really take its toll," Asal said, seeming to read his mind.

"I try not to admit it," he said, "but I'm not always successful. Enough of this. I see that you have a head start on me."

She smiled and picked up her glass of white wine. "I arrived early," she said. "Hope you don't mind."

"Not at all." He motioned for a waitress and ordered his martini.

"What is new about the congressman's son?" she asked, after he'd been served and they'd touched the rims of their glasses.

"Not much," he replied. He wanted to share what he'd recently learned with someone, and Asal's openness and encouraging smile prompted him to do that. But he held back. Instead, he asked something he'd thought about while driving there. "You read that the young woman who blew up the café was here from Pakistan on a student visa."

"Yes."

"A phony one. How does that work? You told me that one of the things your organization does is to arrange for students from the Middle East to come here to study."

"That's right, although it's not the only thing we do."

"No, I'm sure it's not. You bring students here only from Iraq?"

"No."

"Other Arab countries, like—I don't know—Jordan, Saudi Arabia, and Pakistan, places like that?"

Her smile faded. "They aren't all Arabs," she said, "but they are from that part of the world. Yes, we arrange for them to come from other Middle Eastern countries, like Pakistan."

"I'm just wondering how somebody like this young kid gets a set of bogus papers that are good enough to enter the country. She gets here and disappears. How does that happen?"

"I don't have an answer for that, Robert," she said, and sipped her wine.

He shook his head and drank, too. "Who checks on these foreign students?" he asked. "How does the process work overseas? Who makes sure that they're legit? How does your organization know that a student you sponsor isn't coming here to kill Americans?"

Her sigh said that she wasn't pleased with the direction the conversation was taking.

"I'm not suggesting anything," he said defensively. "Maybe your people in those countries do a good job screening young applicants, and I'm sure that you and your agency are careful about who gets entry visas. But I've been gathering information all day, Asal. I need all the info I can get."

"I understand," she said and handed him the menu that had been placed on the table.

"What do you suggest?" he asked, aware that she'd deliberately shifted gears.

"I usually have the Late Harvest salad," she said.

Brixton wasn't a salad guy, at least not as a main course. He told the waitress what Asal had ordered, and chose a Southern Fried Chicken salad for him. "I never had fried chicken in a salad," he said smiling; he wanted to break the tension that had developed over the past few minutes.

"So," he said, "how was your day?"

"Busy, and it isn't over. I have a meeting to attend after dinner."

Brixton wasn't sure whether he was disappointed that they wouldn't be able to extend the evening or relieved. While he was attracted to Asal Banai, he was too battered by conflicting emotions and figments of information, none of which added up to anything definitive, to contemplate romance.

Their meals arrived, and they ate in silence aside from an occasional "How's your salad?" or "This is good." The truth was that he'd lost his appetite and looked forward to when they would leave.

She sensed his mood.

"I wasn't upset about you asking how students get here under false pretenses," she said. "I know that you are looking for answers. I assure you that the students we help come here to the United States to study are carefully vetted."

He was glad she'd brought them back to the subject.

"I don't doubt that," he said, "but maybe you can help me understand. I'm still considered a murderer of an innocent young man who also happens to be the son of a powerful congressman."

She took a few bites of her salad before saying, "The

young Pakistani woman who blew up the café—and your daughter—wasn't one of our students. The minute she was identified in the press, we checked. We'd never heard of her."

Brixton nodded, patted his mouth with his napkin, and pushed his half-eaten salad away. "Do you know anything about a man in Hawaii named Samuel Prisler?"

"No. Who is he?"

"Just somebody I've been told about. There's another guy I've got to track down."

"Who is that?"

"His name is Alvi. I have his first name." He pulled out the slip of paper Kogan had given him. Zafar Alvi."

She stared blankly at him.

"The congressman's kid, Paul Skaggs, was driving this guy's car here in D.C. before the bombing. His name is Middle Eastern."

She said nothing and took a bite of salad.

"You've never heard of him?"

"No. Why should I have?"

"That's strange," he said.

"Why?"

"I'm told he's a pretty well-known guy in Arab-American circles. I just figured that—"

"You just figured that because I am an Arab American I know every other Arab American in Washington, D.C." Her tone now had a slight edge.

Things were spiraling out of hand.

Brixton forced a laugh. "I've never been known for subtlety," he said. "That's another gene I have. When I was on the PD, I was always the bad cop. Whoever I was partnering with was the good cop—smooth, trustworthy, things like that. Me? I always said what was on my mind."

"Which isn't necessarily a bad thing," she said.

"It can be, like tonight. I'm looking for answers from everybody, including you."

"Maybe especially me," she said. "When you are with me you see someone whose people have done this terrible thing to you. I understand that, but it doesn't help you." She looked at her watch. "I must get to my meeting."

As he paid the bill, she said, "You know, Robert, you may never get the answers you want."

She'd said what he'd been thinking all along but hadn't admitted it to himself. Hearing the words was hard to take.

He drove her to a small office building not far from the restaurant.

"Sorry I ruined dinner," he said as they sat in the car.

"You didn't, Robert, but until you've achieved some closure, it is best that we not see each other again."

"Look, if I've offended you, I apologize."

"Am I offended?" she said. "I suppose I am. Because a few of my people do horrific things, I am looked at with suspicion."

"'Suspicion'? I don't suspect you of anything."

"Perhaps *suspicion* is the wrong word. But I am one of them. I can see it in your eyes, hear it in your voice."

"My daughter's wake is tomorrow," he said bluntly.

"I don't envy you."

"It's at the funeral home. Closed casket." He looked away, then back at her. "I'd like to see you again," he said. "Maybe when the funeral is over I can think more clearly."

She opened the door.

"Is there anything new about your brother?" he asked.

"No," she said as she got out. She looked back and

said, "I hope you reach that point when you can think more clearly quickly, Robert. Thank you for dinner."

He watched her walk into the building and realized that another layer of sadness had been added to what he already felt.

CHAPTER

18

No matter what happened in Robert Brixton's life, good or bad, he seldom had trouble sleeping. But this night was an exception.

He poured himself a tumbler of single-malt Scotch over ice, sat on his small balcony, and watched people passing below, couples holding hands, a drunk stumbling home, a boisterous crew of teenagers trying to out-macho each other. He could see into an apartment across the street where an attractive woman passed her window a number of times. She was dressed in pink shortie pajamas, and Brixton mentally created a life for her—single, perhaps divorced, works in some vast government bureaucracy, wishes she were out on a date. The play he was mentally writing ended when she closed her blinds.

He wanted a cigarette; he'd quit smoking just before leaving Savannah, but the urge was always there. He went to the kitchen, poured himself another Scotch, and returned to the balcony, where he sat staring into the night until the glass was empty and it was time to go to bed.

He'd fought against feeling lonely since breaking up with Flo, but he acknowledged it this night, another departure from the basic Robert Brixton. He didn't believe in loneliness. You were lonely only when you were incapable of enjoying your own company. As much as he liked being with people—certain people—he was quite comfortable being with himself. Did the emptiness he felt at that moment mean he was aging and growing soft? He refused to answer the question. After tossing and turning for an hour, he put on the TV and watched the second half of a bad movie until sleep finally came, and when he awoke the following morning, he felt as though he hadn't slept at all.

He skipped breakfast except for coffee, and after checking that no reporter was lurking outside, he retrieved that morning's paper and read it on the balcony.

The murder of the French embassy employee, Georges Quarle, had generated an article. What was of particular interest to Brixton was that the reporter made mention of the other embassy killings and quoted a spokesman from the State Department: "The recent murders of foreign embassy staff members here in Washington are, as you can imagine, of concern. Whether it represents a pattern or is a series of unrelated incidents is under serious discussion at the State Department, as well as with Washington law enforcement."

Brixton mentally prepared for the day. He would go to the funeral home at two. Following that, he was set to have dinner with Charlie McQuaid at his home, where McQuaid would hopefully provide useful information about the cult leader and alleged illegal arms dealer Samuel Prisler. But first, he intended to follow up on the lead Mike Kogan had given him, the man whose car Paul Skaggs had been driving prior to the café bombing.

After doing a series of exercises, he showered, dressed, and called Will Sayers at the editor's office.

"What's up, pal?" Sayers asked.

"I met with Charlie McQuaid last night," Brixton said.

"You call him Charlie? Sounds like you've become bosom buddies."

"That's what he likes to be called. He's a nice guy. I'm having dinner at his house tonight."

"Did he have anything to offer about Prisler?"

"Plenty. He says he'll tell me more tonight. Mike Kogan at SITQUAL gave me some info about Paul Skaggs's movements before the bombing."

"Anything to link him to the bomber?"

"Nothing specific, but I want to follow up. He told me that Skaggs was driving a car around D.C. that belongs to a guy named Zafar Alvi. Ring a bell?"

"No. Who is he?"

"That's what I want to find out. I figured his name might have surfaced with you."

"Sorry."

"I also want to see if I can talk to Lalo Reyes again. Have you come up with anything new about him and Congressman Wisher?"

"No, but working on it. Maybe when you talk to him you can ask about it."

"I'd rather not complicate things. What intrigues me is that he lived in Hawaii for a spell."

"Lots of people live in Hawaii."

"Not with Samuel Prisler."

"He lived with Prisler?"

"That's what I intend to find out."

"What else have you come up with, Robert?"

"That's about it. I had dinner last night with Ms. Banai, the gal who was at the Smiths."

"Oh, ho," Sayers said.

"Nothing like that. She's a nice lady. Just a friendly dinner."

"Sure." Sayers was happy to hear that his old friend was socializing. With what he'd been through—and what was on the horizon—he needed whatever distractions he could find.

"Janet's wake starts today."

"I'll be there."

"You don't have to, Will."

"I know that. What do you make of the recent embassy killings?"

"I don't make anything of them."

"I thought you worked for the State Department."

"Past tense. I have to run."

"Don't forget you owe me an interview."

"After the funeral. Catch up with you later."

Brixton decided to go to the Spanish embassy and see if he could entice Eduardo "Lalo" Reyes to give him some time. The young Spaniard had been skittish when he and Donna Salvos had interviewed him at the restaurant, and he had made a point that he did not want to be questioned at the embassy. It was a long shot but worth the effort.

The six-story embassy, its bottom half a dismal gray, its top floors blue, was located on a corner in the city's West End neighborhood, an extension of Embassy Row. Brixton's genes kicked in, and he found a parking spot on the street close to the entrance. He'd decided that he'd have to establish some sort of official reason for being there. They'd taken his SITQUAL-provided weapon, but he still had his ID card. Using it, considering his circumstances at the agency, wasn't proper, but neither was the blowing up of his daughter.

He flashed his ID and asked the guard stationed inside the entrance for Mr. Reyes in the public-information section. The guard, an attractive, chunky female who looked as though the uniform was painted on her, asked him to wait while she called that division. A moment later she reported that Mr. Reyes was no longer with the embassy.

"That can't be," Brixton said. "Let me speak to his supervisor."

Her sigh demonstrated that she wasn't pleased with being challenged, but did as he'd requested. He was told to go to an upper floor and ask for Señor Marquez.

Marquez was waiting at the elevator when Brixton stepped off. Brixton showed him his SITQUAL card and shook his hand.

"You are with Security?" he asked Brixton.

"Yes. I had interviewed Mr. Reyes following the murder of someone from the German embassy, Peter Müller."

"I know nothing about that," Marquez said.

"That's not what I'm here about," Brixton said. "The guard downstairs said that Mr. Reyes no longer works at your embassy."

"That is correct."

"He worked here a few days ago."

"Yes."

"Don't people usually give a couple of weeks notice before they leave a job?"

"That is customary," Marquez said.

"But he didn't?"

"I don't wish to discuss his departure, Mr. Brixton. It is a matter of employee privacy."

"Privacy, hell," Brixton snapped. "We're talking about murder here."

"You said that was not why you are here."

"Look, I need to talk to him. Where did he go, back home to Barcelona?"

"Again, sir, that is not information that I wish to—"

"Where does he live here in D.C.?"

"I suggest that you contact our counsel for such information."

"I'll do that."

Brixton felt the Spaniard's eyes follow him as he stepped into the elevator and rode it down to the lobby. Once outside the building, he called Donna Salvos's cell.

"What's up?" she said.

"You got Eduardo Reyes's home address before we interviewed him."

"I have it."

"What is it?"

"Why do you want it?"

"I need to follow up on something."

"This isn't kosher, but hold on." She found the address and gave it to him.

Reyes lived in the Dupont Circle neighborhood, popular with the gay community—and with many others too. Brixton located the apartment building, parked, and checked the listings of residents in the lobby. Reyes's name was next to the buzzer for apartment number 2D. He rang. No one replied. He tried again. Still no response. A woman carrying an empty shopping bag came through the door.

"Excuse me," Brixton said, "I'm looking for Mr. Reyes in Two D."

The woman shrugged.

"You don't know him?"

"No, I never heard of him." She walked away.

Brixton pondered his next move. He could locate the building super and use his ID to convince him to open Reyes's apartment. He could use his knowledge of how to break into an apartment, a skill he'd used more than once when he was a cop and private detective. Leave a note for Reyes? No sense in tipping him off. He ruled out all three approaches after checking his watch. He didn't want to be late to Janet's wake, which started at two. He decided to head for Rockville, grab some lunch on the way, attend the wake, and come back to Reyes's apartment later in the day.

As Brixton parked in the lot for the funeral home and walked to the door, his daughter's stepfather, Miles Lashka, all smiles and dressed in a blue suit that might as well have had a price tag on it, greeted arrivals as though welcoming them to a family celebratory dinner.

"Glad you could make it," he said to Brixton and extended his hand, which Brixton ignored.

"Why wouldn't I be here?" Brixton asked, working hard to tamp down his annoyance.

"I just thought that with the pressure you're under you might . . ."

Brixton shook his head and walked past him into the lobby, where a few familiar faces milled about, friends from when he and Marylee were married and who'd stayed in touch with her. He didn't recognize most people. From inside the chapel the sounds of musicians tuning up reached him, and he grimaced. A knot of younger men and women, undoubtedly Janet's friends from her music world, chatted; one laughed at something another said, which pleased Brixton. He'd always preferred wakes where the gathered found something to smile, even laugh about when remembering the deceased. He gave a short snort, realizing that what irked him about Lashka pleased him in the young people.

Will Sayers came through the door. "Hi, pal," he said, slapping Brixton on the shoulder.

"Glad you came," Brixton said.

Sayers started to say something but instead muttered a "See you later" as Marylee came up to Brixton. "We'll be sitting together when the priest talks," she said. "He said he would keep it short."

"That's good. Is your husband still planning to speak?"

"Not here. At the church." She leaned closer to him. "There are people I don't recognize," she said. "I think they're from the press."

"I wouldn't know," Brixton said.

"I hope they don't make a scene," she said.

"Why should they? They just want to cover the story. If they ask to interview you, just refuse, walk away."

Marylee left him to rejoin others, including their older daughter, Jill, who held Brixton's grandson in her arms. Brixton went to them. Jill handed him the boy. He laughed as he bounced him up and down and blew against his soft cheek.

"I didn't know whether to bring him," Jill said.

"No harm," Brixton said, giving him a kiss and handing him back. "He doesn't understand what's happened.

Jill sighed. "Neither do I."

He looped his arm around his daughter's shoulder and gave her a squeeze. "I know, sweetheart."

An employee of the facility came from the chapel and asked everyone to follow him inside. The musicians, three of them, had set up in a corner of the space and prepared to play. The chapel filled up fast. Soon there were more than a hundred people standing around, including a couple of SITQUAL agents, who expressed condolences to their colleague and to Marylee. A succession of men and women paid homage to Janet by going to the closed casket. Some wept or blessed themselves with the sign of the cross or just knelt on the padded riser and slowly shook their heads. Others went to Marylee and said what people usually say in such situations, causing her to cry, to compose herself, and cry again as the next person whispered words of sorrow or sympathy.

Brixton stayed back from the crowd. He was aware that few of the gathered knew who he was; it had been that long since he and Marylee were a couple. He took note of a group of six people, four men and two women, who stayed together. None of them approached the casket or Marylee, and Brixton sized them up to be reporters. He turned his attention to two men in suits who stood by themselves at the rear of the chapel. Were they there to pay their respects to Janet? Brixton was certain that they weren't. He'd had a reputation while on the Savannah PD and as a private detective as someone with a keen sense of people, an ability to look beyond what seemed obvious in order to paint a more accurate picture of them, their true motives, and their agendas, not what they claimed. Government types, he decided. No doubt about it.

Brixton sat with Marylee, Jill, his grandson, and Miles Lashka as Father Monroe stepped to a lectern and spoke briefly about the reason they were there and the greater meaning of Janet Brixton's too-short life. He was mercifully brief; his longer sermon would be saved for church the following day. When he concluded his comments, Lashka, contrary to what Marylee had said, took the priest's place and mentioned the three musicians who would play a few tunes in Janet's memory, including a song she'd written about the fragility of life. *Apropos,* Brixton thought.

He might have stayed if the music came from a jazz trio playing music by Ellington, Brubeck, or Miles Davis, but the opening bars of what the young musicians

played were grating to his ears. He'd considered staying, out of respect for his deceased daughter, but
decided that she would understand if she were alive.
Brixton leaned close to Marylee. "I'll be back tomorrow," he said. "Call me if you need anything." He kissed
Jill and his grandson and left.

He told Sayers that he was leaving and thanked him
again for coming, walked from the chapel, through the
lobby, and stepped into the fresh outdoor air, where
he had a powerful urge to smoke. As he approached his
car, he was aware that there were people behind him.
Sure enough, three of the group that he'd pegged as
media summoned him.

"Yeah?" he asked.

They began firing questions at him about the killing
of Paul Skaggs. Brixton stood stoically, his head cocked,
his lips pressed together to mask his anger. When there
was a momentary break, he said calmly, "My daughter's body is in there in a closed casket. She was killed
by a suicide bomber who was accompanied by Paul
Skaggs, Congressman Skaggs's son. I shot him because
it looked to me like he was pointing a gun at me. If you
want a real story, go out and use your contacts to find
out why a congressman's son would take part in a suicide bombing. If you come up with the answer, let me
know. My name and number's in the book. Failing that,
leave me and my family alone."

A few additional questions trailed behind him as he
went to his car and opened the car door. He looked up
and noticed that the two men he'd assumed were government types stood next to another car two spaces
removed. Brixton had one foot in the car, withdrew it,
and shut the door.

"Nice day for a funeral," he said, approaching them.

The men didn't respond.

"You friends of the deceased, of the family?"

Their response was to look at each other, climb in their car, and drive away.

Brixton now knew that he'd been right about them. The questions were Who did they work for? and Why were they there?

He returned to his own car, started the engine, and pulled from the lot. He'd been successful in sizing up the reporters and the two men in suits inside the chapel, but he'd missed another person who didn't look like he belonged at Janet's funeral—or any other funeral, for that matter. He wore a tan bush jacket over a crimson T-shirt, jeans, and brown desert boots. His tanned face was pockmarked; a small white mustache defined his upper lip. He'd pulled into the parking lot after following Brixton from the District, remained in his car until Brixton had emerged from the funeral home, and fell in behind as Brixton drove back to the District to take another swipe at finding Eduardo "Lalo" Reyes before heading for dinner with Charlie McQuaid.

19

Brixton's second visit to Lalo Reyes's apartment was as unproductive as the first had been. No one answered the bell. Did Reyes's name on the list of tenants in the lobby mean that he was still in town? If so, how long would it be before he decided to head back home to Barcelona, or to some other place? Brixton decided that he'd come back again following his dinner with McQuaid.

After stopping by his apartment to check on messages, he headed for the southwest quadrant of the city and McQuaid's home. What he was confronted with as he pulled up in front of the house was both puzzling and upsetting. A marked police cruiser, its lights flashing, was parked in the short driveway, an ambulance directly behind it. Brixton approached a uniformed officer standing next to the patrol car.

"Robert Brixton, State Department," Brixton said, flashing his ID.

The cop didn't bother looking at it.

"What's going on?" Brixton asked.

"An accident," the officer said.

"Accident? Who?"

The cop pointed over his shoulder at the house. "The man who lives here," he said.

"Charles McQuaid?"

"I don't know his name."

Another uniformed cop joined them, and Brixton asked the same questions, plus a few others.

"Boating accident," the second officer said. "DOA."

"Charles McQuaid?"

"Right."

"Is anybody here from his family?" Brixton asked.

"There's a sister inside."

Brixton entered the house and saw a woman sitting on a couch in the living room. He introduced himself and asked if she was McQuaid's sister.

"That's right," she said. "Mr. Brixton. Charlie talked about you when he came to visit yesterday."

"He told me that he was going to see you, someplace in Maryland, right?"

"Silver Spring."

He joined her on the couch. "I hope you don't mind my asking some questions about what happened to Charlie. One of the cops outside said it was a boating accident. I was out on his boat with him yesterday. He seemed—well, he seemed to really know what he was doing. The boat was immaculate and . . ."

She smiled. "Yes, 'meticulous' is the best word to use about Charlie. He told me about you, and I've read some of it in the papers. You must be very angry at what's been happening to you."

Brixton wasn't sure how to respond. McQuaid had told him that his sister was suffering from terminal cancer, yet here she was raising his problems.

"Look, I'm not important right now. What happened

here? I don't understand this business about a boating accident."

"Another fisherman discovered him out on the river," she said. "At least that's what I've been told."

"Another fisherman? Was Charlie fishing?"

"That's what they say."

He fell silent.

"I suppose Charlie would have wanted his life to end this way, out on his boat, fishing, enjoying the fresh air," she said. "That's a lot nicer than what I . . ." She trailed off. "Anyway, it's good to die doing what you love, isn't it?"

"He was a widower," Brixton said.

"Yes. I felt terrible for him when Sue died. She was a wonderful woman, perfect for him. Isn't that the way a good marriage works, when one spouse understands the other?"

"I wouldn't argue with that, Ms. . . . ?"

"Jeannette McQuaid. I never married. Charlie was always trying to fix me up with someone he said would be perfect for me, but they never were." She managed a small laugh.

"When I was with him yesterday, he told me that he stopped fishing after his wife died, that he preferred getting his fish from local restaurants."

She assumed a thoughtful expression. "Yes, he did say that, more than once. I suppose he missed it and decided to go fishing again."

That didn't play for Brixton.

"What else did they tell you?" he asked.

"About?"

"How Charlie died."

"I'm not sure I remember. When they called they said that my brother had died in a boating accident—he had listed me as his contact should anything happen to him.

That's all they said, I think. I came right away, of course."

"Excuse me," Brixton said, getting off the couch and seeking the officer outside who seemed to be in charge. The ambulance was gone.

"I've been talking to the deceased's sister," he said, "and she's a little confused about how her brother died."

"The guy who found him says he got tangled up in his fishing line and went overboard."

"Did you see the body when it was brought in?"

"Yeah. He had fishing line around his neck. I guess he wasn't too experienced being out on a boat and all." He pointed to a man and woman standing in front of a neighboring house. "That's the guy who found him."

Brixton walked next door, introduced himself to the couple, and asked the man, a hefty fellow with a ruddy complexion, about having discovered the body.

"Doesn't make any sense to me," the man said. "Charlie's been out on his boat damn near every day for all the years we've been neighbors. Can't imagine how he'd get himself caught up in his fishing line."

"He was in the water when you found him?" Brixton asked.

"Yeah. I was cruising by real slow and spotted Charlie's boat anchored in a cove. Good fishing there. I didn't see him on board, so I pulled close. That's when I saw him in the water. Shocked the hell out of me. I passed him only an hour earlier when he was talking to a couple of guys in their boat."

"Did you know those other guys?" Brixton asked.

"No, can't say that I did. It wasn't the kind of boat you usually see around here."

"How so?"

"One of those low, flashy speedboats, you know, lots of plastic, big engine."

"And you'd never seen it or the men before?"

"Can't say that I did. I would have noticed a boat like that."

"The last time I was with Charlie he told me that he'd quit fishing."

The man grimaced. "He quit right after Sue died. I guess he caught the bug again. Probably wishes he hadn't."

Brixton thanked him and returned to Jeannette McQuaid.

"Charlie was going to share things that he thought might help me," he told her. "I know this is an imposition at a difficult time, but would you mind if I took a look around his office?"

"Of course not," she said.

Brixton knew where it was but followed Charlie's sister to the home office in which he and McQuaid had talked the previous day. There was a big difference twenty-four hours later. What had been a pristine, obsessively neat room was now in disarray. A few file cabinet drawers were half open, their contents sticking up crookedly. The desk was a repository of other folders, papers spilling from them. Brixton came around to the chair and saw that two drawers had also been left open.

"Have you been in here since you learned that your brother died?" he asked.

"I peeked in when I got here," she said, "but didn't stay. I was surprised how messy it was. Charlie was always so neat."

"I'm surprised, too," Brixton said.

"Maybe Charlie forgot and was looking for the things he left with me yesterday," she said.

"What things?"

"Papers, files. He brought some files and papers with him and spent some time after dinner going through them. He forgot them when he left and called to ask me to keep them till he could pick them up. I offered to bring them back and was about to walk out the door when I got the call about his accident."

"Where are they?" Brixton asked.

"In my car."

He hesitated before asking, "May I see them?"

"I don't see why not. I'll go get them."

"Tell you what," Brixton said, "how about I take you to dinner? You can give them to me after a good meal."

Her face lit up. "I think that sounds like a very good idea," she said. "There's nothing I can do for Charlie tonight. I've already identified his body and have called his three children. They live so far away; Charlie always wanted to be closer to them. They'll be flying in tomorrow, and we'll get together and make funeral arrangements. To be honest, Mr. Brixton, the shock of this is just now hitting me. I think I'd like to lock up the house once everyone is gone and relax over a good meal. Thank you for suggesting it."

B rixton had seldom met a woman—anyone for that matter—who was as open and self-effacing as Jeannette McQuaid. He'd suggested one of the nearby fish restaurants, but she said, "I would love to go to the Bistrot Du Coin." She pronounced it "bis-trot."

"Bistrot? With a *tee*? Not bistro?"

"I'm showing off, I suppose," she said. "One of the men Charlie fixed me up with took me there on the few dates we had. I know it sounds cruel, but the restaurant was much more interesting than he was. I learned that the word *bistrot* is Russian. It means "quick." The waiter also told me that bistros in France are always painted brown to hide the nicotine stains. That's why they chose the color for their walls, only no one is allowed to smoke there. Do you smoke?"

"I did," he said, not adding that a cigarette would be welcome.

"Would you mind going there?" she asked. "We'll go strictly Dutch."

They drove both cars to the restaurant where they secured a table and ordered from the restaurant's vast menu, with Jeannette translating some of the French phrases.

Brixton felt like a kindly uncle or psychotherapist during the meal. Jeannette told him stories about her brother and her life growing up, of the job from which she'd retired at the Maryland Department of Motor Vehicles, how she'd learned French and Spanish from online courses, and a host of other personal tidbits. Brixton decided that as a single woman who'd lived alone for most of her adult life, she had too little opportunity to talk to people, and he was glad to provide a listening post. It was toward the end of the meal and over dessert and coffee that she mentioned her cancer. "They say I'm terminal," she said, laughing away the thought. "I always thought that only women who had children got ovarian cancer. I guess I was wrong. I'm in a clinical trial at NIH, and I'll bet you anything—any amount, you name it—that my cancer will disappear."

"I'd never take that bet," Brixton said.

"I haven't told you how sorry I am about your daughter."

"Looks like we both have someone to grieve over."

They walked to where she'd parked her car a block from the restaurant.

"Thank you for dinner," she said, "I really did intend to pay my share."

"It was my pleasure."

"Oh," she said, "the things that Charlie gave me."

She retrieved three file folders and a manila envelope from the backseat and handed them to him.

"Thanks," he said. "I appreciate this. If there's anything I can do . . ."

"Charlie wanted to help you prove what you said happened at that café and with the congressman's son. That's what he told me."

"Your brother was quite a guy."

"Yes, he was, even though he was a lousy matchmaker."

She kissed his cheek, got in her car, and drove away.

20

Charlie McQuaid had been murdered.

Brixton was as sure of that as he was sure of his own name. The question was *why* someone had killed the retired Justice Department lawyer and taken great pains to make it look like a boating accident. Did it have to do with McQuaid's obsession about the arms dealer and cult leader Samuel Prisler? That was a possibility, the best that Brixton could conjure at the moment. If so, why had his murder taken place the day after he'd invited Brixton into his home and had made a date to get together again the following night?

Was someone aware that McQuaid was helping Brixton with his struggle to clear himself of culpability in the shooting of Paul Skaggs, and to nail down the young Skaggs's involvement in the suicide bombing? Was McQuaid's death a message to Brixton? If so, who was sending that message?

It had taken willpower to not raise with Jeannette McQuaid the distinct possibility that her brother had not been the victim of a fishing accident. There would be time for that later. In the meantime, Brixton knew that he had to keep probing to pull together the disparate bits of information and speculation that had come his way.

He decided to visit Lalo Reyes's apartment building again before calling it a night. The street in front of the building was relatively quiet considering its vibrant neighborhood. Brixton went to the small lobby and pushed the buzzer for Reyes's apartment. Again, no response. As he pondered what to do, a young couple came through the door. They were so infatuated with each other, laughing and kissing, that they walked right past Brixton, who stepped inside. He walked down a short corridor to the elevator and rode it to the second floor. Apartment 2D was at the end of the hall. Brixton pressed his ear against the door. There was no sound. After checking to be sure that no one was nearby, he used a small device carried by most police and private detectives to undo the lock, stepped into the dark apartment, and quietly closed the door behind him. His eyes adjusted to the room; light from outside filtered through a dirty window at the far end of the living room.

He turned on a table lamp and took in his surroundings. The room gave off every sign that its occupant was getting ready to depart or already had. There were discolored squares on the walls where artwork had once hung. The few tables were bare. Newspapers and magazines were piled haphazardly on a couch.

Brixton went to the kitchen, where dirty dishes sat piled in the sink. An unplugged toaster oven occupied part of the countertop; a small coffeemaker, also unplugged, sat next to it. Half-consumed bottles of booze were on a table, along with glasses, and bottles of club soda and tonic water.

The bedroom was also in disarray. A queen-size bed covered with a garish red comforter was unmade. A flat-screen TV sat on a bureau top. What most interested Brixton were two suitcases in a corner. He picked them up; their weight indicated that they were full.

He returned to the living room and sat behind a white plastic table that functioned as a desk. It was littered with scraps of paper, and Brixton idly went through them. He opened an envelope with the return address of a travel agency and removed its contents. Included was a one-way airline ticket for travel two days hence, destination Maui, the Hawaiian Islands.

The meaning of the ticket wasn't lost on him.

Prisler!

Why was Reyes traveling to Hawaii, more specifically Maui? Was it because that was where Samuel Prisler and his cult were located?

What was Reyes's relationship with Prisler? Was he a cult member, as Paul Skaggs had been and as his sister was? Maybe there wasn't a connection. Maybe— and Brixton was willing to accept the possibility that no connection existed—Reyes had simply lived there in the past and wished to return to a place that he enjoyed.

But why had he resigned his job at the Spanish embassy so abruptly?

Did his relationship with the German embassy staffer Peter Müller mean anything in the larger scope of the recent embassy murders?

Brixton felt overwhelmed as he sat and stared at the airline ticket, but a sound snapped him to attention. Someone was outside the apartment inserting a key in the lock. Brixton sprang to his feet, switched off the lamp, and went to the bedroom, where he secluded himself behind the open door. He heard two male voices, one belonging to Reyes, as they entered the apartment. The man with him spoke with a deep voice and drawl; Brixton thought of cowboy movies.

"We'll miss ya'll," the drawl said.

"And I'll miss you," Reyes said, "but it's time to go; a time for everything. Sorry for the mess."

The second man laughed. "It's not as messy as my place, Lalo. You should see it, dude."

"Drinks are in the kitchen," Reyes said.

"Had so damn much to drink at the party," said man number two.

"I'll miss Marigold's," Reyes said.

Of course, Brixton thought. *That's where he should have looked for Reyes—at Marigold's, the gay nightclub.*

He heard the rustle of clothing and a deep sigh. Were they embracing?

"Make yourself a drink," Reyes said. "I'll get changed."

Brixton tensed. Reyes walked into the bedroom and tossed his jacket on the bed. He sat on its edge and began to remove his shoes and socks. It was after he was barefoot and had wiggled out of his slacks that he sensed Brixton's presence. "What the—?

"Calm down," Brixton said as he stepped from behind the door.

"Get out of here," Reyes shouted.

"What's going on?" the other man asked as he came into the bedroom. He was big, taller than Brixton, and bulky in his tight jeans and fringed yellow leather shirt-jacket. "Who in hell is he?" he asked Reyes.

"It doesn't matter who I am," Brixton said.

The big guy with the drawl lunged at Brixton, hands extended as though to strangle him. Brixton's reflexes kicked in. He stepped aside, allowing the big guy's momentum to carry him past. Brixton came up behind and wrapped his right arm about the man's throat in a stranglehold, causing him to slump to his knees. Brixton maintained his grip and turned, expecting an attack from Reyes, but the young Spaniard stood paralyzed on the other side of the bed, eyes wide, fear etched on his smooth, handsome face.

Brixton released his hold and used his foot to shove Reyes's friend in the direction of a chair. "Tell you what," he said. "Why don't you saddle up whatever horse you rode in on and get lost. I have something to discuss with Mr. Reyes. Shouldn't take more than a half hour, maybe an hour at most. Go back to Marigold's and have a drink to kill the time. I'm sure Lalo will be happy to see you when you get back."

"Damn, Lalo," he said as he struggled to his feet and gently touched his fingertips to his bruised throat. "What's this all about?"

Brixton took a step in his direction.

"Okay, okay, I'm goin'. Damn man, you really hurt me."

"You're lucky you can walk out of here," Brixton said. "And don't even think about telling anybody what happened. Got it?"

He nodded sullenly and left the apartment.

Brixton now focused on Reyes, who'd pulled up his pants and nervously buckled his belt.

"So you're planning a trip to sunny Hawaii, Lalo."

"What? How do you know that?"

"I read your airline ticket. Maui's supposed to be nice this time of year."

"You have no right breaking into my apartment and going through my things." He didn't say it with any conviction, as though he didn't want to upset Brixton.

"You're right, Lalo. I'm guilty of breaking and entering. You want to call the police, nine-one-one?" Before Reyes could answer, Brixton added, "Before they get here, you'll be in a lot worse shape than your gentleman caller."

Reyes looked at the phone next to the bed but didn't reach for it. "What do you want?" he asked.

"Get on the bed, get comfortable. Go on, Lalo. I want you to be comfortable."

"Are you crazy or something?" Lalo said. "Hey, wait a minute. You're one of the agents who talked to me after—"

"Right, after your pal Peter Müller was shot."

"I already told you I didn't have anything to do with that. Peter was—"

"Yeah, yeah, I know, I know. He was your lover. You get around, don't you, Lalo?"

"What do you mean?"

"Your lovers, Müller, a congressman, who else?"

"You have no right asking me things like that."

"I've got every right. What about Hawaii?"

"What about it?"

"You told me you'd lived there once. On Maui?"

"So what?"

"Who did you live with on Maui?"

"That's my business."

"I'm making it mine. You know a woman there, Morgana Skaggs, aka Kamea something or other?"

Brixton had no idea whether Reyes's connection with Hawaii involved Congressman Skaggs's daughter and Samuel Prisler, but he figured that as long as he had Reyes on the defensive, he might as well take a shot. It had worked more times than not when he was a cop in D.C. and Savannah.

The expression on Reyes's face told Brixton that mentioning the Skaggs daughter's name rang a bell.

"Yeah, you knew her," Brixton said. "Let's try another name. Samuel Prisler."

Reyes picked up the phone. "Either you leave or I'm calling the police."

Brixton responded by pulling his revolver from the

holster in his armpit and pointing it at Reyes. He knew that he had stepped far over the line. Reyes had every right to bring charges against him, which would ensure the end of any job Brixton might ever want in law enforcement. But that was irrelevant. Everything was irrelevant except clearing his name and proving that Paul Skaggs had aided and abetted the suicide bombing.

Reyes lowered the phone with a trembling hand. "Don't shoot, okay?" he said. "Please don't shoot me."

"Then tell me why you're going to Hawaii."

"I have . . . I have friends there."

"Friends? In the Prisler cult?"

"I know people there but—"

"But *what,* Lalo? Who do you know on Maui?"

"Sam. I know Sam."

"Sam. Sounds like you know him pretty well, calling him Sam."

"He's a . . . he's a very fine man."

"He sells weapons to terrorists and runs a cult. You call that a fine man?"

"What do you want from me?" Reyes asked. He was close to breaking down.

"Did you know Paul Skaggs?"

"Who?"

Brixton made a show of leveling his revolver at Reyes.

"You know damn well who I mean. Paul Skaggs. The congressman's son, the guy I shot and killed after he helped blow up the café and my daughter. Stop playing games with me. I shot him and I wouldn't mind doing the same to you."

"I think I met him once or twice," Reyes said.

"Where? In Prisler's cult?"

Reyes nodded and sniffled.

"Tell me more about Prisler and his cult," Brixton said. "And take your time. I've got all night."

Reyes gave Brixton an abbreviated history of what he knew about Samuel Prisler, vague statements about how the cult provides a better lifestyle for its members, most of them young; how Prisler loves the members of the cult and makes better human beings of them; how the Skaggs daughter was a loyal member of the cult; and how Reyes wanted to leave Washington and all its nastiness to live a better life.

Brixton took it all in, uttering an occasional grunt and probing a halfhearted answer to simple questions. He brought the conversation to an end when he decided that he'd better leave and not run the risk that Reyes's buddy with the drawl would decide to return with help.

When Reyes realized that Brixton was about to take off, he said in a stronger voice, "I resent this."

Brixton slipped his revolver back in its holster and smiled. "And I resent having a daughter blown up, Mr. Reyes. Enjoy your trip to Hawaii, and be sure to take plenty of suntan lotion."

21

B rixton's adrenaline flowed as he walked to where he'd parked his car on a side street off Dupont Circle. He knew that his unannounced visit had been impetuous at best, a dunderheaded move born of frustration. He had no right to have invaded the young Spaniard's apartment or to have pulled a gun on him and demanded answers. It hadn't accomplished much aside from knowing that Reyes had been a member of Prisler's cult and was in the process of returning. But that left Brixton with more questions than answers.

How did Reyes's involvement with Prisler's cult link to the café bombing and Paul Skaggs? Or was there even a link? Brixton had only his own speculation, his own what-if scenarios as an answer. Could it be sheer coincidence that Reyes and Paul Skaggs just happened to have the Prisler cult in common? Brixton believed in coincidence, but there was a limit.

Were the recent murders of embassy employees connected in some way? The café had been a known hangout for State Department staffers. Had they been the targets of the suicide bomber? And what about the recent rash of murders of individual embassy employees? Brixton had initially believed that those killings were the work of homophobic whackos, and the possibility still existed. He reminded himself to check with Kogan to see whether the two latest victims, the Italian and French embassy staffers, were gay.

And now there was the suspicious death of Charlie McQuaid added to the mix. McQuaid had been murdered. Brixton was certain of that. Would McQuaid's sister, Jeannette, tell the authorities that her brother no longer fished? Brixton doubted it. She had enough on her mind, losing a loving brother, and on top of that facing her own mortality. He decided he'd seek out someone at MPD who might be interested in pursuing McQuaid's death as a possible homicide. From what he'd learned from the cops at the house, and from Jeannette McQuaid, the assumption—and that's all it was, an assumption—was that the retired Justice Department lawyer had died as the result of a boating and fishing accident. Whoever had killed him had done a good job of covering his or her tracks, but that didn't mean that the murder was foolproof. Anger welled as Brixton thought of McQuaid and his offer to help clear his name. Charlie McQuaid was a good and decent man; he deserved having light cast on the truth.

With these thoughts and others swirling in his mind like an out-of-control mental eddy, he stopped in front of a small bar and peered in the window. It was virtually empty; a couple sat at the bar, and only two tables were taken. Brixton entered, took a table as far away from others as possible, and continued his ruminations, hoping that the gin and McQuaid's file folders and papers that he'd carried in with him would calm his jumbled brain and jump-start clearer thinking.

As Brixton nursed his drink and began reading, Annabel Smith was hosting the monthly book discussion group at the Smith's Watergate apartment. That month's assigned book was *My Beloved World* by Supreme Court Justice Sonia Sotomayor. The nine women, including Asal Banai, engaged in a lively discussion that sometimes broke down into political views, which Annabel did her best to avoid. Despite the sometimes sharp bantering, she judged the evening a success.

The group was winding up its debate when Annabel's husband, Mac, walked in. He'd been to Ford's Theatre, where he'd treated himself to its current production.

He'd vacated the apartment that evening because of Annabel's book group. Mac encouraged his wife's monthly involvement. She invariably came away from those confabs energized and filled with ideas. He, on the other hand, enjoyed spending a solo evening out, a spin on "Ladies' Night Out," except that it involved a man, and only one—him. Mackensie and Annabel Lee Smith were deeply in love and savored time spent together. But they were also wise enough to know that having individual interests and spending time pursuing them solidified their commitment to each other.

He'd enjoyed dinner at BLT Steak, a block from Lafayette Square near the White House, one of his go-to restaurants when out on the town on his own. He arrived at Ford's Theatre early and did what he always did when there, perused the remarkable array of artifacts in the small but nicely conceived museum that traced Lincoln's presidency and included the actual derringer used by John Wilkes Booth to assassinate the president as he sat in the presidential box with his wife, as well as the actual clothing worn by the president on that fateful night. Annabel's group was getting ready to leave when Mac returned home.

"Good discussion?" he asked as the women gathered their belongings.

"It was wonderful," one said. "Justice Sotomayor is so self-effacing in the book."

"Reading about her humble beginnings was inspirational," said another.

"I'm just concerned about her leftist leanings," said the staunch Republican woman in the group.

"I have the feeling that she'll put aside politics when it comes to making decisions," Mac offered. "At least, let's hope she does."

Asal Banai was the last to leave.

"Thank you for a wonderful evening," she told Annabel.

"My pleasure, Asal."

"Have you heard from your friend, Mr. Brixton?" Asal asked.

"You talked to him earlier today, didn't you, Mac?" Annabel said.

"Yes," Mac said as he returned from the kitchen, where he'd carried dishes. "We're going to the funeral home tomorrow."

"It must be terrible having to arrange a funeral for a child," Asal said. She saw Mac wince and remembered that he'd lost a son to a drunken driver on the Beltway.

"Robert has so many challenges," Mac said. "Besides burying his daughter, he's trying to prove that Congressman Skaggs's son was involved in the café bombing, because Robert's accused of gunning down the congressman's son without justification. That's a lot to juggle at one time."

"Is he making any progress?" Asal asked casually.

"I think so. He told me on the phone that the son was given a traffic ticket shortly before the bombing. Seems he was driving a car belonging to another man." He turned to Annabel. "What was that name I mentioned to you?

"I'm not sure. It sounded Middle Eastern."

"Please give Robert my best when you see him," Asal said.

"We certainly will," said Annabel. "You never mentioned how things went when you had a drink with him after our dinner party."

Asal was surprised that Annabel knew about that. She hadn't mentioned it to them, but Brixton obviously had.

"Oh, yes, we had a drink. It was pleasant."

"Robert can be abrasive at times," Mac said through a laugh, "but he's a really good guy. I admire him."

He walked Asal to the elevator. "Any progress in your brother's situation?" he asked as they waited for the car to arrive.

"Unfortunately no, but thank you for asking."

"And your agency?"

There is always the problem with money, but we are working on it."

When Mac returned to the apartment, Annabel said, "Asal was so moody tonight. I got the feeling that she has something weighty on her mind."

"She asked about Robert," Mac said. "Maybe their drink together sparked something."

Annabel laughed. "He needs a new woman in his life with all he's going through. It's a shame that he and Flo Combes broke up. I liked her. She seemed to be able to handle his cynical view of life."

"I've given up trying to understand romance, Annie," Mac said, grabbing her and pressing a kiss to her neck. "The only romance I understand is ours."

"Which is good enough for me. Let's finish cleaning up and call it a night."

"Get to bed, you mean."

She smiled. "You're very astute, Mackensie. You might have made a good lawyer."

Asal Banai stood outside the Smith's Watergate apartment building. She wanted to go home, but that wasn't to be, at least for a while. The phone call she'd received earlier that day saw to that.

Resigned, she walked to the taxi stand that served guests of the Watergate Hotel and gave the driver an address on Thirty-first Street NW north of Georgetown. The house he pulled up in front of was Georgian in architecture, an imposing sight set back from the street on a hill. The front door was reached by climbing a steep set of steps. Spotlights illuminated the house's front from half a dozen locations. A narrow driveway snaked its way along the side of the house and disappeared in back.

Asal paid the driver, drew a deep breath, and slowly began ascending the stairs. She was halfway up when a young man dressed in a black T-shirt and jeans appeared at the top. He'd been alerted by her image on one of two security cameras whose field of vision scanned the front of the property. Similar cameras secured the side and back of the house. "You are?" he asked.

"Asal Banai. Mr. Alvi is expecting me."

Another young man opened the door and asked her to wait. "Mr. Alvi will be with you shortly."

Asal hoped that her nervousness wasn't too apparent. She'd practiced what she would say to Alvi from the moment she'd received his call late that morning requesting that she come to his home at eleven. No, it hadn't been a request. It had been an order, politely delivered but unmistakable in its meaning. After receiving it she'd considered canceling her appearance at Annabel's but had second thoughts. She knew that the book club would disband early enough for her to make the appointment on time, and she hoped the lively discussion would distract her from the dread she felt at being summoned.

She sat in a straight-backed chair in the expansive foyer decorated with garish Middle Eastern paintings and furniture, and fidgeted with her handbag until the second young man appeared and told her to follow him. They went up a circular staircase to the second level and into Alvi's study, where the Iraqi sat behind a rococo desk with multiple sections of inlaid woods of different colors. Zafar Alvi was not handsome but he exuded the sort of self-confidence characteristic of more attractive men. His nose was large, deeply veined, and bulbous. His closely cropped salt-and-pepper beard was scraggly; it looked in some spots as though it refused to grow. What was left of his hair ran over his bald pate from side to side and was gelled down. He wore a red and brown button-down shirt, tan cardigan sweater, baggy tan slacks, and gray and red sneakers. Alvi's reputation was not based on his fashion sense or looks. It was his wealth that fueled his charisma and supported multiple homes around the world, most of them in the Middle East.

A sal had met Alvi for the first time at a social gathering six months earlier. She'd certainly heard of him and knew the powerful position he held within Washington's Arab-American community. But while Zafar Alvi was relatively high profile, there had always been an air of mystery about how he made his money.

As a Sunni, it was assumed that he had lost considerable clout in the new Shiite Iraqi government, but rumors abounded about various business deals he had with the new leaders. There were also unsubstantiated charges that he was a financial supporter of and laundered money for rebel groups in Mali, Pakistan, Afghanistan, Somalia, and other hotbeds of discontent.

That introduction to Alvi had occurred during a particularly difficult time in Asal's life. The Islamic Partnership was floundering; donations had dried up, and the group's modest headquarters was behind in its rent. She'd fallen into an easy conversation with the powerful man and was aware that he was physically attracted to her. But her interest in him was anything but romantic. She saw in Zafar Alvi a financial lifeline.

Alvi took her to dinner the next night at a Middle Eastern restaurant in which he enjoyed partial ownership. They dined alone in a small separate room with romantic lighting and music and a special menu served with flourish to Alvi and his guest. It was during that dinner that he asked her to provide a service to him. At first she thought that he might be propositioning her, but he quickly disabused her of that notion. He told her that he needed people within Washington's Arab-American community whom he could trust to provide him with information about the goings-on, particularly political, of individuals he described as "enemies" and "potential enemies."

Asal hesitated to commit herself at first, but by the time dessert was served and he'd offered a sizable amount of money for both the Islamic Partnership and herself, she agreed. After all, she reasoned, what could be wrong with simply telling him what certain people were doing in exchange for a generous fee?

But if she had reservations, there was another more compelling reason to become involved with him—her imprisoned brother in Baghdad. She'd told Alvi about the situation that night at dinner, and he'd suggested that he could use his influence to secure her brother's freedom in exchange for her cooperation. The combination of money and the promise to intercede on her brother's behalf was more than enough to secure Asal's promise to keep him informed.

Asal had little contact with Alvi in the months that followed. Communication with him came through a man introduced only as Kahn, Alvi's chief of staff. Their brief meetings were conducted in public places, a coffee shop, Union Station, and a park. It was like a cloak-and-dagger movie to her, which she found amusing. She had little to offer in exchange for the generous payments delivered by Alvi's representative. Her work at the Islamic Partnership brought her into contact with many people in the Arab-American community, none of whom it seemed to her were involved in anything that would interest Alvi. Still, she passed along innocuous tidbits of information, most of them personal—a leader of the community cheating on his wife, or a woman making comments that could be construed as anti-Islam.

But that changed when she was ordered to meet with him one morning. He told her that he had become active in helping bring young worthy Middle Eastern men and women to the United States for a university education and wanted to work through the Islamic Partnership. Asal's first reaction was positive. His involvement could expand the program and result in more young people benefiting. But once he'd begun to influence the project, she began hearing from Iraq that Alvi's people had virtually taken over the program and were arranging for a select group of young students from various countries to enter the United States with visas arranged by Alvi's colleagues. Losing control of the program dismayed Asal, and she raised her concerns with him. His answer was that unless he had control of the program, he would have no choice but to cease making payments to the Islamic Partnership. It was at that moment that Asal realized the penalties for agreeing to provide her reports to Alvi. She considered ending the arrangement. But after some soul searching, she decided that his money was more important to the partnership than her pride. Let him run the student program if it meant that much to him, she decided, and she continued passing along seemingly meaningless information about his alleged enemies.

But then the bombing of the café occurred, and Robert Brixton was injected into her life.

Alvi got up from behind his desk, took her hand, and said, "Thank you for coming, Asal. I hope that it isn't inconvenient for you at this late hour."

"No, not at all," she said.

"Sit, please," he said, indicating a chair with a high back upholstered in red and yellow silk. "Something to drink? Coffee? Tea? Something stronger?"

"No, I . . . yes, tea would be fine."

He picked up the phone and instructed someone to bring tea and *basbousa* pastries. "With almonds," he instructed.

He sat back, his fingers laced beneath his chin, and smiled. "So, my dear, it seems that you have been spending time with interesting people," he said, the smile not fading. "Tell me about this Robert Brixton."

Asal shook her head and extended her hands. "I don't know much about him," she said. "I've only met him once or twice."

"What were the circumstances?" he said.

"I was at a dinner party with him and we . . . well, we ended up having a drink afterwards."

"At a nice place I hope."

"It was . . . yes, it was nice. The Watergate."

"This dinner party you attended, Asal. Tell me about that."

She'd become increasingly uncomfortable and was certain that her posture and voice betrayed it. He continued to smile, his brown eyes sustaining his questions.

"They're friends of mine," Asal said, "Mr. and Mrs. Smith. He is a law professor and she, Annabel, owns a gallery in Georgetown and is in my book discussion group."

"I know of them," Alvi said. "They are friends of Mr. Brixton."

He sat back and stared at her.

Alvi's sudden silence was disconcerting for Asal. It was accompanied by a harsh expression that replaced the smile. She'd seen him employ this ability to instantly switch gears during previous meetings. His intent was to create unrest in the other person, a threat unstated but unmistakable. It became evident to her that while she was paid to keep tabs on people whom Alvi considered enemies, others were being paid to keep tabs on her. That realization was chilling.

"I can't help but wonder, Asal, why you never mentioned to Kahn your relationship with Mr. Brixton."

"I would hardly call it a relationship, Mr. Alvi," she said, realizing how defensive she sounded.

"What *would* you call it, my dear?"

"I was introduced to him by the Smiths," she said. "Mrs. Smith and I are friends. It didn't occur to me to say anything to Kahn about him."

"Even though he is very much in the news these days? He is, after all, the man who claims that the son of a prominent American congressman was involved in that tragic bombing of the café near the Department of State, and the same man who shot that son in cold blood. It seems to me that befriending such a man would be very much on your mind when reporting to Kahn."

Asal had indeed weighed telling Kahn about her drinks and dinner with Brixton but decided to avoid the subject. She'd withheld the information out of deference to Annabel and because she was attracted to Brixton and hoped he wouldn't be someone who would be of particular interest to Alvi. She was obviously wrong. She'd lied to Brixton when he'd asked whether she knew a man named Zafar Alvi, because she wasn't sure that she was free to acknowledge their relationship.

She hated the situation in which she'd placed herself. She'd become a spy for Alvi. He now controlled her, and as long as she needed the money and held out hope that he would intervene on her brother's behalf in Iraq, she would continue in that role.

"I admit that I am disappointed in you, Asal," Alvi said. "I expect more from people who benefit from my generosity."

"I'm not sure that I understand, Mr. Alvi. It didn't occur to me that Robert Brixton would be of interest to you."

"Well, Asal, you now know that I do have an interest in him. The reason isn't important. What *is* important is that you use your relationship with him"—the smile returned—"or however you wish to characterize it, to learn everything he does, every place he goes, the people he sees, every aspect of his life. Do I make myself clear?"

"I still do not understand. Robert—Mr. Brixton—is a man who has just lost his daughter and—"

"Yes, a tragedy to be sure, but irrelevant. There are

so many tragedies in this world, Asal, so much heartache for our people. Wrongs must be made right. I'm sure you agree. Your brother is a good example."

"My brother," she said. "Why do you raise my brother? You told me that you were working through your contacts in Iraq to free him."

"And I have been making progress, but these things are complex. They take time. Of course, if you prefer to no longer accept my generosity, I'll have no choice but to curtail my activities on his behalf, and on your behalf, too, of course."

"No, I do not want that, and I am grateful for what you are doing for my brother. It's just that . . ."

"Yes, Asal?"

She shook her head. "No, nothing," she said.

"So, suppose you tell me what your social engagements with this Brixton fellow have resulted in."

Asal told Alvi that Brixton had asked about him.

"Did he say why?"

"He said that the young man, the congressman's son, had been driving one of your cars before the bombing."

Alvi scribbled a note on a pad. "Go on," he said.

"That was all."

"Did you say that we were friends?"

"No. I said that I knew of you, that's all."

"What else, Asal?"

She shrugged. "He also mentioned another man, someone named Prisler."

"Who is he?"

"I don't know."

Alvi noted the name on the pad.

"You remain friends with him and with Mrs. Smith?" Alvi asked.

"Annabel Smith and I are friends but I did not plan to see Mr. Brixton anymore until . . ."

"Until what, Asal?"

"Until he has worked out his many problems. He's very volatile."

"I suggest that you make contact with him soon and perhaps *help* him work out his problems. A beautiful woman is often of considerable aid to a troubled man, eases his tensions, renews faith in his manhood."

Asal understood the meaning of what he was saying but did not reply.

"And because Mrs. Smith is his friend, she might be a source of information about his activities."

Asal sat silently.

"Do we understand each other?" Alvi asked.

"Yes". was all Asal said as she stood.

"Here," Alvi said. He handed her an envelope.

"What is this?"

"A bonus for the good work I know that you will do for me and for our cause. Your brother is safe, although I am not sure how long he will be without my direct intervention. I assure you I am working closely with those who possess the power to release him."

"And I am grateful for all you are doing, Mr. Alvi. I would like to call a taxi."

"No need for that. One of my staff will drive you home."

He came around the desk and placed his hands on her shoulders. "We make a good team, Asal. It will be a mutually beneficial relationship. Safe home. Kahn will be in regular touch from now on."

Alvi's conversation with Asal had been recorded. It had also been piped into an adjoining room where Samuel Prisler listened intently. When he was sure that she'd left, he opened the door and joined Alvi.

"I don't understand you, Zafar," the large man said as he took the chair that Asal had occupied and shoved a *basbousa* in his mouth.

Alvi cocked his head.

"Why are you dragging your feet with this Brixton character? You heard her. He knows about you, and he mentioned me to her. He's obviously hell-bent on proving that the Skaggs boy was involved with the young woman you recruited, and has traced him back to me and Hawaii. He has to be gotten rid of—and fast!"

Alvi's face turned hard. "I am not accustomed to being told what to do," he said. "You will remember that I am the one who provides a conduit for the weapons you sell. I suggest strongly that you remember that, Sam."

"You're not the only customer I have," Prisler snapped back.

"Perhaps not, but I am your best customer. I must also remind you of your involvement in the project I have undertaken here in Washington."

"Against my better judgment."

"No matter. The project is under way. You are tied to it whether you want to be or not."

"Which makes my point, Zafar. Brixton is dangerous. He's got to be taken out. If you won't, I will."

"Which will be done in all due time, Samuel. You were equally as concerned about Mr. McQuaid. There is no reason for you to be concerned about him any longer. Now, my friend, I suggest we enjoy some of my best cognac and discuss more pleasant things. You'll be flying home tomorrow. Enjoy your trip and leave everything here to me."

CHAPTER

22

Two young people were being laid to rest.

As mourners crowded the Mississippi church for the funeral of Paul Skaggs, the priest in Virginia at Janet Brixton's church service, Father Monroe, combined a standard Catholic Mass with words of his own. "There's evil in this world," he said, "and evil took the life of this precious young woman. Those who commit acts such as these often claim to have done it in the name of the God they worship. But there is no God who condones the killing of innocent people. To claim this is to indulge in blasphemy of the worst kind. To claim that their God is a conspirator in such senseless slaughter is to slander that God. Janet's family and friends have gathered here together to celebrate her much too short life and to give thanks for having known her. As we mourn her death we . . ."

At the conclusion of the priest's comments, three laypeople came forward to pay tribute to the young woman whose body lay at rest in the closed coffin. The first to speak was Janet's sister, Jill, who managed to get through her remarks, written on wrinkled sheets of legal-size yellow paper, despite frequent breaks to regain her composure. She spoke of her sister's spirit and love of life and the joy.she took from music. She also elicited occasional laughs when she mentioned the differences between her and her sister. "We were so different, such different personalities. I will always remember her infectious laugh, which could always be counted on to get her out of scrapes, while I, the serious one, often took the blame."

Brixton smiled against his tears.

She was followed by Janet's most recent beau, whose trio had performed at the funeral home. He kept his comments short, stressing what a wonderful partner she'd been, both professionally and romantically. Brixton was impressed with the young man's poise and the words he spoke, although not necessarily with what he'd chosen to wear for the occasion—black jeans, checkered shirt with what passed for a tie that came halfway down his torso, and a powder-blue suit jacket that needed a dry cleaner. But Brixton silently reminded himself as he sat in a front pew with Marylee, Jill, his grandson, and Miles Lashka, that this was no time to be critical. Janet's boyfriend had tried to dress appropriately, and his heartfelt sentiments were more important than what he wore. Besides, he was a rock musician on whom a three-piece gray pinstripe suit—even if he owned one—would have looked silly.

Lashka was the final speaker. As much as Brixton disliked the slick lawyer, he had to give him points for smoothly delivering a thoughtful series of vignettes about Janet that her mother had undoubtedly provided him. If you didn't know better, you'd have thought that he was her natural father.

Throughout the service Brixton was aware that a number of worshippers took notice of him, not because he was Janet's father but because of the attention the press had paid him. He was uncomfortable with that and wished that the events leading up to his notoriety had never happened. More than anything he wanted it all to disappear—the café bombing, Janet's death, and the confrontation in the alley with Paul Skaggs. As Father Monroe's amplified words filled the church, Brixton's mind drifted away to another dimension.

The bombing and the chaos surrounding it, and facing Skaggs in that alley, occupied what seemed to be a permanent place in his thoughts; he relived those moments over and over. He wondered whether that would always be the case. Was it a definition of hell? It would do.

As people filed from the church and headed for cars to take them to the cemetery, Willis Sayers and Mac and Annabel Smith came up to Brixton. Annabel gave him a hug.

"A nice turnout," Mac commented.

"Yeah," Brixton agreed. "She deserved it."

"We won't be going to the cemetery," Annabel said.

"That's okay," said Brixton. "I appreciate you coming to the service."

"Thanks for being here," Brixton told Sayers after the Smiths had left.

"I liked the priest's words," Sayers said, "more down-to-earth than what I hear at most funerals."

"Coming to the cemetery?" Brixton asked.

"No. Listen, Robert, you heard about Charlie McQuaid."

"I was supposed to have dinner with him the day he was killed. I ended up having dinner with his sister, a terrific woman, and she gave me papers that he was going to turn over to me when we met. They're all about Samuel Prisler, his cult on Maui, and his arms dealing."

"I was told that McQuaid drowned, a fishing accident," Sayers said.

"Like hell he did," Brixton growled. "He told me the day before that he'd given up fishing after his wife died. He wasn't fishing, and he knew his way around boats and the water. Somebody killed him, Will, and whoever did it went through his office. He was a real neatnik, but the office was a mess."

"Who would have done that?"

"I'm going to find out. Trust me, Will. I will find out!"

"You say he had papers that his sister gave you."

"Yeah. I've read them."

"They indict Prisler?"

"Damn near. No smoking gun, no definitive piece of evidence, but maybe enough to make law enforcement take notice. McQuaid told me that politics got in the way every time he tried to bring a case against Prisler. Prisler has Congressman Skaggs in his pocket, other politicians too. I'm sure he shovels lots of loot to our esteemed congressmen."

"Skaggs kept a case from being brought against Prisler?" Sayers said.

"According to McQuaid."

"I'd love to read those papers."

"Happy to share them with you."

"Robert."

"What?"

"You do realize that whoever killed Charlie Mc-Quaid might have targeted him because of you."

"It's crossed my mind."

"Which means—"

"Yeah, I know. I'll watch my back."

Brixton heard Marylee calling to him.

"Got to go," he told Sayers. "We'll catch up later."

Brixton had originally wanted to drive his own car in the procession to the Greene burial site, but his daughter Jill convinced him that he should be in the black stretch limo carrying the immediate family. It took a while for the procession of vehicles, flashers on, to fall in line, but it eventually pulled away from the church behind the hearse bearing the casket, uniformed officers directing traffic at the two major intersections that the group had to navigate.

Brixton thought he recognized a few reporters at the church, but they had the decency to not attempt to interview anyone. He saw them again at the cemetery, standing apart from the mourners surrounding the open grave site. His son-in-law, Frank, stood ramrod straight, his arm around his wife, Jill. As Father Monroe recited traditional prayers heard at virtually all Catholic burials, Brixton took note of another person, a man with a pockmarked tan face, small white mustache, and wearing a tan safari jacket. He didn't seem to be part of any group. He stood in a clump of trees, his eyes trained on the solemn ritual being performed, and Brixton wondered whether he was one of the gravediggers who'd prepared the plot.

As the mourners walked from the grave site to their cars, two reporters approached Brixton.

"I don't have a comment," Brixton said in reply to their questions.

"Do you still claim that Congressman Skaggs's son was with the suicide bomber?"

Brixton stopped walking and turned to the questioner. "You bet I do, and one of these days I'll prove it."

"Congressman Skaggs says that—"

"I don't care what Congressman Skaggs says," Brixton snapped. "Maybe you should look into his relationship with gun dealers and cult leaders."

"Who are you talking about?"

The rest of the family had reached the limo and called to Brixton.

"Who were they?" Jill asked when he caught up with them.

"Media types. I blew them off."

"I knew that would happen," Marylee said.

"First Amendment, that's all," Brixton said.

"It taints everything" was Marylee's response.

"You mean *I* taint everything," Brixton said.

She started to reply but stopped in midsentence and climbed into the limo, followed by Brixton.

Lashka had arranged for food and drinks at a local restaurant following the burial, but Brixton begged off when they returned to the church.

"You sure, Dad?" Jill asked. "It would give you a chance to relax."

"Yeah, I'm sure, sweetheart. I'm just not in the mood. Look, I'll call in a few days and we'll get together, go out for dinner, something like that."

"Okay." She embraced him and said, "I love you, Dad."

"And I love you, Jill. Take good care of the kid. He's my only grandson."

The turnout in Biloxi, Mississippi, for Paul Skaggs's funeral at the Old Biloxi Cemetery off Irish Hill Drive was huge. Dozens of his father's congressional colleagues traveled to this city on the Mississippi Sound that had suffered extensive damage in 2005 from Hurricane Katrina. Congressman Skaggs had used his considerable power within Congress to see that the city and other Mississippi cities on the Gulf Coast received maximum federal aid. Skaggs was a beloved figure in his state. The funeral was covered by teams from the networks and cable news channels, along with dozens of reporters from the print media. After a church service at which speakers broadcast the service outside to the hundreds of people who couldn't get in, the entourage led by Skaggs and his wife slowly made its way to the cemetery, where their only son was interred.

Members of the press surrounded Skaggs following the service. Appropriately grim faced, he waved off their questions but stopped to make a statement, the sun shining off his silver hair.

"This is a very sad day for me and mah wife and for the good folks of Mississippi and the United States of America. It's bad enough to have had a beloved son gunned down in cold blood by someone charged with keeping the peace, but he's been maligned in the process. Ah am in talks with the Justice Department about looking into the killing of my son and bringing charges against his murderer. Now if you'll excuse me, ah have a lot of good people to thank for bein' here."

As he started to walk away, a reporter shouted, "Why isn't your daughter here, Congressman?"

Skaggs stopped and his face turned redder than usual. He fixed the reporter in a stare that would penetrate lead. "How dare you come here at this time of grief and sorrow and ask about what is a personal family matter? Ah suggest that you go back to wherever it is you come from and learn some manners."

With that he disappeared into the large crowd, which closed ranks around him.

Following the interment, a gathering was held at a local casino that had been rebuilt with federal funds generated by Skaggs. Rumors were rife over the course of his political career that he was closely entwined with the "Dixie Mafia," whose home base was Biloxi and which had practiced its violent control of business in that and other southern cities since the 1960s. Skaggs's rise from local politics to the United States Congress was said to have been achieved with the help of the Dixie Mafia's leaders, but no one had ever made the case against him, including local media, which was said to fear reprisals from Skaggs and his well-oiled Mississippi political machine.

He was having a drink with old friends when an aide whispered in his ear that he had an important call. He excused himself and took the aide's cell phone and his drink to a secluded corner of the casino.

"Skaggs here," he said in his raspy voice.

"It's Sam Prisler."

Skaggs looked around to ensure that he was alone. He was, but he still moved farther into the corner and lowered his voice. "This is a hell of a time to call me," he said.

"Look, Congressman, I know you just buried your son," Prisler said, "but this is important, too. You know what I'm talking about."

"I'm listening."

"Pull back on Brixton."

"What the hell does that mean?"

"We don't need more publicity about him. We don't need any hearings in Congress or lawsuits or anything else that keeps him in the public eye."

"The son of a bitch killed my only son."

"And he has to pay for that, but we'll take care of him in our own way. Keeping him in the public eye makes it more difficult."

Skaggs was aware that others were approaching. "Look, Sam, I can't talk now," he said. "You give me a call tomorrow night at my house in D.C."

"I'll do that, Congressman, but in the meantime, lay off Brixton."

The line went dead.

"Problem?" the aide who'd given him the phone asked.

"No, no problems. Fetch me another bourbon on the rocks, will you, Jamie? This one's got itself all watered down."

*   *   *

Brixton popped a frozen meal in the microwave and watched TV news. A live feed from the Paul Skaggs funeral showed Congressman and Mrs. Skaggs holding hands at the grave site. Brixton hadn't known that the Skaggs funeral was scheduled on the same day as his daughter's, and he found himself choking up as the reporter's voice-over talked of the special tragedy of burying a child. A close-up of Paul Skaggs's father and mother, tears running down the mother's face, the congressman's mouth set in a tight line of resignation, ended the piece.

Brixton retrieved the papers that Jeannette McQuaid had given him from where he'd secured them beneath shoe boxes in the bedroom closet, went to the balcony, and reread them. As much as he understood the prevailing message they contained—that Samuel Prisler was a major conduit for illegal arms and explosives to Middle Eastern countries, and there were tangential references to the role Zafar Alvi might play—much of the legal jargon and previous case histories tested his limited knowledge of the law. Halfway through the papers he dialed Mackensie Smith's number.

"Hello, Robert," Smith said. "Tough day for you."

"Tough for everybody, Mac. I'm calling to ask a favor."

"Shoot."

Brixton explained what he had and asked if Smith would read them and give his take on how damning the papers were for Prisler.

"Sure thing," Mac said.

"Can I run by now?"

"Give me an hour or two to finish up something I'm doing. Why don't you plan to come for dinner?"

"Annabel won't mind a last-minute guest?"

"No, she's used to it. I've always said that the perfect wife is one who doesn't mind last-minute guests, and who doesn't let travel snafus throw her. That's Annabel. Come by at seven."

Brixton had just returned to the balcony when the phone rang.

"Robert, it's Asal Banai."

"Hello, Asal. How are you?"

"I'm fine, but I'm feeling some remorse."

"Over what?"

"Over the way I acted at dinner the other night. I'm afraid I was testy and not very pleasant company."

He agreed, but knew that he wasn't a scintillating dinner companion, either.

"I enjoyed being with you anyway," he said.

"I suppose I'm asking for a rain check, another dinner, you know, to make amends."

"There's no need for that, Asal, but I'd enjoy having dinner with you."

"Free tonight?"

"No. I'm having dinner with the Smiths."

"Another time then."

"I'm sure the Smiths wouldn't mind if I . . . well, if I brought you along. I'll call Mac and ask, but I'm sure it'll be all right."

As expected, Mac told Brixton that they would enjoy seeing Asal again. Brixton called her back at her office and arranged to pick her up at six.

"I should mention," he told her, "that I've asked Mac to go over some papers with me. I want to pick his sizable legal brain. Shouldn't take too long."

"I'm always happy to talk with Annabel. Maybe she'll need help in the kitchen while you two huddle.

"Maybe she will. I don't think Mac spends a lot of time in the kitchen."

"What sort of papers?" she asked. "Or are they secret?"

"I'll fill you in later. Got to run. See you at six."

When he hung up he called Mike Kogan at SITQUAL. "Got a little time?" he asked.

"Depends on what you want."

"I need to run some things by you."

"Like what?"

"Not on the phone. Give me a half hour."

"Not now, Robert. Can you come by at five?"

"I'll be there."

It was three o'clock. Brixton went to the underground parking garage, shoved McQuaid's papers under the spare tire in the trunk, and drove to the address Kogan had given him for Zafar Alvi, whose car Paul Skaggs had been driving prior to the café bombing. He didn't have a plan of what to do once he got there, but he at least had to see where that car had come from, maybe gain a sense of this Zafar Alvi character.

He parked across the street and took in the stately home through a small pair of binoculars he kept in the glove compartment. He saw no one until after a few minutes, two tall, muscular young men came through the front door and peered down at him. Brixton's first instinct was to pull away. But he decided to stay and see what ensued. The men engaged in animated conversation before they started down. Brixton returned the binoculars to the glove compartment and waited.

They came to the car. Brixton leaned out the open window and said, "Hello. Nice day, huh?"

"Can we help you?" one of them asked.

"No, just out for drive and admiring the architecture of the house. Who lives there?"

"Why do you want to know?"

Brixton shrugged and laughed. "No special reason. Whoever lives there has good taste in houses, that's for sure."

"I suggest you leave."

"Leave? Why? Who am I bothering parked here?"

"We can call the police."

"Why would you do that? There's no law against me sitting here, no signs saying it's illegal to stand here. Come on, tell me who lives here."

The men glared at him before turning and heading back toward the stairs.

"Hey," Brixton yelled, "is this the house that Mr. Alvi lives in, you know, the bigwig in the Arab-American community?"

They stopped, muttered something to each other, ascended the staircase, and disappeared inside the house.

Brixton couldn't help but grin. He'd obviously gotten their attention, and he sat patiently waiting to see what would happen next. Minutes later an MPD patrol car pulled up behind him and two officers got out and approached. Brixton did what he'd been taught to do in that circumstance. He placed his wrists on the steering wheel in plain sight to show that he wasn't armed.

"Driver's license and registration," one of the cops said.

Brixton obliged.

"You have business here?" Brixton was asked as his documents were returned.

"No, just killing some time."

"We had a complaint from one of the homeowners in the area," a cop said.

"Mr. Alvi? He called and complained?"

"Not Alvi himself. Look, I suggest you move on unless you're visiting somebody."

"Of course, Officer. Don't want to cause any problems."

The cop standing outside the driver's side leaned a little closer to Brixton. "Are you the Brixton who shot the congressman's kid?"

"One and the same," Brixton said pleasantly.

"You got yourself in one big mess, huh?"

"You might say that. Sorry to have caused you any trouble."

"Take it easy," the cop said.

Brixton watched in his rearview mirror as they left. He looked back at the house and saw the two men standing together at the top of the stairs. Brixton was tempted to extend a middle finger but stifled the urge.

He was early for his meeting with Mike Kogan and passed the time browsing small shops on the same block as the Thai restaurant above which SITQUAL's headquarters was located. At a quarter to five he went upstairs and saw that Kogan was meeting with Donna Salvos, whom he hadn't seen in a while. Kogan waved him in. Donna kissed him on the cheek and asked how he was doing.

"Janet's funeral was today," he said.

"Must have been rough," Kogan said.

"It's been rough ever since the day that crazy young woman and Skaggs's son blew up the café," he said.

"I'll leave you two," Donna said.

"No, stay," Brixton said. "You'll be interested in a couple of things I've come up with."

Kogan asked, "Any progress on linking Skaggs to the bombing?"

"Lots of intriguing stuff, but nothing tied up in a neat bow. You remember when we interviewed Lalo Reyes about the Müller murder?" he asked Donna.

"Sure."

"I caught up with him again."

"Why?" Kogan asked, and Brixton knew that his boss was concerned that he'd done something official even though he'd been suspended.

"I remembered when we talked to him that he said he'd once lived in Hawaii. Seems that Paul Skaggs, the congressman's son, lived there, too, in a cult run by

Samuel Prisler. Mr. Lalo Reyes also spent time in that cult. Not only that, he's on his way back there."

Donna's and Kogan's expressions were blank.

"Congressman Skaggs's daughter is also a member of that cult."

Kogan asked, "How do you know that Reyes is going back?"

"I had a pleasant little chat with him," Brixton said. He addressed Salvos. "You know a guy named Charles McQuaid? You do, Mike." He explained to Donna, "A retired Justice Department lawyer. At least he was until he died."

"You told me that you were getting together with him, Robert," Kogan said. "He died just the other day. There was a small obit in *The Post*. Something about a drowning accident?"

"He was murdered," Brixton said flatly.

"How do you know that?" Donna asked.

"I just know, okay? Prisler, the arms dealer and cult leader—you told me that you know about him, Mike—Prisler was on McQuaid's radar screen when he was with Justice. He built one hell of a case file against him. I have that file."

Kogan's phone rang. He picked up, heard who was calling, and said, "I'm busy right now. I'll call back." He replaced the phone in its cradle and said to Brixton, "I know you're under the gun, Robert, but are you sure you're not going off the deep end?"

"I don't blame you for wondering that," Brixton said, "but these seemingly unconnected things are starting to come together for me. Ready for another?"

"Go ahead."

"You told me about the Skaggs kid getting a traffic ticket while he was driving somebody else's car, this guy named Zafar Alvi."

"Uh-huh."

"There were references to Alvi in McQuaid's papers."

"In connection with Prisler?"

"Right."

"What's the link?"

"That maybe Prisler funnels his illegal arms to militants around the world through Alvi."

"*'Maybe'?*"

"Yeah, maybe."

"Hardly a solid case, Robert. Alvi is an important guy in D.C. He's close to people in Congress."

"Buys them off, you mean, the way Prisler does?"

"I'm just saying that unless you have solid evidence of wrongdoing, you're on shaky turf."

"I know the puzzle is still in pieces," Brixton said, "but it's enough to keep me going. Look, you were good enough to check on how and when Paul Skaggs got to D.C. from Hawaii, and told me about the traffic ticket. I need another favor from MPD."

"What is it?"

"I need to talk to somebody in Homicide about McQuaid's murder, convince them that it *was* a murder and *not* an accident."

"How do you do that?"

"Get a forensics team down to McQuaid's boat, check it out. One of McQuaid's neighbors says he saw two guys in a boat pulled up next to McQuaid the day he died. I'm telling you Mike, Charlie McQuaid was murdered!"

"Because of giving you papers that could be incriminating for certain people?" Kogan said.

"I hope not, but that's a good possibility," said Brixton.

"If that's the case, you're playing with some very powerful people," Kogan offered.

"Yeah, and not of my choosing," Brixton said. "Look, if you'll put me in touch with somebody at MPD, I'd really appreciate it. In the meantime I intend to do some digging into this Zafar Alvi and his possible connection to Prisler, Skaggs—hell, with everybody."

As Brixton prepared to leave, Donna said, "By the way, there's been another embassy murder."

"Open season on them, huh?" Brixton said. "Who this time?"

"A guy from the Danish embassy. His body was found this morning in his apartment, single gunshot to the back of his head, gangland style."

"I'm afraid to ask," Brixton said. "Was he straight or gay?"

"Gay. *The Post* is working on a feature story linking all the embassy murders together. They're concluding that the killings are bias crimes, the work of a homophobe. The Frenchman who got it was also gay."

"Except that not only were the victims gay or lesbian, they also all worked for foreign embassies."

"So what's the motive?" Donna asked. "Homophobia, or somebody who has it in for foreign embassies?"

"You bought the bias-crime angle from the very beginning," Kogan said to Brixton.

"And I gave up on it. What about the café bombing? One of the victims was that gal who's a leader in the gay community."

"It was also a popular hangout for State Department workers," Donna said.

"I don't buy it," Brixton said. "The MO is different. The café bombing was a classic terrorist act: Take down as many people as you can in one swoop. Knocking off individual embassy workers is something else. Not only that, every murder victim worked for a *different* embassy—German, French, Italian, Polish, and now Danish. It would make sense if somebody had it in for a particular country, but this is all over the map."

"Literally," Donna added.

Brixton realized that he had to leave to pick up Asal Banai.

"Thanks for hearing me out," he told Kogan and Donna Salvos.

"I can't promise anything, but I'll run the McQuaid thing past someone in Homicide," Kogan assured.

"Thanks, Mike. You know I appreciate it."

Kogan grabbed his shoulder. "And Robert," he said, "watch your back."

"You're the second one to tell me that today."

Asal lived in a relatively new apartment building in Foggy Bottom. Brixton told the doorman that he was there to pick up Ms. Banai and was directed to the top floor, one of four corner penthouse apartments that were surprisingly small considering the "penthouse" designation, each with an equally small but pleasant balcony that could be accessed from two sides.

"Beautiful place, Asal," Brixton said as she led him into the living room with thick white carpeting, white furniture, and splashes of gold—lamps, chandelier, and tabletops.

"Thank you. I was lucky to find this apartment."

"Must set you back some," he said, immediately realizing that what she paid was none of his business.

"I manage," she replied. "Make you a drink?"

"Thanks, no, I'll wait until we get to Mac and Annabel's. We should leave."

"Yes, of course. I'll only be a minute."

She disappeared into another room, and Brixton stepped out onto the balcony. The view was nice; the District of Columbia's strict ban on building heights assured distant views. He took note of the outdoor furniture, which was also white and expensive-looking. He briefly recalled her comments about how the Iraqi Partnership was always low on funds, but he forgot what he was thinking when she appeared at the door.

"Ready?" she asked.

"Let's go," he said.

"Tell me about these mysterious papers you have," Asal said as they settled in Brixton's car and headed for the Watergate.

"They were given to me by a man named Charles McQuaid," Brixton said. "He was a retired Justice Department attorney who spent a lot of his time at Justice trying to build a case against Samuel Prisler, an arms dealer in Hawaii. I mentioned him to you when we had dinner."

"Yes, I seem to remember that name. Why are you interested in him, this fellow Prisler?"

"It's a long story, Asal. Don't want to bore you with it."

"I don't think you could ever bore me," she said, lightly.

"We'll have to see about that," he said as he pulled into the Watergate's underground parking garage.

Annabel greeted them and brought them to the kitchen, where Mac had set up a bar. "Help yourselves," she said. "Mac will be out in a minute."

They'd taken their drinks to the balcony overlooking the Potomac River when Mac appeared. "Sorry," he said. "A last-minute flap at the university." To Brixton: "Why don't we take care of business before dinner? That way we can relax over our meal."

The two men retreated to Mac's study, leaving Annabel and Asal on the balcony with their glasses of wine.

"You are Robert's good friends," Asal said absently

"Yes, we are. We became involved with him when he was in Washington trying to get answers for a client back in Savannah, Georgia. He ended up being wounded, but he got what he was after. He's tenacious, that's for certain."

"Does he have a woman in his life?" Asal asked casually.

Annabel picked up on the question. She had a feeling that Asal might be smitten with Brixton, which amused her. She'd met his former lover, Flo Combes, when she'd come to D.C. to pick him up and drive him back to New York, where they'd decided to return to live.

"He had a very nice gal, Asal. Her name is Flo Combes. Frankly, I thought they might end up married one day, but they've broken up. She's still in New York."

"Breaking up with her must add to the terrible ordeal he's going through," Asal said.

"I'm sure it hasn't helped."

"I'm afraid that we got off on the wrong foot."

"Oh? How so?"

"He took me to dinner after we'd met here, and I took some of his comments as being anti-Muslim."

"Robert? I don't think he has a biased bone in his body. At least, I've never seen it surface."

"No, Annabel, it was *I* who was wrong. I was too sensitive, looking for examples of people broad-brushing all Muslims because of what has happened around the world at the hands of a few fanatics, and the café bombing here that took his daughter."

"Why don't you forget about that and start new? I mean, here he is bringing you for dinner. Let's just enjoy the evening and let things develop naturally."

Asal smiled. "Good advice. But I would expect nothing else from you."

Mac and Brixton huddled for an hour. When they emerged, Mac made fresh drinks for them and they joined the women.

"So, Robert, did you accomplish what you wanted to?" Annabel asked.

"I think so," Brixton said. "Your husband has one hell of a legal mind."

"His students think so," Annabel said.

"What is this about?" Asal asked, her brown eyes wide.

Mac started to respond but stopped and said to Brixton, "You're better equipped to explain what's going on, Robert."

And Brixton did exactly that for the next half hour, outlining his suspicions and the still-missing pieces of the puzzle.

After dinner of baby back ribs, homemade slaw, fresh baguettes from the Watergate bakery, and key lime pie, the two couples returned to the balcony and sipped from snifters of single-barrel bourbon that Mac had purchased at the liquor store, also part of the Watergate complex. It was a balmy night; fog had settled in over the river and created a mist through which the spires of Georgetown University came and went.

"What you have said tonight gives me a chill," Asal said to Brixton, wrapping her arms about herself to further make the point.

"The problem," Mac said, "is tying together all these loose ends, but what Robert has given me could prove to be explosive."

"I've asked Mac to think about how we can use what's in the papers to bring charges against people like Prisler and the guy who loaned the Skaggs kid his car, Zafar Alvi."

"But how would that help you prove that Congressman Skaggs's son was with the café bomber?" Annabel asked Brixton.

"I don't have an answer for that, Annabel, but maybe putting the pressure on will force someone into making a mistake."

"I am shocked to hear that Mr. Alvi might be involved in something illegal," Asal said.

"You know him?" Mac asked.

"No, no, I don't, but he is a well-known man in Arab-American circles, a very important man."

"I stopped in front of his house before I picked you up, Asal. He sent a couple of musclemen down to ask why I was there."

"Did you talk to him?"

"No. That's next on my agenda. Up until today I almost felt that there was no way to put the pieces together. But Mac has helped me think in—what do you call it?—in a more linear way."

The conversation drifted to other matters at times but kept coming back to Brixton's dilemma. Asal had little to say aside from asking an occasional question about what Brixton had learned about Samuel Prisler and his possible connection with Zafar Alvi. Before leaving, Brixton mentioned that Mac had agreed to keep the papers McQuaid had given him.

"I'd like more time to go over them," Smith explained.

"Better you have them than me," Brixton said.

It had started to rain by the time Brixton and Asal left the Smith's apartment. They got in his car and headed in the direction of her apartment building.

"I'm concerned about you," she said.

"Why?"

"The people who did what you say they did to Mr. McQuaid are bad people."

"Lots of bad people in this world."

"But aren't you concerned for your life?"

"I think about it once in a while, but then I remember Janet, my daughter, how she died, her young life blown sky-high by some demented woman and the guy with her. No, I'm not worried about my life, Asal. My .

biggest worry is that I'll never make the bastards who did it pay."

He pulled into a parking spot close to the building's entrance.

"Thanks for coming with me tonight," he said.

"I was pleased that you asked me. I meant what I said on the phone, that I'm sorry for the way I behaved the first time we had dinner."

"That's old news," Brixton said.

"Would you like to come up for a drink?" she asked.

"Yeah, that'd be nice."

She put on lamps in the living room and slipped a CD into a small stereo unit on a bookshelf.

"Who's playing?" Brixton asked.

"Taylor Swift. Do you know her?"

"She sings western songs," Brixton said.

"Do you like western songs?" Asal asked.

"Not much. I mean, I don't listen to that kind of music. I'm a jazz lover."

"Oh, American jazz. Yes, jazz is very American, isn't it?"

"Actually it's pretty much all over the world," he said as he went to where her CD collection took up one shelf, and he flipped through it until coming to a dozen recordings by familiar jazz musicians. He chose one by the pianist Oscar Peterson and his trio. "Where'd you get this?" he asked.

She came to his side and took the CD. "A friend gave it to me. He wanted me to become familiar with American music."

"Mind if we play it?"

"No, of course not."

The sound of Peterson and the trio playing the standard "These Foolish Things" came through the speakers.

"I love Oscar Peterson," Brixton said. "He's one of the best."

"Do you dance?" she asked.

He laughed. "Not so you'd recognize it. I'm pretty clumsy on the dance floor."

"My friend also taught me how to dance like an American," she said, extending her arms.

Brixton hesitated before allowing himself to slip into her embrace. The lush chords played by Peterson, the soft lighting, and the feel of her against him overcame his reluctance to dance, as they moved back and forth, the smell of her rich black hair, her low voice humming along with the recording seducing his every sense.

The trio launched into something with a faster tempo, "The Lamp Is Low," and they stopped dancing, but stayed coupled. He kissed her neck and she purred. She raised her lips to him and they kissed. Minutes later they were in her bedroom where they made sustained, satisfying love before falling asleep in each other's arms.

23

B rixton left Asal's apartment at six the next morning, drove home, showered and changed, had breakfast in a local luncheonette, and read that day's *Washington Post*. The long feature article about the raft of embassy murders started on page one and jumped to two inside pages. It was a collaborative effort by three *Post* reporters, and the headline said it all: D.C.'S LGBT COMMUNITY UNDER FIRE.

In the article, the reporters cited each of the embassy killings, starting with Peter Müller and ending with the most recent murder of the Danish embassy staffer. Brixton found it interesting that the connection the victims had with foreign embassies was downplayed, although it was mentioned as a possible theory behind the killings. A spokesman for the MPD was quoted as saying, "We have established a task force to look into these murders and are confident that whoever is behind them, whether a single individual or a group of people, will be brought to justice. We are working closely with members of the State Department's security professionals in the event that the victims' embassy connections have anything to do with the crimes. In the meantime, we urge members of the city's LGBT community to exercise particular care. I'll have further details as the task force develops possible solutions."

The overall message of the article was that a demented homophobe or homophobes were on the loose in Washington.

Brixton reflected on his conversation with Mike Kogan and Donna Salvos. It was obvious that no one had come to a firm conclusion about the genesis of the murders—embassy personnel, or gays and lesbians. While *The Post* piece covered both possibilities, it leaned heavily toward the bias-crime scenario.

Brixton's own thought process mirrored this confusion. He'd started buying the bias theory, shifted to an embassy motive, and now had come back to the thrust of *The Post* article. He imagined the difficulty the MPD was having in deciding which scenario to pursue, which was in line with the debate going on in SITQUAL and the State Department's DSS security apparatus.

Yes, the victims were homosexual or lesbian.

They also all worked for foreign embassies.

His years as a cop and private investigator had taught him that motive was a crucial element in solving crimes, especially murder. Motive narrowed the field of suspects, as did access to the victims. As he pondered this he thought back to Lalo Reyes and his relationship with Peter Müller. Will Sayers had also said that Reyes was possibly involved with a closeted gay congressman. Had the slender Spaniard been romantically entwined with other embassy personnel who had been murdered? He made a mental note to check that out with Donna Salvos. If anyone would know, she would.

As he sat in the luncheonette, he reflected back on the

previous evening with Asal Banai. He had been surprised when she'd invited him to have a nightcap in
her apartment, although the possibility of extending the
evening had crossed his mind. He'd been tentative; it
had been a while since he'd been romantically involved
with a woman, going back to when Flo Combes had
walked out. But Asal made it easy, nurturing, inviting,
and skilled. There were moments when he felt guilty at
being in bed with a woman other than Flo, even though
he knew that was irrational. It was over with Flo, and
he didn't have any doubts that she'd found another man
in New York and was spending intimate time with him.

He also acknowledged to himself that he was taken
aback at Asal's sexual forwardness, at least initially.
There you go again, he told himself as he finished his
coffee, *stereotyping people.* He'd read of Arab women
being stoned to death for straying outside their clois-
tered families and being sexually active. But Asal had
been in the United States for ten years. She spoke excellent English and had been exposed to the more per-
missive sexual climate in America than was evident in
her native Iraq.

His reverie was interrupted by the ringing phone.

"Robert, Mike Kogan here. You wanted me to set
you up with someone in Homicide at MPD. Here's the
name. I told him you'd be calling."

"Thanks, Mike. I appreciate it."

"Just don't do anything that'll cause me or SITQUAL
any grief."

"Would I do something like that, Mike?"

"Yeah, you would. Stay in touch, let me know what
comes out of your meeting at MPD."

The detective's name was Quintin Halliday. Brixton called and was put through to him.

"Mike Kogan said you'd be calling," Halliday said.

"It's about the Charles McQuaid accidental death, right?"

"The Charles McQuaid *murder*," Brixton corrected.

"Kogan said that was why you'd call. What makes you think it wasn't an accident?"

"Mind if we don't go into this over the phone?" Brixton said. "Any chance of getting together this morning?"

"I've gone over the paperwork that was filed by the officers who responded to the scene. I don't see anything that pops out at me, but I'm willing to listen."

"That's all I can ask," Brixton said. "How about I buy you coffee at the place across the street from headquarters?"

"I never turn down a free cup of coffee unless somebody's trying to buy *me*."

"I'm not trying to buy anything. Does a half hour work for you?"

"Fine. I'm the tall black dude in a gray suit."

Halliday was already at an outdoor table when Brixton arrived, coffee and a cinnamon Danish on the table. Brixton went inside, got himself a coffee, and joined the detective.

"So," Halliday said, "give it to me straight and fast. Oh, before you do, just so all the cards are on the table, I'm aware of who you are; dragged up your old personnel file. You lasted here four years, and now you're under the gun for killing the congressman's kid."

"He blew up my daughter," Brixton muttered.

"So I hear. Sorry about that. Don't know how I'd react if it happened to one of my kids."

"Probably no different than me. Look, I don't want to waste your time. Here's why I say that Charlie McQuaid was murdered."

Brixton gave a concise recapping of how Will Sayers

had put him in touch with McQuaid, his initial meeting with him, plans for dinner the following night, and arriving at the house and learning of his death. He spoke of McQuaid's sister, Jeannette, and how she'd given him her brother's case file on Samuel Prisler. He finished his summation with, "McQuaid had given up fishing after his wife died. He was an experienced boater. His neighbor saw two guys in another boat in the cove next to Charlie's boat earlier that afternoon. Later, Charlie is dragged out of the water with fishing line wrapped around his neck. Give me a break. Somebody who didn't like that he was trying to build a case against Prisler got rid of him. I was in his office the day before he died. It was pristine. He was a meticulous guy, put Felix Unger to shame."

"Who?"

"Felix Unger, the character on the TV show *The Odd Couple*. Tony Randall was the actor."

"Okay, I know who you mean."

"So after he was found, his sister takes me to his office and it was all messed up. Stuff thrown on the desk. Somebody went through his files after killing him."

Halliday took a final bite of his Danish and sat back. "What you say makes sense, Brixton. The problem is that McQuaid's death has already been labeled a drowning accident."

"That doesn't mean it can't be reinvestigated."

"What do you suggest I do?"

"Bring a forensics team to his boat, see if there's anything on it that points to something other than an accidental drowning. Talk to the neighbor."

"My boss will never buy it," Halliday said. "We're up to our necks with murders."

"But you can give it a try, can't you?"

"Sure, I can give it a try. Mike Kogan's a buddy, and he sure as hell is a fan of yours. But no promises."

"There never are. And yeah, Kogan is one of the white hats. Thanks."

"I'll let you know what the captain says."

B rixton's cell rang at two that afternoon.
  "It's Quintin Halliday. There'll be a forensics team at McQuaid's house at four."

Brixton spent part of the time waiting to go to McQuaid's house on a phone call with Mac Smith.

"The material in these files is compelling," Smith said. "I'd like to run it past some friends at Justice."

"I can't imagine them doing anything," Brixton said. "McQuaid was stymied at every turn, at least according to him."

"And I may run into the same roadblocks. But I also have some friends in Congress."

"Like Walter Skaggs?"

Smith laughed. "Hardly. Just give me the word and I'll see what I can do."

"Go for it, Mac," Brixton said.

Brixton found the phone number McQuaid's sister had given him and called to tell her about the forensics unit coming to her brother's house. He asked her to be there. She agreed.

He arrived at twenty minutes to four and was surprised that there was someone in the house. His knock was answered by a man, a younger version of McQuaid, who introduced himself as Alex, one of Charlie's sons.

"My name's Robert Brixton. Your dad and I were supposed to have dinner the day he died. I'm, ah . . . I'm here because I've asked the police to reexamine your dad's boat."

Alex looked puzzled.

"It's hard to explain," Brixton said, "but it boils down to my not believing your father died in a boating accident."

"What do you mean?"

"What I mean is I think that he was murdered."

Alex did what so many young people do when at a loss for words. He laughed.

"I know this might be a shock to you, Alex, but it's important to know what really happened here."

"Who would want to murder my father?"

"That's what I want to find out."

"Are you a cop?"

"No, I'm with . . . I'm an agent with SITQUAL. We're part of the State Department's security force." He showed him his ID.

"And you think my father was murdered?"

"Unfortunately, I do. I've called your aunt Jeannette. She's coming over."

"Does she also believe that Pop was murdered? She never said anything to me."

"She agrees with me that your father was an experienced guy around boats, and that he'd quit fishing when your mother died. Did he ever tell *you* that he was hanging up his fishing rod for good?"

Alex thought for a moment. "Yeah, he did, more than once. I think he missed it, though. Maybe he decided to—"

"To take it up again? Didn't happen."

They were interrupted when Detective Halliday and his colleagues pulled into the driveway. Brixton introduced Halliday to Alex McQuaid, who asked what it was they wanted him to do.

"Show us the boat your father was in when he died," Halliday said. "Won't take too long."

The son hesitated before asking, "Do you need a warrant to do this?"

"We're not looking for any wrongdoing by your father," Brixton said. "We just want to rule out foul play in his death."

"I can get a warrant," Halliday said.

"No, that's okay," Alex said. "If my father was murdered—"

"You'd want to know," Brixton said, finishing the thought.

Alex accompanied them down to the dock and watched as the photographer began taking photos and as the fingerprint tech went to work.

"Hard to get prints off these surfaces," the tech grumbled.

"Do your best," Halliday said.

The woman in charge of the team slowly walked along the boat's deck, her eyes taking in the small craft inch by inch, as Brixton and Halliday stayed out of her way. She stopped, bent over, then got down on one knee to examine something. Halliday and Brixton moved closer to see what had captured her attention. She pointed at shoe imprints on the shiny, recently painted floor. "More than one," she said.

"McQuaid went out alone," Brixton said.

"How can you be sure?"

"He liked going out alone," Brixton said. "He told me that. But his neighbor said he saw two guys pulled up next to his boat."

"Did he say whether they came on board?" Halliday asked.

"Not that I recall. We can see if he's around when we're finished up here."

The lead investigator instructed the photographer to get close-ups of the shoe prints. While he carried out her instructions, she again leaned over. She motioned for Halliday and Brixton to join her.

"Did anybody examine this boat when we got the call about the drowning?" she asked.

"Nothing in the report filed by the officers who responded," Halliday said.

"Look," she said, pointing to an area of the freeboard wale above the waterline. Brixton got close and took in what she was seeing. The otherwise immaculate surface was scratched and gouged. There was also what looked like dried blood. Further examination of the freeboard indicated that something yellow had scraped against it.

"That sure wasn't there the day before he died," Brixton said. "I was out on this boat with him. It was clean and without any marks."

"You said that the neighbor saw two men in another boat in the cove talking with the deceased," Halliday said. "Chances are their boat had a yellow finish and some of it rubbed off when they bumped."

"Maybe," Brixton muttered. "Why the blood?"

"If it is blood, he could have cut himself," Halliday replied.

"Or someone else cut himself," Brixton retorted. He asked the chief forensics examiner if there was enough dried blood to run a DNA on it.

She nodded. "I'll have to scrape away the portion with the blood."

Brixton looked to where McQuaid's son stood taking it in. "You have any objections to us slicing a small piece off your dad's boat?"

"I don't know. I . . ."

"I don't," McQuaid's sister, Jeannette, said, joining the others on the dock. She put her arm around Alex and hugged him. "We want to know the truth about Charlie's death, don't we?" she said to him.

Alex nodded. "Okay," he announced. "Go ahead." He

turned to his aunt with tears in his eyes. "But I don't want to watch, okay?"

"Of course," his aunt said. "Why don't you wait for me in the house."

Ten minutes later, with evidence in hand, the foren- sics team had driven away. The commotion had been noticed by Charlie's next-door neighbor, who stood with his wife on their patio. Brixton waved them over.

"Wally Fenton," the neighbor said, shaking Brixton's hand. "My wife, Agnes. What's going on?" he asked Brixton, Halliday, and Jeannette McQuaid.

Brixton explained.

"I gotta say I'm not surprised," he said, "Charlie made some enemies when he was working. At least that's what he told me."

"He say who?" Brixton asked.

"Names? Nah. He just said that there were people who didn't like what he was doing. Besides, there's lots of crime around here these days."

"Wally has a gun," his wife said.

"It's legal," Wally quickly added.

"Did you happen to get a good look at the two men you say were with Charlie the day he died?" Brixton asked.

The neighbor's grin was self-satisfying. "I sure did. I took a look through my field glasses."

"Binoculars?" Halliday asked.

"Uh-huh. I always have them with me when I go out on the water; carry my gun too. I've got a carry permit. Used to work security."

"You looked at them through your binoculars?" Brixton said.

Wally nodded. "Well, I was really looking at the boat, but they were on it."

"Wally's nosy," said Agnes.

"It's not being nosy," Wally said, annoyed at his

wife's comment. "But I like to keep an eye on what's going on around here. Like I said, there's too much damn crime."

"I think your neighbors are lucky to have somebody like you to keep tabs on things," Brixton said. "So tell us, what did the two men with Charlie look like?"

"Well, let's see," said Wally. "One was a little guy. The other was a lot bigger."

"You used your binoculars," Brixton said. "You must have seen their faces."

"Sure I did. The little one, he had kind of a thin face, like one of those rodents that people keep as pets."

"Like a ferret?" Halliday offered.

"Yeah, that's it. Like a ferret. The big guy had a tan, that's for sure, and a white mustache. He wore one of those jackets with pockets like they wear on a safari, you know, on *National Geographic* on TV. I thought it was kind of a funny thing to wear to go out on a boat."

It's also a funny thing to wear to a funeral, Brixton thought, remembering the man he'd seen at Janet's funeral standing apart from the mourners.

"Anything else?" Halliday asked. "What was the smaller man wearing?"

"Some sort of Windbreaker, blue if I recall. And he had a hat on, a Nationals cap, a white one. Had it on backwards. I never understand why people wear baseball hats backwards. Looks goofy, if you ask me."

"I know what you mean," Brixton said through a smile. "Thanks for taking the time to talk to me."

Wally's wife took Brixton aside and asked in almost a whisper, "You think that Charlie was murdered?"

"Just checking into all the possibilities," Brixton replied.

"I wish Wally would mind his own business," she said. "I hate that gun he carries with him."

"He seems like a responsible guy," Brixton said. "It's

okay for a guy like him to have a gun. It's the crazies we have to worry about."

"He won't get in any trouble will he?"

"Can't imagine why. Thanks for your time, ma'am."

Jeannette McQuaid stood in the driveway waiting for Brixton to finish his conversation with the neighbor.

"Thanks for coming," Brixton said. He introduced Detective Halliday to her.

"You said the police would be here," she said to Brixton. "Is there a problem?"

"There's a possibility that your brother didn't die in a fishing accident, Jeannette. He might have been murdered."

"So I gathered from what you were discussing with Wally Fenton. Do you really think that Charlie was murdered?"

"Maybe," Brixton said. "Detective Halliday will be following up on whatever was found on the boat today."

"Poor Charlie," she said, more to herself than to them. "I wanted to believe that he died doing what he loved, being out in his boat and enjoying the fresh air. To think that he was killed by someone is terrible."

"We can't always choose how we die," Brixton said. "What I'd like you to do is tell Detective Halliday what Charlie told you, that he gave up fishing, the same thing he told me."

She obliged.

"I'll stay in touch," Brixton told her. "Maybe we can have dinner again."

"I would like that, but now there's a young man inside who needs me," she said, heading for the door.

24

Brixton intended to phone Asal to see whether she was free for dinner, but a call from Will Sayers dashed that plan.

"Hey buddy, how're you doing?"

"I'm doing okay."

"You up for an early dinner?"

"What's the occasion?"

"You promised me an interview. Remember?"

"I was afraid you were going to say that."

"Not only do you owe me an interview," the corpulent newspaper editor said, "I have some information that might interest you."

"About what?"

"Nothing special—dead embassy workers, murdered homosexuals, gun merchants, terrorists—insignificant stuff like that."

"I assume dinner's on me," Brixton said.

"Absolutely."

"Then I pick the restaurant. Let's make it Bobby

Van's Grill on New York Avenue. Best lamb chops in town."

"Sounds like your horse came in."

"Nothing like that. I just figure I'm due some good lamb chops. See you at seven."

Brixton took his cell phone to the balcony and punched in Donna Salvos's cell number.

"It was good seeing you, Robert," she said.

"Same here. Donna, I mentioned that our Lalo Reyes was leaving town, heading for his cult in Hawaii. Have you gotten any information that he might have been romantically involved with any of the other embassy workers who've been killed?"

"No, I haven't. Why? Have you heard something to that effect?"

"Just a wild notion, that's all." He refrained from mentioning that, according to Will Sayers, Reyes might have been involved with a member of Congress. "Any chance of doing a little digging into that possibility?"

"I'll see what I can turn up, only don't expect anything."

"It's the effort that counts," he said.

Brixton preceded Sayers to the restaurant and waited for him at the long bar, sipping a shaken, cold, dry martini with a twist. It had been a trying day, and he felt that he owed himself some pleasant downtime with his favorite drink. Two men to his right also ordered martinis, but theirs were of the vodka variety. The vodka distillers and marketers had done a superb job of changing the habits of martini drinkers, Brixton thought. For him, the only *real* martini was made with gin. Order a martini these days, and it was automatically assumed by the bartender that you wanted vodka. *Another precious tradition left in the dust,* he mused as he savored another sip.

Ten minutes later the editor walked in, came to Brixton, looked down at his half-consumed drink, and said, "Still thinking you're James Bond, huh?"

"Bond preferred vodka in his martinis," Brixton said, "but he drank some with gin too."

Sayers slid onto the adjacent stool and laughed. "Had to be shaken, right?"

"Of course. Did you know that shaking a martini releases more antioxidants than stirring does?"

"That's BS."

"I wouldn't expect you to know such things," Brixton said. "Go ahead, order your bourbon or Southern Comfort. You can take the man out of Savannah but . . ."

Sayers caught the bartender's attention and ordered a single-barrel bourbon on the rocks.

"So," Brixton said, "what's this information I'm paying for in this expensive joint?"

"You chose it."

"That's not the point." He motioned to the bartender for another. "I was at Charlie McQuaid's today."

"Helping with funeral plans?"

"I was with some MPD forensics types going over his boat. He was murdered, Will. I think they'll come up with proof of that, or at least enough to open an investigation."

Sayers nodded and toasted Brixton. "Maybe I should be paying for information from *you*," he said. "How's your love life?"

"I don't have one."

"You and that beautiful woman at the Smiths seemed to hit it off."

"Asal? We're friends, that's all. Let's take a table. I can smell those lamb chops from here."

Settled at their table and having placed their orders, Brixton asked what information the heavyset editor had for him.

"You remember when I told you about the hypocritical Georgia congressman who preaches against the sins of homosexuality but maybe dabbles himself?" Sayers asked.

"Sure."

"You said that Reyes was involved with that German embassy staffer, Müller, who was murdered."

"That's why I interviewed Reyes," Brixton acknowledged. "By the way, I sort of interviewed him again."

"Oh?"

"Not an official interview. Long story short, I suspect that Mr. Reyes is involved with that cult on Maui run by Samuel Prisler, the same one where Paul Skaggs spent time and where his sister lives."

"Maybe the dots are getting closer," Sayers offered.

"Not close enough. Reyes has left D.C., headed back to Maui."

Sayers dug into his salad before saying, "Interested in more about Mr. Lalo Reyes?"

"I'm listening."

"You do know, I assume, that a young Danish guy from the Danish embassy was murdered."

"Mike Kogan at SITQUAL told me."

"Would it interest you to know that your pal Mr. Reyes is rumored to have been an intimate friend of the victim?" Sayers asked.

"Of the Dane?"

"Yup."

"Müller, the Dane, and your congressman. I Googled the esteemed elected official after you told me about him. Nice-looking guy, young," Brixton said.

"Blond, like Müller and the Dane."

Brixton took the last bite of his lamb chops. "I wonder . . . ," he said.

"Wonder what?"

"Reyes suddenly quits his job at the Spanish embassy

and skips town. He didn't come off to me like the kind of guy who kills people, but looks can be deceiving. You come up with anything linking Reyes to the other embassy victims?"

"No. You read the piece in *The Post* about the embassy murders?"

"Sure. The writers alluded to the fact that all the victims worked for foreign embassies, but as far as they're concerned, the murders are bias crimes."

"They may be right."

"Or they may be wrong. Will, I asked you the last time we talked whether you knew anything about a man named Zafar Alvi."

"I did some checking after that conversation. Alvi is a shadowy character, well-connected, with pipelines into Middle Eastern countries and into certain members of Congress. You might say that he's a lobbyist for Middle Eastern interests."

"And a conduit for Samuel Prisler's illegal arms sales?"

"That's one of many rumors about him."

"He's rich, right, lives in a fancy house, has young muscle-boys working for him? Where does he get his money?"

"Why don't you ask him?"

"I'd like to."

Sayers fished something from his jacket pocket and handed it to Brixton. It was an invitation to a dinner honoring Zafar Alvi for his philanthropic work on behalf of the Arab-American charity hosting the event the following night at the Hay-Adams Hotel.

"How'd you get this?" Brixton asked.

"The power of the press. I get invited everywhere, only I turn down most invitations. These dinners honoring someone are all the same, dried-out chicken and long-winded, self-serving speeches."

"You going?"

"No, but I figured you might want to."

"Interesting idea. What other goodies do you have?"

"Your turn to give *me* something, Robert. The interview. I've filed stories back to Savannah about what happened at the café and your involvement, nothing insightful, just what's already known and published. But I need something more personal from you, how you've been handling the pressure you're under, what you've been doing to try and clear your name and avenge what happened to your daughter."

"I don't feel up to doing an archaeological dig into my inner feelings."

"It might be therapeutic," Sayers said.

"Like talking to a shrink?"

"It'd be cheaper talking to me."

Brixton nodded. "Okay," he said. "When?"

"No time like the present, but not here. Let's go back to my apartment. I'll just need an hour with you."

The waiter brought the check, which prompted Brixton to say, "Actually, a shrink would have been cheaper. I feel like I'm paying off the national debt."

Sayers's apartment mirrored his casual approach to almost everything in life, including his wardrobe. Wrinkled clothes were piled everywhere; the sink contained a week's worth of soiled dishes. One corner of the living room had been turned into an office of sorts, with desktop and laptop computers, two phones, and stacks of paper covering every surface of the hollow door on legs that served as the desk. Sayers broke out bottles of gin and bourbon, loaded a pitcher with ice cubes, and plopped two glasses on the edge of the desk. He wedged himself in behind the desktop computer and said to Brixton, who sat in a red director's chair with black arms, "Shoot, Robert. Just talk. I type fast. Just let it come out—your feelings, your thoughts about what's happened to you and your daughter, and how you've been trying to clear yourself since being suspended from the State Department's security apparatus. No holds barred; just spill it."

Brixton talked for an hour and a half while Sayers's stubby fingers flew over his keyboard.

"Enough," Brixton announced, downing what was left in his glass. "That's it—my life story. Think it'll sell newspapers?"

"I don't care whether it does or not," Sayers said. "I appreciate it."

"What are friends for? Time for me to go; past my bedtime."

"It's only ten."

"That's late enough."

Sayers walked him to where he'd parked his car. As Brixton was about to get in, he looked across the street at a white minivan parked there. He narrowed his eyes to better see who was behind the wheel. The driver started the car and leaned back against his seat, allowing light from a lamppost to play across his features.

"Excuse me," Brixton said to Sayers, and started toward the parked car. The driver shifted into gear and pulled away, leaving Brixton standing in the middle of the road. He returned to where Sayers stood.

"Who was that?" the editor asked.

"A guy I've seen before, at Janet's funeral."

"So?"

"Charlie McQuaid's neighbor—name's Wally—says that he saw two guys cuddled up to McQuaid's boat the day he was killed. One of the men he described looks like the guy at the funeral and the guy driving that car."

"You think this guy is following you?"

"Probably not. I enjoyed the evening, Will. You were right. You're a good shrink. Catch up with you tomorrow."

Brixton considered calling Asal when he returned home but thought it might be too late. He took half a snifter of brandy to the balcony and looked out into the night. The woman across the street appeared in her window, followed by a man. They embraced, and she lowered the blinds.

The loneliness that he'd suffered on occasion and that had been held at abeyance all day returned with force.

25

Brixton was groggy when he awoke the following morning. He'd tossed and turned all night and had considered a few times getting up and watching TV. But he'd stayed in bed figuring that even if he wasn't sleeping, he was resting. Sleeping? Resting? It didn't matter. He felt like hell as he made coffee and scrambled two eggs.

He'd just come out of the shower when Mackensie Smith called.

"Didn't wake you, did I?" Smith asked.

"No, I've been up."

"Anything new on the case?"

"No, but I had dinner last night with Will Sayers."

"Has he come up with anything to help your cause?"

"He's always got a few interesting tidbits. He gave me an invitation to a dinner tonight honoring Zafar Alvi."

"Are you going?"

"I was thinking I would."

"Annabel and I were offered tickets by a colleague

at the law school. He had a family emergency and couldn't use them. We declined. Robert, I need time with you."

"About McQuaid's papers?"

"Right. Are you free anytime today?"

"How about this afternoon? Say three?"

"See you then."

Brixton spent the rest of the morning on the phone.

"Hi, Daddy, it's Jill."

"Hi, sweetheart. I was about to call you."

"I beat you to it. How are you?"

"I'm doing okay. How's the little guy?"

"He's fine. I envy him. He's so innocent."

"I know what you mean."

"Mom and I were going through Janet's things. We had no idea how many songs she'd written—dozens of them."

"She had talent, that's for sure."

"Miles wants to pay to have a CD made of them."

"That's . . . that's very nice."

"She would have loved that."

They chatted for another five minutes before the baby started crying in the background.

"Say hello to Frank for me," Brixton said, and the conversation ended.

He made a few calls regarding his car insurance and to protest a phone bill before calling Detective Quintin Halliday at MPD.

"I was going to call you later," Halliday said. "Nothing definitive on the forensics has come back, but we're reopening the case, 'means of death unknown.'"

"Can't ask for more than that. Mind if I stay in touch?"

"I hope you will. Take care, Brixton."

After paying some bills, Brixton called Asal at her office.

"I was hoping to hear from you," she said.

"I've been busy. I was going to suggest that we have dinner tonight, but something's come up."

"It wouldn't work anyway. I'm busy, too."

"How about tomorrow night?"

"That sounds fine."

He had lunch alone in a neighborhood pub before heading for his meeting with Mac Smith. They settled in his study, where the law professor had laid out McQuaid's files in a series of piles, with yellow Post-its on each to indicate the subject.

"You make any sense out of them?" Brixton asked, taking a sip of the coffee Mac had provided.

"The more I go over them, the more sense they make. I'll level with you, Robert. I believe that there's enough here to initiate a probe of Samuel Prisler's arms dealings and the role that Zafar Alvi might play in it."

"You said you were going to run it past a few friends."

"I did, with one. She's a member of a task force at Justice that's picked up where McQuaid left off. They're looking into illegal arms trafficking involving American citizens."

"Including Samuel Prisler?"

"Yes."

"McQuaid told me that certain members of Congress keep thwarting those efforts."

"These things are always complicated. Sometimes our own laws prevent us from doing the right thing. But the new attorney general has more of a backbone than the previous one. I'm told that he's given the task force his full support."

"That's good to know. I heard this morning that MPD is reopening the McQuaid case, Mac. They're calling his death 'undetermined origins.'"

"Good. Here's what I suggest we do as a next step."

Fifteen minutes later Smith had outlined for Brixton

a course of action that he intended to take, using Mc-Quaid's papers as a basis for spurring additional interest in Prisler and his ilk.

Annabel arrived as they were wrapping up their meeting. She was speaking with another woman, the two female voices floating down the hall.

"Annabel must have brought someone home from her gallery," Mac said as he reassembled the papers and piled them neatly on a credenza behind the desk. "Come say hello."

Mac opened the door and preceded Brixton from the study.

"This is a surprise," Mac said.

Brixton stepped through the doorway to see what the surprise was.

"Hi," Flo Combes said.

"Flo!" Brixton said.

"I met her in the lobby," Annabel said.

"What are you doing here?" Brixton asked.

"I came to see you," Flo said.

"It's really not a surprise," Annabel explained. "Flo called earlier to say she was coming to Washington and would stop by. I should have mentioned it to you, Mac, but you were on the phone and I was running late for an appointment at the gallery."

There was an awkward moment as Brixton and Flo looked at each other. Then she stepped forward and kissed his cheek. He hugged her and said, "It's good to see you."

"I missed you," she said.

"Yeah, me too."

"I didn't pick up anything for dinner," Annabel said, "so why don't we go out? I've had this yearning all day for Italian food."

"Wish I could," Brixton said, "but I have this dinner to go to."

"But you'll join us, won't you?" Mac asked Flo.

"I'd love to," she said.

"Where are you staying?" Brixton asked.

"I was hoping that—"

"Stay here," Annabel interjected quickly. "We'd love to have you."

Flo looked at Brixton, who said, "That sounds like a good idea."

"But only for a night or two. I'll find a hotel afterward."

"Maybe you can . . ."

"Yes, Robert?"

"Nothing. Look, I have to go to get ready for this dinner."

Mac read the disappointed expression on Flo's face and said, "It's one of those dinners honoring someone, you know, rubber chicken and lots of speeches."

"Yeah," Brixton said to Flo, "I have to go. It's, ah . . . it's business."

"Sure," Flo said.

As Brixton prepared to leave, he said to Flo, "I'm really glad to see you. Maybe we can have dinner tomorrow night and catch up and . . ."

"Okay," she said. "What time?"

Brixton slapped the side of his head with the heel of his hand. "No, tomorrow's no good," he said. "But we'll do it soon. Got to run." He kissed her again and left.

"There's someone else, isn't there?" Flo said to Mac and Annabel after Brixton was gone.

"No one special," Mac said. "I'm in the mood for Italian food, too. I'll call and make a reservation for three at Notti Bianche." It was a small Italian bistro in the George Washington University Inn a few blocks away, which had become a favorite spot for the Smiths when good Italian food was on the agenda.

Flo excused herself to freshen up after her drive from

New York, leaving Mac and Annabel alone in the kitchen.

"That was awkward," Mac commented.

"And promises to become more so," said Annabel.

"Robert doesn't need this complication," Mac said.

"Whether he needs it or not, he has it," Annabel said. "But it could be worse. Having two lovely ladies is a lot better than dealing with suicide bombers. I'm glad we're going to Notti Bianche. I'm suddenly in the mood for linguini with shrimp—and lots of sauce."

26

Flo Combes's unexpected arrival had surprised as well as confused Brixton. He was flummoxed enough without this complication. As he headed home to dress for the dinner, he wondered why she'd called the Smiths and not him. Although their breakup had been what some would label "volatile," their recent phone conversations hadn't been testy. To the contrary, she'd been loving and caring on those calls. Maybe she wanted the Smiths to be a buffer between them. That was as good a reason as he could muster at the moment.

Before leaving the Watergate he'd almost suggested that she stay with him that night, but Asal entered into his thinking and he thought better of it. He was juggling enough loose ends and baffling scenarios without adding Flo to the mix.

As he showered and changed into a suit, he wondered what the Smiths and Flo would talk about over dinner. He would undoubtedly be the subject of much of the discussion, and he wished he could be there to counter anything she might say about their estrangement with which he would disagree.

He took a cab to the Hay-Adams to avoid having to find a parking space. He'd been to the luxury hotel across from Lafayette Park and the White House for a drink once before and had enjoyed the experience. The building had been created from the merging of the nineteenth-century homes of John Hay and Henry Adams, and was considered one of Washington's best hotels—the second most prestigious address in the District after the White House. Brixton wasn't sure that he'd go that far, but he had to admit that it did possess a certain cachet. During his one cocktail-lounge visit, the bartender had told him that the hotel was haunted by Henry Adams's wife, Marian Hooper Adams, affectionately known as "Clover," who'd committed suicide in the place before it was a hotel. "She walks around the floors at night," the barkeep said, "smelling like mimosa."

That anecdote came back to Brixton as he crossed the lobby—he wondered whether the smell he detected was mimosa from Clover or perfume from an elegantly clad woman who'd just passed him—and asked where the dinner for Zafar Alvi was being held. He checked the written invitation again to be certain that Sayers's name wasn't on it. It wasn't. The press invitation simply indicated that it had been issued to the *Savannah Morning News*. He hoped he wouldn't be asked to produce credentials.

He approached the private room and was greeted by a young woman who smiled widely as she checked his invitation. "I have never been to Savannah," she said.

"You'll have to visit sometime," Brixton said. "I'm sure you'll love it."

She handed him a place card with the newspaper's name on it, and a table number. Brixton thanked her as she turned her attention to the next person in line, and he walked into the room where service bars had been stationed at opposite ends. Tables set with white tablecloths and sparkling silverware and glassware would accommodate a hundred, maybe a hundred and fifty diners.

He navigated his way to one of the bars and waited his turn, until the bartender poured gin over ice and added a lemon twist, which he took to a solitary corner from where he could survey his surroundings.

A dais and speaker's podium had been set up at the far end of the room, presumably where Alvi and those close to him would sit. Two tables directly in front of the dais were already half-occupied; Brixton recognized one of the young men who'd approached his car when he sat in front of Alvi's impressive home. Brixton took note that he'd be seated at the numbered table farthest away from the dais. He went to the nearest empty table, picked up one of the programs that was at each place setting, and looked down at the photo of Alvi on the front cover. "So that's who you are," he muttered as he quickly perused the program's pages before replacing it on the table and returning to his chosen corner spot.

The room began filling up, and a few minutes later Alvi arrived, escorted by an entourage that included the second muscular young man who'd questioned Brixton. A woman came to the podium and asked that everyone take their seats.

Brixton's table accommodated eight, and he found himself seated between two men, neither of whom introduced themselves. Two women and three other men completed the octet. The older of them greeted everyone and introduced himself as a reporter from *The Washington Times*. That prompted others to do the same. When it came to Brixton, he simply gave his name.

"Who do you work for?" the young man to his left asked.

"I'm . . . ah . . . I'm a freelancer," Brixton mumbled.

"What'd you say your name was?"

"Brixton."

The man screwed up his face in thought. "Are you the Robert Brixton who was involved in that bombing in the café?"

"Yeah, but I don't like to talk about it. Who do you write for?"

"The AP. Any chance of getting together after this is over so I can ask you a few questions?"

"I'd rather not," Brixton said. "Like I said, I don't like to talk about it."

A woman across the table who'd overheard the conversation said, "Are you here to write about the evening?"

"You might say that," Brixton replied.

They were interrupted by the woman at the podium, who invited everyone to enjoy their meal, and announced that the formal portion of the event would start after dinner.

It hadn't occurred to Brixton that he would be seated at a table of journalists, and that fact made him uncomfortable. He knew that he'd become the focus of attention, not only among his tablemates, but at other tables too. His seatmate from the Associated Press had visited guests at nearby tables during the meal and had mentioned who Brixton was. People turned to look at him. The reporter tried a few times to engage Brixton in conversation about the café bombing and the shooting of Paul Skaggs but was politely rebuffed, although Brixton found it increasingly difficult to continue to be courteous.

When the meal finally ended—rather than rubber chicken, the entrée was nicely cooked beef medallions—

the evening's emcee took the microphone to introduce a member of Congress, who gushed ten minutes of praise for Zafar Alvi and his efforts to foster better relations between the United States and Middle Eastern nations. Brixton pulled a pad and pen from his breast pocket and pretended to take notes. The congresswoman sat to applause as the evening's next speaker, a Washington businessman with offices in Iraq and Pakistan, lauded Alvi for creating an atmosphere in which American companies could establish businesses in those countries, leading to a better quality of life for their citizens. At the conclusion of his speech, the emcee introduced the reason for the gathering, Zafar Alvi.

Brixton watched the Arab American take the podium and wait for the applause to ebb, before saying, "I am truly humbled to stand here before you and to be honored in such a lovely way." He looked down to guests at the front tables and said, "My life is rich with friends, and I thank each and every one of you for sharing this evening with me."

Brixton strained to make out who was at those tables, aside from Alvi's young assistants, but he was too far away and couldn't see past the sea of heads separating him from the front of the room.

Alvi, who was dressed in what could only be described as a silver suit, white shirt, and red tie, and whose rings glistened when caught by the lights, went on to extol the American people and their efforts to bring democracy to Iraq and Afghanistan. Brixton surveyed others at his table. A few were making notes. Would they really write about the evening, or were they there for a free meal? It didn't matter, nor did it concern him. He'd come to the dinner, compliments of Will Sayers, to see in person this man who might have had something to do with his daughter's grisly death and the slaughter of so many other innocent victims.

Alvi went on for another ten minutes. When he'd finished and basked in the applause, Brixton excused himself and took a circuitous route along the wall in the direction of the dais. He didn't know what he intended to do or what he would say, but he knew that he had to get closer, see Alvi in person and if possible let him know that he was in Brixton's sights.

Alvi was in a receiving line of well-wishers, and Brixton joined it. He took note that the guest of honor was flanked by his two young aides, their faces unsmiling, their eyes taking in each person who extended a hand and told Alvi how impressed they were with his work and his efforts to bring about a better understanding between cultures. Behind Alvi was a tall bulky man in a black suit and shirt, a white tie, and whose head was shaved. His dusky face was a blank slate.

As Brixton inched forward, he kept his eyes on Alvi, ignoring everything else that was going on in the vicinity. It was when he was four people removed from shaking the great man's hand that he saw her seated at one of the front tables, laughing at something a companion had said. He was stunned. Asal Banai was at the table reserved for Alvi's closest friends. *How could it be?* She'd told him that she knew of Alvi, not that she was personally involved with him.

He was now one person away from Alvi. Brixton kept shifting his gaze from Alvi to Asal, who had not yet seen him in the receiving line. The guest in front of Brixton stepped away, and Brixton was now face-to-face with Alvi, who extended his hand. Brixton took it and said while gripping it, "Robert Brixton. You know who I am."

The broad smile that had crossed Alvi's face disappeared.

"I'm the guy who shot Paul Skaggs," Brixton said, leaning close to keep the person behind him from hearing. "You know, the congressman's kid who was driving one of your cars before he and his girlfriend blew up the café and my daughter."

It took the young men flanking Alvi a moment to realize that this was a confrontation, not a congratulatory handshake. They moved closer to their boss, one tucking his hand into his jacket, where Brixton surmised he carried his holster. The other recognized Brixton from the encounter at the car and said, "It's him."

Alvi forcefully pulled his hand free and said, "You are holding up the line."

"That's okay," Brixton said. "I want private time with you, Mr. Alvi. You and I have a lot to talk about."

Alvi's bodyguards were poised to grab Brixton but knew that they couldn't without drawing attention to the scene. The smile returned to Alvi's face as he said, "I would be pleased to meet with you, Mr. Brixton, extremely pleased. Call me and we'll arrange a time."

He turned to greet the person behind Brixton, but Brixton didn't move.

"How about after this nice little affair is over?" Brixton said.

The smile disappeared. "I suggest you make way for someone else," Alvi said, his voice low and menacing.

Brixton realized that there was nothing to be gained by holding his ground. He moved to his left, which brought him closer to the table at which Asal sat. She looked up and their eyes met. Her face flooded and paled in quick succession, and her body language mirrored her dilemma—acknowledge him or bolt? He made the decision for her by approaching the table and saying, "Hello, Asal. Didn't expect to see you here."

"Hello, Robert," she said, forcing a light tone. "I didn't know that you would be coming to the dinner."

He started to respond but she quickly got up, excused

herself to the others at the table, and walked away. He followed. He caught up with her in the vestibule. "I thought you didn't know Alvi," he said.

"I didn't."

He guffawed. "Then how come you're seated at one of his prime tables?"

She'd obviously been shaken at seeing Brixton, but now she injected a steely quality into her voice. "Zafar Alvi has made a generous donation to my organization, and he invited me along with others who benefit from his generosity."

"When did he do that, this morning?"

"I resent your tone, Robert."

"And I resent being lied to, Asal. Come on, level with me. How long have you known him?"

Her deep, prolónged sigh said much. "I refuse to be questioned by you," she said. "Excuse me. There are others I need to speak with inside. You may not be aware of it, Mr. Brixton, but running a nonprofit organization takes time. It takes meeting people with money who believe in what you are doing and who put their funds behind those beliefs."

Brixton lowered his voice. "What about his belief in selling illegal arms and taking care of a guy like Paul Skaggs before he kills my daughter, lending him a car to drive, and who knows what else?"

"I don't wish to discuss this here, Robert. If you still want to have dinner tomorrow night I'll—"

The man in the black suit and the shaved head suddenly stepped between them. "Is there a problem, Ms. Banai?" he asked through a heavy accent.

"No, Kahn, no problem," she said. "I'm going back inside."

Brixton watched her walk back into the ballroom, skirting tables and stopping to greet someone, her wide smile never leaving her. He considered going after her but resisted. He would call her, and if dinner was still on the agenda, he'd pursue it then.

Kahn, who stood a full four inches taller than Brixton, remained at his side, arms folded, face devoid of expression.

"You work for Alvi?" Brixton said.

"Good night," the man named Kahn said.

"Yeah, good night to you, pal," Brixton muttered. When he turned, he saw that Alvi had left the ballroom along with his two young acolytes.

Brixton walked away, aware that Kahn's eyes were boring holes into his back. He felt at a loss. His attempt to shake up Alvi had failed. His brief words with Asal Banai had resulted only in her anger at being confronted. As he walked through the lobby and stepped out onto Sixteenth Street NW, anger welled up in him. He was back in Washington, D.C., where it seemed that nothing good had ever happened to him. He'd spent four years there as an unhappy cop, had married the wrong woman, was almost killed by a psychopath when he'd pursued a case while a PI in Savannah, had lost a daughter in a senseless suicide bombing, and just now learned that he really didn't know the woman he was involved with. "*I hate this city,*" he said under his breath, and for a moment thought he might be capable of going crazy, attacking passersby, screaming invectives, betraying himself.

Instead, he drew a series of deep breaths and walked in the direction of Lafayette Park, also known as the President's Park, part of Lafayette Square across from the White House. He'd spent time there while a D.C. cop, finding a modicum of solace when things went downhill with Marylee or with his superiors.

He had a favorite spot, a fountain dedicated to a couple of obscure Washingtonians of another era—Archibald Butt, a military aide to President Taft, and an artist named Francis Davis Millet. Brixton wasn't into history but he found the men for whom the fountain was constructed in 1913 to be of particular interest. From what he'd read Butt and Millet had shared an elegant house in Washington. (Millet's wife, Lily, spent most of the year in their home in Italy.) The men had died together as passengers on the *Titanic*. Brixton was fascinated about the *Titanic* lore and had often imagined himself on that ship, fighting for survival. Now he was fighting to stay calm.

He sat on a bench and struggled to put his thoughts in order, to decide what to do next. *Was it all a wasted exercise?* he wondered. Was it possible that no matter how hard he tried, no matter how doggedly he pursued the truth, that nothing would change? He'd seen it too many times before in Washington, D.C., crimes buried under layers of lobbyists' cash and influence, elected officials avoiding being called to account for their misdeeds because they belonged to the D.C. "insiders' club." He knew that Samuel Prisler and Zafar Alvi were involved in some way with the bombing. He knew that Charlie McQuaid had been murdered because he'd gotten too close to making them account for their crimes. Was the string of murders of homosexual employees of foreign embassies somehow involved? Was Lalo Reyes in Prisler's cult on Maui? If so, what did *that* mean? Had Paul Skaggs been a member of that cult, too? His sister was. Those facts swirled around in his head like a cyclone, and he knew that making the right connections at that moment was difficult, if not impossible.

He leaned back against the bench and closed his eyes. It was quiet and serene. He thought of Flo Combes at dinner with Mac and Annabel Smith. He thought of Asal seated at a prime table for a dinner honoring Zafar Alvi, someone she'd said she'd never met. He was deep into those thoughts when he sensed that he was no longer alone in this secluded area of the park. There wasn't any noise, no footsteps on the walk, no breathing, no inadvertent cough or sneeze. But he *felt* the presence of someone.

He tensed as he kept his eyes closed, his hand sliding down his leg toward the Smith & Wesson 638 Airweight revolver in his ankle holster. He slowly opened his eyes. As he did, a length of cord was slipped over his head and pulled tight against his throat. It yanked him against the back of the bench with such force that it was almost ripped from its ground anchors. Brixton's hands frantically went to his throat as he tried to pull loose the rope that dug into his flesh and threatened to cut off his breathing. Instinctively, he reversed his actions. He slid his rear end forward, which caused the noose around his neck to move up to beneath his jaw. Simultaneously, he twisted to his right, almost lying down on the bench. Then, he kicked up one leg and directed it at the head of his assailant. That he was able to do this surprised both him and his attacker. His foot smashed into the man's face and sent him tumbling into bushes behind the bench. Brixton rolled off the bench to his knees. He fumbled for the weapon in his ankle holster, retrieved it, and leveled the barrel at where the rope wielder's head had been. He was gone. Brixton stumbled to his feet and stood unsteadily, his revolver pointed into the black void behind the bench. The sound of someone crashing through bushes sent Brixton limping around the bench to where his attacker had stood only seconds earlier. He desperately wanted to follow, but a searing pain shot down his back into his right leg and he dropped to the ground, his chest heaving as he gulped in air. He used the bench to haul himself up again and peered in the direction his assailant had taken, but there was no sign of him. All was quiet and serene again.

Brixton slumped on the seat. He stuffed the abandoned rope in his pocket, returned the Smith & Wesson to its holster on his ankle, and continued to draw in the night air until he was again breathing normally and the pain in his back and leg had subsided. Slowly he got to his feet and walked from Lafayette Square to H Street, where he hailed a taxi that took him home.

27

Brixton stood in his bathroom and examined his neck in the mirror. The braided strand of rope his attacker used had sliced into his flesh, leaving a vivid red line. The pain in his back and leg had returned, and he'd popped a couple of Tylenols, washed down with gin on the rocks.

He had debated going to the police to report the assault but decided it wouldn't accomplish anything. He would mention it to Kogan at SITQUAL, and it would provide dinner table conversation with Sayers and the Smiths. But the resolution would not come from the police or any other agency. It was his problem and his alone.

As vicious as the attack had been, it didn't take center stage in his thinking as he carried his drink to the balcony and looked up into an overcast sky that promised rain before morning.

Asal's presence at the dinner pushed all other thoughts aside. There had to be a plausible explanation for why she had denied knowing Alvi. She owed him an explanation.

He figured the attack had to have been the result of his confrontation with Alvi. It would be too much of a coincidence for him to have been mugged by some street type immediately following the dinner. Besides, muggers didn't usually strangle their victims. This was a planned hit, and it took its place in the jumble of incidents that marked his life these days.

Alvi had said to set up an appointment. He obviously didn't mean it; it was a ploy to avoid the confrontation that was taking place. The last person Zafar Alvi wanted to meet with was Robert Brixton. A better bet was that the mover and shaker wanted Robert Brixton dead. Still, he decided that he would take Alvi up on his empty offer, if only to reinforce that he was still pursuing the Arab American.

Brixton took a swallow of gin and smiled to himself. In a sense, what had happened that night had been beneficial, and a wave of satisfaction washed over him. He was now free of any lingering doubts he'd had up to that juncture about whether Alvi was involved in the café bombing. He felt liberated. Until then he'd been a victim, just as his daughter had been the victim of the crazed young woman who'd blown up herself and others in the name of God knew what. No, he told himself, you've *allowed* yourself to be a victim. That's past tense. It was time to answer all the questions, put the pieces together, identify who was responsible for Janet's brutal murder, and take action.

Brixton wasn't the only person contemplating taking action that night.

Zafar Alvi returned home from the dinner honoring him, went directly to his study, and summoned Kahn from the garage, where he'd been busy running a chamois over the car they'd used that night.

"Well?" Alvi said when his large right-hand man appeared.

"It should be taken care of by now," Kahn said.

"'Should be'? You don't sound certain."

"I don't think that Mr. Brixton will be a problem any longer," Kahn said.

"You'd better be right," Alvi said. He pushed a button on the answering machine on his desk and listened to incoming messages. Two were from Samuel Prisler in Hawaii. He'd just picked up the phone to return those calls, when there was a knock on the door.

"Come in."

Peter, one of Alvi's young assistants, sheepishly entered the room holding a bloody rag to his face.

"What's this?" Alvi demanded.

"I was . . . he was . . . I tried but—"

"He's alive?" Kahn asked.

"I thought I had him, but he was stronger than I figured and—"

Alvi slapped his hand on the desk. "You idiot!" he said.

"I couldn't help it. I thought—"

"Where is he?" Alvi asked.

"I don't know," Peter replied. "We were in the park across from the White House. We were alone. No one saw us."

"Except for Brixton."

"No, he didn't see me," Peter said. "I ran before he got up."

"Get out of here. Get out of my sight!" Alvi yelled.

Peter started to protest, but Kahn physically pushed him through the door and slammed it behind them.

Alvi picked up the phone and dialed Prisler's number in Maui. "I'm returning your calls," he said when Prisler came on the line.

"You're damn right I called. What's going on there?"

"Nothing. Everything is fine."

"Like hell it is. That fruitcake Reyes is back."

"He's a nice young man," Alvi said.

"Did this 'nice young man' tell you that Brixton attacked him before he left D.C.?"

"Hold on a second, Samuel," Alvi said as he switched on a small digital recorder attached to the phone. "Go ahead," he said. "I'm listening."

"Reyes comes back here looking like a scared rabbit. He starts babbling how Brixton broke into his apartment, held a gun to his head, and asked him questions about me."

"I'm sorry to hear that," said Alvi. "What specifically did he tell Mr. Brixton?"

"Who the hell knows? He babbled on, says he told him nothing about my operation here on Maui, but I don't believe a word he says. The point is that Brixton suspects that Reyes is involved with me. What I want to know is who else has Brixton told?" Before Alvi could respond, Prisler said, "I told you that Brixton has to be taken care of, and you said you'd do it."

"I don't think we should be discussing this on the phone, Samuel. Perhaps you could make another trip to Washington."

"Why, to get another runaround from you? Take care of Brixton and anybody else he's been blabbing to, damn it, or I will!"

"I'll speak with you again in a few days, Samuel. In the meantime I suggest that you compose yourself. Men who lose their equilibrium also often lose their lives." He hung up.

Kahn returned to Alvi's study.

"I am very disappointed with Peter," Alvi said. "It would have been better to assign Jacob to take care of Brixton. He proved himself with Mr. McQuaid."

"I'll have him come-in, Zafar."

"Yes, please do. In the meantime add to our security at the house, at least until we can read the tenacious Mr. Brixton's obituary in *The Post*."

B rixton had just left his balcony to refresh his drink when the phone rang.

"Robert, it's Asal. We must talk."

"That's right, Asal, we have to talk."

"I know that you think I've lied to you about Mr. Alvi, but I haven't. You don't understand how important it is to me and to my organization to have the financial backing of such a man."

"You're probably right," Brixton said wearily. "You see him as this guy on a white horse, coming to the rescue of people like you and your organization. What you don't know is that he's someone who deals illegal arms to terrorist groups around the world, and who took good care of Paul Skaggs before the kid brought the suicide bomber to the café that killed my daughter."

"I cannot believe that," she said.

"Tell you what, Asal. We're on for dinner tomorrow night. Let's keep that date, only let's do it someplace private, like your apartment or mine. I'm not up to being in public. Make it my place. I'll order in food and we can hash this thing out. Okay?"

"What time?"

"I'll pick you up at six and bring you back here."

T he following night Mac and Annabel Smith spent the evening at a dinner party hosted by the British ambassador to the United States at the British embassy on Massachusetts Avenue NW. Mac had been on a panel of American and British legal scholars whose mission was to explore the differences between the two country's legal systems, and how those differences impacted relations between them. Recently there had been two cases of Americans tried in British courts who'd been found guilty but whose lawyers had filed appeals based upon the actions of the trial judge.

"We've always had a problem with your judges summarizing the evidence for the jury before it deliberates," Mac commented during dinner. "It can be prejudicial."

"But necessary to ensure that the jury understands the weight of each side's presentation," one of Smith's British colleagues countered.

A law professor from Harvard backed up Smith's view, which led to a strident defense of the British system by another British panel member.

"Gentlemen, gentlemen," the ambassador said, laughing. "I thought this was all hashed out during your meetings."

"I'm not sure that we can ever come to an agreement about it," said the Brit.

"Especially considering the language barrier," Smith joked.

At one point Annabel, a former attorney herself, weighed in and delivered a reasoned view of the debate, which had one of the Brits at the table actually applauding.

And so it went for the remainder of the evening. As the group filed from the stately home, the ambassador and the Smiths engaged in a final conversation.

"A splendid evening," said the ambassador, "despite the tragic event today."

"What was that?" Annabel asked.

"I'm afraid that a trusted staff member assigned to our military attaché office, was gunned down in cold blood."

Mac and Annabel looked at each other.

"When did this happen?" Mac asked.

"Four o'clock this afternoon. I was informed of it an hour before everyone arrived. I'm sure you'll read about it in tomorrow's papers"

"Another embassy murder," Mac commented.

"It does seem that there have been a raft of them lately," the ambassador said grimly. "He was a good chap, extremely well liked by everyone. He'll be missed dearly."

"Do the authorities have any leads?" Annabel asked.

"Too soon, I'm sure," said the ambassador. "I asked to be briefed on a regular basis."

Both Mac and Annabel immediately thought of *The Post* feature article speculating that a gay-and-lesbian-hating serial killer might be on the loose in D.C. Tactfulness kept them from bringing it up to the ambassador despite their being curious as to the sexual orientation of this latest victim. Instead, they expressed their condolences, thanked him for a lovely evening, and drove home.

Flo Combes was watching the TV news in her robe when the Smiths arrived home. The murder of the British military attaché came up in the report and provided some additional information. His name was Geoffrey Thomas, age thirty-eight, married and with two children. His body was found late that afternoon in a parking lot in the Adams Morgan section of D.C. Authorities were investigating his movements leading up to the killing, and canvassing the Adams Morgan neighborhood for anyone who might have seen the victim prior to his death.

"How many murders of embassy people does that make?" Flo asked.

"I'm not sure," Mac answered, silently running through those he knew about. "At least six, maybe seven."

"I'm glad I don't work for an embassy here in Washington," she said.

"It does seem like high-risk employment these days," Mac said. "It's got everyone, embassy worker or not, on edge. Nightcap, Flo?"

"Love one."

"You won't mind if we get changed, too?" Annabel asked.

"Please, get comfortable. Forget I'm here."

The Smiths changed into their nightclothes and carried snifters of cognac to the balcony, where Flo joined them.

"I'll be interested in hearing Robert's take on this," Mac said.

"Despite what *The Post* speculated, this victim wasn't homosexual," Annabel commented.

"Or doesn't appear to be," Mac said. "Being married and having kids isn't a guarantee that he didn't have a second, secret life."

"I know that, Mac, but it doesn't make sense that the gays and lesbians who've been murdered also happen to work for foreign embassies."

"Have you spoken with Robert again?" Flo asked.

"No, but I'll give him a call tomorrow."

"He's . . . he's a good guy," Flo commented.

"Robert?" Annabel said. "We'd certainly agree with that."

"Breaking up with him was stupid," Flo said. "He can be exasperating at times, bullheaded and cynical, but I'm afraid I overreacted."

"We all do at times," Annabel offered.

"I think that leaving Savannah caused the breakup," Flo said. "Robert never especially liked it, but at least he had a presence there that he lost once we were back in New York. He spent twenty years on the Savannah police force and had his own PI agency. Once we were in New York, he seemed to be struggling to find himself."

"From what he's told us, he wasn't crazy about Washington either," Mac said.

Flo laughed. "I don't think Robert will ever like where he is. Maybe that's part of his problem, or maybe that's part of his charm. I've already extended my stay to two nights. I'll get out of your hair tomorrow. I'll move to a hotel. I'm not going to stay in Washington long."

"Then why do that?" Annabel said. "We enjoy having you with us, and there's no sense in spending money if you don't have to."

"That's really sweet of you but . . . well, I'm hoping that Robert and I can find some time for a serious talk about our relationship. I know he's insanely busy trying to work out his problems, but I at least need a chance to tell him how sorry I am that we broke up and maybe, just maybe, give it another go."

"Staying with us might help grease those skids," Mac said. "I can talk to Robert and encourage him to find time to discuss things with you."

"You would do that?" Flo said.

"I'd be happy to."

Flo was silent for a few moments before saying, "There *is* another woman in his life, isn't there?"

Annabel visually checked her husband before saying, "He met a woman here one evening, Asal Banai, and I believe they've had dinner together once or twice. But I wouldn't say that there's anything special between them. That's something you can ask him when you get together."

"What an unusual name," Flo said.

"Asal was born in Iraq, but she's been here for at least

ten years. We're in a book discussion group together. She's very nice. I'm sure you'd like her."

Mac didn't necessarily agree with his wife, considering the situation, but withheld comment.

Later, after everyone had gone to bed, Annabel said to Mac in their darkened bedroom, "I like Flo."

"You like Asal too."

"That's right. I like them both. I just hope that Robert doesn't hurt either one."

"He's a big boy, Annabel, and they're grown women. Whatever happens, happens."

"Good night, Mac," she said, rolling over to kiss him.

"Good night, Annie."

As he turned onto his side, she heard him mutter, "Another embassy murder. What in hell is going on?"

28

Brixton was about to leave his apartment to get breakfast when Will Sayers called.

"How was dinner?" Sayers asked.

"Do you mean the food?" Brixton said. "Not bad. As for the rest of it, I've got a bloody line on my neck from ear to ear and a squashed Adam's apple."

"You've lost me."

"It doesn't matter."

"I'll buy you breakfast. I want to show you something."

"Sounds like a plan."

They met a half hour later at The Diner on Eighteenth Street NW, in Adams Morgan. Brixton got there first, and while he waited he read about the murder of the British military attaché in a parking lot not far from where he sat.

"Another one," Brixton said, pointing to *The Washington Post*'s open page when Sayers arrived.

"I saw it. What do you hear from your pal, Mike Kogan?"

"Nothing yet, but I'm sure I will."

Sayers leaned closer and looked at Brixton's neck. "So what happened to you?"

Brixton gave him a play-by-play of the dinner and its aftermath.

"Did you see who attacked you?"

"No, but I'd bet my last nickel that he was dispatched by the night's guest of honor."

"And you say that that pretty lady we met at the Smiths' apartment was at the dinner, front row center?"

"Right. I'll see what she has to say tonight. We're having dinner. To add to my soap opera life, Flo, my ex, is in town, staying with the Smiths."

"Oh, ho," Sayers said. "You think you have problems with gunrunners and terrorists? Wait until you get in between two women vying for the attention of the handsome, erudite Robert Brixton."

"No one has ever called me that before," Brixton said, laughing.

The waitress broke into their conversation and took their orders.

"You seem to end up in trouble everywhere you go," Sayers said after she'd gone.

"Seems that way. You said you had something to show me."

"Right." He opened his briefcase and pulled out the multipage article he'd written about the café bombing and Brixton's involvement with it, including his shooting Paul Skaggs in the alley.

"It's long," Brixton said, "and you could have picked a better picture of me, like the ones that make me look like George Clooney."

"Don't give me a hard time, Robert."

"This for me to keep?"

"Yeah. I was surprised when the paper's syndicate decided to put it out on their wire."

"What does that mean?"

"It'll be picked up by newspapers around the world. At least it might be."

"Will it make me rich?"

"No, but you'll have dozens of adoring fans clamoring for your autograph."

"Or coming after me with a rope." Brixton grunted, folded the piece, and put it in his suit jacket pocket. Their breakfast came and they ate in silence until Sayers asked, "So, what's next, now that Alvi set his goon on you and gave you a necklace?"

"Not sure what to do next."

"What about Asal? Think she's involved with Alvi?"

Brixton shrugged and finished the last bite of his western omelet. "She says he's just a benefactor supporting her organization. What bothers me is that she claimed she'd never met him, but only a few days later she's at table *numero uno*. I want to give her the benefit of the doubt, but there's something not quite right."

"Sure you're not seeing conspiracies behind every door?"

"That's not me, and you know it, Will."

"*Mea culpa,*" Sayers said. "Where are you going when we leave here?"

"SITQUAL to see Mike Kogan."

"What about your lady friend, Flo Combes?"

Brixton grimaced and drained the last of his coffee. "I've been avoiding that."

"Don't," Sayers said with finality. "I always liked her, Robert. Don't blow her off."

"Advice to the lovelorn?"

"I'm full of advice, my friend. Just don't be a jackass and screw up your life any more than it is." He motioned for the check. "And start sitting with your back to the wall. Whoever gave you that crimson necklace is likely to try again."

*   *   *

Brixton met with Kogan at SITQUAL.

"This Brit who got it," Brixton said. "What's new on it?"

"Not much. MPD came up empty when they canvassed Adams Morgan. The guy was evidently going to his car when somebody came up from behind and put two in his head."

"Nobody knows why he was there in the afternoon? He was a military attaché. Seems he'd be at the embassy doing whatever military attachés do."

"Between us?"

"Do you have to ask?"

"MPD talked to somebody who claims that Thomas—that's his name—that he might have been with a girlfriend just before he died."

"Not gay."

"That's a fair assumption."

"Who's the girlfriend?"

A shrug of Kogan's broad shoulders. "I don't have that information. Wish you were back in the saddle, Robert. We're swamped here."

"I'm yours for the asking. Sure he wasn't playing kissy-face with a guy?"

Kogan shook his head, not in response to Brixton's question, but as a general display of how he was feeling. "Despite what *The Post* says, these embassy murders aren't the work of a homophobe. That's too easy an answer. I've come to the conclusion that there's something far deeper here than bias crimes.

"I won't argue with you," Brixton said.

"How are you making out?" Kogan asked.

"Okay."

Kogan hadn't noticed the thin red line on Brixton's neck until now. "Cut yourself shaving?" he asked.

"No."

Brixton explained.

"And you think that Zafar Alvi put the hit out on you?"

"It's a solid bet that he did. He's not going to like this. I'm an international celebrity now." He handed Kogan Sayers's syndicated piece about him.

Kogan perused the article. "Hollywood's next," he quipped.

"I'll make sure you're invited when I win the Oscar. I'll get out of your hair. Give me a call if you come up with anything new on this latest embassy murder."

Brixton left SITQUAL's office and meandered along the street, gazing in shop windows and trying to come up with his next step. His conflict with Asal would hopefully be resolved at dinner that night. He'd intended to try confronting Alvi again but now thought better of it. He'd been lucky to escape with his life last night, and based upon the attack on him, Mr. Zafar Alvi wasn't likely to welcome another intrusion. No sense walking into the lion's den and pulling his beard.

Having Flo Combes in town posed a new wrinkle. He wanted to spend time with her but wasn't sure how to approach it. That dilemma was resolved when his cell phone rang.

"Robert, it's Annabel Smith."

"Annabel. How are you?"

"I'm fine. I'm calling for two reasons. One, Mac wanted me to tell you that he's at the Justice Department today pursuing the case against Samuel Prisler."

"Great!"

"The second reason is that . . . I mean, I hope you find some time to get together with Flo. I know you're busy, but she came all this way."

"I've been thinking about that."

"I know that I probably shouldn't get involved like

this—Mac doesn't think I should—but she has driven here from New York to see you, and I know how much she cares about you and what you're going through and—"

"Hey, Annabel, no need to explain. I agree with everything you say and I want to see her. It's just that it's a tough time right now."

"Mind a suggestion?"

"Shoot."

"Don't leave her hanging. Either find the time to get together or tell her to go back to New York."

"I can't do that."

"Then get your tail over here."

Her directness caused Brixton to pull the phone away from his ear and look at it.

"Robert, are you there?"

"Yeah, I'm here. I'm tied up tonight, but maybe she and I could have dinner tomorrow."

"I'm sure she'd like that," Annabel said. "Should I mention it to her?"

"Sure, I guess. I'll keep it open."

"Good. Please don't think poorly of me for getting in the middle of this."

"Are you kidding? Me think poorly of you? Come on, Annabel. Tell Flo that we're on for tomorrow night. I'll take her someplace nice where we can talk."

"Good. Hope your day is going well. Thanks for hearing me out."

Brixton looked at his watch. There was still plenty of time to return to his apartment to catch up on paperwork, check his e-mail—which he hadn't done in days—and maybe even squeeze in a nap before heading out to pick up Asal. He'd ridden out the attack on him in Lafayette Park the previous night, hadn't succumbed to the severity of it, but he was feeling it now, and the thought of getting in between the sheets—What had the TV host Jack Paar once said? "They can't hurt you under the covers"—suddenly had powerful appeal.

He arrived at his apartment and went directly to his desk to check e-mails. But after a few minutes online, the allure of the bed won out. He kicked off his shoes, discarded his suit and shirt, and climbed beneath the covers. He was asleep within minutes.

The problem with napping during the day, he knew, was that you woke up groggy. When his eyes opened after his uncharacteristic afternoon slumber, it took a few moments for him to realize where he was. His watch read 4:30. He sat on the edge of the bed until he was sure that everything in his body was where it should be, went to the bathroom, and checked his image in the mirror. Unhappy with what he saw, he stripped down and got into the shower, hoping the hot water would wash away what the mirror had displayed.

While Brixton slept, Asal had sat in Zafar Alvi's study. He had called her and sent Kahn to her office to escort her back to his house. Her initial instincts were to decline, but Alvi's tone, if not menacing, was sufficiently authoritative to secure her assent. Kahn remained present during the meeting, and his looming physical presence unnerved her.

"Did you know that our mutual acquaintance was going to be at my dinner?" Alvi asked.

"I had no idea. I don't know how he got a ticket."

"What were you and Brixton talking about last night?"

"Nothing really," she responded. "He was surprised to see me there, that's all."

"Why would he be surprised?" Alvi asked.

"Because . . . because I'd told him that I didn't know you."

"And seeing you at the dinner caused him to disbelieve you?"

"Yes. We're having dinner tonight to discuss it."

"Good."

"I really don't want to go."

"But you must, my dear. As we've agreed you will keep me informed of what he's up to. Don't misjudge Mr. Brixton. I have no doubt that he can be charming, but keep in mind that he represents a threat to me and to you, not to mention your organization."

She had to fight not to cry.

"He's said terrible things about you," she managed.

"I am sure he has," Alvi said. "Untrue things, of course. A man like him is dangerous, very dangerous. The son of an esteemed congressman is dead because of Brixton. He is desperate to pass along the blame to bring down me and my powerful friends to save his own worthless skin. Believe me when I tell you that by keeping me informed about Brixton you do a great service for our people."

As Asal listened to him her mind swirled, at times threatening to short-circuit. She wished that she'd never agreed to act as a conduit to Alvi about Brixton. What had she gotten herself into? It seemed so innocuous at the time, to pass along tidbits of information in return for desperately needed money for herself and the Islamic Partnership. But, of course, it hadn't only been the money, she reasoned. Her brother was in jail in Iraq, and Alvi had pledged to use his influence to free him. But what had he done? He used the promise to keep her bound to him. She hated the position she was now in. She wanted to save her brother, and she enjoyed the money that her association with Alvi provided. But she didn't have any animosity toward Brixton. She was sympathetic for his having lost a daughter in such a brutal way and for being accused of killing the congressman's son without provocation. She felt trapped sitting in Alvi's opulent home, Kahn fixing her in a harsh stare without saying anything, arms folded, lights shining off his bald pate. She realized that she could easily scream, say that she wanted her brother out of the cruel Iraqi jail. She would scream that Alvi should donate to her organization simply because it did good work, and not in return for being a spy. That's what she was, a spy. The thought chilled her.

"Enjoy your dinner with Mr. Robert Brixton, Asal," Alvi was saying, "and let me know if anything of interest comes out of it. I sense that you're uncomfortable telling tales out of school, or in this case telling tales from dinner. I assure you that your contribution is extremely worthwhile. I also assure you that you will not be in this position much longer."

Asal shivered. "My brother," she said.

"Ah, yes, your beloved brother. I have already put into the works with the right people initiatives that will free him. You have my word, Asal."

"Thank you," she said.

Kahn drove her back to her office. Not a word was exchanged during the short drive. She thanked him for the ride.

"Thank Mr. Alvi," Kahn said, looking straight ahead. "I just do what he tells me to do."

29

Brixton got in the car to pick up Asal and realized he hadn't given a thought as to what he would bring in for dinner. Chinese? That was the easiest solution. Maybe pizza. There was a Moroccan restaurant on the block. Perhaps she'd prefer that. He'd ask when he picked her up.

She buzzed him into the lobby, and he rode the elevator to her floor. She greeted him at the door dressed in a teal pantsuit. She looked beautiful. He wasn't sure whether to kiss her, but she spared him having to make that decision by closing the door and telling him she was busy in the kitchen.

"Why?" he asked. "I thought we were going back to my place."

"I'd rather stay here if it's all right with you."

"I suppose so. Look, Asal, I—"

"I know that we have things to discuss, but can't it wait until we've eaten?"

"If you say so. What are you cooking?"

"A special lamb dish that my mother used to make. I hope you like it. Excuse me. You can make yourself a drink over there." She pointed to a small bar on which various liquors had been poured into crystal decanters, and disappeared into the kitchen.

Brixton noticed that the dining table that occupied a part of the open living room had been nicely set with linen napkins, sparkling silverware, and two tapered white candles. This change in plans was disconcerting. He'd come revved up to confront her about Alvi. Instead, it appeared that she was hosting a dinner party for the two of them as though nothing had happened, as though there wasn't a more-pressing reason to get together.

He plucked cubes from a metal ice bucket, plopped them in a glass, and poured gin from a decanter that had a small etched silver sign hanging from it that announced what it contained. He peeked into the kitchen and saw that she was busy at the stove, went out onto the terrace, and leaned on the railing.

If her intention was to provide him with a romantic, candlelit evening to soften the discussion they needed to have, it was working. As he stood peering out over Foggy Bottom, he questioned whether he was, as Will Sayers had suggested, looking for conspiracies behind every door and in every corner. Was his anger at people like Zafar Alvi, Samuel Prisler, and anyone else who might have played a role in Janet's death tainting everyone who had even a casual connection with them? Maybe she was right when she claimed that being at Alvi's dinner was a last-minute occurrence, that she had not personally known him prior to that. He had trouble accepting that but resigned to give her the benefit of the doubt. He understood the need for an organization like hers to raise money from as many sources as possible. Speakers at the dinner had praised Alvi's generosity as a benefactor to a variety of nonprofit organizations.

He sipped his drink and was deep in such thoughts when she suddenly appeared at his side holding a glass of white wine.

"Enjoying your drink?" she asked.

"Yeah, I am. How's dinner coming?"

"Almost ready. Did you have a good day?"

"As good as they can be these days. I had breakfast with Will Sayers."

She laughed. "Your funny friend. What did he have to say?"

"About what?"

"About anything. Have you made any progress in clearing your name?"

"About shooting Congressman Skaggs's son? No. Oh, maybe you'd like to read this."

He retrieved the feature story Sayers had written about him from his pocket. "He says it's being syndicated."

"Which means it will be read by people everywhere," she said as she seated herself at a table to read the article.

"Quite a story," she commented when he joined her, and she handed it back. "I like the picture of you."

"It's not my best side," he joked. "It's kind of odd thinking of so many people reading about me and knowing what drives me. But Will's a good writer—and a good friend." He took a sip of his drink before adding, "I did something today that I seldom do. I took a nap this afternoon."

"You must have been tired."

"I've been tired ever since the café bombing. Tired and sore. See this?" He raised his chin and pulled open his collar to reveal the fading pink line on his neck.

"What happened?"

"I was attacked after I left Alvi's dinner. Somebody tried to strangle me with a rope."

Asal gasped. "How awful. Did you see who it was?"

"No, but it's quite a coincidence, isn't it, that it happened right after I left the dinner?"

"What are you suggesting?"

"I'm suggesting that your buddy, Alvi, sicced somebody on me."

"Oh, Robert, isn't that—?"

"Isn't that what—paranoia? Maybe so, but it works for me. Look, Asal, we said we'd get together to talk about what's been bothering me ever since Alvi's dinner. I—"

"I don't want to burn the lamb," she said, and left him standing on the balcony.

Ten minutes later they were seated at the dining table enjoying her culinary efforts. Brixton had decided not to raise the subject of Alvi again until they'd finished eating. She told stories about when her brother and she were children in Iraq and what life was like then. He related a few stories of his own about his daughters, especially Janet, and mentioned that her stepfather, Miles Lashka, was going to finance a CD of her songs.

After he'd helped clear the table and had his offer to help load the dishwasher declined—"Men always do such a bad job of it," she'd said—they carried cups of strong Turkish coffee to the living room.

"Is it time?" he asked

"To ask why I was at Zafar Alvi's dinner?"

"That's a good place to start."

She reiterated what she'd told him earlier, that Alvi provided financial aid to her organization but that she'd not met him until shortly before the dinner.

"But you were seated at a prime table with some of

his closest friends. Or *are* they friends? They look to me more like hired thugs."

"I don't know the others at the table," she said, "not very well, and I know nothing of what you accuse Mr. Alvi of being. You paint him as some ogre, some criminal. You say he had someone try to murder you. Why do you say those things, Robert? What do you base those things on?"

"Let's start with his connection to Paul Skaggs, the congressman's son. Skaggs and his sister have been involved with a cult on Maui, in Hawaii. The guy who runs the cult is a known gunrunner named Samuel Prisler. Prisler—at least it's alleged—sells weapons to terrorist organizations around the world through Zafar Alvi. With me so far?"

She said nothing

"Paul Skaggs came to D.C. from Hawaii a few weeks before the café bombing that killed my daughter. He flew into New York. Nobody knows how he traveled from New York to Washington, no trace of an airline reservation, a bus, Amtrak, nothing. Okay, now he's here in D.C., and nobody knows where he stayed, who he spent time with, where he ate and drank, nothing, zippo, zilch. But, lo and behold, he gets a traffic ticket while driving a car registered to your benefactor, Zafar Alvi. Strange, isn't it?"

"Maybe there is a logical explanation for it."

"The only explanation I can come up with is that Alvi was harboring him, feeding him, giving him a car to drive, all in preparation for Skaggs bringing that poor misguided girl to the café and buying her a lemonade before she blew up herself and everybody else in the place."

"But you don't know that for a fact, Robert."

"Do I have proof? Not yet. Charlie McQuaid, a lovely guy, a lawyer who retired from the U.S. Justice

Department, built a case against Prisler for his gunrunning. He gave me his papers, and they included references to Alvi as Prisler's conduit to Middle Eastern arms buyers. What happens to this nice guy, Charlie McQuaid, who's enjoying his retirement on his little boat? He's murdered. Whoever did it made it seem as though he'd drowned after getting entangled in his own fishing line and falling into the Potomac. Didn't happen that way. Somebody killed him, somebody who knew about those papers and who was looking for them in his office."

"Are you saying that Zafar Alvi might have had something to do with this Charlie Something-or-other's death?"

Brixton drew a breath and wished he hadn't quit smoking. He said in measured tones, "Look, Asal, I'm looking for answers. I wouldn't even be thinking about Alvi or Samuel Prisler if it weren't for two facts. One: Paul Skaggs was driving a car that belonged to Alvi shortly before the bombing. Why? Why would Alvi lend him a car? Two: Alvi is alleged to be a conduit for Prisler's arms sales to Middle Eastern countries." He paused and took a breath. "I believe that Paul Skaggs came back to D.C. from Hawaii, where he was a member of Prisler's cult. Did Prisler arrange for Skaggs to make contact with Alvi and drive one of his cars? Questions, Asal. I have questions that have to be answered."

"What can I do to help?" she asked.

Her question surprised him. He wasn't looking for her help. That wasn't why he was there. He needed to satisfy himself that she hadn't lied when she said that she didn't personally know Alvi. But that now seemed almost irrelevant. She was indicating that she was in his corner.

He leaped on it.

"Asal, if you mean that, that you want to help me,

there's a way for you to do it. You obviously have an in with Alvi. He funds your organization, invites you to be at a prime table when he's being honored at a dinner. You might be able to find out what Alvi's connection was with Paul Skaggs."

"How can I do that?"

"Get together with Alvi and ask him, maybe not directly, but lead him into a conversation in which the truth might come out."

When she didn't reply, he added, "I know that you need his money to keep your organization going, and I respect that. I'm not looking for you to jeopardize that on my behalf. Whatever you find out stays with me. I don't mention it to anyone. I promise you that."

"What about your friend, the journalist Sayers, and your friends Mac and Annabel? If I find out what you want and you use it against Alvi, how can you not share it with them?"

"You'll just have to trust me," he said. "And you *can* trust me."

"I will have to think about it," she said.

"Sure, I understand that, but don't think about it for too long. I have the feeling I'm running out of time."

It was natural that both Brixton and Asal were considering whether to repeat their previous romantic evening together on this night. Asal softened after their conversation, and Brixton knew that should he make the advance, they would end up in bed again.

But he steeled against the urge and said, "I'd better leave."

"Sure you don't want to stay?" she said, running her fingertips over his hand.

"I'd like to but . . ."

"But you're tired and sore, as you said."

"Yeah, something like that. I appreciate what you're considering doing with Alvi. I'll call you tomorrow and we can get together again. The dinner was terrific. You're a good cook."

"My mother was a better cook."

With that, she wrapped her arms about him and initiated a long and passionate kiss. He disengaged, touched her nose with his fingertip, and said, "I'm sorry that I doubted you. I'll call tomorrow."

30

As Brixton drove home he second-guessed his decision to leave rather than enjoy being entangled in the sheets with Asal Banai. Lately he found himself vacillating between devoting all his energies to revenging Janet's death and clearing his name, and saying the hell with it and putting together whatever life he could, post-bombing. He hated being indecisive. He'd spent his adult life analyzing a situation, making a decision, and acting on it. That approach to life had gotten him into trouble, but that was better than wallowing in self-doubt and indecision. What did the shrinks say? "Any action was better than no action." At least by acting you stood a fifty-fifty chance of being right.

He pulled into his underground parking space, got out of the car, and checked his surroundings. Since the attack on him in Lafayette Park, he'd become even more conscious than usual of where he was and who might be sharing his space. Confident that he had a clear path to the elevator, he rode it up to his floor, stepped into his apartment, turned on some lights, and checked his answering machine. The tiny blinking red light said that he had messages, three of them.

He listened to the first two—Mac Smith and Mike Kogan. Then he heard the third caller, a woman, speaking softly as though afraid of being overheard. There was a sense of dread in her voice, hesitation between words, not sure that she should be making the call.

"Mr. Brixton, this is Kamea Wakatake. I'm calling from Maui in the Hawaiian Islands." She paused, cleared her throat, and continued. "I have been reading about you. . . . I need help. . . . I can help you. . . . Please call me at this number, . . . Ask for Wayne . . . ; he's my friend. . . . Don't speak to anyone else. . . . Please hurry." She recited the phone number and clicked off.

Brixton played the call another three times and wrote the number on a pad. Kamea Wakatake. It took him a minute to remember where he'd heard that name. Will Sayers had told him that Paul Skaggs's sister, Morgana, had assumed that Hawaiian name after joining Prisler's cult.

Kamea Wakatake!

He went to the bedroom, where he stripped off his clothes, got into pajamas, a robe, and slippers, then returned to his desk and placed the call.

"Wayne," the man who answered said.

"This is Wayne?"

"Yes."

"I'm returning a call from Miss Wakatake."

"She's not here right now."

"This is Robert Brixton. She said it was urgent."

Like her, Wayne also lowered his voice. "I'll have her get back to you when she can."

"Is there somewhere I can reach her now?"

"No, no; you can only call her here. I'll give her your message."

"Tell her that she can call me anytime, at any hour. What is it, a five-hour time difference?"

"I have to go. Good-bye."

"I'll be damned," Brixton muttered after hanging up. What was *this* all about? The frustration he felt was palpable. He paced the floor, stopping from time to time to look down at the phone as though willing it to ring.

He tried to relax, but it was a useless exercise. He flipped through TV channels in search of something to capture his attention, but that too was futile. He took the phone with him to the balcony and sat staring into the black sky. The woman across the street distracted him momentarily as she passed by her window wearing baby-doll pajamas, but after a few minutes she closed the blinds and turned off the light. He thought of Asal and of Flo Combes. But those were fleeting thoughts. Why had Paul Skaggs's sister called? They were furtive calls, no doubt about that. Who was this Wayne character?

He paced again, inside and on the balcony, checking his watch every few minutes and calculating what time it was in Maui—12:30 in D.C., 7:30 Hawaiian time. One-thirty in Washington, 8:30 P.M. on Maui. He considered calling the number she'd left again, but he didn't act on the urge. Why had time so dramatically slowed down? The hands on his kitchen clock and watch seemed never to move.

At two he dozed off in a recliner in his living room but had been out for only fifteen minutes when the phone rang. He awoke with a start, kicked the empty glass that was on the floor next to the chair across the room as he made for the desk. "Robert Brixton here."

"Mr. Brixton, this is Kamea Wakatake."

"Yes, Kamea. I returned your call earlier and—"

"I can't speak long. I read the story about you."

"The one that—?"

"I need help, Mr. Brixton, and I know that you do, too. What my brother did was ... Oh, my God ... I ..."

"Kamea, I do need help and I'd like to help you. Can you come here to Washington?"

"No, no. He would never let me."

"Who, Prisler?"

"Can you come here, Mr. Brixton? I'm afraid for my life. Please."

"Yeah, I can come. How will I make contact when I'm there?"

"Wayne. The boatyard. But only call the number I gave you. It's a borrowed cell phone."

"I'll see what I can set up. I'll call you at that number when I get there."

The line went dead.

Brixton went to his computer and looked up flights to Hawaii. He called United Airlines and was told that they had a coach seat available on a flight leaving from Newark Airport for Honolulu the following day at 6:00 P.M. He booked it and returned to his recliner, where he grabbed a few hours sleep before showering. As he dressed he turned on the TV, where a breaking news story was being reported. There had been a bombing in London at a pub near the U.S. embassy, and another in Italy, this one in a restaurant across the street from the Australian embassy.

Visions of being with Janet at the café, the explosion, and its aftermath flooded him. The memory pressed him down into his chair as though an elephant were sitting on his chest, like in those TV commercials for COPD. He couldn't breathe, couldn't make sense of what was happening, but he somehow knew that the answer might lie on the island of Maui.

He couldn't get there fast enough.

31

MAUI

Wayne Bates managed a charter boat service in Lahaina Harbor for Samuel Prisler, although he wasn't a member of the cult. Prisler had businesses all over the island and earned the loyalty of his employees by hiring those for whom opportunities were limited. That morning Bates had taken out a group of tourists to enjoy a fishing expedition on the forty-one-foot Rybovich sportfishing boat. Returning to the dock, he bid the fishing party farewell and entered the cramped office, where Kamea was filing papers and doing other administrative tasks.

"Good trip?" she asked.

"The usual—one seasick woman and one guy complaining about the size of the fish he caught. You saw the gray-haired titan of industry with his young trophy wife, or maybe she was his girlfriend? They spent most of the trip smooching in the cabin."

Kamea managed a smile. Bates always had amusing stories about his customers on fishing trips, but her smile didn't reflect what she was feeling.

The *Honolulu Star-Advertiser* had carried the syndicated story written by Will Sayers about Robert Brixton. Although she already knew about Brixton—the café bombing and Brixton's shooting of her brother—seeing his photo and reading of his determination to clear his name and avenge the death of his daughter had a profound effect upon her. She'd been on the verge of tears ever since, but her fragile emotional state was nothing new.

"You still intend to do it?" Bates asked.

Kamea swiveled in her chair and gazed out over the harbor.

She had struggled with her decision before calling Brixton.

Since being summoned to the meeting with Sam Prisler where she was admonished for wanting to attend her brother's funeral in Mississippi, she'd been on edge, paranoid, fearful. She knew that her only telephone was tapped and that any mail she received, which was minimal, was being opened and read before reaching her. Credit cards were never allowed for members of the cult, nor were driver's licenses or other forms of identification. Cultists were given a token amount of money each month; all the profits of their work went to Prisler and the cult. In return, they were housed and fed and reminded at daily meetings that they were chosen people, blessed to have found each other and to be able to benefit from Samuel Prisler's wisdom and love.

Prisler's right-hand man, Thomas Akina, a burly Hawaiian with a mean streak, had paid particularly close attention to Kamea when Prisler went to Washington. After his return the surveillance of her became even more obvious and intrusive. Akina seemed to be everywhere she went, and she wondered if he had the means of peering into her small apartment; the thought sickened her.

She was no longer dropped off at her job at the fishing charter service by the usual driver who ferried cult members to work in a stretch van. Akina now personally chauffeured her to and from the compound and frequently showed up at her work to check on her during the day. While others envied her special treatment, Kamea knew better. She was being closely monitored.

Adding to her concerns was Lalo Reyes's arrival back at the cult. She'd known him when he'd initially arrived on Maui and found him to be charming; albeit naive. Openly gay, his flamboyant personality allowed him to easily fit in with many of the cult members. But his return was not greeted warmly. Instead, he was kept under wraps, housed in one of three rooms attached to the main house. He took his meals there, and the only sighting was an occasional glimpse when he sunned himself on a tiny patio off his room and could be seen from the entranceway at the front of the property. Kamea worried that she would be sequestered the same way.

Kamea's ambivalence about the cult had been smoldering since Prisler had dispatched her brother to Washington. Until then she'd believed in Prisler and what the cult stood for. She was one of his most loyal followers, feeling blessed that he'd provided a refuge for her from a life that she'd hated. She detested her father, a bombastic, my-way-or-the-highway type, whose life represented everything that she abhorred. When she'd first joined the cult and changed her name from Morgana to Kamea, the congressman had made what she considered sham attempts to persuade her to return home. He was furious with her choice, and words to the effect of "all is forgiven" were delivered with icy inflection. Her mother, browbeaten by her husband for so many years, had made her own feeble approach, but her weakness and willingness to be dominated by her husband disgusted Kamea, who refused to rejoin their loveless household.

And so she'd settled into her new life and reveled in it, basking in the belief that she'd found an answer to what was surely a corrupt world, escaping her father's hypocritical life as a member of Congress, and the shallow thinking of her peers back home. To her, Prisler was a messiah; Maui was the Garden of Eden populated by loving people who worshipped nature and the human spirit.

She'd found nirvana.

Until now.

"I can't change your mind?" Bates asked.

"No; I have to leave, Wayne. Don't you see?"

"I wish I did. I mean I do understand to a degree. After all, I'm letting you use my phone. Doesn't that count for something?"

"Of course it does." She touched his arm. "I'm no longer happy here," she said, "and I'm afraid."

"Of Sam?"

"He doesn't trust me anymore. You see how he treats me since Paul went to Washington and was killed. I feel like a prisoner. I never used to feel that way."

Bates turned from her and carefully folded nautical charts, saying as he did, "What about me, Kamea? What about us? Doesn't that mean anything to you?"

Since Kamea had been assigned to work at the boat chartering service she and Bates had fallen easily and naturally into a romantic relationship, one that had to be conducted discreetly because it violated the cult's rules.

"Of course it does," she said. "That's why I want you to come with me. Sam treats you like dirt. He pays you half of what other charter captains make. We could leave together and . . ."

He turned and said, "And do what, Kamea? What do I do back on the mainland? Running fishing charters is all I know, and *you* know I'm lucky to have this job. I screwed up. I got busted for drugs more than once. Sure, I'm clean now, but with my record, there's not another charter service in Hawaii that'll hire me. Sam Prisler did me a favor, and he's been good to me. Okay, so he's on edge since Paul got killed, but that'll pass. Give it some time, and things will be the way they used to be. You loved it here."

"I don't want to live in fear again. No, Wayne, I have to leave."

"What if he won't let you?" Bates asked.

"I've thought of that," she said. "No one is allowed to leave if they're not assigned elsewhere. The only ones to get away have had to sneak out like thieves in the night. I'm not naive, Wayne. That's why I want to call Robert Brixton and see if he can help me."

Bates's laugh was dismissive. "He's the guy who killed your brother, for Christ's sake."

Kamea thought before answering. "He's a man who will help me because I can help him. I know things that he needs to know."

"About your brother and why he went back to Washington?"

"That and other things too. You have no idea what I've learned in the past few days, things that can make a difference."

"A difference for who?"

"A difference for—a difference for me. You said I could use your cell phone. Don't let me down now. I can't take a chance using the phone here in the office or in the dorm, and we're not allowed to have cell phones."

"I said I would, Kamea, but I wish you'd think it out before you make the call. But if you insist, let's go outside. You can use my cell once we're under way."

He released the lines tethering the boat to the dock, started the twin diesel engines, and maneuvered the craft away from the dock and into open water. Once away from prying eyes, Bates handed her his cell phone and she made the call, reaching Brixton's answering machine.

"He'll call me back," she said.

"On my phone?" he said.

"You said it was all right."

Bates's expression said that he'd reconsidered that decision.

"Can we stay out a little longer in case he returns my call?"

"I have to get ready for a dinner charter tonight," Bates replied. "Besides, Akina will be arriving to take you back to the compound. What do I say if this Brixton guy calls back?"

"Tell him I'll try to reach him again."

As Bates guided the boat into its slot at the dock, he said, "The caterer will be arriving at six. See if you can get Akina and Prisler to let you work it; tell them I'm shorthanded and need you."

"I don't know if they'll let me."

"You won't know if you don't try. I'll tell Akina when he comes to pick you up."

When Akina arrived, Bates passed along the message to him.

"I doubt if Mr. Prisler will agree," the hefty bodyguard said.

"Ask him. I really need her."

Bates had not heard from Kamea when Brixton returned her call. He considered not telling her about it. Maybe if she thought that Brixton hadn't responded and probably wouldn't, she would stop trying to reach him and rethink attempting to leave Maui. But when Akina drove up in his Range Rover, and Kamea hopped out, he decided not to put himself in the position of having her discover that he'd been dishonest.

"What time will you return?" Akina asked.

"Ten. I always bring these nighttime charters back in at ten," Bates said.

Bates and Kamea said nothing as they watched Akina pull away. When he'd passed from view, Bates told her of Brixton's call.

"Let me have the phone," she said.

"Wait till we're under way," he suggested.

She busied herself helping the couple from the catering company arrange the food in the cabin. Eight guests arrived and were welcomed by Bates and the young man who served as his mate on charters. Kamea acted as bartender in the cabin as they left the dock and smoothly moved through the calm waters of the harbor. Bates summoned Kamea to him where he stood at the helm. "Call him from here," he said.

She pressed into a corner and dialed the number. Bates strained to hear her end of the conversation over the boat's engines but caught only snippets. When she'd finished she handed the phone back to him.

"What did he say?" Bates asked.

"He said he'd come."

"When?"

"I don't know. Soon I hope. He'll call you on your phone."

Her lip trembled and she wiped away a tear from her cheek.

"Not too late to change your mind," he said grimly.

"I know, but I can't stay here any longer. Please try to understand."

"I'm doing my best," he said as he slowed the engines in preparation for anchoring while dinner was being served.

"You'd better help with serving and the cleanup," he said.

What he didn't say was how deeply he resented her calling Brixton to help her leave the island and the cult. She was putting his job in jeopardy. He didn't want her to go. He never should have agreed to let her use his cell phone to make those calls. He was suddenly gripped by distrust and jealousy. He brought his fist down hard on the console and began to conjure what he could do to keep her on Maui.

32

Brixton started his day by returning Mike Kogan's call.

"Hey, pal," Kogan said, "how about stopping by this morning?"

"What's up?"

"I want to ring you in on a meeting I'm having with the staff. Donna will be here, Larry and Luke too."

"I'm suspended. Remember?"

"And I'm unsuspending you, at least for this morning. Is that a word, 'unsuspending'?"

"Doesn't sound like it, but what do I know? I never aced any of my English classes. Sure I'll swing by. What time?"

"Ten."

Before heading for SITQUAL, Brixton printed out his boarding pass, packed a suitcase, and booked a flight to Newark Airport leaving at two that afternoon. He placed a call to the airline informing them that he was a licensed handgun owner and would have an unloaded weapon in his checked baggage, secured in a locked metal box. He would also have with him a limited number of rounds for the weapon. He was tempted to lie and to say that he was an agent for SITQUAL, but he knew that wasn't necessary. Transporting a gun was permitted as long as he followed the rules concerning the locked box and giving prior warning. It annoyed him that he would have to check a bag instead of carrying it on board, but it was a small price to pay for being able to bring his Smith & Wesson with him. All he had to do was remember to place the gun in the box, lock it, and shove it in with his clothing before going through security. The government didn't take lightly to showing up with a weapon in your carry-on luggage.

"I'm going out of town for a few days," he told Sayers.

"Where?"

"Hawaii."

"Taking a few days vacation? No, wait a minute. It has to do with Prisler, right?"

"Right. I'd just as soon not spread it around."

"My lips are sealed."

"Unless there's a prime steak beckoning. I got a call from Paul Skaggs's sister on Maui."

"Whoa. *She* called *you*?"

"Yeah."

"And?"

"And she says she needs help and knows that I do, too."

"What kind of help does she need?"

"Get off your editorial horse, Will. I don't know. She said she'd been reading about me, probably that syndicated article you wrote."

"The power of the press."

"Have you come up with anything new before I go? I'm catching a plane to Newark at two. My flight to Hawaii leaves at six."

"Nothing new on my end. You said that Lalo Reyes

has returned to Hawaii. Maybe you'll catch up with him again."

"Maybe I'll get lucky and won't."

"Anything I can help you with while you're gone?"

"Can't think of anything. Just want you to know that I appreciate what you've already done for me."

"You make it sound like this is our last conversation. How long will you be gone?"

"No idea. I'll give you a call when I get back."

"With Paul Skaggs's sister? If so, I'm first on your call list, right?"

"Right. Catch you later."

W hat's this about?" Brixton asked when he joined the others in Kogan's SITQUAL office.

"We're trying to make sense out of this rash of embassy bombings, come up with a logical motive behind them."

"But they're not bombing embassies," Donna offered. "It's always someplace *near* embassies that they target."

"Cafés are easier targets," someone said. "Embassy security has been beefed up. Tough to get close to an embassy these days. Restaurants and the people in them are sitting ducks."

"Maybe no one from an embassy is in a café when it gets blown."

"But chances are that there will be. They're doing their homework, choosing places popular with embassy staffs. Whoever's behind this always make their move at the end of normal office hours, when it's most likely that people from embassies are enjoying a drink after work."

"Let's go back to those individual murders," Kogan said. "While it seemed at first that they were bias crimes— and I don't buy that scenario anymore—the larger question remains, *Why* were these individuals murdered? If it wasn't because they were gay, then it has to be because of where they worked."

"Which raises another question," Donna said. "Terrorists like to make a big splash, kill lots of people, get a bigger bang for their buck. They accomplish this in the café bombings, but killing individuals hardly follows that MO."

"The homosexual complication still bothers me," an agent said. "Whoever is behind these attacks could be deliberately creating red herrings by killing gays."

They spent the next half hour going over myriad scenarios that might be behind the recent bombings and murders.

"No one has claimed responsibility?" Donna Salvos asked.

"Not so far," Kogan responded. "We've received briefings from the intelligence agencies. None of them knows for sure who's calling the shots. Internet chatter hasn't yielded anything. We do know that whoever it is is targeting embassies in developed countries, nothing like Benghazi or Lebanon or other past attacks. The intelligence folks are trying to come up with a link between the embassies that have been affected. What do Poland, Germany, Italy, France, Denmark, Great Britain, Australia, and us have in common? The attacks are obviously of Middle Eastern origins. The gal who blew up the café near our State Department was Pakistani. The suicide bombers in Britain and Italy were also Middle Eastern. But why in hell would they want to kill that woman from the Polish embassy? Were they the bad guys in their eyes. Poland? Australia? There is no link."

"They're all embassies for democracies of one sort or another," someone said.

"Did all these countries who've had their embassies

hit contribute troops for the wars in Iraq and Afghanistan?" Brixton asked.

"Good question?" Kogan said. "I'll check."

"And I have to hightail it out of here," Brixton said.

"Nice having you back, Robert," an agent said.

"Strictly unofficial," Brixton said. To Kogan: "Thanks for ringing me in, Mike. Got a second?"

They went into the hallway, where Brixton told him of his travel plans.

"What's this all about?" Kogan asked.

"I can't get specific, Mike, but I'm hoping to find some answers to my problem."

"I won't press you, Robert, but keep whatever you're doing unofficial. Keep SITQUAL out of it."

"Count on it. I'll check in when I get back."

Kogan watched Brixton disappear through a door leading to the stairs. "Good luck, pal," he muttered. "You deserve it."

33

As Brixton got into his car he remembered that he was slated to have dinner that night with Flo Combes. That was obviously out of the question, and he dreaded having to tell her. He considered calling the Smiths' apartment but decided instead to break the news in person.

His call was answered by Annabel.

"It's Robert," he said. "Mind if I stop over for a few minutes?"

"Love to see you, Robert. A cup of coffee will be waiting."

Annabel answered the door. "Come in, stranger. What have you been up to?"

"Too many things," he replied.

Flo was in the living room reading the paper.

"Hi," Brixton said.

"Hi to you," she said. "This is a nice surprise. We weren't on until tonight."

"Yeah, I know. That's why I dropped by." He joined her on the couch. "Something has come up and—"

"We're not having dinner?"

"Unfortunately no. I'll be out of town."

Mac heard him as he walked into the room. "A last-minute trip?" he asked.

"Yeah, it is, Mac. I'm going to Hawaii."

"I never considered you the type to like Hawaii," Flo said.

"Don't know whether I'll like it or not. Never been there."

An awkward silence was followed by Flo asking, "Why are you going to Hawaii?" Her voice was tinged with frost.

Brixton decided on the spot to lay it all out for her, and he did.

"So the sister of the man you shot called and said she needs help?" Flo said after Brixton had explained the call from Kamea Wakatake.

"She also said that she knew that *I* needed help," he added.

"Did she mention her brother?" Mac asked.

"She started to but didn't follow through."

"What sort of help do you think she's asking for?" asked Annabel.

"I don't know," Brixton said, "but I'll find out soon enough. I'm taking a flight from Newark this afternoon." He checked his watch. "I'd better get going. My bag's packed and in the car."

"I wish you had a better handle on what the sister wants from you," Mac said, "before going there. Prisler isn't to be taken lightly. I'm sure he won't welcome you with open arms."

"Hopefully I'll be able to avoid him and deal only with Kamea. That's Ms. Skaggs's Hawaiian name. Anyway, it'll be good to get out of D.C. for a little while. By the way, I was attacked the other night."

"Attacked?" Flo said. "By whom?"

"I didn't see him, but he left a calling card." He raised his chin to display the remnants of the mark his assailant had made on his neck. "I'd attended a dinner in honor of Zafar Alvi at the Hay-Adams."

"Who is he?" Flo asked.

"He's a big shot here in Washington who funnels illegal arms provided by Prisler to terrorist groups. Mac can fill you in. Anyway, I'm convinced that it was Alvi who set his goon on me."

Flo had been looking directly at Brixton while he explained the attack. Now she turned from him. He reached and placed a hand on her shoulder. "I'm really sorry about dinner tonight, Flo. I'm sorry that you came here to D.C. and we haven't had time to get together. Hopefully, I won't be away long and—"

"I'm leaving today for New York," she said.

"Don't do that," he said. "Stay a few more days. By then I'll be back and—"

"I've mooched off Mac and Annabel long enough," she said.

"Don't be silly," said Mac.

Flo shook her head. "No," she said, "it's time I left." She turned to Brixton. "It was silly of me to come. I thought that maybe I could help you, but I realize that was foolish, too. You'll do whatever you have to do by yourself, Robert. That's just the way you are. I only hope you won't get yourself killed in the process. If you don't, and when this is over and you've accomplished what you need to, we can have that talk we never had here. Excuse me."

Her last few words were spoken with a trembling voice, and Brixton saw that her eyes had welled up. She went into the spare bedroom she'd been using and closed the door.

"I should have found time for us to get together before now," Brixton said.

"Things just didn't work out, that's all," Mac said. "We'll try and convince her to stay with us a little longer. In the meantime, go do what you have to do. But Robert . . ."

"What?"

"That red circle on your neck is proof that what Flo said is true, that you might get yourself killed while trying to avenge your daughter's murder and clear your name. Don't be a hero. I hope your ticket is round-trip. Whatever happens in Hawaii, make sure you're around to use the return portion."

34

B rixton's flight to Newark was without incident. He boarded the United Airlines plane bound for Honolulu and settled in his window seat in the coach section. It was a full flight, and he was fortunate to have gotten a seat by the window and not one in the center.

Despite having gotten a better seat, Brixton was not happy. It wasn't that he was afraid of flying. He hated the hoops that he had to go through—the security checks, shoes and belts off, nothing in your pockets that might set off the electronic scanning devices, and the cattle-car atmosphere that pervaded every step of the boarding process. Knowing that he was in for a long flight, he'd stopped in the airport bookstore and picked up a couple of paperback mystery novels by authors he'd never heard of. But the covers were nice, and positive comments by other writers on the back gave the books third-party endorsements, provided they weren't the authors' family members or best friends. There he was being cynical again; Flo would not approve.

It wasn't long before the cramped seat became annoying. Brixton wasn't especially tall—a little over six feet—and he wondered how taller men managed. It became even more nettlesome when the passenger in front of Brixton decided to recline his seat, which pushed it against Brixton's knees. He tapped the man on the shoulder and suggested that he not recline.

"I paid for this seat and I'll do whatever I want" was the whiny reply.

"Thanks, pal," Brixton muttered, and briefly fantasized ramming his knees into the seat back on a regular basis. *Don't even think that way. Stay out of trouble,* he reminded himself. *You're in enough hot water already.*

He read, he dozed, ate the two alleged meals that he'd paid for and that were laid in front of him, and he thought—thought of what he would do once in Hawaii.

His only contact with Kamea was through this man Wayne. What sort of guy was he? It was safe to assume, Brixton decided, that he was Kamea's friend, since he'd allowed her to use his phone. Why didn't she have a cell phone of her own? The whole world had cell phones, including kids as young as six. What was the world coming to?

He'd gunned down her brother, for good cause he knew, yet she was turning to him for help. Help with what? It occurred to him that he might be walking into some sort of trap. Was she intent upon avenging her brother's death, luring his killer to Maui and planning to enjoy retribution? That was unlikely—or he hoped so. He remembered what Mac Smith had said about making sure he left Hawaii in one piece.

What about Lalo Reyes? Would he see him again? Was Kamea friendly with the young Spaniard who'd flown the coop in D.C. and hightailed it back to the Prisler cult? And what about Prisler? If he was as vile as he had been painted, he wouldn't be happy to see Robert Brixton on his doorstep, if cults had doorsteps. Prisler and Zafar Alvi were in business together, peddling illegal arms to groups hell-bent on killing as many Americans and their allies as possible. Nice guys. Had Alvi called ahead to arrange this invitation?

Ten hours later, the plane taxied to the gate and its door opened. Brixton joined the long line of passengers waiting to disembark. The flight's captain stood in the open cockpit door welcoming each passenger to Hawaii with "Aloha."

It was tight, but Brixton managed to make his connecting flight to Maui, the last one leaving that night. It was a smaller jet aircraft that covered the short distance between the big island and the smaller Maui in what seemed minutes. Brixton crossed the terminal and went directly to the car-rental desks, where he arranged for a sedan and received driving directions to Kapalua, site of the Prisler cult.

He was tired as he drove and had to fight to stay awake. He hadn't booked a hotel ahead of time before leaving and hoped that he'd find one with vacancies and at a decent price. When he came upon a beachfront property, he pulled in.

"Aloha," the attractive young woman manning the desk said.

"Hi," Brixton said. "Do you have any vacancies?"

She looked at him quizzically.

"I'm not here for a vacation," he said, flashing his most winning smile. "I'm here on a last-minute business trip. I mean, it was *really* last minute."

"We have one garden-view studio," she said. "It's very nice, but it's not on the ocean."

"I don't need the ocean," Brixton said. "I just need a nice room. I have business meetings in Kapalua tomorrow."

"Of course," she said and started the checking-in process.

"How much is this garden-view room?" he asked casually.

"Three hundred and fifty dollars a night," she replied.

He whistled. "That's pretty steep."

Her cocked head asked whether he wished to take the room.

"It'll be fine," he said, and placed his American Express card on the desk. This was no time to worry about finances.

"If you play golf, we're less than a half mile to the Kapalua Golf Club. We also have two eighteen-hole putting greens on the property, and massages are available through the gym, which is fully equipped and—"

"That's all great," Brixton said, "but I'm afraid I won't have time for those things. I am hungry, though. Is the restaurant still open?"

She checked a wall clock. "Yes, the restaurant is still open but not for much longer. We have twenty-four-hour room service."

"I'll head for the restaurant. Thank you."

"Aloha," she said.

"Yeah, aloha to you."

It was a lovely room with a comfortable bed and doors leading out to the garden. A mirror on the bathroom door reflected a weary traveler. He realized that his wardrobe was distinctly non-Hawaiian. He'd stand out on the touristy island in his gray suit, white shirt, green tie, and black shoes. He'd have to find time in the morning to pick up more appropriate clothes.

The restaurant was open-air with tables overlooking the water. He ordered a martini the way he liked it and an assortment of appetizers from the menu. He debated calling the number Kamea had given him. If this guy Wayne was asleep, chances were he'd have turned off his cell phone. Then again he might be a night creature who enjoys barhopping. With his drink and one of the appetizers in front of him, he dialed.

"Hello?"

"Wayne?"

"Yeah." Loud music and crowd noise in the background made it hard for Brixton to hear.

"It's Robert Brixton."

"Right. Where are you?"

"On Maui. I just arrived."

"That's, ah, good."

"Is Kamea with you?"

"No, she's— Where on Maui are you?"

"I haven't checked into a hotel yet," Brixton said, deciding to not tell this stranger where he was staying. "I'll let you know tomorrow. How do I get in touch with Kamea?"

"You mean now?"

"Sure."

"That's impossible."

"She said to arrange to meet her through you," Brixton said.

"Yeah, I know but—hold on." The background noise was all that Brixton heard until Wayne came back on the line. "Look, Mr. Brixton, it's going to be tough for you to get together with Kamea tonight, but she works with me at the boat dock in Lahaina. She'll be there tomorrow at nine thirty, but there's usually somebody from the cult with her. You know that she lives with a group in Kapalua?"

"Yes, I know that. Sam Prisler's cult."

"He doesn't call it a cult."

"I don't care what he calls it. Who'll be with her besides you?"

"A guy from the group. He drives her to work and checks on her during the day."

"I'll keep that in mind. She'll be there all morning?"

"Yeah, in the office. I gotta go. If you come by to-morrow, maybe you can talk to her."

"What dock is it? Must be more than one."

"On Front Street. Wayne's Charter Service. Can't miss it."

He hung up.

Brixton finished his drink and food and stared out over the water. A full moon created a million flashes of light on the ripples. Recorded Hawaiian music through speakers accompanied his thoughts as he pondered what the next day would bring.

He now knew where and when he would make contact with Kamea. What he *didn't* know was what would happen after that meeting. He had to assume that she'd sought his help to leave Maui and the Prisler cult. But that was purely supposition. If it was true, it raised a much larger issue. How would they accomplish that? Obviously, she wasn't free to simply pack her bag, get on a plane, and fly to the mainland. Did the cult have that much control over its members? If so, why would anyone subject themselves to such tyranny?

The waitress informed him that the restaurant was closing. He signed the bill, using his room number, and walked to the pool, where he sat in a chair and prolonged the thought process before returning to his room, stripping down to his shorts, climbing into bed, and succumbing to his fatigue.

He was up as the sun rose into the pristine blue sky. His suit pants and dress shirt weren't proper exercise attire, but that's what he wore to the gym, where he used its equipment to work out his multiple aches and pains, many of which he blamed on having been wedged in that infernal airline seat obviously made for smaller bodies. He showered back in the room and had breakfast on the same seaside terrace at which he'd eaten the night before. A desk clerk directed him to a clothing shop a block away but pointed out that it didn't open until nine. Brixton passed the time sitting by the pool and watching a succession of shapely females dip their toes in the water before quickly heading for lounge chairs. He smiled wryly, knowing that he received strange looks ·in his suit and black dress shoes. The anticipation of meeting with Kamea dominated his thoughts and emotions, and as the time drew closer, his adrenaline level climbed.

He was at the clothing shop on the dot of nine and purchased a yellow T-shirt with ALOHA printed on the front and back, an oversize red hibiscus print shirt with little green, blue, and white birds on it, which the shop owner assured him was authentic Hawaiian—whatever that meant—white athletic socks, underwear, white sneakers, sunglasses, and a ball cap that said MAUI. He was back in his room at 9:40, quickly changed into his new purchases, strapped his armpit holster on, checked and loaded his Smith & Wesson, and was in his car fifteen minutes later driving to Lahaina.

The town was chockablock with tourists that morning, and Brixton had trouble finding a parking spot. He eventually gave up and pulled into a municipal garage, where he fed the meter to its maximum and walked in the direction of the dock. He spotted the sign for Wayne's Charter Service and took it in from across the busy street. A man whom he judged to be in his early thirties was busy doing what boat captains do, and Brixton figured he must be Wayne. In front of the boat was a small office and a kiosk in which a young woman chatted with four tourists. She was a pretty girl, although from what Brixton could see, she wasn't especially well kempt. Her lank brunette hair hung straight down and didn't have that telltale sheen that a good morning shampooing would have given it. She was

surprisingly pale considering that she lived in sunny
Hawaii. She wore a white T-shirt with the charter service name on it.

Brixton waited until the tourists had walked away
before starting to cross. But he'd only stepped off the
curb when she left the kiosk and joined the man on
deck. Brixton retreated and continued his wait. No
doubt about it, they were discussing him, constantly
looking at passersby in search of this guy Robert
Brixton.

Five minutes later people started arriving and were
greeted by the girl, who had them sign documents before escorting them onto the boat, where they were
introduced to the captain. Brixton surmised that they
were about to embark on a charter cruise, and he wondered whether the girl, who he was sure was Kamea,
would accompany them. Another fifteen minutes of
waiting answered the question. The girl resumed her
place in the kiosk, while the fishing boat backed away
from the dock, turned, and headed out to sea.

Brixton crossed the street and approached the kiosk.
He stepped up to it and said, "Excuse me."

The girl looked up, and recognition spread across her
sallow face. "Mr. Brixton?"

"Yeah. You're Kamea."

She nervously looked right and left before saying,
"Wayne said you'd arrived."

"He said you'd be here this morning."

"I work here."

"This is owned by Sam Prisler?"

The mention of his name caused her to flinch. She
nodded and continued her surveillance of the passing
crowd, eyes darting back and forth, lips pressed into a
tight line. Her fear was palpable. If she was leading him
into a trap, she was a world-class actress.

"Look," Brixton said, "can we go someplace to talk, where we can be alone?"

"I can't leave here. I . . ."

Her face froze as she looked to her left. "Be a tourist," she said quickly, spreading out brochures on the counter in front of him. "Ask about charters."

Brixton was confused for a second but then grasped what she was saying, that someone was approaching who shouldn't know who he was. Another second and Prisler's moonfaced "capo" stood next to him.

"Hi, Akina," Kamea said pleasantly. "Can you wait? I'm just giving this gentleman information about the charters." She gathered up the brochures and handed them to Brixton. "I know you'll enjoy it, sir," she said. "Our captain knows all the best fishing spots."

"Thanks," Brixton said, pulling on the peak of his cap and casting a sideways look at Akina, hoping that the big Hawaiian hadn't seen his face in Will Sayers's syndicated article. "I'll think about it."

He walked to a bench opposite the kiosk and sat down. He opened a brochure, donned his sunglasses, and watched Kamea and Akina talking at the kiosk. He wished he was privy to their conversation. After a few minutes Akina climbed into a Range Rover parked nearby and drove away. Brixton waited until he couldn't see the car before returning to the kiosk.

"Who was he?" he asked Kamea.

"His name is Akina. He's Mr. Prisler's assistant and bodyguard."

"He's big. As I was saying—"

"I can't leave here," she said. "Wayne will be coming back, and we have another charter right after this one."

"Yeah, fine, but we have to talk. I didn't come all the way to Maui to have you give me fishing brochures."

"I know that," she said, apology in her voice.

"What do you want from me, Kamea? You said you could help me too. How?"

"I want to leave Maui."

"I kind of figured that. So why don't you leave?"

"I can't. He won't let me."

"Prisler?"

A nod and furtive glances in search of Akina or anyone else she feared.

"And you want my help getting off the island."

"Yes."

"Okay. Now here's what *I* want. I want to know about your brother, about Prisler's relationship with a guy back in Washington named Zafar Alvi. I want to know everything. Who sent your brother to Washington to help blow up a café in which my daughter, by the way, was slaughtered? I want to know about a guy named Reyes, Lalo Reyes? I'm not staying here and helping if you don't come up with the answers."

"Not here."

"Okay, where? When?"

"Tonight, at the center."

"The cult you mean?"

"We don't call it that. You know where it is?"

"I'll find it. What do I do, drive in and ask for Kamea?"

"Oh, no, God no. It's guarded, men with guns. There's a sugarcane field that backs up to the east side of the center. On the edge of it is a shack. I can get there without anyone seeing me."

"How do *I* get there?"

"There's a dirt road leading to it that skirts the center's property."

"How do I find it?"

Kamea placed a map on the counter on which she'd already highlighted the road to the center.

"What time?" Brixton asked, folding the map and tucking it into his pocket.

"Ten."

Brixton looked to the empty boat slip. "What about your buddy, Wayne?"

"He wants to help me."

"Why? You two lovers?"

A couple had lined up behind Brixton.

Brixton wrote his cell phone number on the edge of a brochure. "My cell," he said. He turned to the couple and said, "Sorry. Sounds like a terrific fishing trip."

"That's a very nice shirt," the wife said.

"Thanks. Authentic Hawaiian. Comes with a guarantee," Brixton said. "Good fishing." He waved the brochures at them, smiled, and walked away.

So that's Morgana Skaggs, aka Kamea Wakatake, he thought as he walked to where he'd parked his car. Seemed like a nice enough young gal. How does someone like that end up as a zombie in a cult on Maui? He'd read about cults and knew that charismatic leaders could warp impressionable young people into buying their snake oil. It took a certain type apparently, one like Morgana Skaggs. Will Sayers had told him that the Skaggs family was dysfunctional; how the daughter and son ended up was testimony to that. Didn't take a shrink to figure it out.

Having made personal contact with Kamea was satisfying, but a sense of foreboding settled over him as he started the car and eased into the dense traffic that moved at a crawl. A man wearing a Hawaiian shirt similar to his darted in front of him, causing Brixton to hit the brakes. "Authentic Hawaiian, my ass," he muttered as the man gave him an angry look and disappeared into the throng.

He found a place to pull over outside of Lahaina and

consulted the map that Kamea had given him. Confident that he had a sense of where he was heading, he drove in the direction of Prisler's cult in Kapalua. He couldn't read the map and drive at the same time, but he figured he'd find it eventually, which he did, along an isolated road beyond which were the sparkling waters of Mokuleia Bay and the Pacific Ocean. A small wooden sign with gold letters at the foot of a long winding driveway said PRISLER CENTER FOR HEALING. He slowed to almost a stop and saw a narrow sentry house halfway up the driveway. Kamea had said there were men with guns, and Brixton didn't doubt that there was an armed guard in the structure.

He continued driving past the property, turned around, and passed it again in an easterly direction until coming to a dirt road that circumvented that end of the center. He took the road and soon came to the sugarcane field Kamea had mentioned. He put the car in park and peered into the field. A strip of dirt led down a winding track to the shack she'd referenced. He didn't like the setup. There were no lights. The weather report he'd checked in the hotel lobby before leaving that morning forecast a nasty storm arriving late that afternoon, with gusty winds and drenching rain.

He stopped back in the clothing shop and purchased a blue rain slicker and a floppy white hat before returning to the hotel, where he decided he would hole up until it was time to meet Kamea, figuring that since he was paying for the resort hotel he might as well enjoy it. He sat by the pool under an increasingly threatening sky and called Mac Smith in Washington.

"It's Robert," he said when Mac answered.

"Calling from sunny Hawaii?"

"Not so sunny. There's a storm moving in."

"Sorry to hear it. Are you making any progress?"

"Yeah, I think so. I've made contact with the Skaggs

daughter, Kamea. She's one scared puppy, Mac. Prisler has somebody keeping her on a short leash. I'm supposed to meet her again tonight."

"Glad you checked in. My contact at Justice called me. They're making progress, too, in building a case against Prisler. I also got in touch with Detective Halliday at MPD, as you suggested. Your friend Mr. McQuaid didn't accidentally drown. The case is now considered a homicide."

"Good news all around," Brixton said. "Did Flo leave?"

"No. We convinced her to stay a few extra days. She's crazy about you, Robert, and afraid for you. She's spending time with Annabel at her gallery. She wants to be useful."

"She's good people, Mac. Hopefully I'll be back before she leaves and we can catch some time together."

"I'm sure she'd like that. By the way, Asal Banai called."

In his rush to leave D.C., Brixton had forgotten to inform her that he'd be away.

"Did you tell her where I was?"

"Yes. She seemed surprised."

"I'm surprised that I'm here, too. If she calls again, tell her I'll contact her when I'm back."

"Take care, Robert, and stay in touch. I'll tell Annabel and Flo that you called."

Brixton had lunch at the bar and took a fitful nap. It started to rain and the wind came up, splattering raindrops against the glass door leading to the gardens. He got up and watched Mother Nature do her act, bending palm trees and sending people scurrying for cover. He hoped the storm would pass before his meeting with Kamea. It was eerie enough meeting in the dark in a sugarcane field, without getting soaked in the bargain.

The storm intensified as the afternoon progressed.

Brixton tried napping again but he couldn't shut off his brain for more than a few seconds at a time. He opted for another brief workout in the gym and picked up where he'd left off reading one of the paperback books he'd bought at the airport.

He ordered room service for dinner—*What the hell,* he thought, *I might as well splurge*—and started gearing up to drive to his rendezvous with Kamea. If her goal was to leave Maui, he began postulating how that might be accomplished. Assuming that she wasn't physically prohibited from leaving by Prisler and other cult members, he could buy them both airline tickets using his credit card and fly back to the mainland. But the fact that she had to use a shack in the middle of a sugarcane field to meet clearly indicated that it wouldn't be as easy as that.

If she disappeared from the cult, Prisler would have his people searching for her at the airports and docks. When Brixton had checked on flights, he discovered that there were only a handful of direct ones from Maui to the mainland, leaving from the Kahului Airport, which, according to his map, was at least an hour's drive from Kapalua. Most long-distance flights originated and arrived in Honolulu. But no matter what airport they tried to use, chances were that no flights would be leaving Maui late at night.

He also researched the distance between Maui and Oahu, where the Honolulu Airport was located. It was about eighty miles. How long would it take a boat like the one her buddy, Wayne, captained to make the journey? He had no idea how fast Wayne's boat traveled. Too, would Wayne agree to take them to Oahu? Maybe he would because he was her friend. On the other hand, if Prisler, who owned Wayne's Charter Service, found out, he wouldn't take kindly to it.

After an hour of playing the what-if game, Brixton

decided to let the chips fall where they may. Trying to plan an escape in advance was like trying to slam a revolving door, and he'd abandoned trying to make those kinds of plans years ago.

He drove from the hotel at nine, leaving him ample time to again find the shack in the sugarcane field. The rain had let up but a fine mist hung in the air, sent twirling by gusts of wind. He made a pass at the center's entrance again. This time an armed guard stood outside the guardhouse, visible in harsh lights that lit up the entire length of the driveway. A weapon was slung over his shoulder. Not a good sign.

He retraced his route around the eastern edge of the compound, turned onto the dirt road, and followed it until reaching the path leading to the shack. He stopped and turned off his headlights, causing the shack to disappear from view. He had a decision to make: Drive up the path to the shack, turn the car around and back in to make for a faster getaway, or leave the car on the dirt road? He chose the first option, so that the car's headlights could be used to illuminate the ramshackle building.

Following the path meant the wheels were in brush at its edges, and the sound of some sort of rigid plant life scraping the rental car's side made him wince. He stopped within a few feet of the shack's door and turned off the lights. It was eerily quiet and dark. The sweet smell of fertilizer from the cane field wafted through his half-open driver's window. He waited. There was no sign of Kamea. Was it possible that she'd changed her mind or that her plan to meet him had been discovered and she was being detained?

How long should I wait? he pondered. He got out of the car and looked back at the Prisler compound, where multiple lights appeared and then disappeared in the blowing mist. He felt for the Smith & Wesson as though to ensure that it was still there. Did Prisler feel that the cane field provided enough of a buffer to make assigning armed guards unnecessary on that side of the compound? It appeared that way.

He kept checking his watch. By 10:15 he decided to give her another fifteen minutes. Ten minutes later he heard rustling in the field. He put his hand on his weapon but removed it when she emerged from the tall green stalks.

"I was giving up on you," he said.

"I'm sorry. I had to wait until the time was right."

"We going inside the shack?"

"Yes."

"Why? Let's just get in the car and get out of here."

"There's something in there I need."

She pulled a small penlight from her black leather jacket and trained its beam on the door. Brixton pushed it open. The penlight brought to life a table and two chairs, not much else.

"I need to talk to you," she said.

"I'd rather talk someplace else," Brixton said. "Let's get some light in here."

A kerosene lantern stood on the center of the table. Brixton went to it, adjusted the wick, and put a match to it. Its yellow-orange glow didn't provide much light but was enough for them to see each other. Kamea looked out the door before closing it. They sat.

"Look, Kamea," he said, "I get the feeling that we don't have much time. I came here to find out why your brother came to Washington and escorted that pathetic young girl who blew up the café. You know, don't you?"

"He was sent." She jumped when a gust of wind rattled the door.

"Who sent him? Prisler?"

"Yes. Mr. Alvi told him to send Paul."

"Zafar Alvi, in Washington?"

"Yes. Mr. Prisler often sends people to do what Mr. Alvi wants done. He is Mr. Prisler's biggest customer." She glanced at the door again.

"For his illegal arms sales."

She nodded.

"How come he never sent you?"

"He says that women play a different role in life."

"Thoughtful guy. He only sends men, *young* men, to do Alvi's dirty work. Of course he didn't follow that rule with the young woman who actually carried the bomb."

"I have get away from here, Mr. Brixton."

"Yeah, I gathered that. And knock off the 'mister' routine. You can call me Robert."

She stood, went to the door, looked out, and resumed her seat.

"Was Alvi behind the café bombing that killed my daughter?"

She replied by going to a corner of the shack. She used her penlight to find what she was looking for, a small envelope buried beneath discarded pieces of wood. She returned to the table and handed it to him.

"What's this?"

"A DVD. All the answers to your questions are on it."

"Where did you get it?"

"Someone gave it to me."

"What's on it?"

"The terrible things that Mr. Prisler and Mr. Alvi and their people have done."

"You've seen what's on it?"

"Yes."

"Prisler doesn't know that you have it?"

"No, of course not. It was given to me only yesterday. I watched it on Wayne's laptop computer in the office."

"Prisler doesn't know it's missing?"

"I don't think so. If he did, he would have turned the center upside down, had all our rooms searched."

"Who gave it to you?"

Before she could answer, a car's headlamps sent shafts of light through a crack in the door. Kamea gasped. There was the sound of car doors slamming and male voices.

"We've got company," Brixton said, pulling his Smith & Wesson from its holster and standing behind the table. "Sounds like an army. Here." He handed her the handgun. "Stick it in your pants. They won't search you." He removed the holster and tossed it in a far dark corner as a foot kicked the door open. Standing outside were Akina and two other men carrying automatic weapons, backlit by their car lights.

"Hey, cool it," Brixton yelled, his hands raised. "We're not going anywhere."

Akina entered the shack and kept his assault rifle trained on Brixton, while another man patted him down, ignoring the envelope in his pocket. He turned to look at Kamea, and Brixton thought for a moment that he might frisk her. He didn't. Brixton wondered whether Kamea had set him up. Did she really want to escape, or was she the lure to draw him to Hawaii?

"Put that damn gun down," Brixton told Akina. "Somebody's going to get hurt."

Akina pulled a cell phone from his belt and said into it, "They're here."

Everyone stood in silence until Brixton said to Akina, "Don't you have something better to do?"

"Shut up," the oversized Hawaiian said.

"If you have a beef with me, that's fine, but Kamea hasn't done anything. Let her leave."

The sound of another arriving vehicle put an end to the conversation. The door to the Range Rover opened and Samuel Prisler stepped from it. He approached the shack and stood in the open doorway, his large frame dominating it.

"Ah, I get to meet Sam Prisler at last," Brixton said.

"And you are Robert Brixton," Prisler said, a hint of mirth in his gravelly voice.

"I'm glad you're here," Brixton said. "Maybe you can tell these goons to put down their weapons before they shoot up the place."

Prisler took a few steps into the shack and pointed to the table and chairs. "Sit down," he commanded.

"You just being courteous?" Brixton asked.

"Sit down!" Prisler repeated, this time with greater force.

Brixton and Kamea heeded his dictate and sat at the table. Prisler came close and stood over them. Brixton was aware of the man's size. The kerosene lamp cast flickering light and shadows over his craggy face. What annoyed Brixton was the perpetual tiny smile on his lips, a sign of the superiority he was enjoying at the moment.

Prisler ordered the guards except Akina to wait outside. Akina moved to a corner of the shack and leaned against the wall, his weapon cradled in his muscular arms.

"Why have you come here?" Prisler asked.

"To enjoy Hawaii," Brixton replied. "It's beautiful."

"I don't appreciate your attempt at humor," Prisler said.

"Frankly, Sam, I don't care what you appreciate. You don't mind me calling you Sam, do you? You can call me Robert but never Bobby. I really get pissed off when someone calls me Bobby."

Prisler brought the back of his large hand across Brixton's face, nearly knocking him off the spindly chair. Brixton touched his cheek where he'd been struck. He looked up at Prisler and came up with his own smile. "I didn't appreciate that, Sam."

"I ask you again," Prisler said. "Why have come here?"

Brixton decided to not mention that Kamea had called him. "I'm here to find out why you sent Paul Skaggs to D.C. to blow up a café."

Prisler's perpetual smile became a laugh. "You believe that I would do that?"

"I admit it's hard to believe that *anyone* would do that, Sam, but from everything I've put together, that's exactly what I think you did."

Prisler sighed like a parent disappointed in a child's actions. He said, "Paul Skaggs was a headstrong if silly young man. I was shocked when I heard that you not only accused him of being involved in the bombing of that café but that you decided to take the law into your own hands and kill him."

"Nice story, Sam, but it's bull. I don't know all the details, but I sure as hell do know that you and your pal Alvi are behind what happened in that café. But you know what? I really don't give a damn about whether you run illegal weapons through Alvi to terrorists around the world. The only thing I care about is who's behind the bombing that killed my daughter, and how and why Paul Skaggs was involved."

Prisler's smile returned. "You're full of crazy notions, aren't you, Mr. Brixton? I would have thought that someone like you, who has been a cop, would be more levelheaded. I suppose that's naive of me. But as long as you're here, I suggest that we go back to my home. You can entertain me with your theories and whoever else you may have discussed them with."

He turned his attention to Kamea. "I am so disappointed in you, my dear. This man you've chosen to meet under these murky circumstances is exactly why you left your family and joined mine."

She hadn't said a word since Akina and the others arrived, and Brixton wondered what was going through her mind. Until this turn of events, he was confident that she was committed to leaving Maui and the cult. More than that, she'd provided him with the DVD on which she claimed were the answers to the questions that had brought him to Hawaii. But was there anything on it? If she was being straight, would her resolve hold, or would Prisler's influence over her win out?

Prisler led Brixton and Kamea from the cabin to the cars, with Akina bringing up the rear.

"You come with me," Prisler told Kamea. He instructed Brixton to get into the second Range Rover with the other two armed men.

They followed the dirt road back to the front entrance, drove past the guard post, and pulled up in front of the main house. Once ensconced in Prisler's living room, the cult leader dismissed the other two guards, leaving him and Akina with Kamea and Brixton.

"Make yourself at home," he said to Brixton. "A drink?" He went to an elaborate bar and held up a bottle. "Good whiskey," he said.

"You have any gin?" Brixton asked. "I'm a martini drinker."

"Of course," Prisler said. "You, Kamea?"

"I don't drink. You know that."

"Oh, that's right." He turned to Brixton. "I suppose my darling Kamea has filled you with tales of life here at my Center for Healing."

"As a matter of fact, she hasn't," said Brixton. "Tell me about it, Sam. Maybe I'll get inspired and join."

His laugh was disingenuous. "That could never be, Mr. Brixton. We have very high standards. You see, there are few places of spiritual and emotional refuge in this wicked, wicked world, and there are very few people who refuse to abide by its destructive rules. Take Kamea for instance. She came to me a terribly confused and frightened young lady. Her family personified wickedness, and she was desperate to escape its grip on her. The same was true of her brother, Paul. I opened my arms to them as I have to so many others over the years."

"That's touching," Brixton said.

"Oh," said Prisler, "I don't expect you to understand. People like you are the ones who the young people here are running away from."

"Tell me more," Brixton said, thinking there's nothing an egomaniac likes more than to talk about himself.

Prisler handed Brixton his drink and raised his glass. "Welcome to Maui, Mr. Brixton." He took a chair next to Akina's who sat with his back to an expanse of windows. A row of eight-foot-tall shrubs blocked the view inside the room from the front of the house. The unpleasant Hawaiian looked relaxed, the assault rifle resting casually on his lap.

"I suppose you're wondering what will happen next."

"It's crossed my mind," Brixton said after sipping his drink and smacking his lips. "I'm sure you realize that keeping me here at gunpoint breaks the law."

A deep growl of a laugh came from Prisler. "To the contrary," he said. "You've trespassed on my property. It's *you* who's broken the law."

"So call the police."

"No need for me to do that."

"Actually, I came to meet with Kamea. We met in a sugarcane field, which isn't part of your property."

Another laugh. "I love a man who asserts a fact when it isn't a fact. That cane field *is* part of the center's property, Mr. Brixton."

"I was invited here by one of your cult members, Kamea."

"Please, I would appreciate it if you would refrain from calling it a cult. It is a center for healing the wounds inflicted by governments and callous, greedy government officials."

"Okay, so it's a healing center. Look, Sam, this has all been pleasant and enlightening, but I'm ready to leave, and I think Kamea would like to come with me."

Brixton stood, which snapped Akina to attention, the rifle pointed at him. As Brixton decided whether to call his bluff, a movement outside the window caught his attention. A face appeared for only a few seconds behind Prisler and Akina before disappearing.

"I think that everything we have to say has been said," Prisler said. "Let's take a pleasant little ride."

"I thought you wanted my life story, all the juicy little details," Brixton said.

"I think I know you well enough. Bobby is it?"

Until that moment Brixton hadn't been overly concerned. As far as he knew, Prisler wasn't aware of the extent to which he'd delved into the cult leader's life, the renewed investigation by the Justice Department, Will Sayers's research of him, and his connection with Zafar Alvi. Brixton also figured that Prisler's primary concern would be keeping Kamea at the cult.

Throughout the conversation, Kamea had sat rigidly in a chair next to Brixton, her arms wrapped around herself as though she was cold or thought it was possible to squeeze herself as small as possible. Brixton thought of his Smith & Wesson tucked into her jeans and wished he'd had it now.

Akina stood and pointed his weapon at Brixton as Prisler indicated they were to follow him. Brixton assumed that they would exit the house through the front door, but Prisler led them down a long hallway to a rear door, outside which another Range Rover was parked. Brixton and Kamea stood together apart from Akina and Prisler. He put his arm around her and felt her trembling. "Take it easy," he said into her ear.

"He'll kill us," she said. "He's killed others," she said in a whisper.

Prisler got behind the wheel of the vehicle. "Get in," he said, motioning toward the rear seat.

Brixton and Kamea did as instructed, under the watchful eye of Akina, who now held both the assault rifle and a handgun. The Hawaiian got in the front passenger seat and swiveled so that the handgun was pointed at Brixton. Prisler started the car and pulled away, heading down a narrow macadam road that sloped down from the property toward the sugarcane field on the compound's eastern rim. It struck Brixton that if Prisler was about to order Akina to kill them, the sugarcane field was a perfect place to do it, and he wondered whether there was more planted in the earth there than sugarcane.

They came to a gate. Prisler got out, opened it, got back in, and drove through, not bothering to close it. Brixton felt himself tense, matching Kamea's movements. They approached Brixton's rental car. He had the keys in his pocket.

"Everybody out," Prisler announced like a friendly train conductor.

Akina exited the Range Rover holding the handgun and leaving the assault rifle where he had been sitting.

"If you're about to do what I think you are," Brixton said, "you won't get away with it."

Prisler said, "What bravado. I admire that in a man. The truth is, Mr. Brixton, you are a murderer. Your victim was the son of a very powerful member of the

U.S. Congress. You came here to kidnap one of the center's members and to assault me. We had no choice but to defend ourselves. Isn't that right, Kamea?"

She didn't answer. But Brixton saw her reach down into the front of her jeans. As she did, a figure leapt out of the shadow of the shack and pounced on Akina's back, sending him to the ground, the handgun flying from his hand. Brixton joined Akina's attacker and pressed the Hawaiian's head into the soft soil with his knee.

"Reyes!" Brixton said.

Lalo answered by ramming a fist into the side of Akina's face.

Brixton turned to Kamea, who'd pulled his revolver out of her jeans and leveled it at Prisler.

"Gimme that," Brixton said.

She backed away from him, shaking her head, and crying.

Brixton retrieved Akina's handgun from where it had fallen and trained it on him.

"Give me the gun, Kamea," Prisler said in his best modulated cult leader's voice. "Don't listen to them. I'm the one who saved you. You must never forget that." He took a few steps toward her, his hand outstretched.

The discharge of the weapon in her hand pierced the misty night air. Prisler, his eyes wide, his face elevated, extended his hands as though to embrace Kamea. And then he pitched forward, his face hitting the soil with a thud.

Brixton grabbed the gun from Kamea and now held it and the one Akina had been wielding in each hand. Akina sat on the ground, scowling and muttering what Brixton assumed were Hawaiian curse words.

"Thanks," Brixton said to Lalo. "I owe you one."

"They planned to kill me too," Reyes said.

"Let's get out of here," Brixton said.

"What do we do with him?" Reyes asked, indicating Akina.

"See if there's any rope in the Range Rover, something to tie him up with."

The young Spaniard returned with a ball of white clothesline.

With one of the handguns pressed against Akina's temple, Brixton and Reyes took the Hawaiian into the shack, where they trussed his hands and feet. Brixton tied a length of cloth he found on the floor around his face, tightening it into his mouth.

"What about Prisler?" Lalo asked.

Brixton answered by dragging the cult leader into the shack, where he propped him against a wall. "Sorry it ended this way," Brixton said to the dead arms dealer.

Before exiting he retrieved his holster from where he'd tossed it, extinguished the kerosene lamp, and left the struggling Hawaiian in the dark hut that smelled of sugarcane and fertilizer—and his own fears.

35

Had anyone in the Prisler compound heard the gunshot? Brixton wasn't taking any chances. He hustled Kamea and Lalo into his rented car and backed out to the dirt road. He'd collected Akina's two weapons and laid them on the front passenger seat along with his own. Kamea and Lalo huddled in the back as he drove, lights off, until reaching the paved road that ran past the cult's entrance.

"Where are we going?" Lalo asked.

"My hotel. Nobody knows I'm there. When we arrive we walk in nice and easy, like we all belong there. We'll go to my room and figure out our next step."

After parking, Brixton shoved both handguns into his waistband and concealed the assault rifle beneath his oversize authentic Hawaiian shirt. He led them to his room, where he locked the door and drew the drapes.

"He's dead," Kamea said. "I killed him."

"You won't get any argument from him," Brixton said.

She fell into a chair and wept.

"It's okay," Lalo said. "He deserved it."

Brixton pulled an ottoman up in front of Kamea and placed his hand on her knee. "I know it's upsetting," he said, "but you need to get hold of yourself. We have to figure a way off the island. Where's your buddy, Wayne?"

"I . . . I don't know."

"Prisler must have known that I was on Maui," Brixton said. "Who told him? The only person who knew besides you was Wayne. Did you tell him that we were meeting tonight at that shack?"

She struggled to pull herself together. He handed her a tissue from a box on the table next to her. "No," she said.

"He didn't ask? He wasn't curious? He was the one who helped me get in touch with you."

"He did ask when he brought the first charter back. I told him I was going to talk to you later in the day, but I didn't say when, or where."

"Why did you lie to him?"

"I just felt it was better that no one know except me."

"You don't trust him," Brixton said flatly.

"I don't know who to trust anymore."

Lalo emerged from the bathroom and sat by the windows. "What do we do now?" he asked.

"We get off this island," Brixton said, "and we do it as fast as we can. By morning the police will be all over it looking for Prisler's killer."

"Looking for me, you mean," Kamea said. "Akina will tell them that I shot Prisler. Maybe I should go to them and admit that I did it."

"There's no way in hell you're going to do that, Kamea. I just came close to being buried in a sugarcane field because of you, and I'm not going back without you. Here's the deal: I get you away from Prisler, and you tell the authorities what you know about your brother and Prisler's role in sending him to Washington to help blow up the café."

"The DVD," she said.

"Why did you bother making it? What's on it?"

"I didn't make it," she said. "Prisler had it."

"I gave it to her," Lalo said.

"*You* gave it to her? How did *you* get hold of it?"

"I took it from Prisler's office when he wasn't there. It was easy. He had me staying in one of the rooms off the main house, so I had access."

Brixton asked Kamea, "If you didn't make it, then what's on it?"

"His instructions."

"Instructions? Instructions for what?"

"For sending my brother to Washington, arranging for other bombings and murders—all of it."

"Who gave the instructions?" Brixton demanded.

"I don't know his name. He is from a country in Africa, a terrorist leader."

"Do you know his name?" Brixton asked Lalo.

"No," the young Spaniard said. "I am so ashamed."

"Of what?"

"Of working for Prisler, of doing what he wanted me to do."

"What was that?"

"I was to identify other gay men working in embassies so that they could become targets."

"Because they were gay?"

"So that the government in Washington would *think* that was why they were killed. I didn't know in the beginning that he intended to kill them. I swear I didn't. I loved them. Peter Müller was a fine person. To think that I had lured him into Prisler's trap is . . ." He choked back tears.

Brixton thought of the red herring theory that had been raised at the meeting with Mike Kogan.

"I don't know what prompted you to do what you did tonight, Reyes, taking down that hulk Akina, but thanks."

"I hated them both," he said.

"You didn't hate Prisler when you joined his cult."

"I didn't either," Kamea said.

"I don't get it," said Brixton. "You're both bright young people. How does a charlatan like Prisler bend your mind and turn you into his puppets?"

"He was there when we needed him," Kamea said softly.

"I still don't get it, but maybe I'm not supposed to," Brixton said.

"Let's get back to how we get off Maui," Lalo said. "I won't feel safe until we are away."

"Should I call Wayne?" Kamea asked. "Maybe he can take us in his boat."

Brixton studied her face before saying, "No. You don't trust him. That's good enough for me. Plus, you said that Prisler owns the boat."

"Yes."

"That's another reason for not bringing Wayne into this. He isn't likely to do something to upset his employer."

"His employer is dead," Lalo said.

"Yeah, but Wayne doesn't know that. Once he hears about it he'll be even less likely to help us. How about you, Kamea? Do you know how to operate that boat?"

"I've gone out with Wayne many times, and he let me run it."

"Are there keys?"

"Yes. They're in the office."

"You have a key to the office?"

She nodded.

"What about fuel? How do we gas up?"

"Wayne always fills the tanks at the end of each day."

"If she can't run the boat, I can," Reyes said. "My father was a fisherman in Spain. He used to take me with him."

"Damn," Brixton said, "looks like we have us a seasoned crew. Let's go."

Brixton put the two handguns in his suitcase and concealed the rifle as they left the room and went to the car. Each of them was on edge, waiting to hear the wail of sirens or run into a blockade. Had Prisler's death already been discovered and reported to the police? Had Akina been able to break his bonds?

Brixton drove the speed limit, not wanting to draw attention. Lahaina had emptied out after the day's tourist crush. He pulled up into a vacant space near the dock and looked around. "We're good," he told them.

They walked to the dock. Kamea removed a key from her jeans' pocket and opened the door to the tiny office. Brixton and Lalo remained outside.

"I have the boat key," Kamea called from the office.

"Good," Brixton said. As he did, a car approached, its headlamps casting light and shadows over them.

"It's the police," Brixton said.

The car came to a stop, its headlights continuing to illuminate them. A pair of uniformed Hawaiian police officers exited.

"Hey, what's going on here?" one asked.

"Nothing, Officer," Brixton said.

The two cops slowly approached.

"What are you doing here this time of night?" one asked.

"We were . . ."

Kamea came out of the office.

"Hi," she said.

"Kamea? Didn't see you at first," a cop said.

"Getting ready for tomorrow," she said. "These are my friends."

"Okay," said a cop. "Just wanted to make sure everything was all right."

"Everything is fine," she said.

The patrol car pulled away, and the trio stepped onto the boat. Kamea went to the helm and inserted the key. The twin diesel engines coughed at first, then caught and rumbled, louder than Brixton would have liked.

"I have to put on the lights," Kamea said, "and the lines have to be brought up."

"Lines?" Brixton said. "Oh, right."

He and Lalo carefully maneuvered themselves along the narrow footholds until reaching the mooring lines. He hoped that they could undo them from the boat but saw that they'd have to get back on the dock. With the lines tossed onto the boat, they came aboard again. Brixton gave Kamea a thumbs-up. "I hope she knows what she's doing," he muttered to himself as the boat, its engines in reverse, slowly backed into the channel.

He joined her at the helm. "It's eighty miles to Oahu," he said. "How fast does this thing go?"

"Twenty-five knots," she replied. "Maybe a little faster."

"It'll take us four hours," Brixton said.

"It depends upon how rough the sea is," she added.

"Let's hope it's smooth sailing all the way," he said. "You're the captain, Kamea. Just tell me and Lalo what to do when something needs doing."

The way things had been going lately, Brixton assumed that it would be rough in the open water between Maui and Oahu. He was wrong. The seas were calm. The storm that had hit the islands that afternoon was long gone. An almost full moon cast light down on them as they headed for the neighboring island, home of Honolulu International Airport. Brixton was surprised at how much at peace he felt. He'd never been a boat lover, didn't understand the allure of owning one. But now he began to soak in the pleasure of being out on the water, breathing in its bracing smell, the wind in his face, the engines providing a pleasant, comforting drone. Even the slapping of the craft's bottom when encountering a swell and white caps was reassuring.

He stayed next to Kamea as she manned the helm, neither saying much of anything, just an occasional glance back and forth accompanied by a smile.

Lalo Reyes had fallen asleep in the cabin, obviously at peace, too.

But the benign mood that Brixton had fallen into fought for space in his head with the realities they faced.

Standing next to him was a powerful U.S. congressman's daughter, a member of a controversial cult, and a murderer. It wasn't lost on him that the weapon she'd used to shoot Samuel Prisler was registered to him; his fingerprints were all over it. Would this adventure he'd embarked on end with his being accused of another unwarranted shooting? Prisler obviously had friends in high places, both on Maui and in Washington, D.C. But Kamea had shot Prisler in self-defense, and Brixton was determined to do everything he could to help defend her.

But that problem wasn't of immediate concern.

Prisler had confiscated all of Kamea's personal identification—driver's license, passport, and credit cards. Lalo too had been stripped of any documents indicating who he was. That meant that neither of them would be able to board a commercial airliner in Honolulu for a flight to the mainland even if Brixton were to foot the bill.

Two hours into their escape, Brixton saw Kamea struggle to keep her eyes open. Brixton asked if she wanted him to take the wheel. "I'm not a boater," he said, "but I figure I can keep us heading in the direction on the compass."

She gratefully accepted, wedging a cushion between her head and the wall next to her and closing her eyes. Brixton looked at her and had to smile. She looked like a little kid, the way Janet and Jill once looked, innocent and without concerns. He knew that wasn't quite the case with Kamea: The life that she'd left was hardly free of turmoil. But he hoped that when the adventure was over she'd find a way to resurrect herself and stand alone, shake loose the powerful hold Prisler had on her, and maybe even come to grips with her nasty family situation.

She took over the helm again after her nap, and an hour later the lights of Oahu came into view.

"Where are we docking?" Brixton asked her.

She'd been consulting nautical charts and pointed to an area near the airport. "Kewalo Basin," she said. "I've been there before with Wayne."

"You make a pretty good captain," he said, slapping her on the shoulder.

"I always wanted to do this," she said, "—be in charge. It's been so long since I've been in charge of anything, including my life."

"Never too late to start, Kamea."

They pulled into a slip. On Kamea's instructions, Brixton went to an office on the expansive dock where he found an old man dozing behind the desk. He woke him and paid for an overnight berthing using his credit card.

"Where'd you come in from at this ungodly hour?" the old man asked as he filled out a receipt.

"Maui."

"Where you heading?"

Brixton shrugged. "Back to Maui later today."

"Pretty late to run over here from Maui," the older man said.

"I've got a meeting at the airport. How far is it from here?"

"Five miles or so."

"Can you recommend a motel or hotel nearby? Nothing too fancy. I'm on a tight budget."

He handed Brixton three business cards from nearby motels.

"Many thanks. Have a good night."

Brixton returned and told them that they were going to a motel.

"We could stay on the boat," Kamea offered.

"No," Brixton said. "Chances are they'll be looking for it once your buddy Wayne realizes it's missing. Leave the keys on board."

They went to the closest of the three recommended motels. "I'm traveling with my family," Brixton told the wiry woman behind the desk. "We need three rooms."

She eyed Kamea and Lalo, who looked pretty scraggly. So did he, he knew.

"You have rooms?" Brixton asked.

"Only have two vacancies," she said.

"Well, that'll have to do," Brixton said. "They have twin beds?" he asked, mentally questioning who would bunk together.

"Yes, sir, they do."

With another credit card charge racked up, they headed for the rooms. "You'll take one of them, Kamea," he said. "Lalo and I will take the other."

Lalo looked as though he'd just bitten into a sour pickle.

"That setup okay with you, Lalo?" Brixton asked.

"I guess so. It's just that—"

"That I roughed you up a little at your apartment. Hey, that was then. No hard feelings, huh?"

Lalo broke into a wide smile. "No," he said, "no hard feelings."

Brixton wasn't keen on allowing Kamea out of his sight, but he didn't have an alternative, aside from sharing the room with her, something he doubted she would want.

"You'll be okay alone?" he asked.

"Yes, of course," she said.

"Good. Here's the drill: I'm going to call someone back in Washington who might be able to help us. If he can, you've got to be ready to roll."

He and Lalo entered the room they would share.

"I need a shower," Lalo said

"So do I," Brixton said. "You go ahead while I make the call. I may be awhile in case he has to call back."

Brixton stepped outside and punched in Mac Smith's stored phone number on his cell. It would be morning in D.C. but not too early. Smith answered on the first ring.

"Mac, it's Robert Brixton."

"Still in Hawaii?"

"Yeah. Look, I'm in a bit of a jam and thought you might have some advice."

Brixton couldn't see the wince on Mac's face.

"What kind of a jam?" Smith asked.

"I'll boil it down fast for you," Brixton said. "I'm on the island of Oahu. I'm with Kamea Wakatake, Congressman Skaggs's daughter, and the young Spanish guy from the Spanish embassy. I've gotten them out of Prisler's cult and we took a boat from Maui."

"You chartered a boat?"

"No, we borrowed it. Anyway, in helping them escape, Prisler got shot."

"He's—?"

"Yeah, he's dead. Kamea shot him in self-defense. My problem is that I can't take them with me on a plane from Honolulu because they don't have any ID. We tied up Prisler's henchman, a big guy named Akina, and left him with the body. If they've discovered him by now, the police will be looking for us and the boat."

Smith grunted.

"My two traveling buddies can give testimony that'll nail Prisler to the cross, and that creep Zafar Alvi too."

"Where are you now?" Mac asked.

"We checked into a motel near where we docked. It's just a few miles from the Honolulu Airport."

"It's what, four A.M. where you are, Robert?"

"Or thereabout." ·

"There's someone I want to call who could be of help. Keep your cell phone on, and lay low until I get back to you."

"Got it, Mac. Thanks."

Lalo had emerged from the bathroom when Brixton returned to the room. Brixton figured he didn't have time for a long, relaxing shower and spent five minutes under the hot spray before sprawling on the twin bed, his cell phone on the pillow next to his ear. Three hours later he was awakened by the phone's silly tuneful ring.

"Brixton," he said.

"It's Mac, Robert. Here's what you do. An old friend of mine is a special agent in charge of the Honolulu division of the FBI. His name is—"

"Hold a second," Brixton said as he found a pad of paper and pen provided by the motel. "Shoot," he said.

"His name is Nathan Mumford. His office is in the new FBI building at ninety-one, dash, thirteen-hundred Enterprise Street. That's in Kapolei."

"Where the hell is that?"

"Outside Honolulu, but not far. Nate is expecting you and your entourage. He was happy to hear from me, Robert. He's been deep into an investigation of Prisler and his arms dealing."

"What happens with the local police?" Brixton asked. "They'll want jurisdiction over Prisler's shooting."

"Cross that bridge when you come to it," Smith said. "I suggest that you get to Special Agent Mumford's office as fast as you can."

"I can't thank you enough, Mac."

"Just do what Nate Mumford says, and keep me in the loop."

Brixton roused Reyes from his sleep. "Let's go," he said. "We've got an appointment." He knocked on Kamea's door and told her the same thing.

In his suitcase, Brixton had secured the two handguns he'd been toting and again used his shirt to cover the assault rifle. After Brixton checked out, they walked to a road and hailed a taxi.

"We need to go to a FedEx office where they have a Kinko's," Brixton told the driver.

Kamea and Lalo looked quizzically at him.

"I want a copy of the DVD you gave me," he told Kamea.

"Do we have time for that?" Lalo whispered.

"Yeah," Brixton replied. "I need a duplicate copy."

When the driver pulled up in front of a FedEx store, Brixton said, "You two stay with the taxi." Fifteen minutes later he emerged carrying the duplicate DVD. "The dupe is for us," he said. "No one else needs to know about it."

"Where to next?" the driver asked.

"Enterprise Street in Kapolei," Brixton instructed the driver, "the new FBI building."

Brixton had just enough cash to pay for the trip and to add a tip. "Aloha," he told the driver, who thanked him and drove off.

"All set?" he asked Kamea and Lalo as they stood in front of the imposing new glass building.

Kamea and Lalo looked at each other and nodded.

They stopped at the security desk, where Brixton handed over the assault rifle and withdrew the two handguns from his suitcase. While this was being accomplished, two special agents, a man and a woman, got off the elevator and approached.

"Robert Brixton?" the man said.

"Yes."

"Special Agent Mumford." He shook Brixton's hand and took in the others.

"This is Ms. Kamea Wakatake," Brixton said. "She's also Morgana Skaggs, Congressman Skaggs's daughter. And this is Mr. Eduardo Reyes, also known as Lalo."

"We've been expecting you," Mumford said. "You're the friend Mac Smith called about."

"Right. Mac's a good friend," Brixton said, taking his first easy breath he'd had for a while."

"Follow me," said Mumford. "We have a lot to go over."

B rixton, Kamea, and Reyes spent the next few hours ensconced in a conference room with Mumford and three other special agents. The conversation was video-taped. A variety of breakfast pastries, coffee, and juice were provided.

"Anything else to add?" Mumford asked, after he and the other special agents had exhausted their questions.

"Yes, there is," Brixton said, pulling the DVD Kamea had given him from his shirt pocket and placing it on the conference table.

"What's this?" Mumford asked.

"From what Kamea tells me, it answers a lot of

questions about the attacks on embassies and embassy workers," Brixton said. "You and I will be seeing it for the first time."

Mumford inserted the DVD in a large-screen computer, while another agent dimmed the lights. The DVD rolled, the voice of the man on the screen speaking slowly and with a heavy accent. The seven people in the room sat silently as they absorbed the man's message. When it was finished and the lights were raised, Mumford broke the silence with, "Wow!"

"I'd say that 'Wow!' sums it up," Brixton said.

A woman entered the room and whispered something to Mumford. He excused himself and followed her out.

He returned fifteen minutes later.

"The Maui police are looking for the three of you, as well as a missing boat."

"That's the boat we borrowed," Brixton said. He gave Mumford directions to where it could be found. "I also left a rental car on the street in Lahaina."

"You've left a lot of problems in your wake, Mr. Brixton. According to the Maui police, a witness claims that Ms. Wakatake killed Samuel Prisler."

"That witness, whose name is Akina, was about to mow down Ms. Wakatake and me," Brixton said. "Fortunately Mr. Reyes here saved us."

"There's an APB out on you, and a warrant for your arrest," Mumford said.

"That's no surprise," Brixton said. "But if we're turned over to them, you can kiss your case against Prisler and his colleagues good-bye."

"I'm well aware of that, Mr. Brixton," Mumford said, "and we're not about to let that happen. The Bureau is now in charge of the case. We've assured the Maui police that after we're through with you they can apply for extradition from the mainland. In the meantime, we have to get you back to Washington. I'm assigning two of our special agents to accompany the three of you on the next scheduled flight from Honolulu."

"On the government's dime?" Brixton asked.

Mumford laughed. "Of course. We take good care of important witnesses."

"That's good to hear," Brixton said. "My American Express bill is big enough as it is."

36

Robert Brixton would have gladly maxed out his American Express card in return for another hot shower—a leisurely one this time—a change of clothes, and a chance to stretch out in his own bed. But it wasn't to be, at least until arriving back in Washington. He, Kamea, and Lalo were hustled off in a car to the Honolulu Airport, where they were escorted by the accompanying agents into a room without any identifying signs. The manager of the airport's Transportation Security Administration processed a sheaf of documents provided by the agents and proclaimed that everything was in order.

"We don't have to go through security?" Brixton asked.

"That's right," an agent said. "This is security."

"You mean I can keep my shoes and belt on?" Brixton said, laughing.

They were preboarded along with the infirm and families traveling with little children, and directed to five coach seats near each other. The large jet aircraft then filled up with the rest of the passengers. Brixton couldn't wait until the plane lifted off the runway and headed for San Francisco, where they would transfer to another plane to take them to Washington, D.C.

Between flights Brixton called Mac Smith to let him know what was happening and thanked him again for making contact with the Oahu FBI.

"Looking forward to seeing you," Smith said. "I'll have a cold, dry martini waiting."

"Gin, not vodka."

"Of course. I know my customers."

"And shaken."

"That too. Flo will be happy to see you."

"She's still there?"

"We persuaded her to stay."

"Good," said Brixton, meaning it.

Their arrival at Dulles International was met by three black limousines with tinted windows, four FBI special agents, two men whom Brixton pegged as intelligence types, and a uniformed Homeland Security officer. Little was said during the trip to the FBI building on Pennsylvania Avenue NW, where they were led to a large windowless room on the building's second floor and questioned again at length.

"And you say that your brother, Paul, was dispatched to Washington by Mr. Prisler to escort suicide bombers to their targets?" the lead agent asked Kamea.

"Yes. They—Mr. Alvi and Mr. Prisler—wanted to make sure that the students who carry the bombs and detonate them would not lose their nerve."

"And your brother was willing to do that?"

"He believed in what Mr. Alvi and his people believed

in," she said. "Mr. Prisler had established almost total control over Paul, and Mr. Prisler followed whatever Mr. Alvi instructed."

"And Prisler sent you to Washington, too?" The question was directed at Lalo Reyes.

"Yes," Reyes said, "but not to escort suicide bombers. They wanted me to identify and recruit gay men from embassies. There was a woman too, from the Polish embassy. I met her at a club."

"To have them killed in order to make it seem, at least initially, that their murders were bias crimes," Brixton said.

"I didn't know any of that in the beginning," Reyes said, his head lowered. "I had worked for the Spanish embassy before going to Hawaii and joining the center. When I came back to Washington, the embassy hired me again and I started hanging around bars. When I identified a gay man from an embassy, I would pass the information along to someone."

"Who?"

"I don't know his name. I was never told. I just dialed a number and was given a location where we'd meet. He was a big man with a shaved head."

And so it went for another hour, questions being asked and asked again, tedious repetitions, every detail checked and rechecked.

A break in the interrogation occurred when the DVD was played. There was stunned silence in the room as the image of the terrorist outlined the philosophy and instructions of how this latest attack would be launched against the embassies of countries involved with the invasion of Iraq and Afghanistan: the United States, Britain, Australia, Germany, France, Italy, Denmark, Canada, Poland, and a dozen others.

The silence continued after the DVD had ended.

"It represents a shift from their usual approach," the lead agent said. "They know they can't pull off another nine/eleven, so they'll pick us off one by one. And you know what? There's not a hell of a lot we can do to prevent it. How do you stop them from killing an embassy employee in Los Angeles, or from blowing up a restaurant near an embassy in D.C.?" His grim words matched the expression on his face.

"We don't have any choice but to try," Brixton said.

"You've brought us one hell of an insight into their latest plan," the lead agent said to Brixton. "Good job."

"I did all this because I wanted to clear myself and avenge the murder of my daughter," Brixton said. "Don't make a hero out of me."

"Still," the agent said, "the information you've provided will save lives."

"I'm glad you feel that way," said Brixton, "but what I'd really appreciate is something to eat. Any chance of getting some food?"

A platter of sandwiches and soft drinks was delivered. The food was welcome, but Brixton's knee and back started to act up, and he twisted and squirmed in his chair in search of relief. After another round of questions, he asked when they would be free to go.

"I think we can call it a day," the agent said. "Of course, with the Hawaiian police fighting for jurisdiction, we'll have to ensure that you're available to them once we've finished our investigation."

"Are you saying that you'll hold us?" Brixton asked.

"Investigators from Justice will be here tomorrow to question Ms. Wakatake. Do you prefer to be called that, ma'am, or Ms. Skaggs?"

"Morgana will be fine."

"All right. Justice will want to gain further information from you, Morgana, and from you, Mr. Reyes."

"What about me?" Brixton asked.

"They'll want to talk to you too, of course, Mr. Brixton—or should I call you Agent Brixton?—but you're free to go. We've been in touch with Agent Kogan at SITQUAL and with people at Justice. Based upon everything they've said, there's no reason to hold you as a witness. Of course, you'll have to remain here in Washington."

"Fair enough," Brixton said. "What about my buddies here?"

"Ms. Wakatake—Morgana—and Mr. Reyes will be put up in proper quarters and well taken care of."

"That's good to hear," Brixton said. "I can leave now?"

"Yes, but we ask that you make contact with us each day." He handed Brixton a card with a phone number on it. "Naturally, you are not to speak with anyone aside from authorized special agents and other government officials."

"In other words, not the press."

"*Especially* not the press."

"That doesn't pose any problem at all." He rounded the table and shook Lalo Reyes's hand. "Thanks for what you did back on Maui, Lalo."

"I am sorry for all the trouble I have caused," Reyes said.

"Yeah, well, it's over. When this wraps up, go on back to Spain and go fishing with your father. That's a lot less dangerous than joining cults."

Reyes grinned and assured Brixton that he would do just that.

Kamea stood when Brixton turned to her. She'd offered nothing during the session aside from answering questions with terse, direct language. There were times when Brixton thought she'd lapsed into a daydream of sorts, drifting away into her own special world. Would the hold that Prisler had over her linger, haunt her for the rest of her days? Brixton leaned over and kissed her cheek. "Thanks to you for making that call to me, Morgana. You did the right thing. Everything will work out for you, and I'll be there to help in any way I can."

A small smile appeared on her lips. "I appreciate what you've done," she said. She squeezed his hand. "*Mahalo*. That's Hawaiian for 'thank you.'"

He winked and said, "Aloha, Morgana."

He took a cab to his apartment, where he spent twenty minutes under a hot shower. His authentic Hawaiian shirt, jeans, and T-shirt were tossed in the kitchen wastebasket. He dressed in casual clothes, made himself a drink, and took it, his cell phone, and a bowl of peanuts to the balcony.

"Mac, it's Robert. I'm back."

"I talked to Special Agent Mumford on Oahu. He told me to expect a call from you. Glad you're home."

"Thanks to you. I was wondering whether I could stop over. There's something I want to show you."

"Let me guess. You brought me a lei."

"Would you accept a DVD instead?"

"A DVD of what?"

"Let it be a surprise."

"We're here, not going anywhere."

"I have a few things to do, but I'll give you a call when I'm on my way."

He next called Asal at her office.

"Ms. Banai isn't in today," he was told. "May I take a message?"

"No, thanks."

He reached her at home.

"It's me, Robert. Your office said you weren't working today."

"I'm working from home. Are you back from Hawaii."

"Just got back. Sorry I didn't call you before I left but

it was last minute. I brought something with me that I think you'll want to see."

⸱ "What is it?"

"It's a DVD that shows what your benefactor Zafar Alvi is all about, Asal, the murderous bastard that he really is."

There was silence on her end.

"Are you there?"

"Yes, I'm here. I'm not sure I want to view this DVD of yours."

"I don't blame you for that," he said, "but I think you owe it to yourself, and to me, to look at it."

A deep sigh was followed by, "All right. When?"

"Since you're home, I can swing by now. We can watch it on your computer."

"I suppose that will be all right, but I'll be busy for the next hour."

"An hour is fine with me."

He snacked on the peanuts and sipped from his drink. Having Asal view the DVD on which Zafar Alvi's role in the embassy attacks was confirmed had consumed him from the moment he first viewed it at the FBI building on Oahu. He'd understood her reluctance to believe the worst about Alvi, to think ill of the man who kept her agency financially afloat and who promised to intervene with Iraqi authorities on behalf of her imprisoned brother. He also understood why she would view him, Brixton, with suspicion when he made damaging claims about the man who was in essence her sugar daddy, although it bothered him that she would think that he was libeling Alvi without evidence.

Now there was evidence. Now she would know that what he'd been claiming was honest and accurate. Not that it mattered in the long run. While he found Asal attractive and had enjoyed the time they'd spent

together—including that one night in her bed—he'd
decided that there was no future for them as a couple.
He could never trust her. Besides, he missed Flo and
was pleased she'd decided to stay in Washington. Now
that the hell he'd been through seemed to have an ending in sight, he wanted to explore getting back together
again.

But first there was unfinished business with Asal.

She opened her door without a smile, no indication
that she was pleased to see him. That was okay. He
wasn't paying a social call.

"Come in," she said. Her tone wasn't welcoming.

He stepped into the apartment and saw that the desk
in a corner was piled with papers next to her computer.
An empty coffee cup sat atop one pile.

"I'd love a cup of coffee, if it isn't too much trouble,"
he said.

"Coffee?" she said. "Not a drink?"

"No, coffee would be fine."

She went into the kitchen and returned with a cup.
"I've run out of milk and half-and-half."

"That's okay. I'll drink it black."

"Your trip to Hawaii was good?" she asked.

"Depends on how you view it. It wasn't much fun, if
that's what you mean, but it was successful. I hope
you're not shocked when I tell you that Mr. Alvi's friend
on Maui, Sam Prisler, is dead."

"It was on AOL today. The report said that he was a
prominent businessman and cult leader on Maui and
had been shot to death. It mentioned you. It said that
you and Congressman Skaggs's daughter were involved.
The police want to question you."

"They'll get their chance after the FBI and CIA are
through with me. The congressman's daughter was the
one who shot him. I kind of like the irony. She used my

handgun. I traveled back here from Maui with her and a young guy who helped Alvi and his terrorist friends identify shooting ducks. Want to hear more?"

She stood facing him, arms folded across her chest, her stance decidedly defiant. "You are always in trouble, aren't you?" she said.

"Seems that way, only I don't cause trouble. It just seems to find me."

"So, Robert," she said, "you've come with this DVD and you want me to see what's on it."

"That's right. Have you seen Mr. Alvi lately?"

"He's away," she said.

"Left the country? If I were him, I'd do that, too, only I don't think he'll get very far."

"I have to leave in a few minutes," she said. "Show me the DVD and then go."

He went to her computer, pulled the duplicate of the DVD from his pocket, and inserted it in the slot. He turned to her and patted the top of her desk chair. "Sit down, Asal."

The image on the DVD came to life. The black-and-white image of the scruffy young man, his black beard twisted and oily, cold hatred in his dark eyes, his broken English delivered slowly but with menace behind every word, cast its spell over Asal's living room. She and Brixton watched in silence as the terrorist leader spoke of the need to punish those countries that had helped the invaders and attempted to crush the people of Iraq and Afghanistan. He referenced the attack on the United States on 9/11 but made the point that no matter how much security had been initiated since that fateful day, the infidels would not be able to prevent attacks on their citizens, and that one by one their lives would be snuffed out in retaliation for their evil deeds. "It is the embassies of these corrupt countries that represent them to the world. It is only fitting that those who work for their embassies bear the brunt of our anger."

Much of it was the sort of rhetoric that anyone watching TV over the past years had heard before. But then he shifted to more-detailed plans. It was here that he mentioned Zafar Alvi and addressed him directly. "You, Zafar, and others who believe in our cause will use your position and influence to launch these attacks on our enemies. We will bring true believers to the countries who have slaughtered our people in Iraq, Afghanistan, and elsewhere, students trained by us who will willingly and happily sacrifice themselves to further our cause. We will attack the enemies where they drink, where they eat, and individually on the streets of their corrupt cities and towns. We will kill those whose decadent ways reflect the society in which they live. Through you, our young people will carry out our revenge for centuries of oppression. They will find their targets wherever they are. No nation's security can stop them. Each death will carry with it the message that we will prevail."

When the DVD ended, Brixton turned to Asal and said, "I don't get my jollies deflating anyone's balloon, Asal. I know that you believed in Alvi because he supported you and your project. Maybe seeing what you just watched won't make any difference to you. Maybe you'll still revere him because he's been generous with you. But now you also know that he's a murderer. His victims include my daughter and lots of other daughters and sons. That's why it's important to me that you know this."

She began to cry, fake tears Brixton thought.

"Sam Prisler on Maui was expecting me. I assumed it was a guy named Wayne who'd told him. But it was you, wasn't it? Mac Smith told you where I'd gone. What did you do, pick up the phone and tell Alvi, and he told his buddy Prisler?"

She reached and grabbed his hand, squeezed tight. "Why do you think such terrible things about me, Robert? I knew nothing of Alvi except that he is an important man in Washington who does many good things for our people."

"You can still say that? How is murdering innocent people doing good things?" Brixton asked, extricating his hand and standing.

"You don't understand, do you?" she said. "My brother rots in an Iraqi prison. Alvi promised to help. My Islamic Partnership does good things, too," she continued. "We open up the world to young men and women. We help them become educated and more accepting of all cultures."

"Do any of these young people you help also carry bombs with them to blow up embassy workers?" Brixton said.

She stood and threw her arms about him. "Please, Robert, you must believe me. I did not know anything of Zafar's involvement with terrorism."

"Does he have a say in which young people come here to the States through your organization?"

"No, of course not."

Brixton stepped back. "I want to believe you, Asal. There was a time when I did. But I don't anymore."

He retrieved the DVD and put it in his pocket. Her cheeks were dry now. The pleading look she'd assumed was replaced by a sober expression, her large brown eyes unblinking.

"I wish you well, Asal," he said. "By the way, what you just watched is a dupe I had made in Hawaii. The FBI has the original."

"You have told the FBI about me and my involvement with Zafar?"

"I had to. But if you didn't do anything wrong, weren't involved with any of his terrorist activities, you've got nothing to worry about. Time for me to go. You take care, Asal. I hope everything works out for you."

"What's that supposed to mean?" she said angrily.

He looked at her pretty face and the soft curves of her body that he'd enjoyed holding.

"Whatever you want it to mean," he said, shaking his head and walking out of the apartment.

37

SIX MONTHS LATER

Brixton loaded apple juice, a banana, uncooked oatmeal, maple syrup, and a concoction containing multiple vitamins into the blender in his kitchen. He pushed the button and grimaced as he watched the mixture swirl into unappetizing glop. When it was finished he poured it into two glasses and carried them to the balcony, where Flo Combes sat reading that day's *Washington Post*.

"Breakfast," he announced.

"Thanks," she said and took a sip. "Delicious," she proclaimed.

"It's like drinking soggy beach sand," he said.

"But a lot healthier, Robert. Trust me. You'll learn to love it."

A lot had happened in the six months since his return to Washington from Maui.

When Brixton had played the DVD for Asal Banai at her apartment, she'd informed him that Zafar Alvi was away. That was true, but he hadn't gotten very far. He was seated on a plane at New York's JFK Airport preparing to depart for Cairo, when a team of FBI special agents boarded and took him off in cuffs. Various people in government kept Brixton abreast of the case being built against Alvi and his colleagues, but the wheels of justice turn notoriously slow. Alvi was being held in a federal prison, and from everything Brixton heard, he'd be there for a long time before ever facing trial.

As for Asal, Brixton never saw her again. He knew that she'd been questioned by the FBI, the CIA, and members of Homeland Security about her association with Alvi. Chief among the government's concerns was the possible use of her Islamic Partnership as a conduit for bringing young suicide bombers to the United States, ostensibly to attend school but whose goals were more destructive than that, and decidedly shorter term. She evidently had provided the right answers, because eventually she was told that she was free to leave Washington. The last Brixton heard was that she'd moved to California. Maybe she'd become a movie star, Brixton mused. She certainly was beautiful enough and was a pretty good actress too.

Investigators from the Maui police force traveled to Washington to question Brixton, Kamea, and Lalo Reyes about the death of Samuel Prisler. The story they received was straightforward and honest. Kamea had shot Prisler with Brixton's weapon. Prisler and Akina were about to kill them. It was a clear-cut case of self-defense. Brixton later learned that the authorities on Maui hadn't shed any tears over Prisler's demise, nor did anyone from Washington's Justice Department or CIA. The Hawaiians had never been enthusiastic about hosting a controversial cult and had been trying to build a case against him. The feds were glad to lop off one branch of arms smuggling. A single shot from Brixton's handgun had done everyone a favor, and the Hawaiian police declined to prosecute Kamea for the killing.

Lalo Reyes returned to Barcelona as soon as the authorities allowed him to leave the country. Brixton believed him when he'd said that he didn't know why he'd been instructed to identify homosexuals in embassies and report them to the large man with the shaved head. How Lalo would end up was anybody's guess. All Brixton knew was that by jumping Akina, the skinny, doe-faced young Spaniard had saved his life and Kamea's too.

Brixton took particular pleasure when news broke that two suspects had been arrested and charged in the murder of retired Justice Department attorney Charles McQuaid. A picture of the men being led from police headquarters to jail captured Brixton's attention. One of them was the guy in the tan safari jacket whose penchant was for showing up too often to be a coincidence where Brixton was. Had he and his accomplice killed McQuaid on orders from Zafar Alvi? Brixton didn't know but was determined to keep tabs on it through his contacts at MPD. McQuaid's sister, Jeannette, kept in touch; she told Brixton that the new chemo regimen she was being administered seemed to be working, which brought a smile to his face.

Of everything that was happening in Brixton's life, perhaps the most meaningful was his reconciliation with Flo Combes.

They'd spent considerable time hashing out the nettlesome problems that had led to their breakup in New York, and they decided to give it another try. Flo returned to New York to close down her apartment and to cancel plans to open a dress shop in Brooklyn. Annabel Smith found her a vacant small retail space in Georgetown, and with Mac and Annabel's help, she arranged financing to get her business up and running.

When Brixton wasn't being questioned by authorities from what seemed like a dozen government agencies, he helped Flo whip the dress shop into shape. He had time for it because he was no longer an agent with SITQUAL. SITQUAL no longer existed. Congressman Walter Skaggs, whose committee oversaw the State Department, pushed through a bill stripping the quasi-governmental organization of funding, and the offices run by Mike Kogan were forced to cease operations. Brixton and Kogan had lunch after Kogan had gotten the news of the agency's closure, and it was during that lunch that the next stage of Brixton's life began to take shape.

"I'm really sorry about what happened," Brixton told his former boss, "and I know it's my fault. Congressman Skaggs was determined to get even with me for shooting his son. He closed you down so I wouldn't have a job. As a result, a lot of good agents are unemployed."

"Don't sweat it, Robert."

"What are you going to do, Mike?"

"An old friend of mine, a private investigator, is retiring and selling his one-man agency. I think I'm going to buy it."

Brixton laughed.

"What's funny?"

"You going into that business," he said. "I worked private in Savannah. Not always easy to make ends meet."

"That was Savannah," Kogan said. "This is D.C. With all the corruption, marital shenanigans, and scams going on in this town, there's plenty of work. Maybe you should give it a try."

"I don't like Washington," Brixton said.

"So why are you still here?"

"Because Flo likes it here. She's opening a business in Georgetown."

It was Kogan's turn to laugh.

"Don't say what you're thinking," said Brixton.

"Give it some thought," Kogan said. "Maybe we can partner up."

Brixton and Flo discussed the possibility at length. She encouraged him not to turn away an opportunity, but he had lingering reservations. He'd "been there, done that" in Savannah and remembered how he'd sometimes struggled to pay his bills. He also wondered whether he had the patience any longer to deal with the strange people who bought his services.

But then one night he received a call from Mac Smith.

"I'm calling inviting you and Flo to join us and a few other couples for a celebratory dinner," Smith said.

"What is it, your birthday?" Brixton asked.

"It's a surprise," said the learned law professor. "You'll find out tomorrow night."

Mac had booked a private room at Johnny's Half Shell on Capitol Street NW. Brixton and Flo were flattered to be included. The other guests were Mac's colleagues at the George Washington University law school, and several higher-ups in the current administration. Once drinks had been served, Mac stood and held his glass aloft. "Annabel and I have made a decision," he said.

"Don't tell us you're leaving Washington," a man said.

"No, we're rooted in this city," Mac said. "But I am announcing this evening that I'll be resigning my professorship and going back into private practice."

Once the shock of the announcement wore off, the party became lively, with plenty of drinking and lobster for all.

A few days later Brixton sat with Mac in the soon-to-be-former law professor's study and told him of Kogan's suggestion that he become a private eye again, perhaps teaming up with his former boss.

"Not a bad idea, Robert," said Smith. "If you do, I can promise plenty of work for you as my investigator."

That settled it, although Brixton decided not to join forces with Kogan. Mac Smith advanced him the five-thousand-dollar bond he had to put up, and also loaned him enough money to lease a small office. Brixton passed the mandatory FBI background check and received his PI license from the Metro Police. He also renewed his license to carry a concealed weapon and bought a new Smith & Wesson 638 Airweight revolver to replace the one that had been confiscated by FBI Special Agent Mumford on Maui.

The Washington Post covered Mackensie Smith's return to private law practice.

Flo Combes hosted a ribbon-cutting ceremony and party at the new offices of Robert Brixton: Private Investigator.

Brixton settled into a life of relative domestic bliss. He made regular calls to his daughter, Jill, and carved out the time to watch his only grandchild grow up.

He finally managed to swallow Flo's healthy shakes without gagging.

Maybe I'll even learn to stomach Washington, D.C., he told himself.

But I doubt it.

Turn the page for a preview of

MARGARET TRUMAN'S

INTERNSHIP

IN MURDER

A CAPITAL CRIMES NOVEL

▸ DONALD BAIN ◂

*Available from Tom Doherty Associates
in August 2015*

A FORGE BOOK

Copyright © 2015 by Estate of Margaret Truman

ROCK CREEK PARK, WASHINGTON, D.C.

Washington, D.C., had been good to Capac Lopez. Since arriving twelve years ago from Peru, he'd found the ethnically diverse city a fertile ground for realizing his dream of opening a Peruvian restaurant in the United States. He'd been brought up around restaurants. His father owned a popular café in Lima, and Capac had spent much of his youth washing dishes, prepping food, and accompanying his father to the markets in the early morning to choose fresh ingredients for the café's ambitious menu.

But at the age of thirty, and with a young wife and infant son, Capac made the wrenching decision to leave his parents and siblings to forge a new life in the United States. Now, eight years after a tearful farewell, he was the proud owner of a thriving restaurant in Washington's bustling Adams Morgan area of the city.

It was hard work, leaving Capac little time for recreation. But on many Sunday mornings he indulged in a favorite pastime, an early-morning hike through the woods of Washington's Rock Creek Park, twenty-one hundred acres that cut through the center of the nation's capital, the America's oldest natural urban park.

Being outdoors provided Capac with a sense of freedom. He especially enjoyed the twisting trails in the southernmost section, not far from Adams Morgan and the National Zoo; on some days he could hear the lions roar. On this particular Sunday morning he'd left his house even earlier than usual, arriving at the park as the sun began to rise. It promised to be a lovely day, the city's notorious humidity having dropped to a more comfortable level, the brightening sky a harbinger of what Capac liked to say would be *el día gordo*—a fat day.

Capac loved to breathe in air that was fresher than in the city, observe small animals scurrying about, examine wildflowers, and splash cold, fresh water from streams on his face. Trash left behind by others angered him, and he quietly cursed them in Spanish as he balled up a plastic bag and shoved it in his pocket.

He was heading home when something—a piece of green cloth?—caught his eye. At first he ignored it; he couldn't pick up every bit of trash. Whatever it was had been partially obscured by a layer of leaves. After taking a few steps away, he returned and bent over to see better. He used his sneaker to kick away some leaves, revealing more of what had captured his attention. More leaves were wiped away. Now the cloth came into full view. It was one leg of a pair of green slacks. Capac straightened, afraid to go farther. But then, using his hand to brush off the debris, he briskly, desperately allowed dappled sunlight to fall on his discovery.

It was a body. A woman. Blond. Pretty? Hard to tell considering the shape her face was in.

Capac turned away and gave up his breakfast to the forest floor.

H omicide detective Jason Ewing had been with the Washington Metropolitan Police Department for eighteen years, one of more than two thousand African-American officers on the force. With him in a conference room at police headquarters on Judiciary Square was the department's superintendent of detectives, Ezekiel "Zeke" Borgeldt who, after a long career with the Federal Bureau of Investigation, had been recruited to take over the demoralized and understaffed detective division. The two men, along with Ewing's partner, Jack Morey, three years as a detective after eleven years in uniform, were meeting to discuss Capac Lopez's discovery.

"What do you think?" Ewing was asked by his superior.

"The conclusion the press and public will come to is that we've got a serial killer on our hands," Ewing said. "This is the second vic in the park in the past three months."

"But two homicides don't add up to serial killings," Morey put in.

Borgeldt looked down through half glasses on the tip of his bulbous nose as he read from the report. "This one's twenty-two years old. The previous one was twenty-seven. No obvious connection between them. The older victim had been reported missing by her husband two months ago. No one reported this new woman missing. The ME is still trying to come up with a name for her and where she came from."

"A hooker?" Morey asked.

"Who knows?" Borgeldt said, sighing. "Amazing

how many people disappear and nobody even knows or cares that they're missing."

"Or maybe they're happy to see them gone," Morey quipped.

"Same MO," Borgeldt said, "same cause of death, blunt force blows to the head, both bodies buried in a shallow grave covered with leaves."

"What I don't get," said Ewing, "is why whoever killed these women took the time to dig shallow graves. Those areas are popular with hikers, families with kids, lots of people. Sure, the graves are shallow, six inches deep at best, but it takes time to scrape away that much dirt and lay a blanket of leaves over the bodies."

Borgeldt pulled photographs from the file and fanned them out on the desk. "The ME estimates that this victim was killed within the past two weeks. Nobody walking in that area saw what this Lopez guy saw?"

"Hikers aren't looking for bodies," Ewing said. "Lopez was pretty far off the path when he discovered her."

"You ran a check on him?" Borgeldt asked.

"Sure," replied Ewing. "Family man, came here from Peru eight years ago, owns a popular Peruvian restaurant in Adams Morgan. I've eaten there a few times. Nice guy. Good food."

"What about that Russian guy women were complaining about, the one they say harassed them when they were hiking in the park?" Morey said.

Borgeldt shrugged. "Wouldn't hurt to bring him in again for questioning. Pick him up."

THE SEDUCTION

1

THREE MONTHS EARLIER
DAVIS ISLAND
TAMPA, FLORIDA

I'll have one of your patented Collins drinks," Congressman Harold "Hal" Gannon told party host Lucas Bennett.

"Tom or John?"

"What's the difference?"

"Bourbon or gin? Tom uses gin, John uses bourbon."

The congressman laughed. "Where did Florida's leading malpractice attorney learn so much about making drinks?"

"I bartended during law school, got interested in the subtler aspects of it. Besides, if doctors ever stop cutting off the wrong limb or leaving sutures inside patients, I might need a job behind a bar."

"Bourbon."

"One John Collins coming up. By the way, I only use Meyer lemons."

"As opposed to?"

"The usual lemons. Meyers have a deeper taste, a hint of orange," Bennett said as he prepared the drink behind the marble bar top in his posh waterfront home. "They were invented in China. Some guy tried to grow them in California, but his trees had a virus that damn near wiped out every other citrus tree in the state. They eventually figured it out." He shook the bourbon, freshly squeezed lemon juice, sugar, and ice in a stainless shaker, poured the concoction into a glass, added club soda, garnished it with an orange slice, and handed it to the congressman.

Gannon took a small sip. "Wonderful," he said, smacking his lips. "I know some bars in Washington that could use you."

"I'll send my surrogate," Bennett said as his twenty-two-year-old daughter, Laura, joined him and accepted his embrace.

"She's a lot prettier than you are," Gannon said.

"Which means she'll get better tips."

Lucas Bennett was a big man in every sense. He was overweight, but the pounds were solidly packed on his six-foot-two frame. His flowing white hair gave him the look of an orator of yore. His ruddy face and ready smile belied a keen legal mind and a killer instinct when engaged in an adversarial situation with another attorney. Hal Gannon had been one of those lawyers who'd once felt the heft of Bennett's intellect and the sting of his silver tongue.

But that was before Gannon put his Tampa law practice into mothballs and successfully ran for the U.S. House of Representatives from Florida's Fourteenth Congressional District. He was in his fourth term. In an amusing irony, Lucas Bennett, his former opponent in court, had been one of his most generous backers, and Laura had worked as a volunteer on his most recent campaign.

"Has Laura acquired your skills, Luke, as a—what's it called?—as a mixologist?"

"I make a dynamite cosmopolitan," she said, "and I can pop a cap off a beer bottle in the wink of an eye."

Both men laughed as Bennett's wife, Grace, joined them. "You have to get out from behind the bar, Luke," she said, "and mingle with our other guests."

Grace Bennett was reed-thin but not emaciated. A physical therapist at Tampa General Hospital, she was a workout fanatic, and her sinewy, muscular arms and chiseled face—not an ounce of excess flesh anywhere—testified to a lifetime spent in gyms and lifting paralyzed patients back into wheelchairs.

"I suppose I should," her husband said as he rinsed his hands in a small sink and dried them. Before he followed his wife to where their other guests were gathered on an expansive patio that led down to the water and the slip at which their small cabin cruiser was docked, he said to Gannon, "I know I've thanked you before for arranging Laura's internship in your Washington office, Hal, but I'll say it again."

"Looking forward to having her," Gannon said.

"Just make sure she doesn't fall in love with some knee-jerk Democrat," Bennett said jovially.

Gannon, a conservative Democrat, said, "Even if he's a Blue Dog?"

"Well, that might make a difference," said Bennett. "Enjoy your drink Hal. I'll be back in a few minutes to whip up another round."

Gannon's reference to Blue Dogs reflected his leadership in the House of Representatives' band of right-leaning Democrats who often sided with their Republican counterparts. They'd taken the name Blue Dogs to mock the Yellow Dog Democrats of the early 1900s who were branded with the nickname because it was said that they would vote for anything, even a yellow dog, rather than a Republican.

Gannon and Laura watched the Bennetts go through open French doors to the terrace.

"Your folks are great," Gannon said, placing his barely touched drink on the bar.

"You aren't drinking this?" Laura asked, picking up the glass.

"I don't drink much, just an occasional social sip. Didn't want to offend your dad."

Laura took a healthy swig and smacked her lips. "Yummy."

"I'll take your word for it."

Congressman Hal Gannon would be considered handsome by any standard. He had a shock of unruly black hair that defied taming, which could also be said about his earlier bachelor days in Tampa. He topped six feet in height, and even beneath his red-and-blue-striped sport shirt you could see that he was physically fit. Like Grace Bennett, Gannon was no stranger to gyms, both when he was home in Tampa and when in Congress, where he took full advantage of the House's workout facilities. His jaw was square, his green eyes probing, mouth always on the verge of breaking into a boyish grin. *The Washingtonian* magazine had named him one of the House of Representatives' handsomest men.

"Looking forward to coming to work for me?" he asked Laura, who took another sip of the drink.

"Are you sure I'll be *working* for you?" she said playfully. "When you work for someone, you usually get paid."

"We have rules about that in the House," he countered, "but maybe I can squeeze something out of the budget—if you're good."

"Good at what?" she asked, raising a nicely shaped eyebrow.

"Hal!"

Gannon looked through the open doors to where his wife, Charlene, waved at him.

"I'm being summoned," he said.

"Your wife is so beautiful," Laura said.

"She is, isn't she? Looking forward to when you arrive in D.C. The housing service landed you a prime spot, a two-bedroom on Capitol Hill, only a few blocks from the office, lots of space for you and your roommate. Roseann, my chief of staff, will help get you settled. Ace those final few exams before you come. I like my interns to be achievers and . . ."

"And?" she said playfully.

He shrugged. "Available, I suppose. Excuse me. See you in a month, Laura." He hesitated, came forward, kissed her cheek, and joined his wife.

Laura finished the drink her father had made for Gannon and placed it on a tray of dirty glasses behind the bar. She took in her image in the back-bar mirror. She was her mother's daughter, albeit more fleshy, more womanly. Her legs were long, her waist narrow. Unlike her mother, her bosom was large and amply occupied her pink silk blouse, its top buttons undone to reveal some cleavage. Both mother and daughter were brunettes, although Laura's hair had more of a copper tint to it; she wore it loose and shoulder length.

She turned her attention to the terrace, where what someone had said generated gales of laughter. It was a money crowd. Social gatherings at the house were always attended by her parents' wealthy friends, and Laura knew that she was fortunate to have been born into the Bennett family. She'd never wanted for anything and had been blatantly spoiled. She was in her senior year at the University of Southern Florida, majoring in health administration in its College of Public Health. She hadn't chosen that major. She would have preferred something more artistic, like acting or painting. But her father had convinced her that she should graduate with a usable degree, which wouldn't preclude her from pursuing artistic endeavors on the side. Law school? That's what Lucas Bennett really wanted for his only child.

Laura's attention went to Charlene Gannon, the congressman's wife. No doubt about it, Charlene was a stunning woman—silver-blond hair, lovely figure, and perfectly painted oval face. She and her husband made a picture book couple. The media, always on the hunt for juicy stories about elected officials, pounced on every aspect of the Gannons' private life, focusing most recently on the fact that Charlene spent little time in D.C. with her husband.

"Why would anyone choose to run for office and open himself to such public scrutiny?" Laura once questioned her father after reading that the public's view of members of Congress ranked only slightly higher than serial rapists and below identity thieves.

"Ego," he replied, "pure, unadulterated ego."

Hal Gannon certainly had such an ego. Maybe "self-assuredness" was a better term. Laura smiled as she watched him break into a contagious laugh at something a woman said. If anyone had the right to be self-assured, she decided as she went to the patio and joined in the spirited conversation, it was Hal Gannon, successful attorney, popular member of the U.S. Congress, and movie-star handsome.

A real hunk.

In a month she would be leaving Tampa for Washington to become an intern in his office. Growing up in the opulence of the Bennett family had been wonderful, as carefully measured and nurtured as her father's favorite drink recipes.

But it was time to taste something new.

She couldn't wait.

Forge

Award-winning authors
Compelling stories

. . . .

Please join us at the website
below for more information
about this author and other great
Forge selections, and to sign up for
our monthly newsletter!

. . . . www.tor-forge.com . . . .

Printed in the USA
CPSIA information can be obtained
at www.ICGtesting.com
LVHW090746060624
782456LV00002B/216

9 781250 878083